Please Don't Tell
My Parents
I Work for a Supervillain

By Richard Roberts

OTHERSIDE
PRESS

Cleric nodded his head toward me, although his eyes and his souring frown remained on Echo. "So you want to start a fight in front of a teenage girl?"

"So you admit you're using her as a shield?" shot back Echo immediately.

Ice should have been spreading around these two, the way they looked at each other. If looks could kill, we would be in frozen post-apocalypse mode. Cold, hateful, and calm. Completely calm.

In that spirit of bleak composure, his tone quiet, Cleric said, "That depends on what she wants."

They had to watch each other. I didn't. Two customers were crouched under their table at the other end of the room, phones out, videotaping us. Darker silhouettes crowded up against the dark windows at the restaurant's front.

This was going to be on the news, and no one, not Echo tomorrow at school, not even my family, would recognize the girl in the video.

But everyone would see her.

I'd left the badge on the table. Picking it up now, I hooked it onto one of my armor's leather straps. Standing up on my chair, I stepped up onto the table next. I might as well have flown. My heart sure felt like it was soaring.

"If you're going to spoil my dinner, you can have it." I hooked a sneaker into one of the plates loaded with fancy food and kicked hard. It splattered bits of meat and gooey sauce all over Echo's chest.

CHAPTER ONE

The first day of high school is a long one when it's a school for the kids of superheroes.

I stepped out of the bathroom, buttoning my blouse, to find my older brother Kay giving my hair a critical stare. "Back to pink, Magenta?" Lanky boys like him do "judgmental" well, with his hand on his hip and everything.

Brushing my fingers through my damp dreads, I stuck out my chin in defiance. It's no lantern jaw, but I had plenty of defiance. "If you think I'm not giving the other super powered kids an' enchilada-the-size-of-your-head's worth of spicy first impression, you're crazy."

He slapped a skinny hand on my shoulder, and leaned down a few inches. "I'm telling you, you've got the wrong idea. Upper High is a magnet school for smart kids. Kids like you."

My heaping helping of defiance was unmoved. I jabbed him in the chest with a finger. "Which I got into because somebody knows you're a superhero." A brand-new superhero taking LA by storm. Winning when he should have no chance was my brother's specialty.

He switched to both hands on his hips, and raised eyebrows

of walrus-level despair. "I wish you had half as much faith in yourself as you have in me, Magenta."

I had faith in myself. I just didn't have faith in anyone noticing.

He made a grab for my pink vinyl backpack, and pulled me toward the front door. "Come on." I snatched it back with a big frown, because I didn't want him to know what I'd packed in that backpack, or to know I was afraid of him finding out.

I jogged down the apartment building steps to the sidewalk, and strode proudly to the bus stop at the corner, until he finally stopped watching me and shut the door. There was exactly one other kid in this neighborhood waiting for this bus, and she had long brown hair and her nose stuck in a huge book. Exactly the kind of tumescent, raging brain-child who belonged at a school like Upper High told the public it was.

We stood there for what felt like an hour. My skin felt increasingly prickly-anxious. This day would decide so much about my life. What would the school be like? Could I handle it? How powerful were the other kids? The Inscrutable Machine went to Upper High!

I almost didn't notice the scruffy guy walking up to us, and gave him a suspicious look only in time to see him reach into his jacket and start pulling out a gun.

He got as far as my seeing the handle. There wasn't time to panic. Black smoke snakes writhed in the air, and out of them thrust an arm. The freaky shadow effects faded, leaving a tall woman wearing white leather, with an off-color oil slick of limp, badly cared for white hair, and marred by a haggard, yellow-skinned face.

The stuff that looked like black snakes slithered into the mugger's body. The mummy-woman disappeared. He fell to the pavement and lay there, eyes closed.

The school bus picked that exact moment to pull up. Its door opened, and the woman in the driver's seat looked past us two aghast teenagers to the body on the ground.

She sighed. The bus driver and my brother ought to date. They could do the same expression of much-aggrieved despair. She told us and the world in general, "Every year there's one idiot who thinks robbing kids on the first day of school is the perfect crime. Every year they get caught. I'm sorry you two were unlucky enough to see it."

The genius and I exchanged amused smirks. "Unlucky" wasn't the word I would use. That silent, ruthless heroine had been Mourning Dove, and you could not get more famous or more undead. We'd enjoyed front row seats to the ultimate curb-stomping of petty evil!

I filed onto the bus, found an open spot, and spent the long trip staring out the window. There was no point making a splashy entrance on the bus. Nobody would remember it.

When we arrived, Upper High looked normal. I filed off of the air-conditioned bus into the September heat. The high school loomed, a big curvy H shape in two tall floors of red brick. Across the street it faced Northwest Hollywood Middle, a more squat building in multiple colors. I joined the crowd of children filing up Upper High's multiple sets of stairs and into the building.

Homeroom 111. That wouldn't be hard to find. As I followed the numbers, I scanned my new schoolmates. Most were taller than me, but I was a freshman. That was expected. Other than that, they didn't look much different from my middle school. A few kids had weird hair colors like mine, but they weren't flaunting the powers that came with that. Maybe an unusually high proportion of cute boys.

Ooooh. Sparks crept through a blonde girl in a hurry's hair. I passed a boy with a ground sloth's worth of claws having trouble with his backpack. That's more like it.

Room 111 loomed like an iceberg from the obscuring fog of students. I went in and took a seat near the front. Posters in a number of different languages and even alphabets advertised what was taught in this room.

Leaning against his desk, the studiously casual teacher greeted, "Welcome to Upper High, new students. I'm Mister Carlyle. We won't be spending much time together, but I should still get to know who is who. When I call your name, raise your hand and say 'Here,' and I'll give you your schedule."

He did just that, and with every student he made a little note on a pad.

Finally, he got to "Magenta Slade" and I lifted my hand. He passed me a crisp, official card with formal school lettering.

This was it. This was my moment I learned my destiny at LA's school for the children of superheroes and supervillains:

Advanced English I
Advanced Chemistry I
Advanced Latin I
Lunch
Advanced Social Science I
Algebra II

My mouth fell open. Numbness crept over me.

This...this was a perfectly normal high school, teaching perfectly normal subjects. Nothing about using your powers, fighting, any of that.

Ugh, wait, and Advanced Chemistry? No no no no no no no! I couldn't pass that! All of this, and a class I would fail in my first semester?!

The bell rang, and I trudged through the halls in a daze to English class. Nothing got any more super-y. The teacher took roll again, then started to tell us course objectives. We would start with reading comprehension. Sure, I'd ace that.

Recovering a little, I tried to look around. I could at least make a good impression to my fellow students, right? But they also looked so normal.

The bell rang again. Somehow, English class was already over. My heart tightened and I don't know why I didn't trip over someone on the way to...Chemistry.

The Chemistry teacher took roll as I sat in increasingly paralyzed shock, then rolled down an ancient plastic scroll over the blackboard to reveal...

"We'll dive right into the periodic table today."

I stared up in horror at that gobbledygook pile of squares and numbers. Numbers! The periodic table was insane! Who cared how much an element weighed? This was like trying to paint by looking at Spectro analysis of the pigments! An alchemist cared about their properties, and how the real materials in front of you interact!

I was going to fail. I was going to look like an idiot on day one. Forcing myself to breathe, I tried to force my hand to move, to raise it and explain I was in the wrong class and the inevitable, humiliating explanation why.

Light engulfed me, and I looked up into the face of an angel. My fear drained away as the golden blonde in a sleekly tight white dress laid her hand on my shoulder and gave me a sweet smile. "It's going to be okay. You're having some kind of super power related attack, right? It happens to all of us. Do you need help?"

She glowed with kindness. The girl was…adorable, probably my age, and the hand on my shoulder definitely felt like flesh and blood. Still dizzy, I mumbled, "I can't do chemistry. My power gets in the way. I don't belong here."

The girl lifted my gauntlet out of my backpack and laid it on my desk. "If you made this, you belong here."

My gauntlet. Thick, thick brown leather, old and worn. When worn, it went up my arm to my elbow. The leather glove itself was little more than a structure to rig brass fittings on, tubes and levers and a firing mechanism at the wrist. I shook my head slowly. "It was given to me." By my brother, but I still had enough self-control not to say that out loud.

The blonde girl had the cutest, lip-jutting pout I'd ever imagined, poking curiously at the gauntlet until she opened a chamber and pulled out a little plastic vial filled with cyan goop. Her eyes widened, sparkling, and her grin turned beatific. "No. You're an *alchemist*."

All I could do was nod.

"What's your name?" she asked, turning her soaring sky-blue eyes back to me.

We'd just taken roll call, but she'd already forgotten, of course. "Magenta." Was I going to pass out? I felt so weird and swimmy.

The blonde typed that into her phone.

His voice strained, the teacher protested, "Miss Lutra, you know you are not allowed to use your power like this."

I glanced at him while he was talking, and when I looked

back up, the girl was gone, disappeared from the classroom as if she'd teleported away. Maybe she had.

Students made quiet noises as we recovered from the bout of mind control. The teacher took deep breaths, and when he got his focus back announced, "Still, I'll forgive her for a good deed. Don't worry, Miss Slade—"

The girl in the chair next to me bounced up and down, her chair's metal legs clattering and her arm waving wildly. "Ooh! Ooh! I can help! I know all about super power related learning disabilities."

I blinked. This had not been the classmate next to me before the cute-as-a-button brain blasting blonde showed up. The new girl, uh....

She and the angel could not have been more physically opposite. Well, they had a similar shape, the kind you find on cheerleaders, but other than that no. Rather than blonde, this girl had ink black hair, naturally straight but uncombed like a porcupine with bed-head. Her burgundy blouse shone, obviously fine silk, but frayed and wrinkled. The shirt was actually missing three buttons, and if I'd been seen in school with the gaps that left, I'd crawl under my bed and never come out. The black-haired girl had not a trace of acne and perfect teeth, but badly chapped lips and a maniacally eager grin.

Wow, that grin. We're talking a whole carnival of killer clowns eager. Could I make a bipolar cure potion?

Still reeling from the Lutra assault, the teacher blinked. "I... suppose, Miss Bradley, but Miss Slade, if you don't think that's enough, talk to me, and we'll get this schedule mistake fixed."

With a bunch of loud clonks, Bradley inch-wormed her chair up right next to mine, and laid an open textbook between us.

She pointed at my nose, then jerked a thumb at her own. "You Magenta. Me Marcia. This will be great."

"Do you really know about super power learning disabilities?" I whispered.

Marcia made a *psssht* blowing noise, and rolled her dark eyes. "Oh, please. That was a giant lie. What I have done is read some real old-timey alchemy books and I am positive you can pass this class with someone to help bridge the gap." She waved her hand airily, and added, "Besides, I could take the final now, if I wanted. My old man was big on chemistry."

I shuddered, half a dozen dreadlocks flopping to the opposite side of my shoulders. "I don't think you can make that monster make sense."

"Naah, see, you're thinking about it wrong. It doesn't make sense to most kids. You have one advantage, because the guys who first lined this up were alchemists. These two lines over here are all alkalis. On the other end are the noble gases. Here's the reactive gases. This chunk is inert stuff, and all in here are metals. Don't try to understand the rest, because that will get in the way. It's a chart where you look up numbers. You'll have to do a lot of rote memorization, but you can handle that." She sneered, the kind of sneer that showed contempt not for me, but for a list that thought it could defeat me.

It was all good advice, but this was as bewildering a change of pace as the avalanche of divine Lutra intervention. My eyes wide, I protested, "How can you be so sure? You don't know me."

Marcia grinned again, not quite as manic, but super smug. "Just watch. You'll see I'm right."

We at least got through the rest of class without my feeling like a lost cause. When the bell announced the end of second period, kids all grabbed their bags and swarmed out. Marcia hung her pack off one shoulder, but lingered with me. Squinting shrewdly, she declared, "So, you didn't go to Northwest Hollywood Middle, and you brought a mad science weapon that you partly made. You have a superhero or supervillain relative, and you're a Bad Penny fan."

See? I told you, Kay!

This was my time. Time to get my balance back and make a first impression for the first time. I shrugged, and gave her my own smirk. "You should know I'm not allowed to say, because you have a relative in the Community, you're extremely powerful, and you want to be a villain."

That got a snicker, and a smile more like a snarl. "Good. Bad. I'm the girl with the fists." She smacked one into the other palm, and black slithered around the impact.

We grinned at each other a lot.

Something made faint *pok pok pok* noises. A girl in braids covered in beads stood behind Marcia, shaking her head. She had sharp features, pretty like a statue, with lean but visibly muscular arms mostly bared by her short-sleeved t-shirt. She spoke with flat determination that matched her straight-backed, utterly confident poise. "You are not corrupting the new girl."

Marcia spun around, which revealed the floating bead that had been poking the back of her head, because now it smacked repeatedly against her forehead. Hand on her chest, Marcia declared with a veritable mud storm of truth-concealing wounded virtue, "When did you become my chaperone?"

Nobody would have fallen for it, and this regally serious and determined girl certainly didn't. "When we were assigned to the same class. Speaking of which, shouldn't you be getting to your next class?"

Marcia tossed her head, clean but unkempt hair bouncing, and pointed two doors down. "Oh, please. It's right there."

That scored a conversational hit. The braided girl turned her head a couple of inches, eyes and mouth tightening in worry. "That's my next class." Her hand whipped out, palm up in demand. "Show me your schedule."

Marcia dug a fist into her pocket and pulled out a crumpled piece of paper. She dropped it in her accuser's hand. The braided girl yanked the paper open and read its contents.

Eyes wide with horror, she looked up at my dementedly grinning new friend. The braided girl's voice came out in a whisper. "We have every class together."

Letting out a squeal of glee, Marcia pumped both fists victoriously up and down. "Best rivals united!"

The girl with the braids slapped a hand over her eyes, and dragged it down her face. I was thoroughly unconvinced by her exasperation, but she did at least sound sincere when she raised an eyebrow and asked, "Aren't you Penny Akk's rival?"

Marcia gave a snort of sudden, unexpected laughter, her smile less manic and more a blistering sunshine of amusement. "Oh, please. That was so six months ago. Now I'm that backup teammate that you would trust with your life but you can't completely be friends with because that would spoil the unexpected wisdom sharing thing."

My eyes went wide, and my voice squeaked. "You know Penny Akk? As in Bad Penny, as in The Inscrutable Machine?"

For the first time, the braided girl properly noticed me, with a faint jerk of surprise, no less. She recovered immediately, offering me her hand and an open, friendly smile. "Oh, a fan? I'm Charlotte, by the way."

Marcia nodded at me, now just with a wry smile that turned up on one side. She folded her arms under her chest, and offered, "I can introduce you. Penny is super friendly... for about thirty seconds, and then she goes back to Ray and Claire."

Charlotte grimaced the reluctant grimace of someone who had just heard an unwanted truth.

I shook my own head and waved a hand lazily. "Naah, it's not about Penny herself. It's about what she did."

Multi-colored beads rattled as Charlotte looked up at the clock in the hall. "We have to get to class."

Marcia grinned at her, syrupy with triumphant malice. "No, you have to get to class, good girl."

Charlotte grimaced again, her pose stiff, ready to bolt, but she hesitated. Her arm lashed out, grabbing my shoulder, and she dragged her forehead to mine. In a low voice that Marcia still would have to be able to hear, she told me, "Listen. Half the time Marcia is the kindest person you will ever meet, but the other half she's trouble with a capital 'violence and insanity.'"

And with that, she flew off to the classroom Marcia had pointed out earlier. Not actually, literally flew, but she did move with eel-like grace when she was in a hurry. Freaky. Also, awesome.

Chortling, Marcia pulled up her backpack and started digging around inside it. She looked up at me as she did with a different smile, of sinister anticipation. "*You* like trouble. You're here for trouble, superhero trouble. So here, have some. You'll be fine if you keep it warm." With that she pulled out...a plastic egg, orange, like cheap vending machine toys come in.

I let her slide it into my hands. The egg felt heavy, with

something soft that didn't rattle around inside.

"Now, get to class," Marcia ordered, pointing in exactly the wrong direction exactly as the bell to start third period sounded.

I did, in a hurry. I bet I could get away with this on the first day under "still finding my way in a new school," but not if I was much later.

While I scurried, I looked at the egg. Okay, this was an obvious practical joke, but you know what? I could play. Holding my own backpack awkwardly in front of me, I found my metal safety box of backup potions, and pulled out the liquid sunlight tube. This had been a goat rodeo of trouble to make, and had to be stored in delicate glass, but it gave off plenty of heat. I wrapped it and the egg snugly in the padding of the gauntlet, and tried to tuck that where my textbooks wouldn't bang against them too hard.

My prediction proved true: I arrived during roll call, and escaped trouble because it was the first day. Latin class...was fine. It went by in a blur, just because it was normal. We got an overview of our textbook, declensions, the fact that we were going to be reading a lot of Julius Caesar's writing, that sort of thing. The worst I could say about the class was that I still wish we were learning something like Sumerian. All the cool super powered artifacts had Sumerian writing on them. Maybe wizards like mud. Now my dreams of one day having a team of investigators stare at me in awe as I read the ancient tablet at the heart of the mystery had been dashed.

Most alchemy books were written in Latin, though, so I wasn't wasting my time.

The lunch bell rang! Free time to mingle! I hurried down to the cafeteria. Entering nearly buried me under a stampede of ultra-blandness, and also other kids eager to stake their brand-new social territory. Upper High's cafeteria was a big white room with a bunch of cheap metal tables that had benches welded to them. Woohoo. Passing through the food line was even more bland. Couldn't there at least have been mad science machines behind the counter to cook the world's only actually good school lunch? Nope. Spongy Salisbury steak and green beans for me.

Emerging with my tray of food, I found that the older kids had taken ownership of their long-claimed territories, while us freshmen eyed the existing cliques, wondering where we would fit in. That was way more important than what dully nutritious paste I was served. I needed to break into the friendship circles of the hero and villains' kids. Preferably heroes.

Making real new friends would be nice, too.

In answer to my prayers, I saw Marcia and Charlotte sitting alone and across from each other at a table. Charlotte was eating from a tray like mine. Marcia's idea of food was a cake. A whole cake, of who knew what flavor because it was a smeary mess from being bounced around in a box.

Approaching them I noticed something else. Marcia's blouse wasn't even the worst of her clothing disasters. She'd "forgotten" to wear a belt, her slacks sagged a lot, and both her blouse and slacks had been cut raggedly and inexpertly short, leaving an inch of midriff and her knees and lower legs bare.

How could I not like someone who hit the world like a blockbuster bomb? Or Charlotte, as comfortable in Marcia's mad presence and on the first day of high school as a captain on the deck of her ship?

So, I walked over to them, set my tray down, and took the place next to Marcia as if I belonged there, to let them know I did.

My bravery melted in the blow-torch of their blank, amused stares. Ugh.

This was the moment I'd been pretending wouldn't happen. I'd at least hoped I could put it off until tomorrow.

"Have we met?" asked Charlotte, half-smiling at my daring and pointing a chunk of cornbread at me.

Marcia's one-and-a-half sized grin evened the pair out as she looked me up and down. "Naturally pink hair. Tight dreadlocks, and I know that takes work. Good color sense. Suspiciously lumpy backpack. And attitude for miles. What's your name, girl?"

Ugh again.

They had no idea who I was.

All my effort went into not looking or sounding pained and embarrassed. "Magenta."

Marcia's messy black eyebrows went up. "Whoa, two girls named Magenta in one—"

Charlotte jerked. Extending a hand to me, she stammered, "Oh, no. I am so sorry, Magenta. I have no idea how I didn't recognize you."

The subtle flicker of identifying me didn't interrupt Marcia's grin. On the contrary, she leaned an elbow on the table, smearing her sleeve with frosting, and studied me with even more smug fascination. "I do. It's Magenta's super power. One she can't turn off. That's the only explanation that makes sense."

Charlotte grimaced, and kept her hand out. As I shook it, she told me in a low, sympathetic tone, "Wow, that must be a pain to deal with. Now that we know, we'll do our best about it. I thought you had a potion making mad science power?"

Marcia straightened up again, merely smirking. "She's got both. It's not like it doesn't happen sometimes. I bet she'd rather change the subject, so I vote we talk about me."

The tension I'd been trying to resist let go, and I just barely avoided a sigh. That had been surprisingly painless. I raised my hand. "Seconded."

Marcia scooped a giant fork full of cake into her mouth and swallowed it without chewing, which left only the barest pause before she explained, "I've got two powers, too. One is a physical perfection thing, the other is an energy shock. Of course, I stole mine instead of inheriting them." Her grin came back, gleeful at that detail.

Charlotte flicked a finger. A ring slid off of it into the air, spun around a few revolutions, then went right back into place. More matter-of-factly, she said, "Jewelry control. I can kind of feel them when I manipulate them, and I'm trying to build that up, get a real ability to know exactly where they are around me."

Gulping another steam shovel scoop of cake to free her tongue, Marcia squeed, "Cooool. Jewelry radar would be amazing!"

They both looked at me, not expectantly, but with pleased, knowing little grins. I realized I hadn't eaten a bite, and had been leaning forward eagerly to listen to all of this. Hurriedly,

I imitated Marcia in miniature, and stuffed an entire meat goo patty in my mouth.

Eyebrows up but thankfully without hint of judgment, Charlotte asked me, "You came to us hoping to get into the super powers club, right? If we can get it restarted this year."

Marcia shook her head so forcefully a fleck of frosting landed on my cheek. "I guarantee you Penny won't do it. Not with her power weakened and her parents watching her. Nobody would be crazy enough to let me be club president—"

"Seriously," agreed Charlotte.

Unoffended, Marcia resumed, "—so you ought to open it."

Charlotte folded her arms. "Nope. No way. I have a life, thanks, and I'm getting plenty of super power practice already."

Marcia didn't try to argue, and I already could tell it would take a battering ram driven by twelve caffeine-crazed mastodons to make Charlotte bend on anything. It was hard to feel too disappointed, because this was exactly the kind of conversation I'd come to this school to be part of, and yes, I was digging every second.

After thirty seconds of silence I used to gorge, Charlotte let out a sigh. Her beaded corn row braids slid over her shoulders as she bent her face forward. "I miss everyone, though."

Marcia nodded, finally wiping the frosting off her face with a monogrammed handkerchief. Admittedly, monogrammed with someone else's initials. "Yeah. We'll just have to hunt up the others, at least the ones already in Upper High. It'll be weird without Teddy, though."

Charlotte nodded, perking up again. "I've seen Mirabelle and Cassie, so maybe they'll be in our afternoon classes. Why aren't you and Sue together already?"

Pinching her nose in disgust, Marcia answered, "She's not at Upper High. Her folks sent her to Pep Prep."

Charlotte gasped, and her mouth remained open in shock. "Oh, no way. I'm sorry for both of you."

The cataclysm of awesomeness girl added an eye roll to her scrunched-up disgust, and her voice took on a mocking singsong imitation of upper-class snootiness. "It's half finishing school. Sue's parents are worried she's doing ghastly unladylike things like not being ashamed of having shadow powers." Her voice returned to mere disgusted irritation. "I'm positive they're superheroes, but I don't know who and I can't find out because that would be getting personal."

Charlotte and I nodded in unison. Kay didn't share much with me about his superhero career, but one thing I did know: Personal lives, civilian lives, were inviolate. Hero or villain, crossing that line meant death. Revealing someone else's secret identity included.

Sitting up as tall as she could and looking around, Marcia asked, "Where do you think Charlie is?"

Charlotte hesitated, her mouth tight in uncharacteristic awkwardness. "I, uh...I kind of doubt he made it to Upper High, Marcia. His grades weren't that good."

Marcia glowered, maybe a touch more ferociously than I associated with, you know, sane people. She thumped her fist against the edge of the table, and her knuckles left a dent. "That sucks. He was trying to be a better person, and I respect that."

The anger disappeared as if it had never been, replaced with an excited grin. She bumped her shoulder against mine, and promised, "Don't worry. Me and Charlotte will introduce you to everybody as we find them, and make sure there's no weirdness over the recognition power thing."

YESSSSSS! Exactly what I'd been aiming for. Friends secured on the first day at a new school, and I'd made a good first impression. Now I just had to keep making a good first impression.

It's a super power joke.

So, being friends, I was finally able to level an accusing finger at Marcia. "That outfit. That's rebellion. You're deliberately testing the limits of the dress code, for no other reason than to be difficult."

"Bwa ha ha ha ha. You are correct!" crowed Marcia.

Charlotte covered her eyes with one hand, although the tightness around her mouth suggested she was actually trying not to laugh. She only looked up at me when she'd gone calm again. "Hey, how are your other classes going, anyway?" Yes, we were indeed friends!

"Oh, they're fine," I promised, using my prosaic paper napkin to make sure my face was clean. "I'm no genius, but grades have never been a problem."

Abruptly, Marcia leaped to her feet. She folded her cake box back up, grabbed her backpack, declared, "I'll see you two later," and ran out the cafeteria door.

Before Charlotte and I could recover and wonder what that was about, the end-of-lunch bell rang anyway. On my way out, I passed Marcia. She hadn't actually gone anywhere, just stood outside the lunch room door, leaning against the wall and grinning with evil glee. She barely glanced at me, so I kept walking.

Social Science! Another perfectly ordinary class, without even a mention of super powers. Not even the special laws about heroes and villains.

I couldn't be disappointed. I had friends now. High school would be fine.

There also wasn't much except classwork type facts to remember about the class, so it was with casual good humor that I set out afterwards for Math.

At the hall's T intersection, something thumped inside my backpack.

Uh...what now?

Crack.

Oh, no way. Desperately, I whipped off my backpack, unzipped it, and dug into my gauntlet. Letting the backpack drop, I lifted out the broken plastic shell and the hideous little lizard thing sitting in the remains.

Honestly, cross my heart, I'd been super absolute bedrock of the Earth positive this had been a practical joke.

Boy, the hatchling was ugly. It had a winding, scaly body, long skinny legs, twitchy bat wings, and the grossest, tiniest, wrinkliest bare skin head with mad bulgy eyes and a curved beak.

"B'gak!" it squeaked.

Ow. The noise hadn't been loud, but it made my head hurt. Already people were staring, and they winced too.

It flopped out of the shell onto my hands. Tiny talons

scratched at my skin for a second, and then my fingers went numb.

I twitched them. They did move, but all I could feel was a faint, stiff ache in my joints. The cold numbness spread, inch by inch, past my wrists and up my forearms.

I dropped the little monster and grabbed at my belt. My fingers were so clumsy when I couldn't feel them! I fumbled open the little leather pouch I always, always wear, and pulled out a plastic tube. My fingers couldn't get hold, but I managed to unscrew the lid with my palm and drink half of the thick red juice inside.

Warmth and sensation flooded back into my arms. Petrification canceled. I would live.

People started to shout. Someone moved towards the hideous thing. Oops. I hadn't warned anyone. I'd been busy trying not to die. At the top of my lungs, I shouted, "It's a cockatrice and it will kill you if it touches you! Stay away!"

That worked. The shouts got louder and more frequent, but everyone backed off. The fumbling newborn cockatrice didn't seem too mobile, bouncing and flopping instead of running or flying. Teachers shoved to the front of the pack, and started to pull away the kids who would rather take videos with their cell phones than retreat to safety.

A bubble appeared over the chicken-snake. I couldn't tell who, but some kid with super powers had decided to use them. The cockatrice didn't like that and bounced forward, popping the bubble with its beak, only to have a new bubble form.

A solidly built boy with scruffy brown hair dumped his textbooks on the floor, opening the mouth of his backpack wide as he prepared to slap it over the monster. A teacher grabbed him.

Serpents of black smoke appeared in the air, vague writhing shapes. Out of them stepped Mourning Dove, as cadaverous as she had been at the bus stop. Reaching down, she jabbed her hand through the bubble and lifted the cockatrice up in her fist.

The chicken-snake writhed. The lines of smoke slithered down Mourning Dove's arms and over the monster, into it. When they cleared, only ash remained, falling out of the embalmed yellow heroine's hand. Greedy instinct tugged at me, but if I gathered some there'd be too much fuss.

Mourning Dove disappeared the way she came, silent as the grave.

"What. Was. That?" asked the boy who'd emptied his backpack. That reminded me to recover my own.

A short girl with giant glasses, dull brown hair in braided pigtails, and equally dull brown shirt and slacks slid to the front of the crowd. Her solemn words carried to everyone as if she were a queen. "A warning. This year, we're being watched. If we get out of line with our powers, a suspension will be the least of our problems."

The kids swallowed that silently, until a teacher clapped her hands. "To class, everyone. You're late!"

Movement resumed, mostly away from the intersection.

One person moved against the tide. Marcia ran in our direction, shoving people aside, and only slowing as it became clear everything was over. She had a wide-eyed, horrified expression, as she ought. I headed for her. Late to class or not, Marcia and I were going to have a flaming hail and raining fish tempest of a discussion about this.

Then she shook, a violent twist that ran from her shoulders down her whole torso. Clamping a hand over her mouth, she staggered on barely functional legs into the nearby girls' restroom. Nobody, not even a teacher, seemed to notice.

Uh. Switching from anger to concern, I weaved through the quickly clearing crowd and into the bathroom after her.

I found Marcia on her knees on the floor, arms wrapped around her torso. They couldn't stop her torso from spasming. The girl who acted indestructible was having a seizure right in front of me.

Now blood began leaking from her nose and mouth. In a panic, I dived down next to her, pushed the remaining half of my healing potion up to her mouth, and tilted her head back to make her drink it.

She still had the self-control to swallow. That left her gasping, but the shakes stopped, and she didn't lose any more blood. Or hair. I had several strands decorating my shirt now.

Instinct took over. I snuck the other tube I kept in my belt pouch out, the empty one. First, I scooped a couple of hairs into that, and then wiped the blood off Marcia's nose and mouth with my thumb. I tried to make it look like tender concern, but no, I just wanted to scrape some into my vial. Marcia's body parts would have some crazy properties. Poison, maybe. Or madness. I couldn't pass a sample up.

She took several seconds to become lucid anyway, then looked down at the tube she'd just drank out of. "What was that?"

"Sanguinity," I answered.

Augh, stupid! I'd been paying attention to my samples! Right on cue, Marcia asked, "You mean blood?"

And then, to my surprise, she corrected herself. "Oh, the ideal of blood. Life! It works, too. Whew. Good stuff."

Laying my arm around her shoulder, I asked, "Are you okay, now?"

She nodded. "Yeah, I'm good."

My concern had been sincere, but now it wasn't necessary. I jabbed the side of her head with my finger. "You set me up!"

At least she did look guilty and upset as she looked up, raising her hands to defend against my anger. "You weren't supposed to keep it warm. I didn't think you'd be able to! And I planned on taking it back right after lunch, but I couldn't find you!"

"I'd literally just told you that my super power makes me hard to recognize," I snapped.

Marcia shook her head. "Yeah, but I didn't think it would take effect that fast!"

We looked at each other. Well, I'd been warned. I'd have to let it go. Besides, I was still more than a little worried. Leaning in to peer at her, I asked, "What happened?"

She rolled back to lean against the cold tile wall, and took a deep breath, then let it out in a rush. Lifting the vial, she answered cheerfully, "Oh, my super power is killing me. These potions are great, though. Make me a dozen."

I was pretty sure she meant it. Now it was my turn to tuck my head down awkwardly, embarrassment prickling up my back. "I can't. Partly it's the time and effort. Partly it's the cost. That potion is purified color red. An apple is cheap, but a sack of them isn't."

"Huh. Then I should pay for this one. Here you go," she said, digging into her pocket. Pulling out a wad of green, she dumped it into my hands.

Uh.

My brain froze up.

These were hundred-dollar bills.

Uh.

Marcia kept talking in the background. I stared at the insane pile of cash in my hand, more than adults usually got their hands on at once.

I knew exactly what I was going to do with this money.

CHAPTER TWO

H ome again, home again, jingling jeep.
I was much too distracted to get nursery rhymes right as I unlocked our apartment door and stepped in. The lights were off, but September sunlight poured through the blinds and kept every room but one lit. Our place always smells like old paint, because we never got around to replacing the flaky orange that came with it.

The moment I stepped in, Kay stepped out of his room, walking swiftly but easily up to the door to meet me. Pinching my cheek, he leaned down and asked, "How was your first day of school, Magenta?"

I nodded, cheerful and thoughtful like a wise geezer in an adventure movie. "I'm making friends already. My classes are as blandly normal as Elmer's glue, but fine. Overall a success, but far short of expectations."

He snickered, straightening back up to perch his wiry fists attached to his wiry arms against his wiry hips, oh so cocky. "Told you. I've got to go."

"Now?" I asked, trying to look disappointed rather than excited.

Kay was already taking the door handle from me. "It feels like right now."

Then he was gone, obeying the mysterious calls of his super power. No doubt he had to arrive at exactly the right time somewhere to stop a crime, or catch someone falling off a bridge.

Creeping down to the one dark room, I stuck my head through the gap where the door wasn't quite shut. In this room curtains were hung over every window, blocking out the light. Gently, I asked, "You home, Mom?"

"Who's there?" mumbled a groggy voice from the shadowy bed. Books were scattered over the covers, and she was leaning back against a pile of pillows. Her head didn't even budge.

So. Mom was interning on night shift at the hospital, Kay was out superheroing, and Dad would be working until who knew how late paying for all of us. I'd had quite a day already and badly wanted to rest and absorb, but this timing was too perfect.

The secret of being a teenage superheroine is having three people who all think the other two are looking after you.

First, how would I get there? Bus. We were sitting on an express line. How would I afford bus far? Okay, yes, my pocket seethed like a crocodile hootenanny with filthy green lucre, but not with useful denominations.

Sliding into my parents' bedroom, I watched Mom's still form as I snuck over to their dresser. She was blotto, out like a light bulb eaten by a grue. Medical school had required her every waking moment, and interning was even worse. That left her pocketbook undefended. In extravagant silence, I scooped out all her cash and change, and replaced it with one of the hundred-dollar bills Marcia had given me. She wouldn't look that gift horse in the mouth when she woke up, nope.

On the way out to the street, I buckled my combat gauntlet into place on my right arm, loaded a few choice vials into it, and clipped my container of spare potions onto my belt. As if I were Kay, the bus pulled up the second my foot touched the pavement.

Nobody challenged or even looked hard at a fourteen-year-old girl riding the LA Metro. I was wearing obvious mad science. Sure, it could be a costume, or maybe I could melt their faces off.

Which I could, but I'd have to switch cartridges. Glue was more heroic.

At Jefferson, I stopped just long enough to fit a hundred-dollar bill into a machine and get a TAP pass that would surely meet my transit needs forever.

I had to come up with a flying potion. Riding buses was not the super powered impression I wanted to make on the world. Whatever, I'd reached my destination.

Hidden within the thin line of "good part of town" leading down to the museum, a little brick building with dark windows and no sign sat behind hedges. I didn't even know what the front door was. No, I went down the shadowy path along the side of the building, and to a door with its own dark glass.

As I approached, the door opened and a superhero stepped out. He had short brown hair, a boyish face, but a subtle solidity to his slim body that made him clearly an adult. The orange, brown, and white bodysuit he wore declared his superhero status at the top of its tacky metaphorical lungs. At least it wasn't spandex. No, something more plastic that blended seamlessly into the high-tech machines scattered aimlessly over his body. A helmet, or maybe just a pair of headphones with a really wide headband, completed the look.

The hero gave me a curious stare as he passed, but pass he did. As soon as he'd stepped around the corner, I passed through the door myself.

Bells tinkled as I stepped into a grease-scented spectacle of color.

Blue dominated. Dark blue felt covered the walls, in an attempt by the owner to make the shop look solemn and harmless. Hooks and shelves fastened to those walls, and along with the skeletally simple racks lined up along the floor, they were dull grey metal except for the stains.

Ah, the stains. Stuff so varied and bizarre that only "stuff" sufficed as a description had been stored on those shelves, and left stains of every color. In one fine example, a glass sphere on a stick contained golden arcs like a plasma gold, most of them twisted down to where the glass touched the rack. The metal underneath had turned awfully shiny and yellow, like brass. Char, weird metals, rust, and more conventional stains recorded other oddities long gone.

The current crop of stuff came in its own variety of colors, although brown leather and shiny brass were the most common. Rainbow painted tanks, copper tubes, a stack of red cliché dynamite sticks, altogether it worked hard to overwhelm the somber and practical blue walls.

No sales tags or labels decorated the items on display. In their trickster ragbag of chaos one trait united every scrap: They all looked beaten up. Worn, punctured, dented, cracked, and scarred, every weapon, implement, and artifact had seen better days.

In fact, a heavy metal object that had a bazooka or ray gun look sat on a work table on one side of the room. It consisted mostly of wires, metal tubes, and rounded metal boxes. A woman with flaming red hair and overalls was even now drilling a hole in the ragged edge of a box, through which she stuck a bolt. I got a glimpse of duct tape wound about cables inside before she started bolting two chunks of the weapon together. Fit, thirty-ish, aside from her unusually but not superhumanly vivid hair and unusually but not superhumanly intense freckles, she looked disappointingly normal and practical in this marketplace of oddities. To reinforce that normality, a few signs hung behind her, with two standing out particularly for their messages:

Vendor does not consider mind control an acceptable risk.

Please refrain from Community games.

The former sign had a whole list of signatures, and after seeing her twice today the ugly chipped letters of MOURNING DOVE stood out. The latter sign only had a small stamped figure like an angular spider, and next to it a smiley face.

The woman looked up, eyebrows raised. "So, The Way sent his little...friend with a new donation?"

Yes, I knew about this place because Kay had brought me before. Did he really have to give away for free the supervillain gear he recovered? There had to be such a thing as too good.

Ah, well. Thanks to him I knew about this store and the

Junk Merchant, and I slapped the wad of moolah Marcia The Source of All Unhealthiness had given me down on her table. "No, for a purchase."

Junk Merchant's surprised, curious smile didn't budge. She folded her arms over the weapon, studying me curiously. "The Way needing anything other than his own self is new, but 'whatever works' is practically your—his motto."

Wait. She'd recognized me instantly as Kay's sister. Huh. That had to be a good omen! If the last piece I needed was still here, I would make a splash so big everyone would remember me!

I circled around to the "mostly armor" section, and...there it was. The armor in general was even more damaged than everything else in here, but my target looked functional and fully repaired, with the leather and metal fittings even freshly oiled.

My prize looked more like really old timey football padding, brown leather shoulder plates and about half a vest, but with thin metal boxes of electronics sewn into the padding. Four little vacuum tubes stuck out the back, and a larger tube off of the left shoulder. Squeezing the armor over my head, I tested the buckles. Awesome! I'd have to poke one more hole in the straps, but once I did that it would fit perfectly.

When I had them pulled tight, the vacuum tubes lit up faintly. Yes, this force field generator was functional.

Okay. Now I just had to look confident on my way out the door. Nobody would haggle with Kay, not when he gives so much to charity to begin with. In fact, maybe I should have kept some of that money for myself? Eh. I'd skimmed a bus card that would last until the stars burned out and were replaced with energy-efficient LEDs. Good enough.

As I strode so very confidently past her counter, Junk Merchant remarked with caustic amusement, "Funny that you made sure it fits you personally, since The Way is a foot taller."

My foot stopped mid-stride. Oops.

Junk Merchant gave me a crooked, compassionate smile, and her tone softened. "It's not my place to get personal, but a hero and a villain in the same family leads to big trouble. Everybody loves to talk about heroes and villains dating, but most of them break up fast and hard."

"I don't want to be a villain," I declared flatly and honestly.

She nodded. Her frank, practical smile almost made me shiver. Respect! Junk Merchant sounded just like she was talking to a fellow professional as she replied, "It wouldn't be my place to talk you out of it anyway, and at least you thought about defense. If you can't take a punch, it won't matter how hard you hit. That shock absorber rig won't make you anywhere near invulnerable, but it's a lot better than nothing."

She waved a hand, her gaze already returning to the weapon she was refurbishing. "Anyway, the money was enough. It's yours."

Yes yes yes! Forget striding, it was time to swagger. I was ready to go!

This time I had the shop door half-open before Junk Merchant called out, "So, if you're going to be a hero, have you figured out how you'll find crimes to fight?"

Uh. Er.

That hadn't occurred to me.

CHAPTER THREE

The second day of high school happened.

My bus ride to school was barren of interest. It was a bus. We drove way up near Los Feliz. No criminals were shown the error of their ways. The other girl from my neighborhood read through an entire textbook during the ride.

Okay, probably not, but some people look that smart.

The bus disgorged its heaving vomit of high school students at the front steps, and we flowed up them past the brown-haired guy I'd seen yesterday to the-

Uh.

I looked again. It was that same guy! He had on an awkward, super-nerdy pressed white button shirt, with a gold tag on it that read "Extra Security." His tan slacks were equally perfectly pressed, and he had the smooth face of a college student, with hair parted to the side in a hair style I could only think of as "default."

The pigtails girl had said the superheroes would be watching us. He'd seen a high school girl enter a mad science store last night, and they knew something was up.

My super power held, at least. The guy watched the crowd

with seemingly amicable curiosity, but never actually settled on me.

Er. Yeah. My super power. I trudged stiffly into room 111, sat down in the same chair as yesterday, and waited, getting more tense by the second.

I didn't have many seconds to wait. Mr. Carlyle's gaze slid over to me, and he stepped around his desk to smile in a way he must have intended to be helpful and sympathetic. "Are you in the wrong class, young lady?"

Everybody stopped their early morning bustle and looked at me.

My face hurt. My spine hurt from the effort of not sinking down into my chair in humiliation.

I couldn't explain why he didn't recognize me. Not in front of the whole class. Not six times, since this was going to happen in every single period today, and probably the next few days even if I did explain, and occasionally after that.

I reached up and lifted a fistful of dreadlocks. "This is my class. Magenta Slade. Pink hair. Same chair as yesterday."

His well-meaning, horrified guilt just made it worse. Eyes wide with shock at the mistake, he stammered, "Oh, I'm so sorry. Magenta, of course. Really, I apologize."

Everyone was still watching.

At least homeroom doesn't last long. The bell rang, and I hurried to English.

Where it happened again, and there was a lot longer for kids to stare at me.

The mortifying period of teacher confusion and other students remembering that there's one weird girl who makes a fuss every morning blended into actual learning, but not for long. Soon, I was hurrying to the next stage of humiliation in Chemistry.

In that accursed class with its nonsensical spinning atom posters, I didn't even get to my chair. As I was about to sit down, Marcia leaned over and put her arm across my desk. "This seat is taken."

She said it with a terrible, discordant finality. Yes, she looked casual and comfortable, but that direct stare promised violence if her friendly warning was ignored, violence she was also casual and comfortable with. One day of knowing her was enough to convince me the promise was real. Five minutes would have been enough.

My teeth clenched, I tried to sound confident rather than desperate. "Yes, by me, Magenta."

Marcia's expression barely flickered before she leaned back in her own chair, now casual in her friendliness and wry surrender. "I was prepped for this. I knew I wouldn't recognize you. Your power still got me! I am seriously impressed."

The teacher, at least, had been watching, and gotten over his own confusion by taking Marcia's word. Or just not wanting to argue with her. He went straight to pulling out the Periodic Table of Elements again, and I was grateful for a change of topic.

Getting out my textbook and setting it between us, I untensed enough to notice what Marcia was wearing today. Yesterday, she'd gone for messy and revealing. Today she'd swung hard in the other direction. Well, the other direction from messy. Her glittery golden gown was slit up the sides to the waist, with a keyhole top whose neck-encircling collar contrasted sharply with the diamond shaped cut out in the middle of her chest. Since yesterday Marcia had grown her hair out at least six inches, and now it curled over in an elegant black wave on the left side, all the way to her shoulder. She'd applied lipstick so expertly that if I hadn't seen the chapped mess yesterday, I might just think she had naturally shiny pink lips. Diamond bracelets and high heeled shoes completed the look.

The truth was, Marcia would blend in perfectly walking any red carpet wearing this dress. In a high school...it made me wish I was half as invulnerable to embarrassment as her.

She was all business as she pointed at the table in my book. "Okay, check it. No understanding, just a method. If they ask how many protons phosphorus has, don't think about actual phosphorus. Look for the name Phosphorus in the table. It says 15, so 15 protons. You're just looking stuff up on a chart."

We got to whisper to each other while the teacher droned on explaining this garbage to people who had so-called normal brains. I calmed down, appreciating Marcia's universal acceptance. When I stopped wanting to hide in a trash can, something occurred to me.

"Hey, how much do you know about superheroing?" I asked. Our heads were almost touching. Nobody would overhear us.

That got a smile of wry amusement from the currently exquisite fashion doll. "A lot. A lot a lot. The only way to know more would be to spend three years as a superhero's active sidekick."

My naturally pink eyebrows went up. "I had you pegged as the villain type."

She rolled her eyes, and her head a couple of inches. Exasperation joined the amusement in her smile. "I'd like to be, but I've agreed to stick to heroics."

I didn't have to say anything about the dubiousness that exploded within me at that claim. I only had to look at her.

Rather than shame, that got a bigger grin. "Oh, yeah. There's a whole long story about snakes, child abuse, terminal illness, vampires, and punching people. I'll be happy to regale you with it when we have the time."

Despite my day, now I was grinning. "It's superhero information I needed. How do heroes find villains to fight?" Sure, the question was a trumpeting giant robot elephant herd's worth of unsubtle, but Marcia would have been smart enough to figure out what I was up to anyway, and was never going to tell anybody they had to obey the rules or play it safe.

Marcia pursed her painted lips for a second, nodding thoughtfully. That was good, because it looked like we were discussing classwork. "That's the big question, and it depends on the hero and their powers. Some heroes you don't hear about much because they don't have a way, just stumble onto a supervillain once a year. The ones who can fly can zoom around listening for screams. Lurking in bad parts of town looking for trouble is an option. There's always monitoring police bands, or making deals with alarm companies. I knew a hero who scouted out likely targets for super powered robberies, and put up spy cameras."

"Hmmm," I said, because I wasn't sure any of that helped me.

"Since each hero finds villains to fight a certain way, and each villain has their own pattern of crime, that's why you end up with some heroes and villains who fight each other over and over and become nemeses or boyfriends or whatever. And now, while I am loving this topic, I want you to pass this class so I can feel smug about my virtuous demeanor." Marcia tapped the textbook pointedly, and I couldn't afford to argue.

Class ended. As I headed back to room 111, I realized I was going to have to put up with a repeat of Mr. Carlyle's performance from this morning. Two a day from the same teacher? This would be—

Brown hair in a plain part loomed up out of the milling students. Desperately trying not to stare, I walked past the Extra Security guy, who had found a white lab coat now. He wasn't looking at me. He was looking at his phone, except the phone was more of a tablet, except the tablet was souped up, as thick as a textbook with weird connectors and wires sticking out of it.

Mr. Carlyle was even more apologetic this time. I walked out of the class wondering who in charge I could tell about my power so this could be handled quietly. Ugh. I hated to do it, but Mr. Carlyle had looked so guilty. It was—

The Extra Security guy was at the corner of the hallway where I had to turn to head for the cafeteria, and this time he looked up from his tablet at me. I pretended I didn't notice, but he kept watching me, and kept his tablet turned to point at me, until I passed him and couldn't see without being obvious.

Suddenly, being embarrassed during role call didn't seem very important. I couldn't believe this. It wasn't fair. I'd been caught before I started! And…what were they going to do to me?

I had no idea, but the stakes went all the way up to that cockatrice, reduced to dust in a zombie's hand.

I didn't exactly walk fast while reminding myself that was ridiculously far past anything I could reasonably expect to suffer. Everyone was at the table before I sat down, even having forgotten to buy a tray of food.

Marcia, Charlotte, and a girl I didn't know were all there

already. She had hair pale blonde at the roots, which turned electric blue as it went up. Literally electric blue. This was the girl I'd seen with sparks going through her hair yesterday. It made her hair stand up, but she'd swept it slightly back and to the side so that looked fluffy instead of wild, and wore a matching blue silk blouse and skin-tight dark blue jeans.

Marcia and Charlotte looked up at me as I sat down, amusement exactly like yesterday's starting to form on their expressions, except the blue-haired girl took the lead. Not as manic as Marcia but definitely energetic, she gave me a quick sweep up and down, then asked the other two, "So, this is the new girl you were telling me about, huh?"

They froze for a fraction of a second, then Charlotte nodded as if she'd known me without prompting. "This is Magenta."

Yanking open her backpack, Marcia lifted out a cardboard box the size of her head. She opened it up to reveal a cauldron's worth of Vietnamese flat noodles. Dumping Charlotte's tater tots onto the tray, Marcia stole a carton and set it in front of me, then poured Great Pho Mountain into it. She finished off by passing me Charlotte's as yet unused fork.

Generosity accomplished, Marcia pulled a pair of wooden chopsticks from the box and wielded them with exquisite grace and surety. She speared clumps of noodles, peppers, and nuts too big for a spoon, transferring them to her mouth to be instantly swallowed.

As if these antics were unworthy even of notice, Charlotte continued talking to the blue haired girl. "Where's Will? I was hoping to introduce you both."

The blue girl looked out across the noisy, writhing cafeteria feeding frenzy. With something between a smirk and a grimace she answered, "Pitching woo at Mirabelle, what else? That poor boy. He's beating his head against a brick wall. She likes him, but not a tenth as much as he likes her."

A sarcastic grin split Charlotte's sharp face. "Have you looked in a mirror lately?"

The girl ran her fingers luxuriously back through her own hair, chin lifted in haughty satisfaction. "Three times as much as I used to. Penny and Ray won't be together forever. When they break up, I want it firmly planted in her head how hot I am."

Ignoring Charlotte's unimpressed look and Marcia's snickering, the new girl lunged across the table, extending her hand and warm smile to me. "I'm Cassie Pater. I'm sorry about all that, but I promise you'll know all of us soon and won't feel left out."

It was Charlotte's turn for a gentle smile and nod. "Cassie is good people."

Marcia mumbled something affirmative, ending in a loud, prolonged slurp as pho went into her mouth like a reverse waterfall.

Cassie scrunched up her face and shuddered. "Have some class, Princess Disgusto."

Despite my cares, I giggled. "I looked into the noodle vortex, and the noodle vortex looked back."

Cassie eyed me sidelong, her smile suddenly lopsided, both wary and hopeful. "Are you sure you're safe sitting next to Mighty Mawcules and her Twelve Labors of Lunchtime?"

"Like an iceberg caught in a shark whirlpool. It's terrifying to watch and I'm getting dizzy, but I'm not the one in danger."

Cassie laid her hands flat on the table, and leaned forward a few inches, staring at me hard. "Favorite song?"

"'King and Queen of America,' by the Eurythmics," I answered automatically.

"Ooh, unusual. Fashion?"

"I'd kill for a leather trench coat."

"Sport?"

"Ice dancing. That I can do? Swimming."

"Movie?"

"If You've Got It, Flaunt It with Explosions."

"Do you dance?"

"I don't know how, but I've never let that stop me. I'd love to learn."

"Oh, we are going to be big time friends." Grinning hugely, Cassie held out her hand again, and this time I took it and gave a firm shake.

We settled back into place. Charlotte smiled proudly, arms

folded over her chest. Marcia kept devouring. Reminded that I needed food, I did my best to gobble my own basket of pho. It was lukewarm, but star-dazzled light years better than cafeteria food.

Poking her own fork in Marcia's direction, Cassie demanded now, "Okay, Trouble Magnet. Which of your disasters did this gemstone get caught up in? Because that's the only way you meet anyone."

Trouble magnet.

Everyone jumped, which is how I found out I'd just slapped my hands on the tabletop. That didn't matter. An idea was forming in my head. Not quite a formula...but I could work one out.

However, alchemy had ethics, and...what the galloping glutinosity. If these were going to be my friends, I would have to be able to trust them. Turning to face Marcia, I confessed, "I stole some of your blood yesterday. Can I use it in an experiment of dark science to pursue forbidden goals?"

She lit up like...Marcia in exactly this situation. Let's face it, she was the gold standard of unholy glee against whom all others must now be compared. "Sure! Do you need more? I have gallons!"

Hmmm. I had barely more than a stain, but...no, quantity wouldn't matter. More than a tiny speck would be dangerous even to own, and I could get that out of a crust of Marcia Bradley's blood.

Holding a quivering chopstick in each fist, Marcia babbled excitedly, "So, what are you doing to do with it? A regeneration potion? Disguise yourself to look like me? Mind control?"

"I'm going to distill the essence of Trouble from it," I announced.

All three nodded.

"That should work," conceded Charlotte.

Suddenly, Marcia dove down, hands burrowing into her backpack only to rear back up holding a little bitty pamphlet, which she shoved into hands. "Here! These are Upper High's dress code rules, which I have not yet broken. Do they help?"

Normally no, but because of the link.... "I might be able

to use these to help separate the Trouble from your blood contaminants. Hmmm." My mind chased the recipe I was building in my head further. "I wonder if I can buy a compass on the way home?"

Charlotte let out a loud, long sigh. We all waited as her face twisted in an undulation of conflicted emotions. Finally, she hung her head forward and muttered, "I might as well be drawn into this insanity."

Marcia and Cassie's eyes widened. "Do you think you can do it?"

"Maybe. People use compasses as decorations. I'm going to try." After those soft, solemn words, Charlotte closed her eyes and went still. Her beads twitched as if a breeze rang through her hair, but then that stopped as well.

We waited, until above the growl of cafeteria conversation a girl squeaked, "Criminy!"

Heads turned, including mine. Way in the back of the room, the drab brown pigtailed girl from yesterday sat with a blonde and a boy in black. Something floated in front of her, too small to see at this distance. A compass attached to something else, no doubt.

Her face lighting up in deific joy, Cassie sprang to her feet and waved at the girl, who responded by fiddling with the floating object, then giving us a thumbs up.

Charlotte let out her held breath. A speck flew across the cafeteria to us, and landed in my upraised palm. It was a cheap compass, hardly bigger than a quarter. That was all I needed.

Sinking reluctantly back into her seat, Cassie dragged her attention back to me. Peering across the table at the compass, she asked, "Hey, is it important if the compass magnet is strong?"

I shrugged. This was untraveled territory for me, chasing an inspiration. "Stronger magnet, more accurate compass. That ought to carry over. I think?"

She held out her hand. "My turn, then."

I passed over the compass. She held it in her thumb and forefinger in both hands. Blue sparks glittered over her fingers at first, then that stopped. Nothing else seemed to be happening, although Cassie certainly frowned like she was putting forth effort.

Finally, she let out a puff of exhausted breath, and handed the compass back. "Best I can do."

I peered down at the cheap little tin dish with its diamond shaped bit of iron on a pin. The diamond did look remarkably steady. I turned the dish in a circle. No wavering. That magnet pointed due north, period.

My shoulders shivered involuntarily, and I let out a giggle. "This is great. I have never had friends like this before."

Charlotte laid a slim but muscular arm on the tabletop, and chuckled. "Welcome to the table of kids who wanted all their lives to hang out with other kids who had powers."

I winced as a very unpleasant memory returned. Er. Trying to sound casual even though my discomfort had to be obvious, I asked the group, "Hey, does anyone know what's up with that special security guy?"

Marcia dabbed her mouth with her glittery dress that surely cost as much as all the rest of the clothing in this cafeteria combined. "His hero name is Echo. Not much of a fighter. He's a mad scientist who specializes in detection equipment, especially sound based."

My heart clenched, and my voice squeaked. "So, he could be listening to us right now?"

Marcia nodded, perfect black hair rippling. "Oh, yeah. Easily."

That got a sour squint from Charlotte, who leaned away from Marcia to give her a suspicious look. "Isn't that illegal?"

"Nope," Marcia declared with the assurance of an expert. "This is government property and he's been given permission to investigate."

Cassie smirked, propping her own elbows on the table. Like a well-fed lioness contemplating an after-dinner lamb, she said, "He's easily embarrassed. The supervillainesses think he's adorable."

The lunch bell rang. We'd all been completely distracted. I hurried off to Social Science.

Echo was right. Outside. The cafeteria.

He didn't look at me this time, just peered at his tablet, but I was so jittery in class that the teacher not recognizing me was miniscule tubers. I had to work not to squeeze the compass too hard and break it. Eventually I tucked it into the potion box in my backpack. There was obviously no point in bringing the gauntlet, but still.…. I'd nurtured a mad, self-destructive hope I'd need my supply.

When the bell rang for the final period, Echo wasn't ten feet from the door, and as I tried to walk past, he stepped in front of me and asked, "Excuse me, miss. What's your name?"

My heart turned to ice. My eyes hurt from being opened so wide. My voice sounded far away. "Magenta Slade."

With a serious frown, Echo looked between me and his tablet. His voice held a subtle hiss of static I don't think I would have noticed if I wasn't so close. "Have you seen any other girls with pink hair in this school?"

Worst case was happening. Frozen, I answered honestly and on autopilot. "There's a girl with big pink spiral pigtails. I think she's a senior. I saw another girl with dyed pink hair in a sort of wide mohawk. I don't know their names. They're people I've seen in the hall."

That got a scowl, and that touch of steel to his otherwise cute, boyish face revealed the superhero inside. He looked at his tablet again, then behind me. "Open your backpack, please."

I managed on the second try. Echo pretended not to notice. All I could pay attention to was the faint twitches of his eyes and mouth, up and down, marking how serious and upset the thoughts were going on behind them second by second. Hands larger than I would have expected for his slim build tapped my metal potion case. "What is this, please?"

Very, very carefully, forcing myself to focus on my hands so I wouldn't drop it, I pulled off the lid of the metal box and held it up. He completely ignored the compass, which right now was technically perfectly normal, and lifted up the little bottles one by one to peer at their bright colors. "What are these?"

Desperately, I stammered, "They're for self-defense! The red one is healing. The blue one reinvigorates you. It's like a night's sleep in a bottle. That pale green one is glue. This is a speed potion. This is a sunlight burst. That's acid that eats fabric and metal, but not people."

Echo…smiled. Warm, pleased, impressed, approving. He straightened back up, laid his hand on the top of my head to ruffle my dreads, then yanked it away with a momentary look of guilt. Reassembling his proud smile, he said, "Those are great choices for escaping danger."

That left him actually looking at my expression for the first time, and he jumped with alarm so hard that his lab coat flapped. His own eyes wide now, he lifted both hands and gushed out, "Oh, you poor thing, you think you're in trouble! No! Here, in fact…you're going to need an excuse note for class, right?"

Echo poked and scribbled his finger on the screen of his tablet, and a second later it spit out a piece of paper that he pushed urgently into my hands.

My heart, my whole body, felt like it was melting. For a second, I thought I would fall over, and I stared at the paper without seeing it. What had happened was so clear now. Echo thought he'd seen half a dozen different girls with pink hair, and detected the potions in my bag, and gotten confused. That's all.

Good thing I hadn't brought the gauntlet. Heh.

Lesson learned. My super power would ensure I kept my secret identity, if I was smart and restricted all my crime fighting to after school. Once I'd saved the day a time or two, no one would be in a hurry to shut me down. If the Inscrutable Machine could do this as villains, I could do it as a hero. I could be famous!

Right now, I was in the clear, and ready to build a magnet that points to trouble—*super powered* trouble!

CHAPTER FOUR

"So, is it ready? I want to see a trouble magnet!" Demanded Marcia when I sat down next to her for lunch on Wednesday.

I gave her my most skeptical look, chin down as if I had glasses to peer over in scorn. "I'm separating a trace element with no guide. It won't be done until Friday afternoon."

I was wrong.

I got home that afternoon still stinging from another day of nobody recognizing me. Someone had warned my teachers about my power, and they'd at least recovered quickly without making a big, embarrassing deal out of it.

When the apartment door closed behind me, silence reigned. Eerie, unnatural stillness.

"Kay?" I called out.

No answer.

Walking down to my parents' bedroom, I peeked in the door. Okay, Mom was here, just deeply asleep. This was too early for Kay to have gone out heroing. What was up?

I dug out my phone and turned it on. Couldn't use it at school, right? A text message from Kay immediately popped up on the screen:

My power dragged me out of school. The news will tell you about the explosion. Some superheroes want to talk to me. This could be big. I swear, I was only using my power to help people. This happened naturally. I don't know when I'll get home. It could be morning, even. This is amazing!!!!!

Suddenly I was breathing hard, my hands clenched painfully around my phone. I was glad for Kay. I was. Except, why couldn't I have this?! Why did I have to get the power that guaranteed I would never get fame?

My pounding heart calmed oh, so slowly as I headed for my room to check my alchemy set. I had all kinds of stuff, most of it handmade. Of course, half of all reactions involve heat, and I couldn't leave them running during school. My parents only let me do them at all because my super power knew how to handle flame.

That meant the bits of Marcia had been sitting all day in a vial with a few other ingredients, waiting for solvency and gravity to separate them all, with her dress code booklet on top in case that did push the Trouble down. I gave it a glance to check what kind of layers I'd gotten.

On the top of the top layer of pure alcohol sat a little black dot. Of course! Trouble was attracted to alcohol, and attracted to rules. Marcia herself had leaped on these rules as something to break.

Now my hands trembled, but they stilled automatically as I grabbed an eye dropper and sucked the little dot up, lay it in a ceramic dish, and set that over a gentle flame. Not much heat. I only wanted to evaporate the alcohol, which took a couple of minutes.

That left me with a shiny black glob, smaller than a pinhead but with a glutinous rainbow shine. There was no doubt what this was. It *looked* like Trouble.

Okay, now I really needed extreme care. With my finest pair of tweezers, I poked the spot. It transferred easily to the metal. Trouble is sticky. Lifting it out, I daubed the black goo on the tip of the compass needle.

The compass swung immediately from north to northeast.

My heart pounded and my breathing shuddered again. It worked! It actually worked!

"EEEEEE—"

No! Get ahold of yourself, Magenta! The Trouble attracting this compass could be hundreds of miles away.

"In LA? The sparkling septic tank down which Southern California's super powered madness has been flushed to ripen into glory? Trouble is never far away. Anyway, I don't have to be the hero. I can just show up and help," I said aloud.

But being the hero would be great.

The urgency of the situation struck me. Super powered trouble rarely lasted long. I fit the cover on the compass, and fitted the compass into the slot I'd prepared on my gauntlet. No time to dress up and look cool. I swept my potion collection into my backpack, even the choking gas I was afraid to use, and stuffed my armor on top. Thrusting my hand into the gauntlet happened as I ran for the front door.

What if it was already too late? What if I missed this chance?

No. I had to trust my power. This would work. Maybe no one would know who I was, but I'd get noticed. Big time noticed.

I still had no alternative but to take the bus, and spent the whole time heading north watching the compass. It turned slowly. The Trouble hadn't ended, and wasn't unreachably far. When it turned East, I got off the bus at...

...Jefferson. Weird coincidence. Or not. If Junk Merchant was on this street, who knew what other super powered treasures hid in plain sight, like a freaky Zeus in a flock of geese?

Running down to the split in Exposition, I climbed onto the train docking there just in time. This went way faster. In no time at all the compass swerved, and I leaped off again next to the University of Southern California.

As I power walked, I buckled on my armor, arranged my potions, and checked the loadout in my gauntlet launcher. Glue, itching powder, and my sunlight flash. I had a speed potion in my belt pouch with the red and blue vials. The neighborhood around USC wasn't great, but I could handle drunk frat boys or muggers.

I only had to go two blocks to get to the right street. This was a short row of empty stores. Just one block, not a slum. The houses on the opposite side were multi-floor with lit windows, no doubt student apartments, but the sidewalks were empty.

Bizarrely, I heard a man singing. No, not quite a man. A boy my height, in a knee-length red robe, hunched in the doorway of one of those closed-down shops. Whatever his age, he had a grown man's voice, beautiful as sinuous lightning embracing alien lyrics in serpentine coils. No, I couldn't make sense of the words. Some other language. They would have sounded like joke gibberish if they weren't being sung in that delicious voice.

He held a big book hunched under one arm as he fiddled with the door lock. As I watched, the handle clicked and turned, and the boy stopped singing. Silent now, he slipped inside with all the stealth someone wearing crimson could manage.

What the budding supervillain didn't do was close the door completely and after a few prudent seconds I slipped in after him. Thank you, compass. You had pointed me to where I personally would find trouble, not where trouble was already happening.

The boy had started singing again, and whew, that voice. Even softly under his breath, he sounded like a professional opera singer. Over his head now floated a small, gentle white light as he searched through…uh, a mess.

So, whatever this place had been, its paper-covered windows now hid the fact that nobody had emptied it before moving out. The layout reminded me partly of a second-hand bookstore, and partly someone's private den. Irregularly arranged bookshelves and tables big and small held dusty knickknacks, and that was all I could say about them. Wooden globes of the Earth, tarnished metal scales, sticks, faded butterfly collections, skulls, hats, lamps, pots, statuettes, and of course lots of books. What didn't fit on tables had been stuffed underneath, like steamer trunks and a stuffed moose head.

The red-robed boy let out an excited squeal, lifting a particularly large book off a table and shaking off the dust and unidentifiable triangular implements that had been layered on top of it. "I found it!" he gloated in a teenage squeak that didn't match his singing at all.

Pointing my gauntlet at him, fist clenched and other hand on the firing switch for the glue vial, I ordered, "Great. Now put it down, villain."

The boy spun around to face me, robe flapping. Oh, yeah, definitely a boy, about my age. He had a pale face and squid ink black hair, with delicate, not quite girlish features. Stung, he shouted, "I'm not a villain!"

"I caught you stealing," I answered, arm still pointed. Now that the singing had stopped, the light over his head was slowly fading. I flipped open the sunlight firing tube to get some more light, but honestly even in the dimness filtering through the ajar door and grey papered windows I could see that bone white skin easily.

That caught him. Narrow shoulders writhed with the poisonous torment of guilt. "Well...I'm taking it, but it's not stealing because nobody owns it!"

Yeah, not impressed. "Somebody has to own it."

His chin jutted forward, simultaneously desperate and offended. "It rightfully belongs to me! I am Aikamieli, descendant and heir of the second greatest wizard in history!"

Unable to help myself, I squinted and gave him an oblique stare. "*Second* greatest? Okay, so I guess the greatest was Merlin?"

That might as well have set fire to the kid's robe. His chest swelled in injured pride. His arms twitched, raising the book.

I was having none of that, and jabbed my gauntleted fist an inch toward him, finger on the switch. "I will fire this thing if you move another inch."

He glared rabid animal fury at me, but froze except to complain, "Merlin is cheap pop culture trash! Wainamoinen is the greatest wizard in history, and he wrote this book!" As he got angrier, the teenage villain's voice cracked and wobbled more and more. Sticking his chin out in fury also drew attention to three ugly, out of place dark hairs that might be part of a beard by the time the next ice age happened. Yuck. So much for "pretty boy."

I sighed. This was not exactly the big, exciting, showy public Trouble I'd hoped for, but maybe it would build to something. Aikamieli was singing again, and if he was smart, he would sing everything because I could drown in that voice. The words remained foreign, but it wasn't hard to get the point from the tone. This was the wrong fight to pick. He didn't mean to be a villain. We'd be better off as allies.

Awkwardly, he edged past me with his back to a bookshelf, reading the words he was singing out of the bigger book he'd just taken. The display was so goofy and harmless, I might as well let him go.

No. Absolutely not. I'd invested too much in this. My arm had sagged from firing position, but that was fine. I fired at his feet. Green goop spat out of my gauntlet, spraying over his ankles and feet, which stuck to the floor.

He let out a yelp, and the spell broke. Literally. He'd cast a spell on me! Lunging forward, I shoved the knuckles of my gauntlet right up against Aikamieli's mouth, and snarled, "You do not want me to fire this next capsule. Hand over the book."

At that moment an actual adult man stepped into the room from a doorway at the back of the room, which I hadn't even seen thanks to the shadows everywhere. With condescending amusement, he announced, "If that book is the True Kalevala, you'll be handing it over to me."

I spun and fired another glue blast at him. A book leaped off a shelf and pushed my arm away, sending the green glob to harmlessly splatter a corner instead. The book had flown like a brown, leather-bound blur, and if I hadn't been wearing my force field armor it would have hit a lot harder than "pushed."

My heart went cold. This guy was no goofy kid like Aikamieli. Tall, blonde, he looked athletic but not bulky, although it was hard to tell under a coat of loose chainmail with a black tunic on top. He stood still and balanced and ready, utterly confident but not negligent. An experienced, professional supervillain, and if his power let him throw books, I was standing in the middle of a potential blizzard of projectile defeat.

First, get out of sight! I dived behind a table with enough junk piled underneath to block his view and attacks.

Aikamieli chose to run rather than hide. Flipping hurriedly through the (maybe) True Kalevala, he found something and started to sing. After only a few words, his shoes slipped free of the glue I'd trapped him in.

That was as far as he got. A modern trade paperback smacked him in the face with its pages spread wide. The book bent Aikamieli backwards until he fell into the glue again. From the muffled sounds, paper in the boy wizard's mouth made it impossible to sing.

This kept getting worse. I needed a plan. I wouldn't have time to aim at the supervillain. I'd fire itching powder at the ceiling and let the cloud drift down onto him. Ready. Set. Go!

I rolled up, peeking over the table just enough to confirm my aim as I raised my arm and jabbed the firing button.

Waiting newspapers swarmed over my gauntlet like octopus bees. The itching powder fired, but it didn't go anywhere. With a yelp, I shoved the gauntlet off. I did not want any of my itching powder getting on me. That stuff was brutal!

As soon as the gauntlet fell free, big, thick dictionaries closed on my wrists and ankles and half-lifted, half shoved me against the wall. The impact didn't hurt, but my shock absorbing field did nothing to prevent the grip itself, which held me upright with my arms spread and my feet slightly apart.

The armored villain stood in the middle of the abandoned shop, lighting a dusty oil lamp. He still sounded condescending and amused, but worse, pitying. "You are not ready for this, children."

Leaving the lamp on the table, he walked over to Aikamieli and crouched down. The book on the boy's face slid far enough for Aikamieli to see the supervillain speak to him. "I'm sorry, but you will never be."

Standing, he turned and stepped over to loom over me, now. I gave him the fiercest glare I could, trying to hide the ice running up and down my spine. Thoughtful, compassionate, and thoroughly unintimidated, the blonde man said, "You may be, someday, especially if you find someone to train you. You think and you had a defense prepared. I don't deal in false hope, child. You'll never be a burning beacon of justice, but you do have a spark."

With no idea what to say to that, I kept glaring. Also, I was decidedly out of other options, except to take up a new life as a mortified, dust-smeared scarecrow.

The bad guy continued to ignore me. No, not quite. As he returned to Aikamieli, I noticed he never turned so far that I was completely out of sight. At least he gave me that much credit. He hadn't given it to Aikamieli, who he now bent over. Taking firm hold of the (alleged) True Kalevala, the villain pulled it loose from Aikamieli's grip.

The high school proto-wizard freaked. His arms flailed, grabbing at the book and trying to take it back. When that met exactly zero success, he clawed at the book covering his mouth. After a few seconds of that he received mercy, and the book slid down to let him plead, "Give it back! Please, I need it. It's meant to be mine!"

Blondie the Book Lord watched this performance with a concerned frown. Quietly, with unhidden doubt, he asked, "Can you really use it?"

"Yes!" shouted Aikamieli immediately.

At least Aikamieli was smart enough to stay silent as the literate armies of conflicted emotion marched across the armored supervillain's facial features. At last, the grown villain dropped the magic book into the merely goober villainette's hands and sighed. "Here. Don't waste this book by trying to use it to fight. Be happy with the magic you have."

"That isn't yours to give away!" I shouted.

My guts crawled in anxiety as the villain looked at me directly, his expression now blank. He looked young-ish, like less than thirty, with a face a little too angular to be pretty. He also looked really dangerous.

Aikamieli had his book, and tried to scramble away, but his robe was glued to the floor. A newspaper page slid over to Aikamieli, and sliced its edge through the goop sidelong, sawing him free. That only made my stomach tighten worse.

Until now, the idea of paper cuts hadn't appeared in my head. Now I imagined myself reduced to a pile of exact bloody cubes with a mop of pink dreadlocks on top. That could happen the second this guy's mood turned.

Instead of murdering me, the villain straightened up and said in a mild tone, "In fact, I believe I will purchase this place. I see potential. Then the book will have been mine to give away."

The books pinning me in place fell to the floor, spitting up clouds of nose-tingling dust. The rest of a pile of newspapers wrapped my gauntlet up over and over into a safe package, and it floated around behind me to deposit in my backpack. He answered my confused stare with fatherly concern. "Wash that glove before you—oh, what am I saying. You're smart enough to take basic safety precautions."

The books that had held me flew around to my back, pushing me forward so that I had no choice but to stumble to and out the shop's front door. It slammed shut behind me.

Aikamieli was gone. I leaned against a huge, papered-over window and let my heart calm down. Well. The compass worked. I had certainly found Trouble. I'd thought Trouble would be bigger, but maybe the guy was right and I wasn't ready. I'd been beaten by a man in medieval armor with the super power of controlling books, for pity's sake!

Which was weird. I heard stuff from Kay. Even for super powered antics, that had all been weird. This guy didn't act right.

Maybe I couldn't fight him, but I could wait and see if he stuck around. The paper covering the shop windows was glued to the inside of the glass, but it had tiny gaps and I peeked through one.

The villain was still there, walking from table to table, bookshelf to bookshelf, holding up the oil lamp to examine the contents. Books flew all over the place. In the process, they kicked up dust, which soon became a cloud that made the man cough. Holding his breath, he deposited the lamp where he'd found it and headed to the front door.

In a hurry, I yanked my phone out, leaned against the window, and fiddled with the screen, unlocking it and poking at my messages. Just an ordinary teenage girl he'd never seen before hanging around, that's me!

The supervillain walked right past me without a glance.

One single step right past me. Then he stopped, turned, and gave me a fascinated, searching frown.

My heart tried to climb up my throat with an icicle ladder. I couldn't speak, but did my best to give him a wary stare like any cornered stranger would.

"Is that a potion, or inherent?" the villain asked, his tone almost a monotone of intense thought.

My control cracked, shattered, and exploded in fragments. I stared at him, mouth open, agog. "You recognize me?!"

Still frowning in concentration, close enough that I could hear faint squeaks from his chain mail, he answered in that flat voice, "Knowledge is what I do. You have a deeply interesting power. It isn't mind control. I've been trained to tell. How does it work? No, foolish question. You don't know either, do you?"

"It just does. It has since I was little. No, it's not mind control. It works even in photographs. Facial recognition programs crash when they see me." I was babbling, but his face was inches from mine, he outweighed me by a hundred pounds, he'd just made it zirconium crystal clear that I had no chance against him in a fight, and that image of death by paper cuts still lingered in my imagination. What could I do but talk?

He straightened up to merely loom over me. The intense concentration faded to flat-chinned speculation. After several seconds, he said mildly, even approvingly, "I can see how that would drive someone to want to be a superhero. You have more potential than I thought. My title is The Cleric, and I'd like you to be my sidekick."

An offer like that meant he had no desire to kill me, and that gave me defiance back. I crossed my arms. "I want to be a hero, not a villain."

"But you're not completely sure about that," he countered, obnoxiously confident and completely wrong. Absolutely wrong. For certain wrong. Maybe. It had been a confusing afternoon.

When I didn't have an immediate answer, he took a step

back, becoming slightly less threatening. He was still tall, anachronistically armored, and probably well-muscled. All of the serious, poised bad guy demeanor vanished, and he gave me a lopsided grin matched by a jovial tone. "Tell you what. Give in to your curiosity. Let me take you to dinner and try to convince you. We'll claim I kidnapped you for a couple of hours. As long as you're unhurt, the Los Angeles super powered community won't object."

Yeah, that wasn't suspicious at aaaaaaaall. I sneered back. "And if I refuse?"

"I'll try to talk you into it. If you still refuse, I'll let you go. I want an assistant, not a victim." The playful tone vanished. He laid his hand flat on his dusty black tabard over his heart. With marble-faced seriousness he recited, "On my oath to the cause I serve and the better world I hope to make, you are free, truly free and without tricks or punishment, to leave my service whenever you choose."

I took a deep breath, suddenly weirdly aware of the bright September sun, the empty street, and the distant sounds of traffic.

"Okay."

CHAPTER FIVE

We had to walk to his car. I sneered up at the chain mail wearing supervillain. "What, no horse?"

I'd agreed to listen, but he was still a bad guy and his every word and action would be met with withering skepticism. Salty tornadoes of mummification level withering skepticism.

My sarcasm was met with a tight half-grin of wry exasperation. "I'd prefer a griffon, or everyone to be able to fly, or for the teleportation technology horded by mad scientists to replace the LA Metro system and be used for mass transit. For now, I make the best of it."

Cleric gestured at his car, and must have been carrying a hidden key because the doors opened. They were funky doors that rose like wings instead of tilting out. It was a funky car, low and sleek like a sports car, but not low enough and way too angular. If it had ever had room for back seats, they were now filled with vents, electronic readouts, vast numbers of buttons, and a glass case containing an oversize fuse.

He slid into the driver's seat. I...hesitated. Was I really going to get into a strange adult man's car? When all I actually knew about him was that he was a supervillain? That was the only reason I was considering it. Supervillains that preyed on teenage girls were found dead very quickly. My brother hadn't had much contact with other superheroes so far, but he had been absolutely clear that there were things that were Not Done or Else, and anything horrible done to a superhero's little sister was right up at the top. Cleric had me at his mercy in the shop and had no need to take me anywhere else.

If I didn't go with him, I would be giving up.

Forget that. I got in the car.

The doors lowered with a *woosh* sound. Cleric ignored all the fancy equipment and pulled out into traffic like a normal person.

A normal person in a not normal car. I could stop worrying for a few minutes to appreciate how different the view through his windshield was. Other cars had eyes, swerving around their surfaces. Echoing trails and arrows protruded from them. Ghostly animals crawled over and through the metal shells. Some cars had dragons, lions, weasels, seagulls, mice, rabbits, all kinds of things. One car passed us gnashing a mouth full of fangs. Another sported a black aura and lettering in…Sumerian. Of course.

The arrows predicted where the cars were going to go. I got that pretty quickly. Weasel cars changed lanes a lot. The rest remained a mystery.

I'd been so busy watching this show that I'd completely lost track of where we were. Low buildings that weren't grungy. Distant hills on two sides that had to be north and east. This could be a thousand neighborhoods in LA.

Cleric finally paid attention to something other than his car's regular equipment. He drew his finger in a squiggle over a blank screen, and said with the distracted tone of someone talking over the phone, "I'm sorry to do this at the last minute, but I need the King's Reservation." Pause. "Just the two of us. It's not a formal occasion."

I gave him another suspicious stare. "Where are we going?"

He grinned. It looked weirdly…honest. Enthusiastic. He sounded merry but not quite gloating. "Let me enjoy this. It's fun pulling out the stops and making a dramatic first impression."

As much as I wanted to, I couldn't argue with that. That did leave me weirdly surprised and a touch on edge again when we pulled into the lot of a boringly normal shopping center. Maybe slightly on the low end, since I'd never heard of any of these stores and at least three different non-English scripts were featured. None of them were Sumerian, either.

The doors *woosh*-ing open again were cool. I hopped out and fingered my belt pouch for the speed potion. That was one reason I had agreed to this. One false move from Cleric, and I was gone like snow in the abyssal Marianas sulfur vents.

Boy, could he grin. On his rectangular face his eagerness looked bizarrely childish. Stepping up to a door with unreadably overdone cursive script on it, he opened up and stood back for me.

Even from the parking lot, I could see this was a restaurant, so I stepped through the door...

...into luxury. Into the wellspring from which all velvet and gleaming varnished wood was born. Lots of reds, but dark, tasteful, muted reds. A few purples, especially on the uniforms of the waiters.

So. Many. Waiters.

Three descended on us immediately, but Cleric waved two away. "No, thank you. I have nothing to take and I think my dinner companion would rather keep her belongings with her."

He followed up by giving me a curious, questioning look, and only when I nodded did two of the waiters disappear. The third led us to a table near a wall covered in elaborate tapestries. Unicorns, guys with lances, stuff like that. Most of the art was terrible, in that Ye Olde Authentic way.

The table sported a burgundy tablecloth, china plates, what I would swear was an actual gold candlestick, and more silverware than I could identify. The moment I sat down more waiters appeared, carrying trays that glittered with fancy appetizers.

We weren't the only diners, and while nobody else seemed to be getting quite as intense a fawning service, having the wait staff outnumber the customers was clearly the restaurant's strategy.

A waiter without a tray stepped closer to the table. He bowed to me, then asked Cleric, "Would you like the King's Selection?"

Cleric, still looking like the cat that ate the buttered bluebird of happiness, nodded back. "Please, but I'm sure the young lady does not want wine...?"

Another curious stare, yellow eyebrow up. I answered, "I want cola."

The fancy waiter did not bat an eye. He whisked away without even a moment's hesitation. Maybe I should have asked for cockroach juice, to see what he did. Or dragon's blood. Oh, what I could do with dragon's blood.

In the back of the others, a waiter began to play the harp. The music wasn't loud, but was definitely intricate.

Waiters appeared with our drinks, both in bottles. One poured green wine into a fancy glass for Cleric, and the other set a glass tumbler in front of me, and flicked the lid off of an unlabeled brown bottle covered in frost. I reached out and took the bottle instead, downing a swig. Wow, it really was just above freezing, and I didn't recognize the brand. Wouldn't it be crazy if they made their own cola on site?

My tumbler was plucked off the table as nimbly as it arrived, but left on one of the hovering trays in case I so much as shot a longing glance in its direction.

Burgundy menus appeared. That was all I could say about the process. Nothing listed was in English and there were no prices. Fine. I could play this game. I opened it to show one of the tray waiters and pointed at five random lines. He fled, replaced within a second by a waitress with his same tray. Someone else absconded with my menu.

Grabbing a bread-cheese-and-sugar thing kind of like a danish from one of the appetizer trays, I took two bites and washed it down with more cola.

That was enough playing around. I gave Cleric a hard stare. "Now, tell me who you are and what you want."

His menu was gone, so he must have ordered. A small smile ruining his otherwise businesslike air, he answered, "As I mentioned, I am known as The Cleric—"

He was not getting to own this conversation. I interrupted,

"—as in 'clerk', a scribe or librarian, with the priest part being optional."

I might as well have tickled his rutabaga, the way he lit up with joy at that answer. Great. Now I was getting points for being smart. And trying hard not to enjoy that.

He didn't even praise me. The jerk knew I knew he approved. He just resumed his speech. "—and I am here on a mission to perfect a system of transferring information in and out of books."

I leaned forward, elbows on the table. The waiters didn't cringe, but I knew they wanted to. Scowling, I demanded, "And what do you want from me?"

He stifled the smiles. Not that his approval disappeared, but Cleric's face went solidly businesslike to make clear his next words were serious. "To answer that, I need to know why you want to be a hero."

Lying would be pointless, and I could tell a supervillain what I could never tell my parents or brother. "I want to be famous. I want to force everyone to remember me, even if they can't identify me." My gut clenched saying it. Kay was out there right now being celebrated. I'd lost a fight in an abandoned souvenir shop.

Food arrived, plate after plate of unidentifiable stuff. I mean, I could tell that there were bits of carrot and thin slices of cucumber in one of them, and that one dish was mainly beef and another chicken, but they had sauces and lumps and who knew what. I picked up a fork, and tried a bite of the beef stuff.

Nothing I'd ever tasted was half so savory. Oh, yum. At least I would get a good meal out of tonight. I dug in.

Cleric knew it was his turn to talk anyway. "Good. I can give you fame. I can use your super powers. I'm confident an alchemy power as strong as yours will be compatible with my work. Can you make a potion to restore old, faded books?"

Good question. Well, really, it was just a purification. Complicated, maybe. I could conjoin new materials where the old had been lost. Swallowing a bite of the syrupy sweet chicken, I said, "Yeah, but it would require a lot of squid or octopus ink. Like, a *lot*."

"I can get squid ink by the gallon, and without harming any squid," he said confidently, then moved back into business offer mode. "Your other power is even more useful to me. You can run errands and perform distractions that would attract violent attention if I did them."

He paused a moment. A puzzled frown flashed over Cleric's face. Lowering his voice and looking me right in the eyes, he added, "Most of all, I value the way your alchemy power makes you see the world differently from other people."

Laying my fork down, I met his gaze, eye to eye. "You're hiding something from me, and I don't appreciate it."

Yeah, that stung him. Cleric's sleek composure disappeared, replaced by a frown of guilt that turned to a wry grimace. "I was enjoying the build-up, but you don't want to be led around like a child. Understandable. I'm offering you this."

Palming it from under the table, Cleric laid a badge a little smaller than my hand on the table, and gave it a push so it slid over to *clink* against my plate.

I ought to give him an earful for still being mysterious, but the badge was too fascinating. Badly scratched metal was engraved with a couple of knights on horseback, complete with lances. It had been painted white and red once. "It looks old," I said aloud.

"It is an authentic badge of the Knights Templar, yes," he answered solemnly.

My train of thought hit an iceberg. "Knights Templar—you work for Tyrant!"

I felt momentarily guilty for shouting that, then momentarily embarrassed for the squeak in my voice, and then realized: Forget all that. Tyrant. Cleric worked for Tyrant. Everyone in the world knew who Tyrant was, because Tyrant had tried to take over that world three times, and that was just the count for this century.

Cleric bowed his head. "I have the honor of taking orders personally from Tyrant and no one else."

I pushed my plate and silverware and cola bottle away, and my chair back. "Nope. I'm not interested in committing crimes and I'm certainly not interested in helping anyone conquer the world, and you promised I could leave when I want."

Cleric still looked calm and serious, and was still giving me that direct stare. "Tyrant didn't send me here to help conquer the world."

"Uh, that's what Tyrant does," I shot back.

The supervillain straightened up a little more in his chair. His face got, not angry, but very grim. The waiters hadn't shown the slightest surprise, but other diners were fussing at other tables, hurrying up to pay their checks and get out. Of all the weird things to notice, my cola had been replaced with a fresh, new, frost-covered bottle.

Not angry, but as solemn as he could get, Cleric told me, "Not quite. Tyrant wants to change the world. He dreams of a better world, a world of honor and wonder and adventure. A world where beauty is more important than numbers and everyone has a chance to prove their ability, if they want to. My lord long ago decided that he was unlikely to accomplish that without conquest, but if he can change the world without ruling it, he will do so gladly."

He meant it. He sounded like a preacher, but more so. Inspired. Bowing his head in reverent gratitude, he finished, "I am in charge of one of those projects."

Impressed despite myself, I sat back in my chair and stared at him. After a couple of seconds, I found traces of my sarcasm. "His name is literally 'Tyrant'."

That got a smirk. A fierce, blazing-eyed smirk, but humor. "And if he called himself the King of Beauty and Kindness, what would you think?"

I wanted to give that one a snappy retort, but.... "You have a point, but...Tyrant?"

Cleric touched a couple of fingers to his forehead, then waved them away. It was a weird, vulnerable idiosyncrasy. "His actual words were 'Dann lasst sie mich Tyrann nennen', but in context he meant that whatever people call him, he'll help them anyway."

Whoa. No liking the bad guy. I folded my arms and tried another glare. "Still not interested in crimes or conquest."

He nodded acknowledgment. "I'm fine with that. I don't

want you to commit crimes." Now a smirk crept back up on Cleric's face, and a bit of whimsy into his voice. "Granted, mainly because no one ever thought forcibly copying anyone's knowledge into a book needed to be outlawed. I need a technical assistant and someone with an unbreakable secret identity to show off, because I can't. My lord has too many enemies."

I took note of "copy." Not "steal," or—

"CIVILIANS,   EVACUATE   IMMEDIATELY.   SUPER POWERED BATTLE IMMINENT," bellowed one seriously loud and familiar voice.

The customers were already on their way out the door. Our waiters stood in rigid terror, watching Cleric. He gave them a shooing wave, and they ran for the kitchen with expressions of gratitude.

Now with a heavy sigh, Cleric rubbed a hand over his face. It left red marks. "Case in point."

The door slammed open, with a hand bracing it. Echo entered, in full costume and covered in unidentifiable mad science equipment. He had something strapped to his left arm that looked like a combination stereo, boxing glove, and cannon, which he pointed immediately at Cleric. Flatly, Echo asked, "Will you surrender or fight?"

I tried to crawl back into my seat, spine a mass of ice as Echo glanced at me...and then looked back at Cleric, without a hint of recognition.

Of course. He had no idea who I was. Why did I ever think superheroes would be different that way?

Scooting back up to the table, I pulled my plate back and took another bite of the beef stuff. It was still delicious, even lukewarm. Echo didn't know who I was, but he could see me clearly, and his expression turned disbelieving—while still never actually taking his eyes off of Cleric.

I poked a fork at Echo. "Do you mind? This is the best meal I've had in...ever."

It felt so *good* to mouth off to the hero who'd scared me all week. I felt dizzy from the relief. To disguise that, I took a bite of something spicy and lumpy I hadn't even tried yet.

Annoyed and disbelieving, Echo asked, "Do you know who

this is? He works for Tyrant, and he's using you as a human shield."

I ignored him and kept eating. Cleric raised a hand slowly and mildly. "I'm not the one who attacked an opponent who's eating dinner and committing no crimes."

Echo didn't get mad, or adjust his aim in the slightest. He answered with professional calm. "Your presence is a threat to everyone in this city, hero and villain. I'm not inclined to wait until after Tyrant invades."

Cleric nodded his head toward me, although his eyes and his souring frown remained on Echo. "So, you want to start a fight in front of a teenage girl?"

"So, you admit you're using her as a shield?" shot back Echo immediately.

Ice should have been spreading around these two, the way they looked at each other. If looks could kill, we would be in frozen post-apocalypse mode. Cold, hateful, and calm. Completely calm.

In that spirit of bleak composure, his tone quiet, Cleric said, "That depends on what she wants."

They had to watch each other. I didn't. Two customers were crouched under their table at the other end of the room, phones out, videotaping us. Darker silhouettes crowded up against the dark windows at the restaurant's front.

This was going to be on the news, and no one, not Echo tomorrow at school, not even my family, would recognize the girl in the video.

But everyone would see her.

I'd left the badge on the table. Picking it up now, I hooked it onto one of my armor's leather straps. Standing up on my chair, I stepped up onto the table next. I might as well have flown. My heart sure felt like it was soaring.

"If you're going to spoil my dinner, you can have it." I hooked a sneaker into one of the plates loaded with fancy food and kicked hard. It splattered bits of meat and gooey sauce all over Echo's chest.

I had to give him this, Echo's weapon didn't budge its aim, even as shocked as he sounded. "Do you know what you're doing?"

Elegant china plates crunched and silverware clattered as I walked two steps across the table, and jumped down between Echo's gun and Cleric. Looking right up into the superhero's dark goggles, I stuck my chin out in defiance. "No. The question is, are you willing to go through me to get to my master?"

Still professional, Echo silently lowered his weapon and walked back to the door and out, watching us until the door closed behind him.

Cleric spoke first, his hands on his knees and his face and voice grim. "I am sorry. I am sincerely sorry. I didn't expect things to explode this quickly. My honest intention is to keep you out of fights, but you'll have plenty of chances to impress people like him who wish they could fight you." Reaching to his hip, he dug for a minute and pulled out a black but utterly prosaic leather wallet. Pulling a few bills out, he laid them in my hand. "Also, it looks like I already owe you for two hours at your new part-time job."

Caught off guard, I flipped through the money. Forty dollars.

Expression touched with guilt, Cleric said, "If twenty dollars an hour seems cheap, it's an income you can show your parents. I promise generous benefits and unofficial bonuses. That is, if you still want to work for me?"

I had to hand it to him. His sober face didn't show hope and left the answer entirely to me.

Me, I was bubbling with hope. "Can we leave in triumph?"

Cleric nodded, standing up straight and brushing at his black tunic with a cloth napkin. "We can."

The shape against one of the outside windows looked distinctly like a camera. Grabbing the only still-loaded plate of food from the table, I threw it as hard as I could to splat against the glass.

CHAPTER SIX

True to his text, Kay didn't come home that night. Dad came home exhausted, and went to bed immediately. I had time to think about what I was going to tell people, at least.

Not that I came up with any good answers before school the next morning.

Echo wasn't at the door of Upper High today. Instead, a woman in a denim jacket and shorts over a grey and black spandex bodysuit waved a camera over the crowd. The moment it passed over me, it let out a buzz and its little green light turned red, then shut off. That meant a face recognition program.

The heroes were trying to find me.

At the corner of the hall past my homeroom loitered another hero. He managed to look like an average guy much better, but any adult hanging around in a high school sticks out.

Two of them. With identification tech. LA's superheroes weren't just trying to find me, they were serious about it. Yes, I had my super power, but this couldn't be creepier if the heroine's head had turned backwards to watch me as I walked by.

On my way between English and Chemistry, I passed a

third hero in a security uniform that fit badly over his many, many muscles. He was swearing quietly and shaking a pair of sunglasses that must have had technology hidden in the lenses.

Stepping into class presented me with a different problem. The teacher already had the roller with the periodic table pulled down. Despite all that had happened, this was still the first week of class, and we were still learning the period table of elements, which was still idiot gibberish that I desperately needed Marcia's help to deal with.

At least Marcia was ready and waiting with her desk pulled up next to mine. After three days of embarrassingly inappropriate outfits, today she'd gone with a loose white knee-length dress with a belt and ties at the wrists for the poofy sleeves. More of a tunic, really. Not something you ever saw high school girls wear, but unless shins were your idea of excitement completely modest.

Oh, wait, I got it. There was nothing wrong with this dress and Marcia had moved on to trolling everyone. Her determination to be difficult felt like a rock I could always stand on in the violently undulating and salt-water piranha filled seas of life.

Marcia also did a great job of assuming the girl sitting next to her had to be me, and launched into her whispered explanation of the teacher's nonsense. "This is all the stuff we've discussed already. Look at the chart, plug in a number. Think of them as phone numbers or a grocery list. It's just a fourth-grade math word problem."

The hoarse edge to Marcia's voice turned my relief to concern. I took a good look at her face. Her eyes had gone bloodshot, and bruises crept across her throat as I watched.

My own eyes wide now, I whispered, "Are you okay? That's a rhetorical question, because you're not."

"I made my choice, and I don't have even one regret," she croaked back.

I pawed at my belt pouch. "I have another red potion—"

She shook her head and interrupted me. "I don't need it." That came out in a growl too emphatic for me to argue, especially as Marcia reached down to fiddle with her own backpack.

Out came a figurine, like a metal action figure. I saw enough to guess it looked like a superhero before her fist closed. Her mouth twisted, and she snarled like an animal. Quietly, yes, but with a deranged hate I'd never seen before in anybody. Her arm quivered.

Suddenly it ended. Marcia relaxed, and gave me a cheerful smile again. Her hand opened to reveal a glob of now unidentifiable deformed metal. The whites of her eyes were sparkly clean again, and she had become the picture of health and good humor. Tapping the textbook, she said cheerfully, "So, let's start with this one. How many neutrons in silicon?"

After that, I did not have the guts to tell her about yesterday.

Latin's patient memorization and reading that Gallia est omnis divisa in partes tres gave me time to settle down. Plus, I saw no heroes at all on the way to the cafeteria.

So, how to break the news to my friends that I was official? I could take the badge out of my backpack and lay it on the table, then watch their faces when they figured it out. That would be *fun*.

My eager swagger faltered as Marcia, Charlotte, and Cassie gave me blank looks when I reached our lunch table. I would never stop hating this part.

"Magenta?" Charlotte asked cautiously.

"Yes." Anything else I said would make it worse.

Cassie boggled, staring at me in shock as she got her first experience of my super power.

Charlotte and Marcia took it in stride. The crazy girl stuffed fistfuls of mixed nuts into her mouth. Charlotte changed the subject as smoothly as if she'd been waiting to ask, "So, what is up with the hero invasion? And where is Echo?"

Now Cassie boggled at Charlotte. "You don't know?"

Charlotte tilted her face forward to look up past her braids at the blonde. "Don't give me that. Non-powered family, remember?"

Lowering her voice to confidentiality, and leaning forward over the table to make the secrecy a little clearer, Cassie told the three of us, "It's the Tyrant agent. That's all anybody in the superhero community is talking about."

Charlotte sank back as she understood. "Oh, that. Yeah, my parents were freaking out until the news reminded us that there are always Tyrant agents in the city. *And* Cossack. *And* the Queen of Swords."

Marcia, who had been focused on shoveling down a superhuman volume of nuts until now, commented, "I punched one, once. He made it past the traps to my front door and tried to sell me cookies."

My nervousness was back. Trying to sound casual, I held up a limp hamburger, but didn't take a bite. "How does that translate to added security everywhere? And where is Echo?"

Charlotte frowned thoughtfully, then cocked a finger in my direction. "It's got to be about the teenage girl in those videos, right?"

She was just answering me, but that finger pointed in my direction did not make me feel any safer.

Cassie hunkered down even more, smiling widely with the joy of secret gossip. "I heard the heroes want to find that girl, bad, and so do half the villains. Echo's in disgrace. He was just barely in bounds picking a fight in that restaurant because the agent was in costume, but everyone figures he was such a bad example that he pushed an innocent kid into doing something stupid. Now he's too embarrassed to show his face, and superheroes and villains are combing LA's high schools to identify the girl."

Keeping my voice even and not squeaky at all, I asked, "Isn't that getting personal?"

Cassie wagged her head in denial. "They're treating her as a victim, not a villain."

Charlotte's thoughtful frown became an angry scowl. Straightening in her seat, she smacked her fist into her palm. "Well, she is. The heroes need to find that poor girl and get her away from that Tyrant agent."

I was now deeply, uncomfortably aware of the badge at the bottom of my backpack. Not only could I not show it off, what if someone saw it by accident? Even my friends weren't with me on this.

Cassie leaned back and gave Marcia a sly, eyelids-lowered

smirk. "I'm surprised you have nothing to say. Surely the Death Murder Zombie Death Chaperon of Death is all over you about this."

The black-haired weirdo shrugged; the only person who looked completely uninvested in the topic. She even swallowed another scoop of nuts without chewing before she answered. "The Death Murder Zombie Death Chaperon of Death hasn't said a word. She knows that joining someone else's army isn't my style."

Charlotte looked right at me suddenly, her eyes piercing like ice-crusted titanium javelins, her frown merely curious. "What do you think, Magenta?"

Scratching the back of her head and sending blue lines arcing through her hair, Cassie gave me a sheepish grin. "Yeah, sorry. Every time you open your mouth, we push you back out of the conversation."

I would have been happy if they were pushing me out. This conversation kept going in dangerous directions, and I was afraid every time I opened my mouth, I would reveal my nervousness. Still, I had to say something, and preferably something true. "I don't really like surveillance gear pointed at me."

Marcia paused with a hand full of nuts and snickered wickedly. "You don't need to worry too much about that. Haven't you noticed? Someone's messing with their equipment."

Uh. Should I say something about that?

I didn't have to. Cassie's face skewed in a sheepish grin, and her hand stayed behind her head, elbow out to the side. "That would be me. Spotters trying to recognize the kid from the video I can handle, but any time they get near me with spy equipment, I do the magnet thing I've been working on and short them out. A bunch of other kids are doing the same thing."

A lot of tension let out of my back and neck. It was reassuring to know nobody would be scanning the contents of my backpack or taking stealth DNA samples or whatever. Still, I couldn't believe how this job had blown up before I even started, and to be honest with myself, I wasn't sure if I was more scared, or angry that I was being treated like a child who couldn't make her own decisions.

But I had sure made a splashy first impression as a villain!

That candle flame of satisfaction slowly melted the cage of icy nervousness around my heart, and stayed with me through the rest of lunch and even lurked during Social Science.

Arriving at Math class drove it away. I stepped through the door and remembered we'd been given homework yesterday. The math teacher, Mrs. Stakes, did not fool around, and had thrown us into the thick of education already. From the moment I got home, I'd spent yesterday afternoon focused entirely on my debut as a heroine that had turned into a debut as a villainess.

From the moment I got home. That's right. I'd done my homework on the bus ride home. The ups and downs of the last twenty-four hours were really messing with me. Relieved, I took my seat and tore the page of quadratic equations from my notebook.

That made me look up and notice that the black-haired superheroine from this morning was standing in the room, looking up and down between a completely different little techno-pad and the class. Not just "at the class." In my direction.

The badge. She was following the badge itself. Of course it would have mad science buried in it, or be magical, or something. Cleric had made it clear Tyrant wasn't the type of guy who gave out normal, boring insignia.

Mrs. Stakes, looking cautious but less sour than usual, asked the heroine, "Can I help you?"

Pffzzt! Snap! A spark flew out of the base of the detector, followed by wisps of smoke. Every kid in the class, including me, adopted identical expressions of innocence. Cassie had been right.

Scowling in irritation, the heroine muttered, "No, thank you," and walked back out the door. Before it closed, I saw her get out her phone and start talking, but her words didn't carry and there wouldn't have been time for more than a couple anyway.

Dismissing the interruption, Mrs. Stakes clapped her bony hands. "Homework, please!" I took pleasure in walking up and laying mine on her desk.

The roller coaster of my mood took its next swing when

school ended. The heroes seemed to have vanished, but when I took the first step out of Upper High's front doors, a hand grabbed my shoulder.

I let out a yelp and jumped into the air. So much for my attempts to look innocent.

I landed facing Cassie, who owned the arm that held my shoulder. Charlotte and Marcia lurked behind her. None of them even looked tempted to laugh. I had lucked into the best friends a girl at a new school could hope for.

To continue that theme, Cassie jerked her thumb at her own chest and drawled confidently, "Soooo, I wanted to cement your status as part of the team by inviting you over to my place for the afternoon. My sister will drive you home, the Polar Opposite Pals back there will be coming, and a couple of kids I'd like to introduce you to."

Uh. Another curveball in this chaotic maelstrom of a day. A pretty awesome one this time. Could I? Mom and Dad wouldn't even know. Cleric wasn't expecting me until tomorrow. That left only one thing, and I explained it out loud as I dug for my phone. "I'll just have to text Kay, who…is right over there."

Yes, that was Kay. One lean, dark seventeen-year-old boy in a soot-stained grey t-shirt and loose jeans, walking up the grassy slope toward Upper High in an extremely unexpected way while looking left and right over the milling students all intent on getting as far away as possible as fast as possible.

To show up in exactly the right time at the right place like this, Kay had to be using his power, which he never, ever did for personal reasons. I wove through the crowd, waving my arm at him and shouting, "Yo, big brother! Come meet my new friends!"

Kay didn't respond, and when I skidded up in front of him, he looked right over and past me, still searching the crowd.

I waited, my guts squirming. My friends were watching as my own brother failed to recognize me, and failed hard. Of course he did. We weren't at home, where he could safely assume that the strange girl who just walked in was his sister. Out in public, my family was as helpless to identify me as anyone else.

I really, really, really had not wanted my cool new friends to find that out, and this just might be the worst moment possible.

Seconds crawled. He noticed how close I was, and took a step back.

I looked like the biggest idiot and loser who had ever lived.

No! Refusing to give in to the hot, heavy weight of shame trying to paralyze me, I grabbed his hand and looked back at my friends. "Hey, come here and meet my brother, Kay!"

That was enough of a clue, at last. With fourteen years of experience, Kay slipped smoothly into pretending he'd always known who I was and gave my friends a winning smile.

They, in turn, pretended I hadn't just looked like the biggest idiot and loser to ever enter high school. Cassie put her fists on her hips, looking Kay up and down and grinning with equally friendly charm. "I'm Cassie. Magenta didn't tell us she had an older brother."

Charlotte clapped a hand on my shoulder, and oozed relaxed confidence. "I'm Charlotte, and we're taking good care of her, I promise."

"Marcia Bradley," declared Marcia as if it were a threat, and stabbed her hand forward to offer a handshake. When Kay took it, she bared her teeth in one of her crazier grins, and kept pumping his hand up and down, up and down.

She was trying to crush his hand, wasn't she? At least when Kay stopped looking surprised and pulled his own hand back, she let him go.

"So, hey, since you're here, can I go to Cassie's place this afternoon?" I asked, waving at the blonde, whose hair had turned blue in the last sixty seconds and was now only blonde at the roots.

Now it was Kay's turn to look awkward, his grin turning crooked and his hands clasping together. "Ah. Actually, I was hoping to ride home with you on the bus. I have had the craziest twenty-four hours, and I wanted to tell you about it."

In all the insanity, I had totally forgotten he'd been having just as dramatic a time. It was bad enough I couldn't tell anybody about my adventures. I couldn't do that to someone else, especially Kay.

When I looked back at my friends, Cassie gave me an

immediate shooing wave, and an understanding smile. "Not a thing, Bubblegum Mop. My sister is cool. We'll be hanging out soon and often."

"In that case, we'd better run!" I shouted, and did just that. The school buses were almost fully boarded.

Kay and I were the last two onto mine. As we climbed the stairs Kay began to explain, "So, it started during English class."

The door closed behind us, and the bus started moving before we even found our seat. That had to be his power again, telling him exactly the right thing to say to make the bus driver think he was an Upper High student and let him on. Then again, he was a student, just not at this school, and it's not like she could possibly know everyone.

This was the bus that went all over the place for the students who weren't from anywhere close to Upper High. There weren't that many of us and finding an empty seat for me and my brother was easy. As we settled in, he kept talking, warming up to a passion. "I had heroing on my mind, and I don't hold back my power on that. All of a sudden, I knew I had to go, and I ran out of school. I don't know what Ms. Marshmallow thought. My power has never been that emphatic, and it even made someone stop and offer me a ride."

"Wow," I responded, and meant it. The whole point of Kay's power was that it guided him through the easy way to accomplish things. What could have been worth this much effort?

He was so excited his hands waved as he talked. "I got out up near Santa Monica Boulevard, walked into the big building right in front of me, and smelled gas."

I shuddered. "At the front door?"

"I got lucky. Walked in just at the right time to catch it," he said. When I nodded at that, he continued. "Still, it was obviously a huge leak. I got the receptionists to announce on the PA a building evacuation. When that was under way, I went to the buildings next door. I don't know where the leak was, but it was way too big to cap. We managed to clear the block before it went up."

My eyes hurt from bugging out. Until a Tyrant agent was

spotted in full uniform with a teenage sidekick, that explosion must have been the news of the day. I couldn't imagine the destruction.

He saw my expression, and hunched down closer to me, his voice getting quieter but if anything, even more excited. "The thing is, a few minutes before it blew, Mech and Marvelous showed up! They'd heard about the evacuation and saw me getting people out. They and some other heroes put shields up and only four buildings were destroyed, but they knew I was the reason no one died. They came back and told me so, and said I should meet some other heroes."

I whistled. Mech and Marvelous were big names. Personally, I'd thought Marvelous was famous more for her combination of beauty and elegantly minimal costuming than power, but if she'd held back a gas main explosion that big, she had to be the real deal. Whatever the case, she was the top of the golden mountain of prestige.

Kay's voice kept dropping until it was just a loud whisper, and he jabbered like he would die of excitement. "I met so many heroes, and they've been keeping track of the work I've done and they think I'm amazing. They all wanted to welcome me to the superhero community. Three fourths of it all was secret and I can't even tell you, and it was such a whirlwind I ended up falling asleep exhausted on Marvelous's couch. But here's the big thing."

I didn't get a chance to comment. Kay grabbed my hands in his, leaned close, and looked me right in the eyes as he whispered, "They're giving me a scholarship. A full scholarship. Living expenses, everything."

"Whoa." I grappled with that. "A scholarship to where?"

"Anywhere I qualify for. Some of the heroes are rich. Absolutely loaded. The retired ones especially like to use their money to encourage the next generation. They're giving it to me as a reward for all the hero work I've done, and because I did it just to help people. I swear I didn't use my power for this, Magenta. I swear."

He wouldn't. I didn't know what happened when he was fourteen, but using his power for his own benefit had left him so tortured with guilt that he only ever used it to protect others.

"Whoa," I repeated.

His hands shook as he explained giddily, "It was the best night of my life. Do you know what this scholarship means? A future. A good job. Our folks not having to worry about whether they can put me through college. I may even be able to help when it's your turn."

I had never seen Kay so happy. He looked like he might burst from it, or float away out the window as a chorus of angels sang. He deserved it. Kay was a great guy, certainly better than Echo. I should be just as happy for him.

Except a little worm of an emotion finally burst its cocoon and sprayed my heart with acid bile. Jealousy. I could barely hold still as it ate me from the inside. Kay was the toast of the hero community. I was being hunted, and not even because anyone respected me. I couldn't even tell my friends! Kay got the hero power, and I had to flail around with my pathetic potions and annoying unrecognizability. He got the dream life handed to him, and I got twelve heart attacks in one school day.

I should be happy for him. I should.

But if Cleric asked me to burn LA to the ground right now, I would consider it.

Kay was so happy he bought pizzas for supper that night, and Dad arrived home just as they arrived. Mom hadn't left for her intern shift at the hospital, and we all got to sit around at the table eating like a family while Kay told them the story.

Mom looked stunned. Leaning back in her chair, she told the ceiling, "A full scholarship."

Dad got up, walked around the table, and put his arms around Kay for a long, tender hug. "I'm so proud of you. I can't tell you how proud I am."

My heart writhed. I couldn't take it anymore. I broke in. "I got a part-time job."

That derailed the conversation, hard. Everyone stared at

me in astonishment. It was Mom who asked, "Where?" She sounded like she wasn't sure she believed me.

Well, it was true. I waved northeast. "A used bookstore off of Expo. Very used. Real antique books, like hundreds of years old, some of them. The owner saw my potions, and he's been looking for some mad science to help protect and restore the oldest ones, and he thought I'd be perfect. It's twenty dollars an hour. You don't pay minimum wage for even teenage mad science."

Everybody still looked stunned. Not happy stunned. Maybe even suspicious. Mom didn't bother to hide her doubt when she asked, "How will you get there?"

I gave that question the sarcasm it deserved. "Uh, the Metro? I'm getting paid now. I can afford bus fare."

Dad at least looked torn, his face twitching from warring emotions. "This doesn't sound safe, Magenta."

Kay raised his hand immediately. "I'll check it out and make sure this guy's trustworthy."

My parents stopped arguing. After all, Kay the super hero could fix my mistakes, right?

I ate fast, went back to my room, and went to bed early, my stomach a knot of anger.

Bring on the villainy, Cleric.

I would show them all.

CHAPTER SEVEN

School doesn't care what mood you're in. You still have to show up for class on Friday morning.

I eyed the heroes by the door with spite on my way in, and noticed I wasn't the only one.

Stewing with resentment, I didn't even take the chance in Chemistry to talk about anything interesting with Marcia. So, I was very surprised when, just before we walked out of the classroom door, she yanked me aside and whispered, "Pretend we're having a conversation."

Uh. Improvising wildly, I got my textbook back out, opened it, pointed at a random page, and mumbled inaudibly faint gibberish, just so my lips would move.

Why were we doing this? I didn't see anything interesting happening, and Marcia wasn't doing anything but grinning madly.

But there was something to hear. A man—it had to be a hero—right outside the classroom complaining, "She didn't say anything. She just looked at me."

An angry heroine replied, "She can read souls! She could

find this kid in a heartbeat! Why is she ignoring this?"

His voice rough with strained patience, the man repeated, "I told you, she didn't say. Not a word."

Despair and worry sharpened the heroine's tone. "We're never going to find that poor girl."

"If it's a girl."

"Looked like a girl to me," answered the heroine with scorn.

The hero just got more insistent. "Did it? Except for the hair that was the most generic teenager I've ever seen, and in armor to boot."

The heroine dropped to a hush. "Do you think it might have been a robot?"

I could hear the hero's sneer, bloated and smug with the arrogant fruits of knowledge. "Working for Tyrant? No. But it could have been something a lot weirder."

At that Marcia cackled. Grabbing me by the upper arm, she dragged me out of the room and into the hall. "I love chaos!"

The hero and heroine who had been in discussion gave her a resentful look, separated, and disappeared into the milling students. I didn't receive so much as a glance.

"Get to class," Marcia instructed me, then strolled casually off to hers, still laughing like a witch and drinking in the stares of children and adults alike.

My seething funk broken, I got to class, and was mostly able to pay attention. I even went to lunch in a merely scowling mood.

I got my lunch tray, and emerged to find Marcia, Charlotte, and Cassie already at the table, along with a red-haired boy. Apparently, I would always be last.

When I reached the table, I got a look at the boy. The arms projecting from his short-sleeved shirt were freakishly cut, in the muscle sense, and the unfastened top button gave a peek at similarly hard chest muscles. What didn't make sense was how skinny this boy was. You got muscles like that on body builders, not teenagers who looked like they were made of pipe cleaners.

Such a weird look. I wasn't sure if he was attractive or gross.

I finally dragged my eyes up to the boy's face at the same time he dragged his up to mine.

Shame crawled over my cheeks and down my spine. We'd gotten caught checking each other out.

At least he looked awkward, too. I wasn't actually interested, and maybe neither was he.

We hadn't been the only ones to notice. Cassie slapped the boy's shoulder with the back of her hand. "Have some class, Bug Eyed Bill. She's not a piece of meat."

He smirked back at her, eyes alight with defiance. "I forgot you used up the drool watching Penny walk by."

Cassie swiveled in her seat to glare at him just as imperiously. "This from the boy who spilled his drink down his shirt the first time Mirabelle patted the chair next to hers."

"Sorry, are we trading embarrassing stories? Should I tell them about your squeak?"

Cassie's mouth opened and closed, and her cheeks turned red, but she didn't say anything.

Victorious, the boy turned to me, preening so hard that if he were a chicken, his feathers would have stuck out everywhere. "I'm Will."

"Magenta," I answered, putting my plate down.

Marcia, Charlotte, and Cassie jumped when they heard my name. Okay, it was more like a twitch, but it didn't help my mood at all.

"Great, you're here!" Beaming, Marcia shoved my food tray, and I barely caught it before it went flying off the edge of the table. In its space, she set a tall metal box, then drew the cover off to reveal an elaborate spiral rack holding slices of pizza. Hot pizza. I could tell just looking at it.

A girl who could afford to shove hundred-dollar bills into my hand probably had custom pizza carrying gear handy.

Marcia followed up by dropping a slice into my hands, and as I fumbled it trying not to burn my fingers she drawled, "Soooooo. It's Friday. Is the compass done yet?"

"I said Friday afternoon," I snapped back, then sighed. "But...."

Way back in my halcyon childhood days, when the pure sunshine of naivete shone down upon my frolicking innocence, and specifically when I still believed I'd be able to actually tell my friends I had a cool job working for a supervillain, I'd thought I should show them the compass. So, now it was in my potions case, and only took a few seconds to dig out.

I laid the compass on the table, since smacking that flimsy little thing was out of the question. While they ooh'd, I stole a few bites of pizza, which turned out to not only be hot, but fresh. Marcia could get pizza delivery at school? Eh. That wasn't the tenth strangest thing about her.

Nobody else cared about pizza, only my Trouble magnet. Even Charlotte couldn't completely hide her eagerness as she asked, "Does it work?"

Through a mouthful of cheese, I mumbled, "It works. One problem." With my one free hand, I pushed the compass around the table. Everyone watched the needle, which stayed resolutely pointed at Marcia.

Thanks to a mouth full of pizza, no one would spot from my expression that I'd only noticed this trait seconds before they did.

Charlotte scowled in disappointment while stealing a slice of pizza for herself. "A Marcia detector. That will be useful if Marcia ever stops shouting and breaking things every five feet."

Swallowing, I assured her, "It points at the nearest source of super powered Trouble. We just have one sitting right next to us."

Cassie and Will snagged pizza for themselves, but the blonde girl ignored hers to lean over the table and give me an excited grin. "So, if we ditch the Fist Freak after school, we can track down a super battle?"

I shook my head. "I start my part time job this afternoon." And I sure wasn't missing that. I would find something to brag about to my friends!

Cassie sank back, pouting. "Aw. It will be Monday before we hear how it works! Unless you want to come visit Chinatown with me this weekend?"

That I had no idea what chaos this afternoon would unleash or how it would affect my weekend was not a useful answer. Unfortunately, I had another one I'd have had to trot out anyway.

"Too far. If you're offering a ride, maybe once my parents are used to me having new friends."

Charlotte nodded in sympathy. "That's a lot to spring on regular kids' parents at once."

Marcia snickered, no doubt at Cassie's look of abject disappointment.

As Cassie retreated in defeat to the safe territory of devouring free pizza, Charlotte scrunched up her nose and said, "A bus ride that long must be boring."

I shrugged and answered honestly, "I do my homework."

"Good system," said Will, and everyone nodded together.

Having stuffed a slice of pizza down her gullet in record time, Cassie shook her head in furious bafflement. "I swear I got more homework at Northeast West Hollywood Middle. Not that I'm complaining."

The conversation diverged into normal school topics, and I focused on eating Marcia's pizza and wondering if I could skip time straight to meeting Cleric again.

No, but close. It's amazing how stewing in resentment and anticipation will cause the minutes to crawl and the hours to fly. My homework should have taken five minutes, and took the whole bus ride home, which caused more time to disappear.

I had to go home to pick up my gear, since, apparently, I was in danger of being searched if I showed up at school with it in my backpack. Trying the hero's path got me nothing, and trying the villain's path got me only one thing: The hilarious look on Echo's face when I kicked expensive meat paste onto his shiny costume.

I could do with more of that.

When my phone beeped during the train ride along Exposition, I nearly leaped out of my seat. If I'd been wearing my gauntlet, I'd have splatted somebody with whatever I had loaded.

Instead, my bare hands dug the phone out, and I looked at the text. Not from Kay. A number I didn't know. Weird! And it said:

It's me, Aikamieli!

Surprise and confusion drained the stormy tides of my anger, only to have them rage back in a boiling tsunami. Stabbing my finger at the screen, I called back, listened to the phone ring, and as soon as it picked up snarled, "How did you get this number?!"

The nervous, cracking voice I remembered stammered, "I—I—I'm sorry, maybe this isn't who—"

You know what I was also sick of? Not being recognized. "This is the girl you met at the shop. How did you get this number?"

He sighed in relief. "Oh, wow. Sorry, you sound totally different over—"

"How. Did. You—"

"There's a spell for it!" he squealed. His voice got quieter halfway through, and I could see him in my mind's eye, raising his hands in defense then realizing he was holding his phone in one of them.

Surprise and confusion sucked the anger back again, assisted by a temporary dike of skepticism. "There can't possibly be a spell for learning someone's phone number in an ancient grimoire."

Immune to my bad mood, Aikamieli enthused, "Wainamoinen wrote a spell to learn a girl's contact information. It's meant for courtship."

He couldn't see me glare, but I did it anyway. "Not interested."

Desperately, he squeaked, "No, no! It's not like that! I'm not into dating my enemies. Romance is too serious for that."

He'd managed to reduce my seething anger to exasperation. "So why are you calling?"

"Because you're the only person I can talk to about this."

Oh.

The train was at a stop. I looked up...and we were at the university already!

"Not right now, bye!" I yelped at him as I picked up my bag and ran to the exit just before it closed. Shutting off my phone, I stuffed it into my pocket (always wear loose pants if you're not sure whether you'll be committing villainy) and hurried down the back street to where I met Cleric.

Nothing had changed. Despite being almost downtown, LA's population shunned this block like death. The pigeons, crows, and seagulls shunned it like...life, I guess?

Life that welled up within me again as I reached the front door and pushed it open. Unlocked. I stepped in...

...to discover Cleric had cleaned up the place. The lights worked, the dust had vanished, almost nothing was scattered on the floor, and many of the shelves and tables had been arranged in sensible order. In fact, Cleric was filing books onto a bookshelf as I entered, actually sorting them into their proper places. Not that I knew how he defined those.

His face lit up with delight when he saw me. "I'm glad you decided to come. I do want to repeat: You can back out of this at any time."

I shook my head so hard my dreads slapped my cheeks. "I want this job."

Wow, I sounded vehement. So much emotion poured out into those words.

Cleric let go of the books, which shelved themselves as he indicated a table against one wall, next to a paper-covered window whose edges had been scraped so that it could open. On the table lay an assortment of glass beakers and tubes, plastic beakers and tubes, Bunsen burners, alcohol burners, wire meshes, medicine droppers, magnifying glasses, miniature fans, and more. Alchemy equipment.

Standing next to an alchemy table, with shelves of crumbling books behind him, Cleric and his black tabard and chainmail looked at home. A notepad with a pencil tucked into it floated across the room and lay on the scarred brown surface of the table as Cleric explained, "The first thing I'd like you to do is figure out what equipment you'll need, or even might want. There's no telling what I'll need you to concoct, and no need to be reserved. My lord is anything but poor."

Where had my anger gone? Because it was gone. Awkward sheepishness, slightly uncomfortable, warmed my heart and had me rubbing the back of my head like an idiot. "This is not a complaint, but I'm surprised you're not having me clean up."

He waved his hand in military grade sharp dismissal. "Waste of your talents. If I want a domestic, I'll buy a homunculus. Speaking of which, there's a refrigerator in back with raw meat in it, and a bin of wood, potter's clay, glass, and scrap metal, for when inspiration hits."

I scrunched up my nose in disgust. "Yuck. Make a homunculus? I've seen the recipes for that and they're gross. Also, stupid. The most important ingredient is blood...." My voice trailed off.

Why had I said that? I'd known something, and then it disappeared.

Hands folded behind his back, smiling like a proud teacher, Cleric asked, "You've had your power all your life, correct?"

Still off balance, I hedged. "I mean, it didn't show much when I was six, but yeah."

My backpack jiggled. The zipper buzzed, and out floated my gauntlet, held up by my chemistry textbook. Ironic. Cleric reached out and slipped a cyan vial from the firing tube. "By embracing your power, you have traveled well along the road to mastery already, but it will grow as you do. A mad scientist's first big breakout is usually making life, and alchemy is science, not magic." He tucked the vial back into place, and my textbook floated the gauntlet over to sit on the table. With a wry nod, Cleric finished, "Different science, but still science."

I just gaped. Literally. My tongue might catch a cold from the draft. "Yes! I can't believe you understand that. Nobody gets that."

Cleric shrugged, a bit of embarrassed pride melting the edges off his stiff, imperial bearing. "I've met other alchemists. Your focus on color is unusual, and I like it. Science should be strange and beautiful."

Now he was back to smiling, and he swept with airy, theatric grace. He lifted a chair with black struts and faded red cushions out from behind a bookshelf, and set it in the middle of the shop's biggest open space. A seriously big book, so big and so old and ratty that "tome" barely described it, floated in from the back, accompanied by smaller books with metal instruments sticking out. After placing the table, Cleric pulled a lectern up behind it, and the fifty-pound behemoth volume landed on that, making the wood creak.

Cleric laid a hand on the book of largeness, and went back to stiff and formal, maybe even a touch worried. "Speaking of which, I was hoping you would help me with an experiment."

Doing stupid, dangerous things sounded good right now, but if he was cautious maybe I should be cautious. I raised a (yes, pink) eyebrow. "What kind of experiment?"

His blonde eyebrows set like a ridge of limestone. "I don't want to be mysterious, but I don't know how to explain without making something harmless sound sinister. I won't require you to do something I can't prepare you for, so this is completely optional. I also would not do anything to you that I did not know for certain I can reverse. The experiment is at worst a little bit scary and uncomfortable for a few minutes."

That was such a watered-down room temperature weak sauce explanation that I had to smirk, which felt good after all the frowning. "Does this have to do with your secret project?"

"Yes. It all centers around this book." He patted the mega volume of ancient decrepitude.

After an explanation that creepy, pathetic, and unconvincing, what could I say? "Let's do it."

On the theory that the chair must be important, I threw myself down into it and gripped the uncomfortably knobby arm rests. Cleric leaned over me from behind, and I felt tiny metal pricks on my scalp. When he changed position, I got a glimpse of old-fashioned calipers.

Then they stopped and he moved away. From behind he asked, "How do you feel?"

Nothing felt different. No, wait. "Maybe a touch dizzy. Did you do something to my eyes?"

Standing up from the chair, I looked around the shop. Everything did look weird, but I wasn't sure how. The depth of dark brown stain on the alchemy table stood out, as did its scratches. If grizzled, ancient resilience could have a color, it would be that. The lamp in the ceiling caught my notice next. That was not the color of electric light, although I couldn't tell you what hid behind the frosted glass cover.

Hints of grey dust still marred the edges of books, all dryness and decay. This shop had a carpet I'd never noticed before, maybe because of its meaningless purple color.

While I stood there noticing, Cleric said, "No. I transferred your alchemical knowledge into the book."

That sounded as bad as bad could get, but he did promise he could and would reverse it, so my voice merely fluttered as I asked, "You took my super power?"

"No, and what I did take I will give back," he answered, flatly and immediately. Yeah, he knew how important it was for me to hold onto that fact.

Returning to the more gentle and technical, he continued, "What transferred into the book is your knowledge. The visual confusion you're experiencing is because your power is rebuilding its understanding of the world from scratch. Would you like to come and see?"

"Oh, yeah." This wasn't the public spectacle I'd signed on for, but it was almost as good. I walked around to the lectern where Cleric had his special magic book. To my hyper-alert power, it...didn't look like anything much, really, which is how I knew it had to be magic.

The contents, on the other hand, were all kinds of interesting. Traced out on the open page was a bizarre geometric design of lines and tiny circles. The words "scrawl" and "labyrinth" came to mind, it was so complex.

All of those lines were traced in vivid black. The opposite side looked much more like I would expect of a book this old, with holes in the paper and illegibly faint writing.

Not daring to touch what might be wet ink or something equally vulnerable, I pointed at the design. "Can you read that?"

Cleric shook his head sadly. "No. I was looking for the True Kalevala because it has spells for gaining knowledge that might have helped." Suddenly, he relaxed, and flashed a grin. "Can you imagine someone with the super power to understand all written languages? They could change the world. Great men and women would fight over them."

I squinted, trying to make something out of the book's condition. "How many brains can this thing hold? It looks a little, uh...ratty. It looks a lot ratty. It looks like sixteen rats, seventy-two mice, three voles, a family of decadent gerbils and a capybara held a wild party between these covers."

Seriously, the pages even had that crisp look that made me wonder if bits turned to powder every time he opened the covers.

That got a barking laugh. Running fingers through his hair, Cleric gave me a suddenly disarmed grin. "Bingo. I think you can fix it. If you can, the book will be able to copy rather than just steal. Robbery is trash. I want to share."

Weird. I thought about that, while trying to ignore the rich depth of black in Cleric's tabard's fabric, and the tiny edges of corrosion in his chain mail that meant it was forged of pure iron. "So, to train people?"

He went stiff again, chains clinking under his clothes. The smile stayed, but got a lot more formal. He waved one arm in a slow arc over the book, indicating...everything. "No, to change how they see the world. Yours is one of the knowledges I'd like to share with everyone. They won't be able to use your recipes, but they will understand that matter is more than just atoms."

I stifled a chuckle. Give him half an excuse, and Cleric launched into speeches on his cause. He reminded me of a preacher.

"But right now, you need your knowledge back." We didn't quite say it together, but we both spoke at once and the point was basically the same.

Not needing instructions, I sat down in the chair. He fiddled with the calipers for a few seconds. Nothing much happened, until I realized I knew now what could be done with old wood and darkness. From the black of Cleric's clothes, from traces of iron and the enduring stubbornness of old wood shavings, I could make armor.

File that idea away, Magenta. It could be useful.

"Wow. As simple as that?" I asked, then felt a bit stupid for saying it.

He didn't get down on me for being so obvious. No, Cleric's beatific smile reveled in the chance to sing the praises of his discovery. "As simple as that. The book does the work. It is one of the greatest treasures of mankind, and if you can restore it, I can use it."

While he did his True Believer thing, I wandered back to look at the page that used to hold my alchemical knowledge. Now it was just blank. Since it was in way better shape than the page across, I lifted it caaaaarefully up to peek underneath. More blank pages. So, this book could hold quite a lot of brains.

My phone rang in my pocket. Seriously, Aikamieli?

But another phone was ringing outside. The shop door opened, and Kay walked in, with his phone out. He followed the ring to look right over and identify me.

I hadn't actually told him where I worked or when I was leaving.

He recognized who and what Cleric was immediately. A blind man could, with that full medieval costume. Taking two steps forward, Kay held out his hand and shouted, "Magenta, get back! I can protect you!"

I'd never seen Kay in combat mode before, had I? His face might be twisted in lines of concern for his little sister, but the rest of his stance stayed relaxed and loose, almost slouched.

Cleric folded his hands behind his back, staring at Kay in a cold, searching way. For the guy who controlled books, in a room full of them, that counted as a fighting pose. It was also perfect for scolding and cold contempt. "You would be The Way. The young lady has not told me what pseudonym she wants, yet, but you should know better than to use her real name."

Kay didn't watch him. Kay didn't have to. Kay watched me, eyes wide with concern verging on desperation. "She doesn't need a pseudonym. She's your victim, not a villain."

For two, three seconds no one moved or said anything, just long enough for the pause to become glaringly noticeable and for me to realize I'd frozen in panic. Then, quiet and mild, Cleric asked, "Miss, may I have your permission to defend you, or do you want to do it yourself?"

My whole body felt cold and stiff, and my brain sluggish. It didn't help that this was the last question I ever expected. All I could manage was, "Sure, go ahead."

Cleric's hands let go, and he placed one on the lectern, gripping the edge with increasing force. His searching, thoughtful frown turned into a frown of acid disgust that locked onto Kay and should have melted him on the spot. "How *dare* you. Your civilian connection with her is personal, but you obviously have one. Is this how little you trust her?"

That caught Kay off guard, but not as much as it did me. It at least got his eyes on Cleric as he snapped back, "Enough to know she doesn't want to be a supervillain."

Cleric's lip twisted. The imperious pride was replaced by forward leaning, natural anger. He certainly didn't hesitate. "Then maybe your problem is that you don't know her. Did you ask what she wants?" The hand not squeezing the lectern flew up, palm out in refusal. "Don't tell me, it's not my business. She isn't a toddler. She accepted an offer, and made it crystal clear to me where the line of good and evil is that she won't cross. That she even has that line proves she's sophisticated enough to make her own decisions."

"But she's—" Kay started to say, then stopped. Whatever he'd wanted to say would be personal. Forbidden.

Cleric drew himself back up arrogantly again, his face back to granite contempt. "Welcome to secret identities, The Way. If you're lucky, she might choose to explain to you why you're wrong about everything, but you are not even allowed to ask."

Kay's growing tension released, and he took another step forward. "However, I am allowed to fight you."

Cleric nodded, but the contemptuous glare didn't fade. If anything, it got a touch sarcastic. "If you catch me performing any crimes, yes, but maybe in not having enough faith in her, you didn't bother to wonder whether any crimes are going on."

Kay looked over at me, and my skin crawled. I felt bad for him, because Cleric was so right, that was kind of why I was here in the first place. Even in the mood for trouble as I'd been today, I'd have refused anything actually bad.

Whatever my expression looked like, Kay clearly didn't find any comfort in it. He looked guilty, too.

Cleric let out a huge sigh. His shoulders and face relaxed, and he rubbed his nose, and looked a lot older than maybe thirty. More sad than angry now, he said, "Lord save me from well-meaning children. Just go, and maybe you should not only let her make her own decisions, you should wait and let her prove they're the right ones."

"Please," I begged, my hands squeezed together so hard they hurt.

Kay could lose with dignity. He didn't say another word, just turned and walked out the door.

Cleric leaned his backside against the alchemy table, looking tired physically as well as emotionally. He gave me a sober, apologetic stare. "I tried to settle that in a way that wouldn't ruin your relationship. I still don't want to know what that is."

"Thanks?" I squeaked, still lost, but starting to realize Cleric might have saved me from Kay's disappointment.

Pushing upright again, Cleric snorted in dark amusement. More to himself than me, he said, "Besides, Tyrant would have been ashamed of me, and I would be ashamed of myself."

Starting to recover, I tried a nervous giggle. "One down, the rest of the city to go."

He pushed himself, walked over, and laid his hand on my shoulder to give me a reassuring squeeze. Man, up close he towered, and he was way stronger than his geeky priest look suggested. "The heroes will respect the rules. All the big cities have similar truces, and I looked up the details of LA's before coming here."

I shook my head, grimacing. "The rules don't count, because they all think I'm a victim."

"They all think that?" asked Cleric distantly, talking to himself.

His expression changed. It happened slowly. First his hand tightened, then he stiffly took it off my shoulder so as not to hurt me. That let his fists clench, and his face normally leaning to boyish went stony, then as tight as his fists with anger.

My heart seized up and turned to ice. I hadn't seen anything like this from Cleric before. This was true fury that left my childish resentment in the dust.

He calmed down again, fists and face letting go, although not relaxing. "Alright," he said gruffly. He looked down at me again, his eyes blazingly intense, but not angry at me. He lingered emphatically over every word as he asked, "Do you want to stick that belief in their virtuous craws, and corollary, are you willing to work weekends?"

CHAPTER EIGHT

Saturday afternoon after my first week of high school, I set foot into dreaded, fabled Chinatown.

Actually, neither dreaded nor fabled. I'd found out all of two hours ago why Chinatown is closed on weekends. Before that, who cared? Business hours are always infuriatingly stupid, so finding out that they were decided by nefarious masterminds to further the cause of evil was not exactly a surprise.

Also, yes, I felt a little jaunty, approaching the roadblocks with a swagger in my step and a swish in my brand new ankle-length brown leather trench coat. The matching dark brown shirt and pants were too thin to be actual leather, but I was still boiling in the September sun and I did not care. Cleric had provided this outfit, built my armor with its straps and vacuum tubes into the coat, and the right sleeve fit perfectly into my gauntlet. The coat also had padded pockets for my potions.

I looked official. I looked hardcore. I had style for days. And I was only slightly creeped out that every piece had been tailored exactly to me, and when I asked Cleric how he got the measurements he'd only answered, "Knowledge is what I do."

This was actually the back-up outfit. He had correctly guessed that the black outfit with the long skirt and the white crow mask would not be acceptable, but said he'd been obligated to try. If he knew so much, he should have known I need skin on display for my unrecognizability power to work.

I did spare a moment of envy for the air conditioner built into the crow mask. Wow, I was hot. Dragonsbreath magma sauna on Mercury hot.

Chinatown is not a small neighborhood, but a fence surrounds it entirely. A huge wooden arch stands over the only road in or out. Under that arch, behind the barricades, hunched a wizened old Chinese man straight out of Hollywood's Uncomfortable Stereotypes Department.

As instructed, I walked between the roadblocks and ignored him. I had so many instructions. Okay, not that many, but it seemed like it. Do not fight. Deliver the letter. Do not talk to Spider, or go see him, her, or them.

Chinatown looked as closed and empty as it claimed on the main street, but I saw someone down an alley and ducked that way into sweet, sweet shade.

The next street was not empty. A woman in a slinky red gown with a huge red hat leaned against a closed shop. A seven-foot-tall wolf and a pretty blonde guy in a shiny breastplate stood nose to nose, arguing. A girl maybe just college age, her pigtails a riot of colors and wearing either a truly skin-tight rag doll costume or a terrifying collection of scars, played jump rope in the middle of the road.

They all looked at me. Grinning as madly as the doll girl, I took my Tyrant badge out of my pocket and fastened it onto my coat.

They kept looking. The red dress woman kept her hat tilted low, but green fire marked her eyes watching me from just under its brim.

I headed for the hunched white shape of the mall in the center of Chinatown. I passed more villains. They all watched me, and I heard mumbled conversations behind my back.

Bless you, Cleric. This was everything I'd signed up for.

The crowd got cooler and freakier near the mall. On the far

side I saw stacked cages. On the near side, a bunch of rough looking villains gathered in a ring, watching a show in the middle that made a lot of pained grunts and thumps.

As big as the men were, a woman head and shoulders taller than them stepped out of the center, mopping her face with a towel. Her nudity hardly mattered, since she seemed to be made out of white plastic or metal decked with rainbow glitter. She had muscle, while remaining sleek and womanly.

A guy who looked like he ate rebar for breakfast whined up at her, "Come on, you can't be out of steam after four fights."

Her voice sounded like a movie femme fatale, not a seven-foot amazon. A tired femme fatale, admittedly. "Despite three score years my beauty remains perfect, but I too grow old."

I plucked a royal blue vial from one of my coat pockets, and lobbed it in an easy arc over to the crowd. The colorful woman snatched it out of the air. Without a question or a glance at me she downed the whole potion. Swiveling like a shark, she stepped back into the ring out of my view. Something thumped as loud as a car wreck, and a man flew up out of the ring, over the next building and out of sight.

"Throwing is cheating!" shouted another crowd member.

Out of sight but not out of hearing, she lustily drawled, "I did not throw him. A lesson in kinetics: Delicious hits hard."

Something much smaller than a man came flying out of the crowd right toward me. Was she returning my vial? I caught the thing in both hands, to find it was a sharply pointed chunk of rigid white material with tiny pink and blue and purple spots. Ooh, living candy. That had to have alchemical properties I could exploit. I tucked it into a pocket for later.

Cool, air conditioned air hit me as I walked around the corner into the big open entrance at this side of the mall. Alternatively, a supervillain might have hit me with an invisible beam that turned my sweat into a layer of frost over every inch of my skin. If so, I would have to thank him. What bliss.

The only stain on this perfect moment was that hardly anyone in the mall was paying attention to me. I couldn't have that, so as I walked in, I lifted the wax-sealed scroll I'd been given and announced, "I am a messenger!"

Oh, yeah. That got everyone's attention.

I suddenly realized I did not want some of these people's attention. A fine example would be the man in the ridged iron mask and sharply pressed blue suit who walked up in front of me. Matching blue velvet gloves encased fists that could wrap around my skull and crush it into pulp. "Tyrant is not welcome in Los Angeles."

That voice. Even through the electronic distortion, it husked with threat, the anger of a man barely restraining his desire to hit me. My spine turned to ice, and my knees to water.

Two animal women drifted sinuously up to join us. One rich violet, the other scarlet red, they wore black leather biker jackets and shorts. It was hard to pay attention to details other than the wickedly hooked claws and teeth like knives, especially when they sneered.

I had to speak loudly and firmly just to hear myself over the pounding of my heart. "But not forbidden."

The masked man's gloves and muscles creaked as he leaned forward, fists bunched up until they quivered. "Leave now, or I will break you," he rasped.

That should have terrified me, but all my fear was now occupied by the more subtle way the animal women moved. They might have shifted position no more than an inch, lower on their digitigrade legs, fingers farther apart, fanged grins wider. Poised and ready to kill.

Don't fight, Cleric said. That was not going to be a worry. It took all I had not to run away screaming.

But I did not run away. I stood in place, and looked up into the slotted grey mask where eyes might be hidden behind it.

The red animal woman propped an elbow in one arm, raising the other hand to caress her own cheek with a claw tip. It should have drawn blood. A few strands of red fur did flutter down, shaved by that casual touch. When she spoke, it sounded surprisingly human and calm, with no hint of growl. "This is not the same girl from the video."

The purple woman leaned closer, past the man in blue. He did not object. Maybe he was as scared of her as I was. Her rough, rectangular tongue slid over her teeth thoughtfully, and she sounded sly and eager. "Who are you, little girl?"

"I'm just a Pawn," I answered. When Cleric gave me the name, I hadn't liked it. Apparently, Tyrant had a thing for chess. Now, the way it combined with my super power for utter anonymity felt like a life line hauling me from brightly colored furry shark infested waters.

The masked supervillain straightened up. He sounded electronically sour. "If there's more than one, then this is a trick. I'll take her out and give her to a hero."

Okay. Deep breath, but don't be obvious about it. You can do this, Magenta.

I held the scroll up in my fist again. "Not until I deliver my official message."

The purple monster absolutely purred with glee. "Oh, we would love to take you to Spider." She raised a hand over me like an arcade crane game, deciding where to grab.

"The message is for Retcon," I answered, as if I knew who that was.

The scarlet beast shook her head lazily. "Retcon doesn't come to Chinatown."

A sober, thirty-ish Asian woman in a pinstripe suit who would have looked like a textbook lawyer if not for her knee length black hair stepped crisply between the villains, plucking the scroll from my hand and unrolling it. As she did, she explained blandly, "Normally true, but after I read the letter, I've been here all day."

The lawyer snapped loose the wax seal, unrolled the parchment, and read. I didn't actually know what it said, since Cleric had written it in flowery Church Latin, but Retcon's translation matched what Cleric told me. "The girl is, indeed, a Pawn, acting under her own free will in a traditional sidekick assistant role. I will have to get Spider's judgment and present this to the heroes, but Spider's judgment will be that the heroes have gone too far. If only mentally competent, rational decision makers were allowed, there would be no heroes or villains at all."

The purple animal woman snickered. No longer threatening me, merely standing lazily and watching Retcon, she still looked like something I did not want to be within arm's reach of.

Speaking of Retcon, he rubbed his hand over his sandpapery shark scalp. Man, that lawyer was big. He really did look like an illustration of a lawyer, maybe out of a political magazine. A shark in a suit, right? He kept reading, and describing his reactions. "The super powered community would rather adults not fight teens this young, but if Cleric has children who are truly willing to operate as non-combat adjuncts, there are well established precedents."

"Like you," the scarlet wolf woman pointed out, literally pointing at Retcon.

"The same rules that protect you from being attacked," added her vaguely feline purple companion.

Retcon bowed, tucking the scroll into his crocodile skin briefcase. Adjusting his collar, the skinny, nervous, blonde young man sweated visibly as he agreed, "Those exact rules. The heroes won't like it, but they'll see reason. They are, after all, the good guys." I had to admit, his was a good look for a lawyer. You would so easily underestimate him.

Something about Retcon told me not to. Something nagged about this conversation, that I couldn't put a finger on.

Business complete, Retcon walked away, a process I did not get to see more of because the villain in the blue suit and metal mask loomed over me again. His arms folded across a chest that barely fit into his suit, and the voice from his mask only sounded slightly less furious than before. "Tell your master that if Tyrant tries to take over Los Angeles, both sides will be against him."

Taking inspiration from Retcon, I tried to sound patiently bland. "I am not at liberty to discuss Cleric's plans."

He walked off. The animal sisters had already disappeared. I was alone, sort of. Alone in a big hall populated by the most intimidatingly cool people in the city famous for intimidatingly cool people, many of whom were still watching me. Their expressions varied, but none of those were "contempt."

I'd done it. I was in. Sort of.

Supervillains seemed way more social than heroes. There had to be two dozen just inside here, and it wasn't night time yet!

Mind you, maybe half that two dozen sat at tables clumped around the sides of the hall, and looked an awful lot like vendors. I wandered over toward them, at first out of curiosity, then in a bee line when one specific vendor caught my eye.

A soft, dusky old man in a grey suit and cream shirt, top button unfastened, sat behind a sparse display of...bottles. Bottles with liquids in them.

I'd found another alchemist.

He was at one end of a clump of vendors, most of them weird looking. One guy had a mechanical arm, another wore almost as much leather as I had on, a woman had an oversized red robotic eye, that kind of thing. My target looked relatively normal, although up close I could see the old-fashioned alchemical symbols printed in darker tan on the cream shirt.

His bottles sported labels and price tags. Price tags with many zeroes, but right now money didn't matter. I picked up the empty-looking but not empty-feeling bottle labeled "Invisibility," and my brain churned as I stared at it. "Purified water. You had to purify water to make this. How did you make water more watery? And you had to do it in a high-pressure oxygen environment. Both elements would need representation."

He stopped staring at my badge, and gave me a pleased and surprised smile. His busy grey eyebrows lifted dramatically. He sat up straighter, and sort-of-answered, "I put too many years into working out that secret to surrender it so soon to the next generation. With instincts that strong, you'll figure it out yourself someday." He waved a hand at the specially designed pockets on my coat. "Interesting focus on color in your work. May I see?"

Nervous, I plucked out a red potion and passed it over. This guy was the real deal, me plus a lifetime of practice. Would he like it? Was I about to make a fool of myself? Should I have stayed a mysterious minion?

Thoughtfully, and at least not yet with disapproval, he said, "Fascinating. The color is not a gimmick. You've actually bottled red. Apple skins, of course, but also the seeds, to reverse the cyanide. Some scale insects. I would have to put thought into the rest. I imagine some people are allergic?"

"Yes, but the healing effect keeps them from choking to death, so it's not a disaster." Now I was talking to another supervillain alchemist as equals. This was so trippy, in the very best way.

He was thinking the same thing, if more calmly. "I'm glad Cleric found you, Pawn. I don't get to meet a lot of my own kind. Cybermancer doesn't count."

The alchemist waved at the man in brown leather, who was about half his age and twice my age. The leather-clad guy—Cybermancer, nodded back with a friendly grin. "I don't."

My eyes drifted down to the display again, and caught on the tags. The least expensive bottle labeled "Cleaning" was three thousand dollars. It had never occurred to me that someday my measly, almost useless for fighting power might make me stupid rich. One bottle with particularly thick protective crystal sides didn't even have a price, just the label "Imprinting."

I picked it up, and swirled the glittery contents. Imprinting?

Ew! Suddenly disgusted, I put it back down. "Ugh. I'm sorry, Mister. I'm sure that's great stuff, but I am not melting down baby birds for any recipe."

Um. What if I'd offended him? No, he kept smiling, and shrugged. "The enzymes I extract are powerful enough to be worth it."

The woman with the big red eye, who was closest anyway, leaned over to peer at the bottle. "Oh, yeah, that's the stuff you got Audit with, right? For three whole months she thought you were her partner, not Brainy."

The alchemist straightened up more, grinning in obvious pride. "That's why I'm the first name on the list of villains who've defeated her."

Cybermancer put his boots up on his table. Business was clearly slow this afternoon. "There's actually a new name on the plaque."

The red eyed woman cocked her head. "What, really?"

The other mad scientists murmured similarly curious surprise. Even my fellow alchemist had his eyebrows up again.

A bushy-bearded guy with a mechanical arm shook his

head emphatically. "No way. She's been retired for fifteen years. Who was it?"

Cybermancer shrugged. "Someone named Fortuity."

The red eyed woman snorted, scooping her arms around her display of ray guns built around big crystals. "Yeah, it would take the luck powers you need to win the fight just to get her to fight."

One man had been standing at the back of the crowd. On the lean side, in a long, gleamingly white and pressed lab coat, he looked like a stern professor. He sounded merely mild as he spoke up. "I defeated the Audit once."

Everyone gave him a long look, clearly impressed. The woman with the red eye smirked. "Got lucky?"

The professor guy chuckled, his smile small but tightly emphatic. "Oh, yes. Deliberately lucky. I've always liked to buy unopened boxes from estate sales, you see. Every once in a while, you find something absolutely unique."

The red eyed woman grinned wider. "I'm starting to see where this is going."

His hands behind his back, really looking exactly like a professor lecturing about his favorite topic, the lab coat guy continued his story. "Once, almost twenty years ago, I opened a box and a voice told me that I had released it from its prison, and it would do me one service. It turned out to be an invisible air monster."

The red eyed woman barked a laugh. "Yeah, that's as out of left field as it gets."

Professor guy nodded. "Exactly. Setting out to and successfully defeating the Audit would make my reputation. I found a type of crime she'd been stopping, and lured her into attacking me. She knew something was wrong, but how could she prepare for a wild statistical fluke like an invisible air monster grabbing and immobilizing her?"

"But what did you do the next time?" asked the red eyed woman with a sneer.

"I made sure I never, ever fought her again."

That solemn pronouncement got a lot of understanding nods, even from the woman with the robotic eye.

Wow. So, this is what supervillains did when they got together. They gossiped. Chinatown was just a big school cafeteria for adults with powers.

With that thought in mind, I almost wasn't surprised when Cassie shouted, "Hey, you!", grabbed me by my shoulder, and spun me around.

"C-gkt!" I just barely managed not to shout her name. Her wild, excited stare included no hint of recognition, after all.

Now dancing from foot to foot jiggling her fists, Cassie exclaimed, "This is great. This is great! My first superhero gig! I'm going to start my heroic journey right now, by defeating a soldier of Tyrant!"

Stamping her feet still, she leveled an arm, pointing her index finger right at my nose. I took a quick couple of steps back so that didn't touch, and good thing, because white arcs of lightning flowed down her neck and across her arm to that finger, which began to glow.

I held up both my hands, palms out in caution. "Whoa! Ease up! I just went through this, and it was agreed that I'm out of bounds."

Cassie wagged her finger in negation, and I had to take another step back because she took another step forward. She smiled with a beatific glee I would have expected from Marcia. "No, the adults agree you are a villain, not a victim, and even bad guys don't want to pick a fight with a little kid. But you and I, we're the same age."

Mouth pursed in disapproval, the red eyed mad scientist raised her hand to object. "It's still bad form to pick a fight with a noncombatant. Grudges get built over that kind of thing."

"Tyrant has a grudge against absolutely everyone who doesn't knuckle under," declared Cassie with giddy determination. Arcs of electricity were now crawling all over her.

I had my own pride. Lowering my arms, I raised my chin instead and told her flatly, "I am under orders not to fight."

"Then that's just your bad luck, huh?" giggled Cassie, drunk with manic glee, or possibly lightning build-up.

Her arm was glowing awfully bright, after all.

I was about to get electrocuted into two Wednesdays after

last Tuesday. Uh. My message was already delivered. Maybe a strategic retreat was very much in order right now, so that my new almost-best-friend didn't put me in the hospital.

With a soft thump, the purple hairy monster woman dropped off an upstairs balcony and landed in a crouch right behind Cassie. My breath choked off, which at least kept me from screaming.

The beast straightened up with lazy grace, lifted its clawed hand, and grabbed a fistful of Cassie's hair.

"Ow! Ow, hey! What are you doing? Let me go!" yelped Cassie. All her electrical arcs went dark. If they'd zapped the animal woman, the monster had shrugged them off like an aircraft carrier ignores a piranha.

I was not an aircraft carrier. I was a guppy, or possibly a chunk of raw steak, and very glad that the two had each other's attention, but...maybe I should do something for Cassie?

Before I could follow that thought further, the animal woman snarled, "This is a *truce zone*, Cassie, and I do not want my little sister decapitated or injected with a quart of neurotoxin!"

Everyone ignored the secret identity breach, so I did, too.

Cassie bared her teeth. She swiped and scrabbled at the fist in her hair. After a few seconds of that, she slumped. The manic energy disappeared, and with a miserable grimace she muttered, "Yeah, okay."

"Now, apologize!" The purple monster shook Cassie once, and I winced in sympathetic pain at that hair pull.

Anger hardened Cassie's face again, and she opened her mouth to argue, then paused. After a few seconds of that, she slumped again. Miserable and now guilty, she looked back up to me. "Sorry. I got carried away, but you need to understand something, Pawn. You weren't named by accident. When your boss tries to take over the city, you and the other Pawns will be sacrificed."

I stared at her, the fear fading, replaced by the last emotion I expected. Anger bubbled up out of my stomach, hot and bilious. Sacrificed? Seriously? My job was to restore a book. I was actually hired to make something less harmful. Cleric's orders had all been aimed at keeping me safe, and were working. Cassie didn't know what she was talking about. None of these people did!

Gritting my teeth, I refrained from yelling all of that only because it would be spilling Cleric's secrets, and so far, he was the only person who'd considered my feelings since I made that stupid Trouble magnet, which had clearly worked beyond my wildest dreams.

My anger only stiffened Cassie's resolve. When her furry purple sister let go of her hair, Cassie brushed that hair back down and gave me a fiery, defiant stare, adding, "Anyway, there are lots of kids who want to be superheroes. One of us will meet a Pawn outside of Chinatown." She grinned with sudden, vicious hope. "Maybe today."

I didn't answer that. I turned and walked away instead, right out of the building, and I did it with my chin high. Why? Because absolutely everyone was watching me. As angry and betrayed as I felt, I had hit this place today like a mile-long comet slamming into Jupiter at one hundred thirty-four thousand miles per hour on July sixteenth, Nineteen Ninety-Four.

And once I was out of sight, it would probably be a good idea to climb out over the fence. One sip of my orange strength potion should be enough for that.

Afterwards, sitting safely in Cleric's car, I told him everything. He smiled, raised his fist, held it out to me, and said, "I'm proud of you, Pawn."

I bumped his fist back, but I giggled the whole car trip long about it.

CHAPTER NINE

The first blow to my victory high came on Sunday. Just a little one. I was on the couch going through meaningless word puzzles from Chemistry and trying not to make sense of them, just do them by formula like Marcia taught me.

Dad had let himself not go to work today, and was in the kitchen somewhere. Kay lounged in Mom's overstuffed chair, which was faded blue and badly worn from loving use. He had a notebook out, scratching away at his own homework occasionally. Mostly he stared dreamily at the ceiling with the big smile of someone whose life is working out perfectly.

Dad stopped being in the kitchen somewhere and walked into the living room, smiling blearily at his children. His clothes were all a rumpled mess, and I liked to see him that way. It meant he was relaxing.

He put his hands on the back of the couch and leaned over it to look down at me. "How's the new job, Magenta?"

Now it was my turn to grin, with the fiery enthusiasm of a conquering battle maiden. "I. LOVE. It. Not that it's really gotten going yet. You can't just leap into alchemy. The books Mr. Clark wants me to restore are fascinating. They're super old.

Hundreds of years old, ancient tomb old, and exotic. Plus, he gives me *respect*." I could not put enough emphasis in that last word!

Dad frowned, and sourness suddenly itched amidst my pride. I mean, seriously? Dad's reaction to my finding a great after school job was to get suspicious? Why suddenly could he not be proud of me? Instead of congratulations, he looked over at my older brother and asked, "You checked Mr. Clark out, Kay?"

Kay snapped into the present, and his dreamy smile turned dour. "I think there's something skeevy about him, but even using my power I can't find anything that suggests his interest in Magenta is inappropriate."

I rolled my eyes. Yes, okay, it was something my family should worry about. I'd been worried about it for maybe sixty seconds. It took that long for anyone to see that kind of thing never crossed Cleric's mind.

Kay's face hardened a little further. "If there is some kind of trouble, I'll get between it and Magenta, I promise."

I didn't hide a groan. Kay was being so stupid. Whatever. Kay could waste his time guarding the world from a reading themed supervillain.

Dad finally started to smile, if only a little. It looked tired and showed off the streaks of grey in his short hair. "What's your schedule look like, Magenta?"

I waved a hand, as lofty and dismissive as the princess of the moon. "We're still sorting it out. There's not a lot to do until the first restorative batch is ready. I figure a couple of hours a couple of days this week, and a lot of Saturday afternoons when I have the time to do intricate work. We're feeling it out day by day, since I can get off the school bus around Exposition and take the Metro home after."

Then Monday hit.

I arrived at the street corner where I waited for the bus in the unspeakable hour of the morning whose name dare not be spoken, the time of sleep deprivation when those of us who have a long, long bus ride to school must suffer. In this bleak, grey limbo our neighborhood consigned only one other girl and I to wait.

To my considerable surprise, this morning she looked at me curiously and asked, "Are you the same girl who's here every day?"

I sighed, trying to keep it as mild and undramatic as possible. "Yes."

She eyed me for a few seconds, as if trying to memorize my face, which would be useless. With a contemplative frown, her high forehead, massive glasses, and button-down shirts she achieved the physical limit of looking nerdy. She even sounded smart, like a scientist analyzing research. "A super power makes you look different every time. Uncontrolled shapeshifting, perhaps. No, it could be that or a dozen other things."

These were normally my least favorite conversations, but this time I smirked. "You must have a super power to have recognized me."

That got a giggle. Compared to my lunch friends, she had an open, easygoing smile, even while energetically shaking her head. "Nope, not me. My brother does. He can control how electrically resistant his skin is. We always laugh about millions of years of ancestors who had this power, just waiting for touch screens to be invented."

Now she squinted at me again, maybe trying to see me through those gigantic lenses. "But that's the point, isn't it? If a different girl shows up at the bus stop every day for a week, she must be the same girl looking different."

The bus finally pulled up. I barely glanced at it as I climbed the steps, still talking. "I wish everybody was that smart."

The girl went back to her "thoughtful analysis" face, staring hard at nothing while her brain worked. "It might be easier for me because I don't know you. I'm not expecting you to look like anything." Snapping to alertness, she returned to her casually friendly smile and held out a hand. "I'm Tonika, by the way."

"Magenta." I returned the smile, returned the handshake, and we went to find seats. She sat by someone else, but I didn't mind. I had to work on my formula for Cleric's book potion. I almost had it figured out.

I did get a final recipe written out just as we arrived at Upper High. Climbing the steps, I noticed something that made me grin: No superheroes guarding the door. That perked my smugness at Saturday's performance right back up.

Then I bumped into Aikamieli outside of homeroom.

Literally.

Reeling backward a step, I gawked at the last thing I'd expected, a skinny wizard in a too-long red shirt and slacks that looked a lot like his costume.

"What are you doing here!?" I demanded.

He gawked back at me. "You know I'm not a student!?"

His eyes betrayed not a flicker of recognition. Of course.

I pushed past him and took my seat before the bell rang. Aikamieli slid into an empty desk and chair right next to mine. The teacher didn't notice, and counted attendance as if Aikamieli had always been there. It was me who got the doubtful look.

Again, of course.

Homeroom lasts all of ten minutes, so as soon as the bell rang, I ducked out the door, leaned against the wall next to it, and waited. He emerged, standing up on his tiptoes and craning his head around to look at the crowd. I grabbed him by the scrawny shoulder.

Aikamieli let out a squeak, but a quiet one at least. The look he turned on me was filled with wide-eyed hope, not panic. "Excuse me, have you seen a girl with pink...uh...well, she's hard to describe, really."

I flipped by dreadlocks up with one hand and glared at him. "Yes. It's me."

He let out a gusty sigh, and leaned against my grip. "What a relief. Boy, did I remember you completely wrong. Where is English class?"

My mouth hung open as I stared at his soft, earnestly

curious boyish face, trying to twist my own brain through the multiple conversational derails. I locked onto one. "How would I know where your English class is?"

"Well, I have all the same classes as you. That's how the spell works. At least, I think that's how the spell works." His eagerness drifted into awkward, pinch-faced, and distant voiced anxiety. Oh, mighty bastion of willpower and unbreachable confidence, thy name is not Aikamieli.

Personally, I groaned. "This is another spell?"

He lit up with apprentice wizard enthusiasm. "Oh, yes! It lets you spend time with your beloved." My face must have been a horror movie, because he quickly started waving his hands and corrected, "It doesn't actually target who you love, just the person you're trying to get to know!"

I dragged him toward English class, because I personally was not going to be late just because of a wizard invasion. Half angry and half disturbed, I asked, "Is this whole book full of creeper spells?"

"Courtship was very important in Wainamoinen's age!" Aikamieli squeaked, stumbling after me.

Reaching Advanced English interrupted our conversation. With any luck, he would find the topics and lessons unendurably confusing since these weren't his classes, but I didn't pay attention to him to find out.

That didn't change the fact he was still here when class ended, but I left him behind and headed to Chemistry. Halfway down the hall, I heard his magnificent singing voice crooning gibberish words behind me, soft and smooth.

After a little of that, he fell in next to me, matching steps, and asked, "Is that you, Magenta?"

Great. He knew my name. "Yes. Do you know how messed up these stalker spells are?"

Nervously, he swung his—also red—backpack around and clutched it defensively to his chest. The True Kalevala must be in there. Stung, guilty, and desperate, he argued, "They're not meant for inappropriate purposes! These spells were written over a thousand years ago, when how you met a girl was completely different! I take romance seriously and I want love, not to force my attention on a strange girl and besides, that's not what this is. It's just that, like I said, you're the only person I can talk to about the superhero stuff...."

He trailed off, giving me guilty, hopeful puppy eyes. They didn't work on me. What did work was that I completely understood his point. Toning down to merely exasperated, I flipped my dreads back and gave him a scolding but not furious glare. "Okay, but you're not making a good first impression."

He lowered his eyes meekly. "It's better than making no impression at all."

Yeah, all right. I'd felt that every day of my life.

We'd reached Chemistry. I took my place next to Marcia, and at least Aikamieli's freaky spell hadn't pushed her out of her place. Marcia looked reassuringly normal, in the sense that she looked wild-eyed and embarrassingly underdressed. She did seem particularly smug today, but as I started to say, "You look like the lioness who—" the teacher interrupted me.

"Pop quiz, children!"

The Chemistry room echoed with complaints of various levels of strength, none of which forestalled our fate by even a few seconds. We received our test papers, and got to work.

It was awful, but I remembered Marcia's instructions and kept checking the Periodic Table on display behind the teacher's desk. This electron shell question meant...no, it didn't mean anything, but for questions like this I counted from the end of the row. Three squares. Okay.

I was pretty sure I passed, but I sweated bullets like a Gatling gun the whole hour, and that's how long it took me. I handed my paper in dead last, right as the bell rang.

I felt drained walking out the door, and dealing with Aikamieli would be more effort than I wanted to spend, but if I didn't approach him, he'd just track me down with his stalker boyfriend magic.

So, I grabbed his arm again, and said brusquely, "It's me. Magenta. Now's your chance. What did you want to say?"

That startled him, but whatever was going on in his head about not recognizing me, he didn't share it. Instead he gave me a blank stare, and flapped his hands. "Well...it was scary, wasn't it? I hadn't imagined how scary it would be to face a real supervillain."

He was right. He was more right than other kids would understand. I nodded sheepishly, swimming through memories. "Yeah. It was terrifying. I hadn't expected to be so scared."

"I heard about the Inscrutable Machine and thought I could be a hero, but I have no idea how they faced adults," he squeaked.

I nodded again, more enthusiastically this time. "Yeah, they inspired me, too. When Cleric showed up it was like stepping off a cliff. I wasn't prepared, and he didn't need to be prepared. He brushed us both aside like little kids."

We reached Latin class. Aikamieli had my curiosity up enough that I snuck a few glances back at him. His spell hadn't managed to put him beside me here. He flipped through the book and wrote answers to exercises with ease and all signs of enjoyment. Yes, of course he was a language nerd.

I felt nothing but jealousy at that, of the friendly sort, even. I'd love to have a talent for languages.

Hmmm. Maybe Cleric had a book on Sumerian. Language is what he does, right?

After Latin I dragged Aikamieli physically to lunch, since I didn't have much choice in the matter. I didn't mind as much this time. I got him into the cafeteria and was heading for the food line when he shook his backpack. "I'll share mine. My mom keeps saying that boys with super powers need to eat three times as—wow."

I stopped and blinked at Aikamieli, standing still and bug-eyed in his protowizardly tracks. "What?"

He answered by raising his arm and pointing. When I saw why, I had to shove his arm back down. "Do you think about nothing but girls?"

"It's not that!" he protested, still staring like a hypnotized frog at, yes, a girl. Unmistakably a girl. A girl with an hourglass shape unmatched by any other high school student I'd ever met, although maybe the knee-length bell skirt and tight corset made her look more voluptuous than she really was.

Then his words broke past my cynicism. "I'm...I'm jealous. If you knew magic like I do, you would understand. She radiates power. It fills the room, like if a dragon was hiding inside her. A chaos dragon. How can a high school student have that much magic?"

Now that I knew he wasn't being as creepy as his ancient hero Wainamoinen, I could admit to myself that I was also jealous. Not of this girl's looks, of her clothing. She dressed like someone carrying a hydrogen bomb's worth of dark power, who ruled from a haunted castle over a barren kingdom of eternal night. The short bell skirt flaunted multiple layers of petticoats. Her striped knee socks were tied with bows. The gown had poufs and trailing ribbons and pockets and many, many laces, all in black with only carefully placed white crosses as contrast. I could just barely spot brown roots in hair dyed black but with small pink, red, and purple stripes here and there. A metal collar with a dangling ring encircled the girl's throat, because an outfit like this needed a touch of the actually disturbing, and she had the guts to go there. Guts, style, and money. Goth wouldn't be what I did with it, but I envied how much of all three she had.

I promised myself that with Cleric's help, I would catch up.

For now, I just wanted to not drool as obviously as Aikamieli, and I yanked him aside and dragged him over to my lunch table, where Marcia, Charlotte, Cassie, and Will waited. When we approached, Cassie pointed a fish stick at Aikamieli and said, "You are definitely not Magenta."

"I'm Magenta," I supplied, trying not to sound stung, because…as sarcastically certain as her words were, Cassie had hesitated the tiniest bit, her voice not one hundred percent completely able to tell me apart from a boy.

Marcia, today eating from a bag of mixed candy, still looked as smug as she had in Chemistry class. Cassie looked almost as happy. It was only Charlotte who gave me a serious frown and spread her hands in helpless apology. "I wish you could see yourself, Magenta. I promise, we try to prepare. Natural pink hair is so rare you should be obviously you, but when we see you the one person you absolutely don't look like is Magenta Slade."

I sighed, and started to take my seat. Marcia interrupted that by yanking Aikamieli down onto the bench next to her, looking him over with one raised, calculating eyebrow. Maniacally focused calculation, sure, but still calculating. As slyly as if she were expecting a romantic confession she asked, "So, who's your friend?"

As awkward and anxious as anyone sitting hip to hip with Marcia's smile should be, he fumbled, "Oh. Uh. Aikamieli. I'm Aikamieli. Yes."

"He's visiting," I filled in, finishing the process of sitting down.

It hadn't been much of a fill-in. When was the last time one high school kid "visited" another school? Nobody but me noticed the implausibility. My immunity had to be because I was the target of the spell. Yeesh. Whatever Aikamieli said about the goth girl, this spell seemed seriously powerful and subtle to me.

"So, what are you into?" asked Charlotte, waving her own fish stick curiously.

He ran his hands over his black hair, looking stunned by all the girls talking to him. "I'm…uh…I'm a wizard, actually."

Everybody perked up, even Will.

"Ooh," said Cassie, eyeing Aikamieli with much the same calculation as Marcia.

Charlotte nodded. "Nice, but…."

All eyes turned.

Charlotte leaned forward, scowling and pressing a fist to the tabletop. "I hate to short the new kid, but why has no one asked the obvious question, yet? Where are all the super powered guards?"

Well, uh. Find an excuse fast, Magenta! Any excuse? Please, brain?

Except Charlotte's attention didn't focus on me. She squinted at Marcia, whose grin kept getting bigger. Pointing her finger across the table, Charlotte demanded, "What do you know?"

Abandoning her candy, Marcia leaned back on the bench, clasping her arms behind her head as she drawled, "Weeeeell, the Construction Workers robbed a hardware store yesterday."

Charlotte snorted. "Those losers?" She did not abandon her suspicious stare directed at Marcia.

Cassie lifted a fish stick, noting airily, "They were big, once. Steamshovel was the first villain to officially defeat Cyber Angel in the 80s. When you've had a team for forty years and it keeps changing members, things go downhill. I don't see what that has to do with anything."

Marcia turned her grin up to the ceiling. "Someone may have put on leather armor, dyed her hair pink, and then punched their getaway van. Oh, and she threw pieces of it at them. Large pieces. Like doors and carburetors. Or so I may have heard."

Her eyebrows still flat as a ruler, Charlotte folded her arms and glared at Marcia. "You are not good enough to take a whole team, even if they're C-listers."

Marcia plucked a jawbreaker from her bag of candy, flicked it into the air with her thumb, caught it in her mouth, spat it six inches back up into the air, caught it in her mouth again, and swallowed, savoring holding us in suspense. Straightening back up, she said, "Didn't have to. I only had to slow them down until Stalwart showed up, and make sure lots of people saw me do it."

Charlotte rubbed her face with one hand, voice turning rough and pained. "I'm going to regret asking this, but why did you do that, besides the excuse to break things?"

Like a flipped switch, Marcia's whole attitude changed. She bared her teeth and thumped her own knuckles into the tabletop, leaving dents. The answer came in a snarl. "Because it ticks me off that the adults are treating some kid as if she didn't have a choice. Whoever that girl in the video was, she deserves to make her own decisions and face the consequences, good and bad."

"Pawn," said Cassie. "Her name is Pawn, and there's more than one."

Marcia, Charlotte, and Aikamieli turned their heads to stare at Cassie. Uh, oops. Better do that, too. Besides, I was more than a little tickled to have my adventures be the subject of rumormongering and tales told. That was why I'd gotten into this business in the first place!

Will ignored Cassie entirely and kept eating. You could tell they were best friends.

Cassie explained to the eager faces, "I met a Pawn, right up close. The heroes are actually gone because Tyrant complained that the Pawns are no different from sidekicks…"

"Which is true," Marcia declared, pointing a finger emphatically.

"…and noncombatants," finished Cassie.

"Not anymore," Charlotte observed, giving Marcia an accusing glare.

A repetitive squeaky noise caught my attention. They came from Aikamieli, whose smile of rapturous epiphany should have summoned a sparkling corona from heaven. When he found his voice, it was to stammer, "This—this is perfect! Perfect! If the Pawns are sidekicks, what *should* happen is that a team of hero sidekicks should stop them, right? We can be those sidekicks!"

Jerking up off her seat, Cassie slapped the table in triumphant eagerness. "Yes! I'll start my hero career, impress Penny, and get some valuable practice for the day I can finally fight her heroine-to-villainess!"

Will covered his face with both hands. Charlotte stared up at Cassie wide-eyed, brows together, amused and incredulous. "You are obsessed. Did you know that?"

Dropping back onto the bench, Cassie grinned back at her. "Of course! No one becomes a hero or villain who doesn't have serious obsession issues."

Marcia nodded at that happily, and shoved another handful of candy into her mouth.

Charlotte scowled, lips pursed, her stare turning distant and increasingly worried. I knew what she was thinking. What did that say about her?

I wish I had time to worry about what that meant about me, but a different concern pushed that aside. My friends had just formed a superhero team specifically to be my enemies.

This was a disaster. An utter disaster. I might, just maybe, be able to take Cassie in a fight, if I was lucky. Marcia could break a car. She would cream me. She would reduce me to a blood splatter. If I somehow managed her, I had no chance at all against Charlotte.

I'd never seen Charlotte do anything threatening. I didn't

have to. She moved like Cleric, like someone who knew what she was doing.

If I confessed, would they call it off? No way. Not with those grins. Besides, they all seemed to think working for someone who worked for Tyrant made me either a stormtrooper or a pathetic dupe. Admitting the truth could end our friendship.

No. No, no. That thought was even worse than getting beaten to a pulp by them. I'd finally made cool friends who were like me. No matter which way I looked at it, this was going to end badly.

I tried not to wince as Charlotte said, "Well, anyway, I'm in."

Will shrugged.

Cassie, Charlotte, and Marcia looked at me. While, of course, I sat there looking horrified. Suspicious much, Magenta?

At least here my brain activated and gave me an excuse. Sounding as miserable as I felt, I shook my head. "Part time job, guys."

Yes. A part time job getting punched by Marcia. Urgh. Unless I quit and gave up everything Cleric had given me. It was a horrible option, but an option.

Cassie waved that off with a literal wave of her hand. Untroubled, she promised me, "When the time comes, odds are good you'll be off work."

Charlotte frowned. Goofy relaxation time with her friends was over. She sat up straight, with the seriousness of a leader thinking ahead. "Whenever that is. How are we going to know when the Pawns are active for us to stop? By the time we see a news report, even online, it will be too late."

Everyone else looked disappointed, but all I felt was relief. Of course, they had to find me to fight me, and good luck doing that.

"Magenta's Trouble magnet?" suggested Cassie.

I shrugged, trying to look disappointed but philosophical. "You can have it, but we'll have to leave Marcia behind, and I don't think a bunch of kids called Pawns will ever be the biggest source of Trouble for it to point at."

"I can help!" declared Aikamieli. "My magic is all about learning and knowing things!"

Pins of anxiety marched up my spine. Aikamieli's book full of stalker boyfriend spells would point them right at me. I might as well give them a slobbering bloodhound and rub myself with meat. I'd have a better chance of hiding.

My friends' smiles of victory matched my rising panic. Marcia hooked an arm around Aikamieli, crowing, "Oh, yeah. We are exchanging phone numbers right now. I'm Marcia, and you are not getting away."

"Can we eat?" asked Will pointedly, the only person not terrified or gleeful.

The need to stuff our faces quelled the conversation, although I didn't have much appetite. This conversation had also dulled my interest in talking to Aikamieli for the rest of the day. When Marcia physically tackled him as he walked out the front door of Upper High at three o'clock, I snuck away to my bus without a word.

Walking into Cleric's boarded-up shop and not very secret lair half an hour later taunted me with bittersweet relief. This was what my life was blowing up for: A room full of antique oddities, books that got older and more impressive every time I came here, and a beautiful, beautiful table full of glassware.

I stared at it, trying not to whine with longing. Arranged against the wall, Cleric had bought for me a complete alchemy set, everything I'd asked for and more. Beakers. Glass, rubber, and plastic. Vials with stoppers. I would actually have more than one alembic to use at a time, and not have to worry about contamination mixing things in an old coffee mug.

Walking up to it with silent, reverent steps, I ran my fingers adoringly over a gas cylinder the size of a propane tank. An actual, professional chemist quality pressure tank, not something I'd cobbled together that broke half the time. It had gauges. Wonderful, wonderful gauges.

I could make so many exotic chemicals with this set, and

Cleric had cleared out the next two bookshelves to fill them with ingredients. I admired a man who knew how much power fresh orange peel contained, and had bought them without even being asked.

Right now, my villainous employer was actually up on the alchemy table, twisting screws that fastened long metal brackets to the ceiling. They hung down like stalactites, and even weirder, surrounded a rectangular block of grey clay. A big rectangular block, the size of the whole table, currently floating in the air supported by hovering books.

He greeted me with a slightly strained smile. "Ah, perfect timing. This is our fume hood. It will absorb everything but the proper percentages of oxygen, nitrogen, and carbon dioxide. Also, an excellent deodorizer. Set it at the height you want it, please?"

Cleric dropped to the floor, and I hopped up in his place, very slightly more limber than a man twice my age. He handed me some dowels, and in a few seconds, I had the scratchy-feeling block pinned in place high enough to be out of my way, but low enough to contain dangerous fumes. I didn't have to ask how well it worked. Touching it left my hands feeling raw from having the oils sucked off of them.

Back on the floor, I pulled my backpack around, fished out the notebook page I'd scribbled up on the bus, and handed it to him. "So, uh…here's the final list of ingredients. I'm going to have to do a lot of concentrating. I mean, concentrating the active properties from—"

He held up a hand, smiling gently. "I understand."

I guess a muscle-bound nerd in chainmail would understand what I meant, yes. I left it at that because honestly, I just wanted to get my hands on this equipment. Yanking ingredients off the shelves, I set them up in different bottles. Mostly, this first round involved filtering, running gasses through water or alcohol, rinsing water through tea leaves, that sort of thing. The brown from tea held power to strengthen paper. You found well cared for old books and people who drink tea together, and they had associated properties.

A loud grinding followed by the softer slithering of a heavy weight on carpet caught my attention. Cleric backed out of the shop's kitchen, sweating with effort as he dragged a metal barrel more than half his height.

I knew what that contained without having to look, and my draw dropped in awe. "How—*where* did you get a fifty-gallon barrel of squid ink!?"

He laughed, leaning against a bookshelf as I scrambled to set up the pump (Eee, I had a pump now!) and concentrating equipment for the ink. Wiping his forehead with his wrist, he replied playfully, "From a squid, of course. You know how the super powered community keeps a lot of weird, rare things to itself. Speaking of which, would you be willing to go shopping for me sometimes? It's safer than my doing it."

"Reading off a list to a guy who's half cyborg and cynically inspecting his boxes of magic swords sounds awesome to me." More importantly, being seen doing it, especially with a touch of being respected and feared because of my boss's boss.

I got busy fastening tubes together. Then I had to soak paper in salts. Which ones? I'd forgotten, but it was all written down. Something to bind the blackness out of the ink. It would take the purest essence of ink to seek out not where ink on a page was, but where it used to be.

After a while, Cleric murmured from behind and above me, "You have a remarkable talent, and an even more remarkable dedication. My quest would be much slower and more difficult without you. I would have found a way, but instead the way found me."

The Way. Eesh. Might as well say it out loud. "I'm worried about The Way."

He laid his hand on my shoulder, squeezed, and removed it immediately. "I'm not. I've studied The Way's powers, and they're considerable, but they have to be directed. He can do one thing perfectly. The way to defeat him is not to engage him in that direction. In this case, I'll stop him from stopping me from doing anything morally wrong by not trying to do anything morally wrong." Stepping around me, he leaned his hip against my alchemy table and grinned merrily. "Strange, yes, but we're helping people and making the world a better place."

This was it. While we were on the topic, I should tell him my friends were hunting me, waiting to pounce the next time I appeared in public as a Pawn.

My heart froze, and instead I said, "You're really dedicated. I heard heroes and villains are all obsessives."

You're such a coward, Magenta. Super powered errand girl is all you're good for.

But I was good at it, and I loved it.

Thankfully, Cleric missed my inner turmoil. He was too busy grinning and nodding at what I'd said. "I don't deny it. My life is dedicated to my cause and to my lord, in that order, and that's the way Tyrant wants it."

I smirked, propping my hand on the table as fluids dripped and gurgled next to me like good little reagents. "So, no hobbies?"

Cleric shrugged, his armor clinking under the tabard. "I read a lot."

Okay, that made me laugh. "Ha! No surprise there."

The villain straightened up, his eyes getting distant as he went into preacher mode. "I go to movies as well. They help me see the shape of what the world could be."

Huh. I thought about that as I turned a Bunsen burner flame up to juuuuust the right level. "You want the world to be just like movies?" Because movies were kind of crazy.

Cleric nodded sharply, chin hard and prominent, and he clenched a fist in front of him as his idealistic passion surged. "Yes. Everyone should have a chance at the adventure and wondrous things that heroes keep to themselves." That hand swept to the side, and his voice softened...slightly. "Not that I blame them, but the whole world deserves a chance to live that way."

The fit of zealotry faded, and Cleric relaxed into an almost normal person again. "You're helping me do that without violence. Your powers are filled with wonder, and I want to help you unlock that."

That turned my attention to the table, and the multiple reactions I had running. I didn't have much more time this afternoon. Some of them I could easily leave like this, but others....

Except I wasn't at home, and wasn't Cleric living here? Upstairs somewhere? So maybe…. "Hey, if I leave these heating, can you turn them off on a schedule and generally make sure the place doesn't burn down?"

"I absolutely can," he answered, with no hesitation.

Yes! I pumped my fist. This was so much better than working on my crummy bench at home.

Clearing my throat, I looked up at my employer and tried to pretend my dignity had never cracked. "Good. I'll have to make a quick stop here tomorrow to switch things out, and I bet the potion will be ready before the weekend."

CHAPTER TEN

The potion wasn't ready on Wednesday. It was ready on Thursday.

I stopped at the door to Cleric's hideout and looked up and down the weirdly deserted little street. It remained weirdly deserted. My friends hadn't said a word about Pawns since Monday. Yesterday at lunch they'd tried to introduce me to someone named Claudia, whose only reply had been "I'm sorry, I have to feed my shark." No one had treated that as a joke.

No sign of Cleric, but he would be downstairs soon. I checked my reactions where I'd left them on the alchemy desk.

Nothing. Still nothing. The black liquid sat in a lump on the clear sparkly liquid, showing no sign of dissolving. Shaking hadn't worked. Mixing hadn't worked. The ingredients were right. The ink essence ought to combine and allow its potential to be sublimated, but that wasn't happening.

Cleric's footsteps thumped on the stairs, and seconds later he entered the shop's front room, or the den, or my workroom, or whatever he considered it. He didn't even glance at the unsuccessful potion, only at my face, and he sounded concerned. "You should take a break."

"I can't take a break when I'm not doing anything!" I complained, glaring at the reagents as if willpower had anything to do with alchemy.

"You can. Have some ice cream," he said mildly, hands behind his back.

I glanced at the kitchen. "Is it in the freezer with the pile of meat?"

His armor clinked, betraying a fidget. "Well…yes."

I stuck out my tongue. "No, thank you."

With a long, pained sigh, I ran my hands back through my dreadlocks. They felt dangerously dry. I would have to use my last hair potion on them when I got home, and then buy some regular moisturizers. My face twisted in a sudden grimace, and I barked, "I don't know what's wrong! I don't know, and I don't have time to experiment and find out. Schoolwork is a bear. A zombie bear with machine guns that shoot bees strapped to its shoulders. I don't know what my family was thinking moving me to a smart kids' school!"

Cleric's pale eyebrows raised, and his voice got even more mild. "Are you getting bad grades?"

My own forehead hurt from furrowing, and I shrank my head down between my shoulder blades. "Well…no. We've only had time for two quizzes, and my homework is getting Bs, but it's a lot harder than it was last year."

Cleric stepped up next to me, his head almost as high as the blocky grey fume hood, as if his size might comfort me. "So, what you're saying is, you feel like you're failing, even if you're doing better than anyone could reasonably expect of you."

I didn't want to hear it. Staring gloomily at the mixing jar, I thumped it over and over, listening to the glass clonk. "I'm failing at this. I thought I knew how to do it. My powers are garbage, and I should resign myself to a life of mediocrity."

Bang! Cleric's knuckles slammed against the top of my work table, so hard the shudder went through wood and glass and split little bits of black off of the blob in my jar. "You are not a mediocrity, and your powers are not garbage! You're fourteen years old, Pawn. Do you think your power—"

"SHUT UP!" I shrieked. He did, his pale face falling into

vertical lines of sorrow and pity. I grabbed those cheeks and yanked them down to the jar. "Look!"

The black bits were starting to drift back into the mass, so I resumed thumping the jar. They floated away again, and two, no, three of the specks disappeared, dissolved into the sparkling fluid.

He went still as he got it. I let go of him, turning and resting my back against the table, hand on my forehead. I laughed, a squeaky, weak laugh of desperation turned to relief. "Of course. I'm such an idiot. I was only thinking about the physical, but books aren't just paper and ink, they're knowledge. Knowledge is patterns."

Cleric nodded, barely moving and voice soft, as if I were as fragile as an egg made of glass, which was probably right. "Yes. Don't spread this around, but my power can't control blank paper. It holds no information."

He'd just told me his power's weakness, hadn't he? He was telling me how much he trusted me. Did I deserve that?

"I said SHUT UP!" I screamed again, this time at myself.

Thumping the oversized beaker relentlessly, I babbled as I processed what I saw and heard, following this new line of thought. "Vibrations. Patterns. Writing. The scratching of pen on paper. That's what I need! No, it would take years to do it that way. The components would dry up. Could I record the sound, speed it up and amplify it on a speaker? No, I'd be testing that over and over again until I found the right speed. A tuning fork!"

"I have a tuning fork," said Cleric. Several things thumped and something crashed upstairs, but seconds later a small children's book flew into the room holding the fork I'd asked for.

I whacked the prongs against the table, setting them ringing, plunged them in the black goop in the jar, and signed my name. Big letters. Flowing, dramatic writing. I wasn't restoring instruction manuals, here!

The black shattered, swept into the wake of the tuning fork again to form letters as I wrote them, only to fade into the mixture completely.

"The vat!" I yelled. Cleric helped me lift the big containers, pouring the reagents into a glass dish as long as my arm and a foot deep. After that, I poured the successful mix in to help start the reaction, and repeated my tuning fork performance. I had to write my name three times before the black fully separated, vanishing into the clear mass with its little sparkles that now moved even though the mix itself sat still. Finally, I poured the teapot full of brown into the dish and watched it meld instantly, perfectly in with the rest.

The resultant liquid had the light, even, opaque tan of an unbleached page of paper, except that dark hints of letters kept forming and disappearing on the surface.

I squealed! "I did it! I did it! That's what it's supposed to look like! No, it's not done until it's tested." I pounced on the nearest bookshelf, yanking off books, glancing at them, and throwing them away. Most of them were old, but not old enough. When one cracked as I pulled it open, and the paper snapped when I turned a page, I knew I had the right one. The ink had visibly faded, and some words weren't readable anymore.

I shoved the book into the goop, explaining, "It won't hurt your hands unless you have tattoos. I don't know what it would do to tattoos." Six, seven, eight, nine...ten seconds. I pulled the book back out, and flipped it open randomly.

Bright, fresh pages turned with supple ease. Every word was printed crisp and black. The book might as well be brand new.

Cleric said nothing. He only held out his open hand toward the kitchen, until a slim, purple-bound book flew out of the back room and into his grip. He opened this new volume and I got a peek at pages blank except for a broad smudge at the top of each one. Ten seconds later, he lifted the book. It looked pristine now, even the leather cover now shiny royal purple. Except, the pages were now blank.

My eyes opened wide. "I don't understand—" I started to say, but Cleric cut me off with a raised hand. He couldn't stop my anxiety. Was this potion good enough for regular books, but not magic? Would it not work on his all-important knowledge taking tome?

Cleric stepped out into the exact center of the open area of the shop. When he swiveled sharply to face me, he held not just the book, but a rectangle of pure black paper. He pressed it to the upper half of a blank page, where it stuck. Then he walked back to the entrance to the kitchen, and beckoned me with a couple of fingers. "Come look."

I wasted no time. He put the book in my hands, open to the page he'd attached the rectangle to. That rectangle was no longer black. It showed a photo of the room, and particular my alchemy desk. Below, writing in a language I'd never seen before filled the rest of the page, set at odd angles like someone making notes, and with little crude drawings of bookshelves and alembics and the fume hood. One was definitely a human head, and with the dreadlocks probably me, but the face had been viciously scratched out.

"Touch your face to the window," Cleric instructed.

I did. By the time it occurred to me to wonder why or if this was safe, I found out. When my nose touched the photo on the page, the room tipped upside down, and I found myself standing, or at least staggering, in the middle of the room, in the exact spot where Cleric had put the black rectangle into the book.

I glanced down. The photo and notes were still there. Presumably, I could do this again, and again, always bringing me back here.

Cleric's boots thumped on the carpet as he stomped up to me, grabbed my shoulder hard enough that it hurt, and snarled in eyes-blazing anger, "NEVER call yourself a mediocrity again!"

Uh. What could I say to that? What should I feel?

He didn't give me time to figure that out. His tabard flapped and chain mail clinked as he swept over to a heavy chest in the rear corner of the shop. Opening it with two keys, he pulled out the book. Huge, heavy, old, and the reason I had been hired. Without a pause, he carried it over to the potion tray, and laid his treasure into the fluid.

I stared. I had never in my life impressed anyone like this, or been trusted like this. The chill of anxiety crept into my skin. What if my potion failed this final test and Cleric's book was ruined?

Unable to watch, I squeezed my eyes shut and clenched my fists. How long could ten seconds take?

Liquid sloshed. Cleric's breathing got louder, heavier.

"Look. Look what you've done," he murmured. The words were terrifying, but his tone soft and filled with awe.

Oh, please, let that mean it worked. I forced my eyes open, stumbled over to the table, and looked at his ancient volume of magic or mad science or maybe a power no one even had a name for.

Not ancient anymore. The pages, thicker and softer than regular paper, shone a pale cream. When I turned them, they felt like silk. If the lettering in the purple book had been weird, these complicated glyphs were insane, but whether or not they made sense, they were every one dark and distinct and gleaming with colorful highlights like a wet crow's wing. The empty pages that filled the back of the book remained blank, but perfectly intact, with no holes or smudges.

I screamed. I couldn't help it. With stiff legs I stumbled away from the table, my fists waving in the air as I yelled out my wordless triumph and relief.

My scream stopped. Cleric and I said together, "Test it."

I grabbed a creaky wooden chair, set it in front of the podium, and plopped my but down onto its faded red cushion. The podium clacked and pages whispered as Cleric messed with the book. Then cold metal pinpricks signaled him touching me with the calipers.

I felt nothing else unusual at all.

"Did it...?" I asked.

"Yes."

As I got up to look, Cleric stepped up and collapsed into the chair. Leaning his head back and closing his eyes, he whispered, "I'm sorry. I need this."

I lingered half a second just to stare at him. He looked suddenly old, tired in a way I hadn't seen before.

Lingering over. I scurried around to look at the book. There, laid out on the page, was the same weird geometric design as before. Maybe some bits of it reminded me of alchemical symbols I'd seen in books, but mostly it just looked like someone liked drawing mazes. This was what my alchemical knowledge looked like.

Except this time.…

I looked at the cushion Cleric was sitting on. A weak red. Not much sanguinity in that. Maybe I could use it as the beginning of a healthy posture cushion. And sugary blueberries were the starting ingredient of my energy potion.

Stepping up to the chair, I waited until Cleric opened his eyes again. I pointed at the book. "It's there." Then I tapped my head. "And still in here."

He straightened up, grinning wearily at me. His eyes slowly regained their usual intense focus, although his voice still shook a bit. "You've changed everything. I wasn't expecting to get this far, this fast. I think I know how to put the knowledge into other people's heads, but I need equipment that I can't get without drawing attention."

Drawing myself to attention, I whacked my forehead in an over-eager salute. "I volunteer. Or you could use me as a distraction. Isn't that what your Pawn is for?"

He thought about this. Slowly, his face lit up with the glee of inspiration, and he pushed himself fully upright. "No. I'll be the distraction, while you carry out my real plan."

Chapter Eleven

"Come one, come all, to the Army of Tyrant's free information retrieval program! The past and future king of the world wants, not your body, not your mind, but your most ridiculous secrets! Skills, ladies and gentlemen, and the stranger the better! Can you juggle? Good. Can you garden? We'll take it. Do you read Sanskrit or Sumerian? I personally would take it as a favor if someone, anyone who reads or speak Sumerian steps up. Are you a spelunker who has seen the world's hidden cave paintings? Now we're talking. Have you read every fictional novel about Catlantis and Ancient Mew? You are exactly, exactly who we're looking for!"

Putting down my crude plastic cone megaphone, I took a swig from a juice bottle that I only adulterated with a few teensy drops of energy potion. While my throat refreshed, I straightened my easels and the placards which advertised the harmlessness of my endeavor.

In full costume, including my Knights Templar badge, I'd gotten plenty of stares from the college students lurking or strolling or hurrying between buildings. They were the perfect prey, which was why I'd set up on a nice, sunny spot on the grassy lawns of the University of Southern California, mere blocks away from the Cleric's lair.

Those stares were hotter and more uplifting than the sunshine, and with drunken glee I leveled a finger at a guy walking past, attracted by his purple t-shirt featuring a striped, bespectacled cartoon snake and some unidentifiable fluffy animal with a big, round head. "You, sir!" I yelled. "How well do you know cartoons? Would you like to take part in a probably safe but completely unethical mad science experiment? Remember, you keep your knowledge. We just want to copy it down!"

The jacketed girl walking next to the boy snorted laughter into her stack of books. He hesitated...and walked up to me! Hesitantly, sure, asking, "It's not painful, is it?" but I had his attention!

Taking off my hat for a moment, I slapped it against my leather coated chest. "No, sir. I've had it done to myself, and don't worry, I was already a brainwashed minion of evil. Also, ninety percent of the helmet is fake. We thought it wasn't worth your time without a bunch of colored lights and beeps."

That got the boy laughing, too, and as his girl friend (girlfriend?) watched, he sat in the folding cloth lawn chair I'd set in front of a plastic table holding The Book. I set our gaudy padded helmet on his head, and attached the clips that themselves attached to wires that attached to the helmet onto one of The Book's blank pages.

As promised, the helmet beeped and booped. Lights flashed their way up antennae. Lines bloomed on the page, drawing themselves into weird patterns that made no sense to anyone but The Book's creator, if them. When the drawing process stopped, I unclipped the page and took the helmet off my guinea pig. "All done, sir! Would you like to see?"

Still snickering but caught by their curiosity, the pair of students joined me at The Book. Their laughter stopped when they saw the page containing his information. His eyes got wider and wider as he stared. Touching a finger reverently to the lines, he traced them around, saying, "There's Chloe Coral

Snake. Librarian Valkyrie Holly. Ghost Cat Solvin' Mysteries!" Personally, I thought you could make out any pattern you wanted to see in that mess, but this was literally his area of expertise and no doubt he knew what he was talking about.

"So, it's not painful?" the girl asked him, shockingly mistrustful of a teenager in leather armor who worked for one of the world's most notorious supervillains.

He shook his head and reported honestly, "I didn't feel anything. I thought it must be a fake until I saw the page."

Raising my juice bottle again in respect, I declared, "I told you it was completely harmless, sir, although Tyrant does not guarantee that your knowledge of cartoons will not be used for nefarious purposes!"

The girl inched closer to me, toying with her hair bashfully and looking down at the ground instead of at my face. "Well, uh…you see…I'm actually writing my thesis about the history and cultural spread of Catlantis legends." Her favorite topic engaged, her eyes lifted, clicking on me with sudden fire. "But you know they're only legends, right? There have been more than two hundred archaeological expeditions exploring every supposed site, and that's not including satellite imagery. Catlantis never existed. People just like stories about wizard cats."

I spread my arms welcomingly wide. "And that is why Tyrant wants your knowledge, miss, because people love stories. Have a seat!"

She did, and I set up the helmet. The boy held her hand as she waited nervously. Yep, definitely dating. I clipped the clips, and let the helmet provide its fake show as the book drew…

…a map.

Uh.

This was clearly, blatantly a map. An ocean map, spreading out from a big black X.

My hands fidgeted as I waited for the book to finish, and when it did, I turned the page before anyone could see it.

Extending my arms again, I told the crowd, "Two satisfied customers, myself and Tyrant! Who else would like to give tribute of knowledge to our eventual overlord?"

I had a crowd now. Dozens of people all gathering around and looking at me and my strange equipment. Basking in that attention, the patter flowed easily, like butter squeezed from the world's fattest dog.

A young man I guessed a mere ten years older than me raised his hand. He was one of those people who looked naturally awkward, but had an infectiously sincere grin. "I'm part of a club of internet sleuths who find forgotten race tracks. There are a lot of them."

"I didn't even know that was a thing. Perfect! Take a seat!"

A couple of recordings later, the first heroine arrived. She came running up the lawn, gouging chunks of grass out with her stone boots. That's right, stone boots. She deserved more stares than me. She wore the strangest suit of armor I'd ever seen, all made of grey and green stone. It wasn't just that it covered about a third of her skin, or was wildly lopsided and asymmetrical. Every inch of stone was carved into elaborate bas reliefs of cats.

On the other hand, the stone shield nearly as tall as the young woman looked like a great defense if you could lift it as easily as she could. Most importantly, she pointed a stone sword at me that I did not want to get hit by, even if she were as soft as she looked rather than someone strong enough to lift several hundred pounds of goofy rock.

Cleric and I had prepped for this moment. Picking up my megaphone, I spun around in a circle, announcing, "Wonderful! Ladies and gentlemen, a round of applause for one of Los Angeles's finest superheroines! You can rest easy now that if my experiment turns out not to be harmless after all, someone is here to defeat me and save you all!"

"Finest" might be an exaggeration. I was sure she could take me in a fight, but this girl—younger than the Catlantis expert—wore a bug-eyed, lost expression at my antics. She didn't know what to say, and her sword wavered uncertainly.

Maybe more friendly bombast would make sure "uncertainty" didn't become "crushing my skull?"

Rescue came to us both in the form of another hero. Where this woman with her curly brown hair bulging out of a helmet that didn't fit had to be a university student, this man was probably a professor. His face only held hints of lines, but thick white streaks ran back through his hair from his temples, along with subtler, thinner white streaks I could spot in his ponytail. Most relevant here, along with a white lab coat he wore mad scientist goggles in leather and brass, and a pair of gauntlets that strongly resembled the single gauntlet I was wearing right now. More metal flashed under the coat when it billowed around him.

He moved with all the calm self-assurance that the girl didn't have. He held up a hand to her as he looked me over, and said mildly and with wry humor, "Not yet. Beating up a teenage girl unless we absolutely have to would look terrible, don't you think?" He reminded me of Echo, if you added twenty years and a sonic-powered wheelbarrow full of dignity.

The heroine looked even more lost, and when the professor hero glanced over and saw it, his attention turned from me to her. Laying his hand on the shield, he turned it aside enough to give her a smile. "We can cover each other's back. You keep your sword out and watch the girl in case she tries something. I'll examine her equipment to make sure it's not trapped."

She swung up her sword, barely missed whacking him in the face with it, and offered a beamingly delighted salute. Then she settled into watching me with a firm, resolute glare. I had a strong feeling I had more experience as a supervillain than this girl did as a hero.

This all suited me just fine. I beckoned to the professor. "Right this way then, sir! Observe as I copy down the exotic knowledge of these innocent fools. If you can figure out how it works, you'll be the first, but it does work. Who's next?"

"Me!" squeaked a skinny girl with badly dyed pink hair, deliberately ragged clothes, and piercings in everything I could see. She leaped into the cloth chair as if it was a throne, and chattered, "I have a huuuuuge scrapbook of heroes wearing impractical armor. Can you get that straight from my brain? Her name is Persea."

That last came with a flick of her head toward the heroine in the stone armor, and a stare that went past enthusiasm to hunger.

"That skill is bizarre, useless, and a little disturbing. Everything we're looking for!" I assured the volunteer, applying the helmet and clipping it to an empty book page. The mad scientist hero watched curiously as lines drew themselves. Were we getting the contents of the girl's scrapbook? Who knew?

Business was booming. As soon as one person vacated the chair, another took it. The professor hero spent as much time assuring the heroine that she was doing a good job at watching me work, but they both guarded me responsibly, or guarded the crowd from me, anyway.

A pair of teens my age squeezed their way to the front of the crowd. I did a double take. One of them was the egg head girl from my bus route, Tonika! She stood shoulder to shoulder with a boy our age that I didn't know.

I'd forgotten to hide the shock of recognition from my face, and was even more shocked when Tonika got the same look. Wide-eyed, she pointed a finger at me and said, "You're—" but stopped when I slapped a finger over my lips with desperate urgency.

The hero in the lab gave Tonika a reassuring smile and explained, "We never reveal anyone's secret identity." He touched his hand to the heroine's stone gauntlet, who at that cue smiled and nodded as well, looking happy that this at least she knew.

I waved the hero away, and stepped so close to Tonika that I was almost whispering in her ear. "How do you know!?"

She whispered back the same way, "I told you! I recognize that I don't recognize you! You're that person who doesn't look like anyone I know."

Even my family couldn't pull that off. Maybe she was right about it working because she only saw me at the bus stop. Or maybe it was the more obvious explanation. "Are you sure you don't have a super power?"

She sighed wistfully, and bowed her head. "I'm sure."

"She's just wicked smart," promised the boy next to her, who did look vaguely familiar. I'd probably seen him around at Upper High. Speaking of which, what were either of these two doing down here at USC? Okay, yes, it was after school on

Friday, a good time for anyone to be wandering around, but USC?

While I resisted the urge to grill her, the boy threw out his own question. "What are you going to do with all that knowledge?"

I threw out my arms, because it was time to be a minion again. "We're going to give it to people. Maybe everyone!"

His expression lit up with feral eagerness. He'd been a completely unremarkable boy in knee-length shorts and a t-shirt, but now he was poised like a cat about to pounce. "Can I be first? I'd love to be a superhero someday, but I don't have any powers, either."

That question hadn't occurred to me. What would Cleric say? What would he want? This was his mystical goat brain rodeo. I was just an errand girl.

Cassie's yell interrupted my thoughts. "There she is! We're not too late!"

Oh, no.

I turned, helpless. The crowd spread out, maybe to avoid the sparks that flew occasionally from Cassie's body. There she was, breathing hard as she jogged up to my display, wearing a blue-grey spandex jumpsuit with blue-white lightning bolts painted on it. That was bad, but it got much worse. Accompanying her were Aikamieli in his red wizard robe and carrying the (rumored) True Kalevala, Charlotte in businesslike (and when combined, modest) leotard, denim pants, and a denim vest covered in pockets, and Marcia in a karate gi decorated in brain-destroying black and white checks, stripes, and dots.

Aikamieli smiled with gormless delight. "I can't believe it. I didn't think the book would lead me to someone I don't know."

Charlotte eyed him sidelong, smirking just a little, or maybe sneering. "I believe it. That whole book is about harassing girls you don't know."

"Not you, too!" squeaked Aikamieli, horrified by the accusation.

Cassie ignored their banter, skidding to a halt on the opposite side of the folding chair, her head turning to look all around. "Where are the other Pawns?"

There aren't any other Pawns...is what I absolutely could not say. I put on a show of brisk, official irritation, since that was better than knee-quaking terror. "My master only sent one of us. I'm not here to fight."

"We are!" Cassie barked, putting one fist on her hip and throwing off a dozen electrical arcs into the chair and the ground around her.

So much for avoiding knee-quaking terror. Every one of those arcs looked like it would hurt a lot. My heart sped up until I could feel it in my chest.

Calm. Stay calm. I had to talk them out of this. I folded my arms and gave Cassie a wounded, angry glare. "There's no reason to fight. I'm not doing anything wrong. Why do you think the adult heroes are just standing around?" I waved a hand at the lab coat professor and inadequately covered student.

"Because it's too embarrassing to fight a kid," answered Cassie immediately.

Charlotte waved and lazily twirled one hand. Beads flowed out of her pockets, orbiting it in rings. She sounded as calm and even-tempered as Cassie did eager. They reminded me a little of the adult heroes. "Your signs say that this is a scheme by Tyrant. It is our duty as heroes to stop you. I would accept a surrender."

No way was I surrendering. That would be as bad as getting beaten up. Besides, if I was with them for a couple of hours, something might trigger them figuring out who I am.

I turned a pleading look up to the adult heroes. The scientist frowned, alert but thoughtful, then squeezed the swordswoman's arm, and pulled her back a few steps. Solemnly, he told us all, "We'll make sure things don't get out of hand."

Cassie opened her mouth, but Charlotte talked over her, with the loud, stiff rhythm of someone doing so deliberately. "Three on one isn't fair. I will round up the suspect, since I can do it gently."

"I told you, I'm not a noncombatant!" I barked at Charlotte. I'd expected her to be reasonable, at least.

Beads whirled in a complicated orbit as Charlotte pointed at my leather and brass potion launching gauntlet. "Is that a weapon?"

At least she didn't recognize it. The glove did look like a million others superheroes and villains wore. It also obviously wasn't a regular glove, so I had to admit, "Yes, but only technically. I'm no good with it!"

"Then hold still, and you won't get hurt."

Charlotte's hands both shot forward, and marbles fired toward me like a glass giant's shotgun pellets. I managed two desperate steps backward before they caught up, whirling around me in a tornado that would hurt much worse than rain if I tried to break through it.

I stood there, taking deep breaths, trying to think. Charlotte had me in a cage, but that gave me time. Grabbing my potion box, I opened it with shaky hands and pulled out the blue-grey speed potion and the green glue potion. I would drink the speed potion, splatter the beads with glue to create an opening, and run away.

"BORING!" shouted Marcia, and launched herself at me.

The wall of beads dissolved, giving me a clear view of Cassie and Charlotte's shocked expressions, and Marcia charging forward, teeth bared and fist raised. She knocked the chair aside, and the pedestal, sending The Book flying to be caught by Tonika in both arms. I stumbled back over my poster easels as that fist got bigger and closer.

The heroine shoved me out of the way with her hip, thrusting her huge stone shield out to block Marcia's punch. Fist met stone with an ear-splitting bang, and the heroine went flying backward over the lawn.

The hero in the lab coat reacted instantly, flying—literally flying—after to catch her.

With the heroes gone and Cassie and Charlotte twenty feet away, Marcia and I might as well be all alone. I lay on my hands and knees where I'd fallen over the easel. Marcia crouched in a groove her own feet had dug from the force of the punch. Her knuckles weren't so much as skinned, and her face...even glimpsed moments of Marcia's anger had been disturbing, but this twisted snarl of animal hate turned my heart to ice. Until now, all the talk about Marcia being violently insane had just been talk.

"Marcia, get a grip!" shouted Charlotte. Beads leaped up from the ground, wrapping around Marcia's face. I remembered myself, and crawled for my dropped speed potion. Move, arms and legs! Please!

Something happened I barely glimpsed out of the corner of my eye. Black flashed, and beads shot everywhere, leaving Marcia's face free. She screamed, wordless and incoherent with rage, and ran toward me again.

Tonika's boyfriend kicked a few marbles under Marcia's foot just as she took her first step. For the briefest flicker I wondered if that would work in grass. It did. Marcia slipped, and her punch hit the ground instead of me, spraying up sod.

A memory clicked. This was the same boy who'd been about to catch the cockatrice in his backpack.

My clumsy hand closed on the speed potion. Wrenching the top off, I drank as much as I could in one swallow, leaped to my feet, and ran. First to Tonika, grabbing The Book which she held out for me. Abandoning everything else, I raced to the street, up the street, crossed the corner in a gap between cars, around the block, around a different block. Everything whirled and raced, because the potion made me physically faster, but not mentally faster. I just had to dodge around pedestrians as best I could and hope.

It only took a couple of minutes to circle around to the abandoned block holding Cleric's shop. The potion was wearing off, but my shaky hand was still so clumsy I could barely open the unlocked door.

Cleric wasn't here. He was out doing whatever he thought of as a distraction, and would be for a while. I set The Book on its wooden pedestal, and sat down in the red-upholstered wooden chair.

After that I did nothing, thought about nothing, just tried to calm down.

It might have been an hour, or two hours. Eventually Cleric walked in through the front door. Physically, he was a mess. He had a big bruise on one cheek up over his eye. Jagged rents turned his tabard into dish rags. The chain mail underneath also had holes torn in it, but I didn't see any blood on the padding underneath. He moved carefully, wincing a lot, but with a smugly triumphant smile.

That smile disappeared the instant he saw me. Rushing over, he kneeled down in front of the chair, brushing dirt off my face with his thumb and looking me over. "Are you okay?"

My fingers were still trembling just a bit when he picked up my hand to examine. In my ears, my voice sounded dull as I answered, "I'm not hurt. I ran away. I lost everything but The Book. I did get a lot of goofy scans."

"Then you succeeded perfectly. What happened?" His encouraging smile didn't match the worry in his voice as he took my face in both hands and examined my eyes.

I wasn't hurt, though, and talking was bringing my energy back. I shook his hands away and said, "My friends have formed a superhero group just to hunt me down."

Cleric digested this news for several seconds, his face cold and serious. Finally, he said, "You should quit."

That kicked me in the gut. I gawked. "You're firing me?"

He threw his hands up in the air in frustration, and climbed to his feet. "No! Do you have any idea how hard it is to find assistants smart enough to know they're not fighters? I'm giving you advice!"

My fists clenched, pressed into the chair's wooden arm rests as a dam burst inside me and a new emotion spilled out. Anger. My voice shook as I yelled, "We're not doing anything wrong! No one will listen! You're just trying to let everyone share each other's goofy hobbies so they'll know what potential life can have!"

He watched me as the rage burst out, then drained away. When my jaw unclenched, he said quietly, "Yes. That is exactly what I'm doing. Are you sure you want to stay? I meant it. You can leave at any time."

"Yes!" I squeezed my fists again, shaking, then let it all go. Head hanging, I sighed. "I don't know what I'll do about my friends. Something."

Cleric tensed, got a little more stern. "I admire anyone who follows what they believe, but it is my job to protect you." With a breezy *woosh*, the purple book flew into the room. He caught it in one hand, and held it out to me. "Here. This belongs to you, now."

Uh. I accepted the book with nerveless fingers. This thing was priceless. Literally priceless. No one would sell something this unique and powerful.

They just might give it away.

Strolling around me, Cleric lectured, "Next time, use that at the first sign of danger. Leave the Book." He patted his huge knowledge stealing tome affectionately as he passed the podium. "If I have to, I can recover it. If it's destroyed, I'll find a new way to help the world. You are irreplaceable. In fact—"

Having circled all the way back in front of me again, Cleric held out another of those black paper rectangles. I took it cautiously. It felt like notecard paper, sleek and stiff, but deep, featureless black.

"—go home, and use this. Being able to go back and forth between there and here might come in handy," he finished.

I shrugged, a hint of giggle creeping into my voice. "I'll still need to take the bus to do my homework."

Cleric didn't join my growing smile. Instead the tall, fit blonde supervillain watched me with a concerned frown on his bruised face. Quietly, he asked again, "Are you sure you don't want to back out?"

Anger sparked in me again. I scowled, and declared, "I'm sure. We're the ones doing the right thing."

He held out his hand. "Then will you help me make Los Angeles a better place?"

I looked up at him. I was dirty, grass-stained, and scared, but unharmed. He'd been beaten black and blue, nearly cut open, but still stood strong and proud and ready for more, driven by his cause.

I placed my hand in his, and gave it one hard shake.

"Yes."

CHAPTER TWELVE

Before I finished the bus ride home, I got a reminder that this wasn't over. My phone rang, and when I picked up a breathless Cassie exclaimed, "Guess what just happened!?"

I gave the safest answer I could think of. "Uh...."

That was good enough for Cassie, who launched into gleeful recap. "We caught up with one of the Pawns, then got our butts kicked because Marcia flew off the deep end and tried to kill her!"

Marcia interrupted, "Hey! She wouldn't have died. She was wearing a force field projector!" Her voice wobbled in and out, accompanied by soft bumping noises like two people fighting for a phone.

"Uh...." I said again, since it worked the first time. I was trying not to remember Marcia's fist heading for my face. My pathetic "force field projector" would not have stopped that from exploding my head.

"It was my fight. Let me tell her!" shouted Marcia.

Cassie shouted back, "You broke your phone!"

The faint grunts and thumps of struggle got louder, then the line abruptly hung up.

Stretching my arms over the empty seats around me, I leaned my head back and groaned. Okay, just relax. I had all weekend to figure out what to say to my friends. Right now, I felt tired and wired at the same time. How could my brain and body ache, I needed the world to shut off and give me a break, and yet I was lick-my-lips eager for more?

For maybe an hour, I had owned the USC campus. Everyone had one focus: me, as the girl bringing awesomeness to their lives. Then I came within inches of death. So maybe tired and excited was the right combination here.

The gentle rumble and passing scenery of a sparsely populated bus did feel good.

When I got home, I headed straight for my room. Was anyone home? Didn't care.

Alone, door closed, I pulled the purple book out of my backpack, and the black rectangle Cleric had given me. The rectangle wasn't sticky. I'd rarely felt anything this slick but not wet, or seen a surface as solid, matte black.

Flipping to the last blank page in the purple book, because I'd rather not have my bedroom stand out as a destination, I faced the door and laid the rectangle to the top of the page, holding it down to the paper with my hand.

This time, I was close enough to hear the faint scratching sounds as notes in an alien language wrote themselves below the window I'd just created. It had a sketch of my unmade bed, my old rainbow striped teddy bear, my closet with lots of mysterious label arrows pointed at it, a tiny, extremely simple sketch of my alchemy set, and another picture of me from shoulders up, so badly scratched out that I could just barely identify my dreadlocks.

The window matched my view from where I stood. Time to take a few steps away and try the teleport function.

Before I could do that, a knock sounded on my door. Two calm raps. Kay.

The teleport book. Where would I hide it!?

Don't get desperate. Aside from the lack of title, it looked like a regular old book from outside. Closing the cover, I set it on my bed by the pillow. Kay wouldn't touch anything there, if he even looked twice.

Cover-up, covered up, I opened my bedroom door.

Sure enough, Kay stood on the other side, alone, with his hands in his pants pockets. He looked uncharacteristically awkward. He sounded uncharacteristically awkward, even guilty. "Can I come in? I'd like to talk, and hopefully not like I'm accusing you of anything."

"I'm tired from doing things you don't approve of," I answered sourly. Except, he looked so serious. That was not the expression of someone trying to nag me. "But…okay. I don't think this will go anywhere, but you can try."

Kay crossed over to my closet door and leaned against it, giving me lots of space. From there he stared at my feet and said quietly, "I'm sorry for not trusting you. I trust you as a person, Magenta. I'm just worried. Supervillains and superheroes get hurt. It's not just part of the job, it's the point."

I sat down on my bed, trying to figure out how to take this. Uncertainty made me detached and calm. "I know, Kay, but if it's possible to keep me safe, Cleric will. He would take a bullet for me without thinking twice." That I was absolutely sure of.

Kay wasn't. His face flickered into anger and disbelief, but as he opened his mouth it all settled back into guilty reservation again. Animated more with hope than skepticism, he peeked up at me. "You trust him?"

He was listening. Honestly listening. That lifted my heart considerably. I answered with a nod. "Yes. I trust him absolutely. He's the most moral person I've ever met, including you. He avoids the word honor, but word or not, he's obsessed with it."

Kay thought about that for several seconds, looking up at the wall now, hands still in his pockets and frowning as he turned that over. That pose shifted from guilt to casual conversation, and his tone turned to confidential, friendly—no, professional advice. "I can't make the decision of whether Cleric is trustworthy for you, but I've met several supervillains by now. Not just fought, but talked to. Some of them seem nice, but they wouldn't be villains if they weren't mixed up in something seriously bad. It was hard to believe someone who's so into fair play that she surrenders just to reward a clever fight was the same woman I caught wrecking a toy store."

A dismissive snort suddenly bubbled up out of me. "Kay, Cleric is a giant book nerd whose evil scheme is to help people enjoy being nerdy. If Cleric didn't have a crush on a real supervillain—" because that was so obviously why Cleric worked for Tyrant, "—people would think he's a hero. A weird hero, but a hero."

Kay nodded. "I hope you're right."

I raised my hands in amused surrender and reassurance. "Look, I know I'm not a fighter. You got the fun power, the automatic win button. This job, this is what I can get. Let me have it."

Kay went stiff, his face tightening in grim disgust. His pants pockets bulged from clenched fists. "Fun? Being a superhero isn't fun. It feels good to know I helped people, but only a crazy person would want to be a superhero for the fun."

That…described Cassie and Marcia accurately, and maybe Charlotte. Charlotte didn't have that manic edge, but something beyond reason was driving her. I gave Kay a mild smirk and reminded him, "At least you know you'll win."

"I wish." He shuddered, and his hands came out of his pockets, lifting up to cover his face. Then he went very still, and his voice came out haunted. "My power is incredible. It's one of the big ones. I could be rich and powerful with it, get anything I want. From moment to moment it leads me to the easiest way to accomplish what I'm trying to do. In a fight, I'm in the right place at the right time."

Kay paused. I'd never seen him this vulnerable. I'd entered a part of his life that his family couldn't understand until now. Quiet and bleak, he continued, "Except when I'm not. No one's power is perfect. Mine isn't. The same way you can't make any potion you can imagine, mine doesn't always work when I want it to, or need it to, or it does what I ask and I find out I asked for the wrong thing. The easiest way to stop a mad scientist's machine may be to stick my arm in the gears and choke it with my mangled flesh. I've had close calls. I'm always scared of the next one. I do it because it's the right thing to do."

He rubbed his hands up and down his face, then let go. His smile was back, subdued but there, as he returned to more pleasant details. "That's why the heroes gave me a scholarship. There aren't enough people who do this because it's right and not because they're crazy."

I thumped my own palm on the scratched wooden post at the corner of my bed, and said honestly, "Well, Cleric is doing what he's doing because it's right. As for me...." I scrunched up my face, the injustice of it burning past the excitement of my day. "I don't even have the option to decide. I can't fight crime, because I can't fight, and I know it. But at least I have some way to do something with my power now. I *need* this, Kay."

He pushed up from the closet, walked over, and slid his arms around me for a tender hug. After a second, I hugged him around the stomach fiercely, trying to bleed some of my unidentifiable feelings into him.

His face bent over me, Kay said, "I hope this works out for you, and that Cleric is as trustworthy as you think. Just don't blame either of us if being a hero and a villain brings us into conflict with each other."

I didn't know what to say about that.

Wait, yes, I did. Bracing my hands against his chest, I pushed Kay toward the door. "Thank you. Now, get out of my room so I can lie in bed and try to make any sense whatsoever of my day."

Chapter Thirteen

My super powered book nerd employer did not need me on Saturday. Maybe he thought I deserved a day off. Maybe he was taking a day off to put posters of Tyrant all over his bedroom. Cleric didn't strike me as the kind of guy who took days off, though. He would be out there doing...something toward his goal of helping everyone share a world of fantasy.

That left me at loose ends, and after lunch I felt rested enough to start wondering what to do with the day. Studying was an option.

While I puckered my lips at the unattractive option of picking up the abominable vortex of stupid misdirection that was my Chemistry textbook, the doorbell rang. Kay—we were the only ones home, so it had to be him—opened the front door, and I heard Tonika ask, "Is Magenta home?"

Uh. Well, that was unexpected. After a quick round of making sure I was sufficiently dressed, I walked out into the hall. Tonika stood at the door in a simple purple dress, hands clasped in front of her over a book and generally the picture of a well-scrubbed, wholesome neighbor who anyone would want their daughter hanging out with. As soon as I emerged, she gave me a beaming smile and greeted, "Magenta! You are home!"

Kay stared at her like she'd grown a fourth head. Yeah, welcome to the club, and thanks for sending me to a school for geniuses, Kay. I'd met the genius's genius. While I smirked and tried not to look stunned myself, Kay asked in an awed hush, "How did you do that?"

I took Tonika by the elbow and pulled her into my room, taking just enough time to tell Kay, "I'll be sure to ask that question when we're alone." Then I shut the door on him.

Although to be fair, my life would be a lot less embarrassing if Kay could learn Tonika's trick.

With the door closed, I whirled and propped my hands back against my dresser, voice lowered to hopefully not carry into the hall. "No, seriously, I could use another explanation, because I do not get it."

Tonika nodded, her puffy pigtails bobbing. "I've been thinking about how to explain. It's a meta process. I don't remember what you look like. I remember what it feels like to look at you and see a complete stranger. It's not the same sensation as just seeing someone I don't know."

That both made sense—barely—and sounded ridiculously impractical at the same time. She might as well learn to identify my shadow.

As weird as super powers could get, maybe someone would do that. Maybe that was how Junk Merchant, the only other person to ever be casually able to recognize me, had done it. Cleric hadn't said how he recognizes me yet, but it was probably Tonika's technique.

He'd pulled it off with a lifetime of training. She figured it out after a week of noticing something weird going on at her bus stop.

As I digested that, Tonika drifted over to my alchemy equipment. As she peeked around the seams of my makeshift pressure chamber and the peeling red and white warning stickers from the parts I'd built it out of, she explained, "This is how I knew where you live. Who else but the potion girl would have a chemistry set in her window?"

Before this went any further, I glanced at the door to my bedroom. Not that Kay was the type to spy, but....

"He's not there," Tonika assured me.

I wasn't sure I wanted to know how she knew, so I edged around it. "Are you really absolutely pinky and ring finger swear cross the cockles of your heart sure you don't have a super power?"

Tonika gave me a tight, embarrassed smile, with one raised eyebrow. One sneaker scuffed behind her. "Well, there are common side effects that accompany super powers, such as anomalously colored hair—"

"Like mine?" I asked, dryly amused.

Tonika paused, and looked at me. She squinted, looking closely. Then she gave a little jump, and her eyes drifted away, back toward the door. "Oh? Oh, right! Pink! I've been trying not to pay attention to what you look like because that would make identifying you harder."

I made a 'pfft' sound. "You really weren't kidding about meta."

She giggled quietly, and stubbornly returned to the subject. "Alcohol resistance is another one that confirms super powers. There are others. I don't have any. I'm a smart person from a smart family, but when does that become superhuman? There's no definition, and you don't actually need any of the side effects."

"Well, what's your IQ?" I tried.

Her jaw tightened. Her shoulders twitched. Tonika did not like this question. She answered with exaggerated, strained calm. "That stops having meaning when the number passes 180. IQ doesn't have much meaning ever. You've only seen me be clever. If we get to be friends—" I gave her a thumbs up at that prospect, and she continued with a weak smile, "—there will be times when you don't think anyone could be as stupid as I can be."

She still looked tense, like someone expecting to be hit. This girl had a major fear of rejection. I crossed over and gave her shoulder a squeeze, followed up by a direct grin. "Well, since we're going to be friends, I'll just have to help you fix things when that happens. Can't be worse than the explosions my power causes." Once. Okay, twice. Usually alchemy failures were a lot weirder than that, or just poisonous.

Tonika signaled that talking about her time was over by bouncing up straight and asking eagerly, "Hey, can I see your costume?"

I snickered, dreads flapping as I shook my head hard. "Nope. It's back at my not very evil master's downright benign lair...but I can show you this." Heading over to my closet, I flipped the door open, reached up on my tiptoes, and pulled a large cardboard box down from the shelf. Setting the box on my bed, I opened it up and pulled out a full body length of black faux-leather with a white mask. "*This* is the costume I refused to wear."

Tonika floated over like she was being pulled by strings, or by her outstretched right hand. As I held up the costume, she ran her fingertips down its form, murmuring, "Tyrant loves his anachronisms. The loose skirt will allow mobility, while emphasizing the inhuman element by keeping the legs hidden. Can I try it on???" The last came in a sudden, gleefully eager squeak, her face jerking toward me with a pleading grin.

"Uh, sure. It's not my style, but that doesn't mean there's anything wrong with it."

I scarcely had time to hold out the dress before she yanked it out of my hands. Sixty seconds of clumsy struggling, including putting it on backwards the first time, and Tonika had the costume in place. It looked a bit lumpy with her clothing underneath, but the slim black figure with its pointed white mask gave off an aura of death. Potions in its sewn-in holsters would look like grenades. Tonika was right, this costume was intimidating.

Still not my style, though.

And if only Tonika didn't keep her hands folded and her feet together and lean slightly away all the time. Cripplingly shy death was a lot less scary.

Running her now gloved hands over the mask, she exclaimed in a breathily distorted voice, "Ooh, air conditioning!"

Okay, now jealousy tightened my stomach and I was just a

little tempted by this costume. Of course I'd chosen the sweat factory outfit!

As Tonika fought her way out of my unwanted medieval combat cosplay, I looked around my room until a harsh truth settled over me. My room was boring. This was not a fun place to hang out with a new friend. Maybe after we'd known each other for a few years and could sit around talking for hours. I'd heard that was a thing, but it's hard to hold onto friends that long when they're never sure if you've left or not.

Alchemy tended to involve hours of grinding powder or moving liquids with eyedroppers. Not excitement city, and it was most of what I did in my bedroom.

Ah, but my life was so much more exciting now.

Nudging Tonika with my elbow, I suggested, "Hey, do you want to go somewhere? I've got an after-school job. I have money!"

Free from black super science leather substitute, Tonika shook her hands with the urgency of an anxiety-laden windmill. "I couldn't let you spend your money on me. We don't know each other well enough yet." Touching a fingertip to her chin, she swerved from self-esteem crisis into problem solving. "We could go to Exposition Park. It's a long trip, but a bus and train provide plenty of time for conversation. Or we could go to No Man's Land. That's not far. Sean and I like to go there. Of course, it's not safe, but Sean is good at spotting crumbling wreckage and it's easy to get out if a super powered battle starts."

Inspiration flashed in my head like a magma mermaid whose actinic blaze disintegrates seashells. "I know! I wanted to test this anyway. Come on!"

I grabbed my backpack, my purple book, and Tonika's hand, in that order. As we fled to the front door I shouted, "We're going out!" to Kay, wherever in the apartment he was. There. That should be enough cover.

We did go out, but only far enough to pull Tonika into the walkway between my apartment building and the next. It wasn't even wide enough to be called an alley, but it got us out of general sight for sixty seconds. Flipping open the book to the picture of Cleric's hideout revealed a still image with no Cleric in it. Good. Would he even be in the picture if he was in that spot in real life? Whatever. Putting an arm around Tonika's shoulder, I said, "Press your face to that photo in three. One...two...three!"

There was just enough room to fit two teenage girls' heads against the page. We hit it at the same time, and were flung violently apart—but violently apart inside Cleric's commandeered book shop.

I lay there on the rough carpet, propped up on my elbows, and laughed in triumph. It had worked! If it hadn't, no big deal. Tonika was smart enough to figure out the book, or I could have teleported back to my room and gone around to get her. But it did work!

Tonika got up first, brushing off her skirts because no effort of Cleric's could remove *all* the dust this place had built up over the years of abandonment. She looked around the shop, particularly at my fancy professional alchemy set and up at the grey waxy fume absorbing block above it, and asked, "Is this a place you shouldn't have taken me?"

Oops. That part hadn't occurred to me. Um. "I'm trusting you with my secret identity already. Maybe we'll take the long way next time." Leaping to my feet, I hurried out the front door, making sure to relock it behind me and doubly sure I had my purple book safely in my backpack.

Outside, Tonika stopped on the sidewalk, her eyes a little wider. "I know this spot. We're by the university, which means we're by Exposition Park. Golly, that book is convenient, and impressive. Very impressive. Teleportation is a big deal. Even the mad scientists who can make it can't do so consistently."

Tonika probably knew all the science there was on teleportation, which was...weirdly charming, like Marcia's utter inability to feel embarrassment.

Plus, she gave me a warm, admiring smile, and who ever got tired of those? I grinned, and maybe strutted a little. "Yeah, my boss really trusts me. I hope I didn't betray that trust by bringing someone else along."

Tonika shook her head urgently, hunching forward merely thinking about that guilt. "I swear, I won't tell anyone anything about your supervillain job."

I did the 'pfft' again, and rolled my eyes. "Supervillain's errand girl. They're cool errands, but they're still just errands. Doing the evil stuff is not my job."

We crossed the street into Exposition Park, which is not so much a park as a labyrinth of paths between museums and the stadium, with decorative greenery.

As we strolled around on the higher levels, enjoying the rich green of non-desert trees and bushes, and warm sun without the leather steam cooker that was my costume, I offered, "Okay, so I get that you don't like someone you're still getting to know spending money on you, but how about we go to a second run movie theater next time? It's cheap, and my other new friends wouldn't go for something that boringly normal."

"Your normal social circle are the kids from the superhero club," she said, looking away from me at the fountain we were passing, a grid twenty feet wide that spat bubbles into the air and provided a breeze as deliciously cool as the sun had been relaxingly warm.

Not quite sure what to say about that evasion, I tried, "My super power is why you approached me."

That scrunched her face into thought, and she lifted it up, arms tucked behind her back and still holding whatever that book was she carried so faithfully. Detached and speculative, she said, "Maybe, in a roundabout way. Certainly, it's what caught my attention. What kept my attention was that you seem smart, you don't fit in, and you don't judge. That's what you were using your powers for, after all. You were learning things and making people happy, while other people gave you trouble for it."

I raised a pink eyebrow now, tickled by amusement. "It sounds like you want in."

She actually jumped into the air, her sneakers thumping when they hit the concrete again. With a squeak in her voice, Tonika denied, "Oh, no no no no! Not me! That's Sean. He envies heroes and villains, because of all the action. I hate action. When I play a computer game, I always identify with the person giving out the quests. They collect the information and solve the puzzles. The protagonist just does the grunt work."

Yep, she'd described my situation with Cleric pretty well. But she'd also flashed a target that made me grin even wider. "So, Sean is your boyfriend?"

"No!" she squeaked again. Her dark eyes flickered over my expression, and she relaxed enough to giggle, "Yes." Then she curled a hand around to the back of her head, smiling bashfully, eyes no longer directed at me but dreamily up at the sky. "Extremely yes. I may be addicted to how smart he thinks I am."

Which was such a twisty way of describing things that I gave her the side-eye. "Is everything meta to you?"

Instead of answering, Tonika jerked a little straighter, stumbling one step as she exclaimed, "Oh! That reminds me! If you tell your super powered friends that you're friends with me, they saw me at the incident, and you can tell them that I told you all about it. That will cover in case they catch you knowing things that you shouldn't. Not just this time, but on a wider scale. They have no way of knowing what I do and don't know or could tell you, after all."

Yeah, I definitely kept up the side-eye. "Just how smart *are* you?"

Tonika tittered, cheeks pinched. "About useful things like making breakfast, not being loud when someone's trying to sleep, or making new friends? I'm painfully stupid."

I nudged her with my elbow. "You're making friends with me pretty well."

Tonika laughed now, finally merry rather than nervous. "Golly, yes, and look what it took for me to have any idea of how to say hello. I spend two thirds of my time reading alone. Before Sean came, nine tenths."

I pointed a finger at her. "Well, now that we are friends, I'm going to force you to let me buy you a ticket into the Natural History Museum, so that I can watch you be smart about the exhibits. I happen to enjoy smart things myself."

She pursed her lips, then smiled. "Only if you'll tell me the alchemical possibilities of the minerals display. I happen to find super powers like yours interesting."

"Deal."

Chapter Fourteen

That plan lasted five minutes. Specifically, the five minutes it took us to slowly navigate the Exposition Park pathway maze around to the front of the museum, and its big, open lawn, during which time we discussed nothing more exotic than the view.

When we got out onto that lawn, the view suddenly got a lot more exotic. A girl in a purple rubber bodysuit with long, straight purple hair and purple eyes stepped in front of us. Not dull, dark purple like Tonika's dress. Glaring violet that might glow in the dark and caught the eyes. The black metal crossbow slung over her back, as big as her torso, also caught the eyes.

Tonika and I must have been deeper in conversation than I thought to not see this girl coming, but now with her only ten feet away, it was too late to run.

The purple-haired girl leveled a finger at Tonika, arm straight, and said in a flat voice with an odd, scratchy edge, "You are a Pawn."

Tonika did her jump and squeak. "Me? No!"

I took a half step forward, elbows out, trying to look tough.

"No, that's me." It's not like anyone could identify me as Magenta Slade.

Face as cold and stiff as ice, Purple Girl remained pointed resolutely at Tonika. "I tracked you from a local Tyrant facility."

I gawked. Was every kid with super powers in LA waiting for a chance to hunt me down?

I still wasn't letting Tonika get in trouble for me. Raising my voice, I growled, "No, I'm the Pawn. She's a civilian bystander."

Purple Girl didn't budge, telling Tonika, "California belongs to Organism One. Tyrant will not be allowed to gain the upper hand in a new resource. You will come with me."

Uh.

She said "Organism One."

I knew who Organism One was. I'd better, he'd mind controlled me and everyone else in the city when I was, what, six? Tyrant wasn't the only "take over the world" level supervillain with his own army. There were four of those big names. Tyrant. The Queen of Swords. Cossack. And Organism One, history's greatest example of life created by mad science turning on its creator—and in this case, its creator's entire species.

The threat level of my after-school job was skyrocketing. Having my friends hunting me was bad enough. And…by "new resources" Organism One meant teenagers, and was going to start with Tonika.

Not going to happen.

Stupid as it was, I grabbed Purple Girl's shoulder. I actually got ahold of the paper-thin rubber, which felt unpleasantly chalky. Then she moved, faster than I could keep track of. A second later my back and head bounced off the thankfully soft sod, and Purple Girl had the point of a crossbow bolt pointed at my eye, a mere six inches away. Somewhere in that process, she yelled, "Ambush!"

More than human strength, more than human speed, and a weapon. Even dizzy, I felt the creeping chill of being wildly outmatched.

But Tonika wasn't just wildly outmatched, she was innocent, so I repeated, "Me. I'm the Pawn. That girl is a bystander who does not work for Tyrant, or anyone."

The Purple Girl watched me as fixedly as she had Tonika, and her voice had turned just enough raspier to be noticeable, but less monotone, with traces of emotion. "Yes. The unit with the cloaking field must be the Pawn. Be warned, my biological half sees through your cloak. That trick will not work again."

I had to stay on topic, for Tonika's sake. "So, you'll let her go?"

Still as a statue except for her mouth, the girl in purple answered, "I was sent to convince the Pawn, but if the bystander wishes to become an agent for Organism One, she will be allowed to state her case."

I blinked. "'Convince' is not a word I was expecting."

Now, finally, the corners of my attacker's mouth twitched up, and she asked almost normally, "Why shouldn't you come to Organism One willingly? Organism One is offering you something that Tyrant can't and won't: Immortality."

"Well, this conversation has taken a drastic turn," I said honestly.

That slight smile became a slight frown. Cold, but at least with a little emphasis and glaring purple eyes, my slim, fit, and rubber-sheathed attacker declared, "That is because mortals do not understand Organism One's intent. Flesh rots. Organism One offers you now a chance to upload. Your body will be strengthened, and when it dies, you will get a new one and live on."

For the first time I really looked at this girl. That bodysuit was awfully close to the skin, and had no fasteners, like it wasn't intended to ever come off. Her violet hair, hanging well past her shoulders, was too straight, too stiff, and a little too thick. Those were fiberoptic threads. The purple of her eyes didn't have normal striations, and no red in the sclera. Those eyes were robotic. Plus, faint purple tracery, like circuits, crept out around the girl's hairline.

My heart sped up and my breathing quickened as I took in what had been done to this girl, a teenager my own age.

"And this offer is voluntary?" I asked.

The girl's voice became almost normal again, stubborn but also haunted, and her eyes slightly unfocused. "Organism One would prefer willing service. Willing agents adapt faster and perform better. I am still adapting, still not thinking clearly because the world is so much bigger and I experience it more clearly." Her humanity drained away in an instant, back to the robotic monotone and perfectly still stare. "Willing or not, Organism One will not let Tyrant have an advantage of Pawns. If your body is sufficiently fresh it may be possible to save much of the brain's contents after revival."

Tonika hadn't moved in the whole conversation, except to lift her fist to her mouth and chew on her knuckles. She looked terrified. Welcome to the club, but for both our sakes I had to keep this cyborg distracted. Mouth dry, I swallowed and licked my lips, both useless except to buy a few seconds. The flutter in my voice stood out painfully as I said, "This is a lot to take in. You know that from personal experience."

It nodded, ever so slightly. "I do. You are being offered an escape, and a master far superior to Tyrant."

Light-headed, it occurred to me that my already wobbly voice and terrified expression were great cover for what had popped into my head. "Let me discuss it with my friend. Please. I have a book. I'll move slowly and won't make any attempt to dodge or run. I won't even point it at you. You can watch me get it out."

Very slowly, as promised, I climbed back to my feet, unzipped my backpack, and got out the purple book. The crossbow bolt remained pointed at my eyeball, a black dot promising death and resurrection as a mechanical slave if this didn't work. Edging sideways, I opened the teleport book to the picture of my room, and crept up shoulder to shoulder with the whimpering Tonika.

I'd pushed my luck to the end. The cyborg said, "I do not see the relevance of this book. Show it to me."

We were out of time. I brought the book up. Tonika and I thrust our faces downward.

I heard the elastic snap of the crossbow firing.

But we spilled out into my bedroom alive and unperforated. Like the last time I teleported two people, we were flung apart and I hit my alchemy table, spilling a beaker and sending a mug and two vials rolling to the floor.

That didn't matter. We'd escaped, and there was no way the cyborg could follow us, or knew who I was.

Tonika and I climbed very slowly and carefully to our feet. She wrapped her arms around herself to stop her hands shaking, and stuttered, "I—I—I need to go home. This isn't—isn't a rejection. I still want to be your friend. I just wasn't prepared to be hunted by Organism One's cyborgs."

I nodded, and helped her to and out my apartment's front door. After closing it behind her, I leaned against the wood and listened to my still racing heartbeat as it gradually slowed.

I wasn't prepared to be hunted by Organism One's cyborgs either.

Chapter Fifteen

When my alarm woke me up Monday morning, it hit me: I had to go to school. It just seemed so strange that I could go back and forth from my life of magic books and being hunted, to the life of a high school student very slightly in over her head with advanced classes.

But that was the point, wasn't it? High school didn't know or care about my job working for a supervillain. I'd sweated blood-covered bullets to keep that true.

When I walked through the front doors of Upper High, passing into its massive red brick embrace, in a crowd of teenagers who did not have that second life, I realized...I didn't have to have one, either. I didn't have to be hunted by heroes and villains both. I could quit my job, and no one but Cleric and Tonika would ever know who the Pawns had been. I could be free.

All it would take was abandoning the only adult who'd supported me and his cause of making a better, weirder world.

I wasn't going to do that.

But it was so, so tempting.

Classes happened. Normal classes where my teachers reminded themselves that the girl sitting in my chair must be the one on the attendance list, and we were asked questions about ancient books that were mostly lists of who fathered who. Chemistry happened.

Chemistry, where Marcia was waiting in her chair pulled up next to mine. I sat down next to her trying not to remember her speeding toward me with murderous super strength.

The teacher pulled a new poster over the blackboard, announced, "Today, we're going to start chemical bonds," and a new horror unconnected to violence crashed over me. All those little lines and numbers! Chemicals didn't work like that! Why would anyone stick carbon and hydrogen next to each other in a picture that was hard to even focus on because—

Marcia's hand grabbed my arm by my elbow, and squeezed, gently but firmly. "We've got this," she whispered to me with absolute confidence.

Half the time Marcia was pure destruction, and half the time she was the best friend you could have. I desperately needed that friendship right now.

Holding my wrist as well, Marcia whispered to me, "Now, close your eyes. Don't look at the board or listen to him. You got through memorizing a bunch of meaningless test answers. Now we're going to memorize how a game works. We'll call it Ballsticks. It's just collecting a bunch of letters, depending on which numbers they have. It's geometry, not chemistry. You can do math."

I could do math. Yes.

We made it through with the single bonds and the double bonds, and Marcia making sure I didn't listen to the teacher and accidentally learn what "bonds" were. I could handle them as lines on paper.

I still staggered out the classroom door with a sense of deep relief, and Marcia still holding my arm. The moment we passed the doorway, her concerned frown turned into a manic grin, and she squeed, "Friday was so awesome. I got to—"

But Charlotte was waiting, and grabbed Marcia's arm, talking over her. "No. The story is too long. Magenta's class is too far away, and she doesn't have time."

Marcia pouted. Charlotte glared, resolute. Tonika and Sean passed by.

Uh, wait. What was that last part? Yes, that was them. Was this always their route between classes, and I'd just never had reason to notice?

Well, now I did. Pulling free of Marcia, I waved an arm in front of Tonika and shouted, "Hey, Tonika! It's me, Magenta. Meet my other friends. This is Marcia and Charlotte."

I'd been out of it and hadn't paid attention on the bus. Now, Tonika turned and looked at me and...smiled, not the least bit afraid. "Magenta! You're even harder to identify in a crowd. It's a pleasure to meet you properly, Marcia and Charlotte."

Marcia lit up with another one of her beatifically social smiles, grabbed Tonika's hand, and shook it furiously. "Oh, I remember you! You were at the university where I technically won that fight because my opponent ran away. And now you're terrified of me and you also really wish I'd put on more clothing, and both of those feelings are perfectly natural."

Tonika pulled her hand gently free, and bit her lip nervously. "Am I that obvious?"

Of course, Marcia was totally easygoing about it. Rather than teasing, she puffed out her chest and rolled her head in pride. "Let's just say I'm not just a pair of pretty fists."

Sean and Charlotte weren't paying attention. Or rather, they were studying each other, and I seriously doubted that was desire. As if by secret signal, they shook each other's hands.

"Sean," said Sean.

"Charlotte," replied Charlotte.

Conversation completed, Charlotte grabbed Marcia by both shoulders and hauled her away, chiding, "And now, Magenta, Tonika, and Sean have to get to their classes."

Sean gave Tonika a little push on her backpack, telling her firmly, "She's right. You especially need to hurry."

Her class must have been on the opposite side of the building, because she didn't argue. She just scurried off into the crowd and disappeared.

That left me with Sean, an awfully bland looking boy with

his short, brown hair, logoless grey t-shirt, darker grey slacks, and black and white sneakers. What he did have was a wickedly expressive frown of solemn confidentiality as he murmured just above the noise of the crowd, "Tonika doesn't have her own phone. Here." Pulling a little pad and a pencil out of a side pocket of his backpack, he scribbled down some numbers, ripped off the paper, and handed it to me. "That's her parents' phone number, and that one's mine. If it's personal, you might be better off calling or texting me. Now I've got to run."

He disappeared, and I looked at the phone numbers. That had been weird. No, it had been thoughtful. Not having a phone number must be one of the many things that embarrassed Tonika. Her apartment was probably a mess somehow, too. That would be why we'd never exchanged contact information.

Poor thing. I had all the sympathy for someone whose life was full of embarrassment.

Latin wasn't exciting. It rarely was. We did declensions. So many declensions. I sensed that if I stuck with Latin, I'd be doing declensions for years to come.

School was starting to feel normal again when I got to lunch and saw my friends at their table. Well, so much for that. It was time to listen to what my friends wanted to do to me.

Except...who was that new girl at the table? She had to be a girl, in that old-fashioned, ankle-length brown hobble dress, right? With the ruffled shoulder puffs and the bow at her neck? But gloves and a wide brimmed hat tilted forward concealed everything.

Marcia was just dumping a plate of barbecued ribs in my spot at the table, saving me from needing to get in the lunch line. As I approached, the mystery girl raised her head until I could see her face.

She was...transparent. Transparent and sparkly, like an exquisite glass sculpture, with thick curly hair that looked solid rather than like real hair. My eyes got used to that enough to make out the details of her face, and it was delicate and graceful and feminine, almost sensual. She was stunning, in every sense. No wonder Will, sitting next to her, stared at her like she was a living goddess he wasn't worthy of being that close to.

She also had a tail, just as transparent, which flicked out behind her. A cat tail, it looked like. Yes, and little pointy cat ears almost hidden by paper flowers on her hat. Unlike everyone else in the lunch room, the spot at the table in front of her was empty, and she showed no sign of being hungry.

With a warm, gentle smile, she looked up at me and asked in an equally warm, gentle voice, "You must be Magenta?"

Marcia and Charlotte stared at me blankly for half a second, then grinned in welcome. Cassie corrected, "No, Magenta—uh, hi, Magenta. Sorry."

Ignoring that, Marcia pulled me down into the seat next to her, and waved at the new girl. "This is Mirabelle, we knew her in Northeast West Hollywood Middle, and yeah, she's as sweet as she looks."

Without thinking, I started to ask, "Are you...?"

She handled it graciously, with a slow nod. "Made of glass, yes. Please be gentle."

Oh, yeah. I of all people got it. "They probably mentioned my power," I told her with a grimace.

She nodded again, with that small smile. "Yes, which is why we'd both like to discuss something else."

I grinned. She understood me, and I understood her. That felt good.

Cassie, at the farthest end of the table from me, leaned forward and brandished a chunk of chicken impaled on a fork. "Mirabelle is too sweet a person to want action even if she were capable of it, but you have got to get in on our Pawn hunting."

Marcia clenched her fists and growled, "Yes, thank you, finally a segue!"

So grateful for the excuse, I paused in the act of picking up a spare rib to say, "Actually, Tonika already told me all about it."

Whack! Marcia slammed her forehead against the tabletop, splattering barbecue sauce on herself. At least she didn't dent the table this time. As if that hadn't been painful at all, she pouted like a six-year-old and whined, "Aw, man!"

"Okay, but you have to go with us next time. You have to!" insisted Cassie, sparks flickering on her pale eyebrows as they squeezed together.

I clenched my teeth. Time for the embarrassingly accurate excuse. I didn't like saying it, so I stared at my beef as I did. "The honest truth is...I'm not much of a fighter, guys. I'm mediocre at best, and that's not good enough."

Airy and unperturbed, Cassie replied, "I'm a mediocre fighter—"

"—headed for an embarrassing career in four years—" interjected a cynically smirking Charlotte.

Cassie bulled on, "—but that's not the point. It's not about whether you help us fight. You just have to be there. We want to do this with you."

Charlotte's smirk turned into an honest, approving smile, and she folded her arms and nodded.

Barbecue sauce dripping down her face, Marcia grinned at me and bumped me with her shoulder. "It's about shared experiences with friends, my girl."

Resuming her role as spokesgirl, Cassie jabbed her chicken-bedecked fork around, but not as emphatically as she spoke. "We probably won't even find a Pawn next time. It was a miracle that Aikamieli kid's spells spotted a Pawn when we were all together and could do something about it. What we want is to go out as a team with you. You can stand around and laugh at us as we make fools of ourselves again."

"We sure did that," murmured Charlotte with that wry smirk again.

Cassie finished her speech with a fork pointed at me. "We want your company, and we want you to be part of something with us."

Mirabelle's own natural smile widened, just a little. "I think they like you, Magenta."

My mouth opened. My mouth closed. My cheeks burned hot. I couldn't deny it. This was so, so sweet, and weird sweet, which was the best sweet.

You know, if I'd been a better friend myself, I might not be in this situation. We might have been too busy having fun for them to want to hunt Pawns.

Cassie leaned back, taking my silence as proof of her victory, which it was. Her attitude turned more casual. "I don't want you to feel like we're making fun of you, Magenta, so I'm going to move on to making fun of Will, who's been gawking at Mirabelle so hard he hasn't heard a thing we've said since she arrived."

Will jumped. He twisted to glare at Cassie. "Don't treat her like that!"

Mirabelle, on the other hand, raised gloved fingers to her mouth and giggled.

Charlotte leaned forward around Marcia to ask me, "Hey, do you think we can get Aikamieli to transfer here?"

Marcia nodded enthusiastically. "Yeah, he was gormless, but I kind of liked him for it."

Charlotte half-grimaced, one cheek pulled back. "I wish we could invite your new friends to sit with us, Magenta, but we're out of room."

With normal conversations like that and the strange sensation of having lots of people actually like me in my head, I spent the last two hours doing normal stuff like making up study lists for my other classes. I felt weird and out of place slipping into an empty restroom when the final bell rang, to stick my face into my purple book and teleport to my after-school job being evil.

CHAPTER SIXTEEN

I lowered the book to see Cleric standing in the back of the room, rubbing his hair with a towel. I'd never seen him without his armor and tabard, although the undershirt was far from shocking. He had all the muscles the shape of the armor had offered. Not that he was "Will" level cut, but Cleric was seriously physically fit. Seeing me, he headed into the back rooms, asking with an amused tone, "Decided to take the direct route this time?"

I was less than thrilled about being seen entering or leaving this place right now, but if I told him about the cyborg...he would fire me. Period. No question and he would do it instantly. Cleric would not let me face a danger like that if he knew about it. I had to hope Organism One remained very low key, because if even one hero found out a teenager had been forcibly cyborged, there would be a city-wide freak-out that Cleric could not miss.

Plus, it would be too late to help whoever that poor girl had been.

So I answered, "Eager to find out what the next stage of the plan is," because I was.

Iron clinked and cloth rustled in the back. Cleric's voice called out, "Well, for your duties, I'd like you to make more of that book restoration potion. I have a lot of other books I'd like fixed. That is a background task I'm sure will take little of your attention, since you've already mastered the recipe. I spent the weekend gathering different types of knowledge from the exotica I sent you after. Sword fighting, opera singing, that sort of thing. The arts that everyone should know. Now it is time to find a willing guinea pig to try to implant this knowledge into. No, not you. No one whose knowledge is in the book already. I have some semi-public errands for you coming up as well. We'll require equipment and knowledge to give this gift on a scale large enough to make a difference to the world."

Something clicked in my head as he talked. I had an idea. Well, a proto-idea. I was besieged on all sides. I had friends, but I needed allies.

So I asked, "Do you trust me enough to bring in two trustworthy people?"

Cleric reappeared in the doorway, tying his tabard into place. He looked at me with one raised eyebrow. "You certainly have me curious. Go ahead."

I got out my phone and the piece of paper Sean gave me, and called him. It rang a couple of times, and he picked up. Before he could say anything, I blurted out, "Sean, it's me, Magenta, and no you don't recognize my voice, that's part of my power. I hope I'm in time. Have you and Tonika gotten on the bus yet?"

"We both have," he answered. My heart sank. "We're heading over to USC, to hang out until my older sister gets out of classes in a couple of hours."

My heart rose again, lifting like a rocket powered helicopter possessed by a dragon's ghost. I gushed, "That is perfect. Would you be willing to take the risk of getting mixed up in super powered danger if I can offer you something almost like a combat super power?"

Cleric did not correct me.

Sean's voice fluttered. "Are...you serious?"

Oh, yeah, I was, but I had to explain this to him responsibly. Treat him like Cleric had treated me. "I can't offer you a job working for my boss's boss, but I can't rule out that you might get an offer. I can guarantee you won't be forced to take that job. That's the only thing I can guarantee. What I'm offering might not even amount to a super power, but I thought you might want the chance."

"Yes. Yes, I do," he answered, voice now the hurried kind of shaky.

"Then have Tonika take you to The Place when you get to USC." And with that, I hung up.

Okay, now it was time to look up at Cleric for his reaction. He stood in the same place, still looking curious, and not the slightest bit angry. At my searching gaze, he said mildly, "You have interesting friends, and I look forward to meeting them. I assume these are not the ones who attacked you on Friday."

I shook my head, calming down now that I knew he was on board. "No, these are the ones who helped me escape."

He beckoned with one hand. "Then let's get set up before our guests arrive."

That meant going upstairs to help him move equipment down from his living quarters. While removing a full-length standing mirror, I got my first good look at Cleric's bedroom. It was everything I had expected. Candles, books on pedestals, weapon racks, lots of black and white, mysterious displays of crystals, everything electronic hidden in an animal sculpture, and my number one bet paid off: At least half a dozen paintings and posters of Tyrant decorated the walls.

I hoped Tyrant was half the man Cleric thought he was.

But, I didn't work for Tyrant. I worked for someone who worked for Tyrant, and there was a big difference there. We got to work building a knowledge transfer set in the shop, which mostly involved exactly arranging mirrors around a chair, and attaching a bunch of wires between Cleric's calipers and different pages of The Book.

As we got all that in place, he chatted, "When the book was created, transferring so much knowledge involved a ritual with a dozen people and a coffin with dull spikes to touch pressure points of the recipient. We have to improvise."

"Huh. So, this has been tried before?" Which made sense.

The Book was centuries old, right? It hadn't spent all that time damaged.

Cleric chuckled, measuring distances on his calipers to attach wires. "I don't know what the creator wanted, but the second person to own this book used it to erase the skills of his super powered enemies and give those skills to himself. Unfortunately for him, it only transfers knowledge. One of his memory-wiped victims remembered she hated him at an unexpected moment, and blew them both up with powers she didn't remember she had and couldn't control."

"Fire?" I asked curiously, putting a fresh cushion on the chair. Sean might as well be comfortable.

"Shapeshifting, actually. The history I read said they found him in a room covered in gore, nailed to the wall by dozens of sea urchin spines the length of a man's arm. Poisonous spines, no less. He was very dead, and no amount of stolen knowledge could do anything about it." Cleric smirked, evidently not sympathetic. The man in the story did not sound like a hero.

A knock sounded at the door. Cleric raised his voice. "Come in."

Tonika and Sean slipped inside, and Tonika made sure the door opened as little as possible and closed immediately after them. Sean… looked a little too excited to remember that kind of detail, walking out into the middle of the room and looking around with wide eyes and an open-mouthed smile.

My cue. "Cleric, these are my friends, Tonika and Sean."

Cleric bowed. Thanks to the armor, it looked natural on him. In a grand, formal tone he said, "Welcome, both of you." Looking up at the anxiously fidgeting Tonika, he told her, "If you do not wish to be here, you may leave without repercussions. Please let me know if there's anything I can do to make you comfortable. Tea is already heating. I take hospitality seriously." His attention turned to Sean. "Do you really, truly want to do this, lad? I believe it's safe, but I can't guarantee it. I am reluctant to perform this on a child, but I see in you someone desperate to live adventure. I've devoted my life to providing the key to those who seek it, and can't turn you down."

Sean nodded, too excited to do anything else.

Something—presumably a tea kettle, although I hadn't seen him set it to boil—whistled in the kitchen. Cleric waved at the chair amidst the mirrors. "Then have a seat, please."

Cleric retreated to the kitchen. Sean sat down, still too fidgety and overwhelmed to speak. Tonika sidestepped up to me, and asked only just above a whisper, "Does he mean all that?"

I nodded emphatically. "Yes, with all his heart, or I wouldn't have called." I hesitated a moment, but had to follow Cleric's example of honesty, adding, "I have ulterior motives, but I think you'll understand having ulterior motives for doing the right thing. It's…well, meta."

Tonika nodded, still subdued but less twitchy and tense. "This is what Sean has always wanted."

Sean got enough strength back to speak, looking from side to side at the mirrors and The Book's pedestal. He was surrounded by reflections of himself. "So, what exactly is this going to do?"

With Cleric still in the back, it was my job to explain. "It's going to give you knowledge, and knowing my boss, it's the knowledge of an adventurer."

Cleric emerged, with a fancy silver tea tray and a gleaming white china teapot. I'd have bet my twenty dollars an hour both were more than a century old. He set the tray on my alchemy table, poured tea into two china cups, added milk and sugar to one and just a tiny bit of sugar to the other. I got the first cup, and Tonika got the second.

I sipped. Mmm, rich.

Tonika seemed pleased as well, inhaling deeply and sighing with a weak smile of relief after her first sip. Turning her dark, heavy-lashed eyes up to Cleric, she said, "I guess the skill of predicting what kind of tea someone prefers would seem important to someone who wants to be what old-fashioned gentlemen should have been but never were."

Cleric smiled at that, widely, his eyes gleaming in the kind of pleasure usually directed at me when I'd done something dramatic. He sounded just as pleased, almost purring. "Exactly."

Turning to Sean, his mood changed instantly to formal, and businesslike—no, gentlemanly, like Tonika said. "I'm sorry, young man, but you'll be better off with an empty stomach. Are you ready?"

Sean jumped at the suddenness of that question. Boy, was he eager! Face lit up like a puppy dog covered in steak, he asked, "How long will this take?"

"Seconds," Cleric replied.

For the first time, I got to watch Cleric do his thing. As Sean sat mostly still, Cleric delicately used the calipers to measure Sean's head at various random angles. That's what it looked like, anyway. Just touch, touch, touch, with no sense I could see.

Sean threw himself forward out of the seat, screaming.

Tonika and I rushed from side to side. What should we do!? Sean held his head, staggering, then falling to his knees, whimpering and bent forward, trying to crawl with only his legs.

I swiveled to Cleric, anger swelling inside me. "Reverse the process! Now!"

"No!" shrieked Sean. He fell on his side, arms wrapped over his head as he shook it emphatically. "No, don't. I won't let you!"

My jaw worked helplessly. What should I do? Cleric stood still, arms folded behind his back, with no expression but solemn interest.

Breathing hard, Sean uncurled his arms. They shook visibly, and his voice wobbled as he squeaked, "I'm sorry. That...was a lot. I think—I'm sure I know who I am and which memories are mine, now."

The boy rolled to his feet, staring around the room with the same wonder as when he'd first entered. No, not quite the same. That was excitement. This was more calm. Mature. Appreciation more than surprise. His voice a little steadier, he went on, "The room is so different. It's hard to process. Just your alchemy knowledge is...everything looks different."

Tonika walked over to him slowly, like she was creeping up on a wounded animal. Just as delicately, she asked, "Sean?"

He staggered to his feet, getting less wobbly by the second. With intimate tenderness, he put his arms around Tonika, hugging her to him. Soft and warm, he murmured, "I'm fine, my love. This is wonderful. You did the right thing taking me here. I might even know a third as much as you do, now."

That got Tonika to giggle, and he pulled back enough so they could exchange smiles. He kissed her very briefly, very lightly on the lips, then slipped free. Approaching me now, he took one of my hands in both of his, and flashed me a smile like a charming movie rogue. Did—yes, of course that's the kind of skill Cleric would consider essential. In a more friendly and less romantic way, he said, "Thank *you*, so much. You've made a friend for life."

And then he stepped back, held up a hand, and declared, "Sword."

Cleric was ready. He scooped a wooden but otherwise real looking sword off a bookshelf, and tossed it over. Sean fumbled the catch, bending over and managing to get hold without it quite hitting the floor. He straightened up, and held the blade forward in both hands, then above his head, then back behind him. He kept shifting to different positions, most of them double handed, with the tip way out in front. Suddenly, he switched to short jabs, then longer thrusts, and a few sweeps.

After trying out a few dozen moves, Sean said in the distant tone of someone really talking to himself, "I see. Stabbing moves less, so it's faster. Faster means I hit before they get a chance."

Cleric nodded, still solemn. I wasn't sure Sean could see him.

Sean held the sword out at arm's length, and dropped it. Carpet muffled the clatter when it hit the floor. He held up his hands, curled down like limp fists, and staggered to the right. Then he staggered to the left. His arms waved around haphazardly.

Was he having a relapse? I took a half step forward, but Tonika grabbed my elbow and shook her head, hard and serious. Okay, this must be deliberate.

Merely wobbly on his tiptoes, Sean tilted around and looked at Cleric. "Hit me." The words were as firm as his body looked unsteady.

Cleric didn't argue. The tall, brawny adult stalked forward like an impatient panther, and threw a straight punch at Sean's face. The brown-haired boy lurched out of the way as if falling over, and flailed an arm. That arm curled around Cleric's forearm, and Sean spun. Cleric flew off his feet over Sean's shoulder, while Sean's other hand came up in a fist under Cleric's chin.

The adult hit the ground in a clank of metal rings, slipped his arm free, and rolled away to hop right back to his feet. That was fine, but if he'd been a fraction of a second slower, or twisted the wrong way, that fist under Cleric's chin would have rammed him head-first into the floor, with both Sean's strength and Cleric's weight behind it.

What had I just seen?

Sean answered without me having to ask out loud. Staring in awe at his own hands, he said, "Drunken Kitty Style. I'm a master of Drunken Kitty Style. No, I know Drunken Kitty Style. Knowledge isn't enough. If you'd really been trying, that wouldn't have worked. I need practice. I need to build up my reflexes. But…I can do this. I can!" By the end, he was whispering in awe, eyes shining in hope.

He lurched again, falling over, or at least looked like he was falling over. In the process he grabbed the hilt of his fallen sword, and spun back up again with it raised in one of the positions I'd seen, hilt close to his chest. He resumed the wobbling around he'd called Drunken Kitty Style, but now stabbing, twisting, and making small slices with his wooden blade as he did.

Without waiting to be told, Cleric drew his own sword, whose blade was metal, simple, and looked intimidatingly sharp. Stepping forward with the sword held two-handed as well, he stabbed at Sean a few times. Each time, Sean's apparently confused weaving meant the boy wasn't where Cleric struck. Their blades met and slapped at each other a few times, but I didn't know what it meant.

Cleric stepped back, raised his sword in salute to Sean, then sheathed it. Sean stopped staggering on his toes, and returned the same salute at attention.

Turning his head to me, eyebrow raised and with an unmistakably amused tone, Cleric said, "He has the instinct of a warrior. You knew."

I bowed my head bashfully. "I don't, so I couldn't be sure, but…yeah."

Smiling now, Cleric clapped Sean on the shoulder. The blonde man loomed over the brown haired fourteen-year-old boy like an approving god. "I can give you opportunities to practice, lad, train you in fighting, and hire you as a Pawn if you're willing to further my cause of giving everyone the opportunities you now have. Like you, whether they shine will be up to them, but at least they'll know how."

Sean stared up at Cleric in awe for several seconds, then dropped suddenly to his knees. He held up his sword, laid flat across both hands, and started to say something in German.

"*Nein!*" yelled Cleric, cutting him off.

Sean raised his head, eyes wide in shock. Scowling, Cleric swept a hand through the air in furious denial. "Not yet. You are not thinking your own thoughts right now. Even if your mind was clear, you are at an age for experimenting and learning what you want. I would not take an oath from anyone under their majority, and maybe not for years after that. Being a Pawn will give you a chance to find out what is right for you, and my other Pawn could use protection from harassment her own age." Calming down, he added in a merely grumpy growl, "I am worried about your secret identity, however."

And with that, inspiration hit me again. I grabbed my purple book off the table and yanked it open. It took only seconds to teleport back to my bedroom, grab the costume box out of my closet, and teleport back to Cleric's lair. I did come out almost on top of Sean, but not close enough that it bounced us apart.

Unrolling the black costume with the white mask, I urged Sean, "Try this on!"

He didn't hesitate for a second, even with the outfit's long skirt. He shimmied the whole thing on over his head, and adjusted it until it fit. A little lumpy with the clothes underneath, but it did fit. Sean was close to my height, if the wrong shape.

"The material does have a fair amount of flexibility," Cleric commented in a thoughtful tone, which explained that.

Sean raised his sword. He did a little of his Drunken Kitty sword-fighting stuff. The skirt swirled around him, but never caught his legs. There were tights and boots still in the box, but he didn't need those yet.

Leaping into the air, Sean tried a front flip, and fell on his butt on the carpet, laughing.

"Practice and exercise," advised Cleric with a proud smile.

Sitting there with his hands propped behind him, Sean announced suddenly, "Oh, hey, I know how to pick locks, now!" His voice had that scratchy sound through the mask.

"A skill for any adventurer," commented Cleric, smile widening. Then he straightened up formally, and lifted a hand, addressing me. "You have done the right thing today, Pawn. Now the three of you go rest. Your fellow Pawn won't be ready for anything more until he's had at least one good night's sleep."

When we left the shop, Sean de-costumed but still clinging to his precious wooden sword, Tonika looked up and down the street anxiously. I couldn't blame her, but I saw no sign of the cyborg.

The door closed behind us, and Tonika whispered into my ear, "If Sean is going to help you fight, then I'll help you plan. I have some thoughts about what to do about your dangerous problems."

Some of the tension I'd been carrying eased. A little, at least. Stage one of my nebulous almost plan had succeeded: Get desperately needed help.

Maybe I would survive this after-school job yet.

Paranoia still tickled me and I tried to keep an eye on everything at once until we got to campus, where lots of adults could see us and too many superheroes would be watching for the cyborg to try anything.

Chapter Seventeen

"You would not believe my weekend. I'll tell you at lunch," I whispered to Marcia as I took my seat in Chemistry class.

She gave me a look as hungry as the wolf Fenrir on a hands-free diet. Step one of Tonika's plan was a complete success.

By gathering my things quickly, I managed to exit Chemistry before Marcia and Charlotte could intercept me. An hour later, when I stepped into the cafeteria, five faces were already turned, awaiting me. Marcia held up an entire roast chicken, and pointed at my seat at the table. Further delay would not be allowed.

"So?" demanded Cassie as soon as I sat down. A scowling Marcia ripped the chicken in half and dumped one of those halves in front of me. Charlotte fixed me with eyes like pointy, pointy gimlets. Mirabelle smiled faintly, amused, but she smiled at me.

Even Will leaned forward on his elbows, intent on me rather than the girl of glass next to him. His brilliant red eyebrows went up, and he asked in a guilty rush, "Please tell me you're actually Magenta."

A sudden grin spasmed across my face. Normally I hated that people had to guess who I am, but this time it was funny. "I am Magenta, yes. Congratulations. You caught the correct pink hair."

"You're drawing things out," observed Charlotte.

She was one hundred percent correct. My survival depended on this plan working, and I wanted to live, thank you very much.

There was such a thing as too much delay. I leaned over my hot, savory-and-spices smelling half a bird, and lowered my voice. "Okay. It's not quite a story, but I guarantee you want to hear it. After I got off work on Saturday, I met up with Tonika by the university."

"Oh, but you haven't been available for us!" complained Cassie, glaring at me with a furious pout and gripping the edges of the table.

I waved that off with an unabashed smile and a literal hand wave. "I'm getting to that. The thing is, we saw a super powered confrontation in Exposition Park. Between teenagers. It's not just the Pawns and us out, now."

All complaints stopped, and everyone waited in silence for me to continue. So I did, and my desire to survive this mess gave my voice convincing emphasis. "One might have been a Pawn, but the other was a girl with a crossbow, purple costume, and purple hair. But that's not the big thing. She wasn't…right." I waved my hands, pretending to be helpless to describe it. "My alchemy power interprets things, and she was wrong. Like, I don't think she was human."

I had them, and now I leaned way forward and lowered my voice to a whisper to finish, "We got out of there, but before we did, Tonika swears she heard the purple girl mention Organism One."

Everyone sat back, except Mirabelle who merely relaxed the pointy transparent cat ears that had been turned toward me. Cassie smiled, and the smile kept growing. She lifted her hands and cracked her knuckles in anticipation, then drawled, "So, what you're saying is, now we have twice as many targets to hunt."

My speech done, my hook baited and cast, I turned my attention to tearing off bits of chicken meat that were not touching the tabletop. As always, Marcia had not gone halfway. This was rich and oily, some other bird besides a chicken. Nice.

Frowning in thought, Charlotte observed, "Crossbow. This new girl is officially a combatant."

"Altered by Organism One to be a combatant, the poor thing," murmured Mirabelle.

Pausing with a strip of cooked mystery bird in my greasy fingers, I added, "This is why I'm telling you, and only you. When the adults find out, they'll do something about her fast. Right now, only we and the Pawns know."

Chewing and swallowing that bit of bird as fast as possible, I gave them a cheerful smile and announced, "Which ties into the other thing. I've got Wednesday afternoon off from work. I've got Family Time stuff at 7pm, but I'd like to get some time with my friends. Will that work?"

Cassie slapped the tabletop, crowing, "Yes! We can do that. We will do that! You're all in, right? You'd better be in."

Charlotte nodded. Marcia nodded too, with a huge grin and a big chunk of freshly ripped off bird in her teeth.

Will said nothing and Mirabelle sighed, shaking her head sadly, but I'd gotten the important people and pumped my fist excitedly. "Yes!"

Charlotte still looked thoughtful. "Do you think we can get Aikamieli at this short notice? We can use him to check if either the Pawns or this Organism One follower are active."

Licking her bird-stained lips in predatory joy, Marcia purred, "I can do it. Aikamieli has a crush on me."

Charlotte's eyes narrowed. "By which you mean he's terrified of you."

Marcia shrugged, a suddenly graceful movement, with her pretty face tilted at an angle that made her wild hair hang with a softer femininity. It was like watching a mugger turn into a cheerleader. The same with the coy drawl in her voice. "I have a way with boys."

Charlotte wasn't having any of that. "Yes. Hitting them."

Cassie swiveled in her seat, one hand pushing Will back as

she leaned over to plead with the glass cat on his opposite side, "You've got to come along, Glitter Girl. You never go out. It will be fun!"

Mirabelle sighed again, face turning down to stare at her gloved hands folded in her lap. "I am sorry. There is no way my parents or my brother will allow that."

Will smirked. "Entropy has heard all about Marcia."

Marcia, unashamed but maliciously knowing, poked a bird bone at the blonde opposite her. "He's *met* Cassie, and knows how safe she isn't."

Will's smirk just grew. Cassie abandoned the topic, and instead reared up, slapping her hands on the table again. "Wednesday afternoon it is, right after school." Pointing a finger at me, she ordered, "Bring your potions, Magenta Slade."

Chapter Eighteen

I walked out of the front doors of Upper High on Wednesday, right past Cassie on one side, and Marcia and Charlotte on the other. They waited, scanning the crowd, looking for me.

Standing there watching Cassie eventually got her to give me a suspicious and annoyed look, so I waved. "It's me, Magenta."

Cassie slapped her forehead, then dragged her hand down her face. "I thought for sure we could grab the first pink haired girl who came out. It worked once."

Arms flew around my neck. I stifled a scream.

I was a little nervous, yes, what with the whole being hunted thing.

They were just Marcia's arms, and she leaned over my shoulder to give Cassie one of her manic smiles. "So, where are we going?" This close, Marcia smelled like roast bird, but to be fair, I'm sure I did too.

Cassie stepped around us, beckoning as she walked down the slope to a car parked at the curb. "There's a foreign film showing at the El Capitan that I've been wanting to see. It should let out juuuust in time to get Magenta back home." Smugly, she tapped the side of her head.

I didn't know cars, but this one was a big family sedan type, shiny and purple. A woman stood next to it, stiffly upright but watching us with a calm smile. She had boyishly short hair in a brilliant but not inhuman red, and was dressed in a plain cream blouse and calf length dress, not loose or tight. I couldn't admit I'd seen Cassie's sister the big purple monster, but surely this couldn't be her.

Charlotte waved at the woman, fell in beside Cassie, and gave the blue-and-blonde an elbow nudge. "New car?"

Her shoulders tightening awkwardly, Cassie answered with forced lightness, "Yeah, the last one had a business-related accident."

The red-haired woman gave the most barely noticeable chuckle. She turned her mild smile to me, and held out her hand. "You must be Magenta. I'm Rachel, one of Cassie's guardians."

First impression time! I took her hand and shook firmly, flashing my friendliest grin. She waved me to the open rear doors of the car, cutting off anything I might have said by adding, "I wish we had time for proper introductions, but we have to get moving if we're going to pick up Aikamieli."

"Still nice meeting you," I assured her as I slid into the car.

Rachel nodded, then frowned with a puzzlement as mild as her smile had been. She lifted her palm to her nose, and sniffed it.

Oh. Oh, no. Red hair. This was the other monster, Cassie's sister's partner. I all too vividly remembered the claws and fangs and wolfish snout. She must have an enhanced sense of smell. Did my unrecognizability power extend to my scent? The question had never come up!

Cassie whacked Rachel in the bicep with the back of her hand, scolding, "Don't be weird," and to my great relief, Rachel stopped sniffing and got into the drivers' seat.

We all piled in, Cassie in the front passenger seat and me, Charlotte, and Marcia in the back. Charlotte took the middle, no doubt to protect me from Marcia.

If today worked, maybe being protected from Marcia would stop sounding like a good idea.

The car got on the road, and we all scrunched around until we were comfortable. When that settled down, Cassie twisted to look back at me over her seat. "So, Magenta. Make any more cool new potions for your part time job?"

Rachel let out the aggrieved sigh of an adult putting up with children. "Super power talk? Really? I know what my best friend and I talked about when I was your age."

Cassie folded her arms and sneered defiantly. "How bad my parents are and how you would run away."

Marcia lurched up, smiling beatifically and raising her hand to wave it as high as she could in a car. "Oh! Oh! I can do that! My old man has hired a lawyer to try and convince the hero community that Mourning Dove shouldn't be allowed to threaten him!"

Everybody went silent for a moment, during which the car merged onto the freeway. Charlotte was the first to recover, scowling and giving Marcia a side-eye touched with concern. "That does not sound good."

Sitting back on the well upholstered seat with a thump, Marcia flapped her hand in airy unconcern. "I'm safe. It won't work for two reasons. First, the old zombie doesn't care. She does what she thinks is right no matter what anyone else says. Second, nobody likes my dad. No one. One hero told him that if Child Protective Services gets involved, they'd have to tell CPS how my dad treated me."

Grimacing, shoulders pulled up, Charlotte said, "Marcia, as your friends we do need to know this stuff, but can we change topics? This is supposed to be our first fun day out with the new girl. I'd like her motivated to stop acting like a hermit."

"I've got one. How's dance class going?" offered Cassie immediately.

For the first time, Charlotte lit up in open enthusiasm, leaning forward toward Cassie. "Oh, it's great! I came out to my instructor about my powers, and he is the coolest. He's letting me integrate my beads into my practice. As a civilian he's not as hardcore restricted from getting personal like we are, but I have no fears about him spilling my identity when I grow up."

Marcia's eyes widened in a much less crazed delight than

usual. "I've been dancing since I was six. We should dance sometime! Not fight dance, dance dance, you and me!"

"I want to learn to dance," pouted Cassie, hands clinging to the edge of the front seat.

"Me, too!" I echoed, because I always had. "Maybe I can get in on those classes once my after-school job is done? It won't last forever." I was pretty sure Cleric was getting out of LA as soon as his book scheme succeeded.

A car horn caught my attention a quarter of a second before the car lurched. I looked around to see a car pull up into the gap we'd been about to merge into.

In the driver's seat, Rachel growled. It was an animal sound, like the way her hair suddenly rose off of her head. With a whirr, our car sped up, tilted right, and angled in front of the car who'd cut us off. Desperately, they pulled off the road onto the shoulder, and we had the spot.

We didn't keep it. Rachel yanked on the steering wheel, and we swerved back into the lane we'd come from, then left again, cutting off someone else pulling forward. Still growling, Rachel stepped on the gas again, zooming us up ahead of the car we used to be behind, only to slam back to the right ahead of them. They couldn't hit us because the violent redhead was still stomping on the pedal, racing forward.

My eyes so wide they hurt, I clung to my seat in frozen panic. Voice high and wobbly, Cassie held onto a handle by the passenger seat with both hands as she squeaked, "Rachel, calm down! You know this is why we haven't been letting you drive. When Ruth finds out you lost it with me and my friends in the car, she'll take away your keys!"

Rachel snarled in return, mouth wide. I caught a glimpse of white but inhumanly sharp teeth, and silvery lines glowed as they crawled up her neck to her cheeks.

The rest of the drive went by in a blur of terror, and also a literal blur as the car rocketed down the 10 freeway like a vengeance-crazed cannonball. Other cars' tires squealed, horns honked, and they pulled this way and that to get out of her way, leaving a desperate mess behind us.

I did notice when a police car pulled up behind us, lights

flashing and siren shrieking. Rachel pulled one hand off the wheel, and punched her fist through the ceiling above her head. Whatever gesture she made, the police lights went out. They wanted nothing to do with that, and I did not blame them.

Her driving calmed down about the time we got off the freeway onto surface streets. When she obeyed the first stop light, relief hit me like a bucket of ice water. Everyone except Rachel let out deep sighs.

We eased quite delicately into a parking spot somewhere in West Hollywood, or maybe a little farther West than West Hollywood. Rachel pushed a button that unlocked all our doors, declared, "This is the address," and got out with the same mild near-formality as when she'd met us at school. Except for the hole in the roof of the car and everyone's cold sweat, nothing might have happened.

Cassie got out, glaring at the college age redhead, who looked maybe the tiniest bit abashed, but only the tiniest bit.

This was a weird neighborhood. The buildings were narrow, pressed together, three or four stories tall, and wood. It looked like photos I'd seen of San Francisco.

We didn't have to do anything. Aikamieli, in one of his knee-length red shirts and pants, holding his oversize "True Kalevala", came hopping down the front steps of one of the houses. The boy had a theme and stuck to it.

Still shaking just a touch, I looked around. We had one car and six people. Ever practical, Charlotte asked first, "Where's he going to sit?"

Marcia raised a hand immediately. "On my lap!"

Charlotte gave her a hard look. "No."

"I'll sit in his lap?" Marcia suggested brightly.

By now, Aikamieli was standing by the car, blushing to match his scarlet clothes. My cheeks felt a bit hot too. This was nothing compared to Marcia's daily campaign of shamelessness, but sometimes she managed to shock me anyway.

Cassie, ignoring Marcia's highly successful attempts to tease poor Aikamieli, solved the issue by squeezing into the back seat with us. Aikamieli took the passenger seat with obvious relief, and Marcia and Charlotte ended up sharing a seatbelt.

When Rachel got back in, Cassie leaned way over and tapped the back of her head. "Keep your temper this time? Please? Pretty please? I want Magenta to enjoy herself!"

"I'm actually having a ball," I said, voice a bit hoarse, but to my surprise I meant it. Yes, I'd been scared out of my wits, but these lunatics were my people, and I'd never had a "my people" before. I'd be having a lot more fun if I wasn't constantly, naggingly aware that my people wanted to hunt me down and beat me senseless. But today would fix that. Hopefully. If I survived.

Wordless, Rachel started driving again, with the faintly whistling hole above her head the only evidence she wasn't steady, cautious, and reliable. Satisfied, Cassie turned her attention to Aikamieli. "So...? That's the book, right? Do that spell to find a Pawn!"

He chuckled awkwardly. "I knew that question was coming." If it sounded a little bit accusing and sarcastic, he sat up with more than a little pride in his smile as he opened the book to exactly the right page.

Aikamieli sang, and we all sat and listened, even Marcia. No one wanted to interrupt that sinuous voice curling around its gibberish words like a glittering oiled snake. I even jumped an inch when he snapped the book closed and apologized, "Sorry, ladies. It's not telling me to go anywhere. There must be no Pawns active."

Or one was right here already.

Charlotte took a deep breath, and blew it out slowly through pursed lips. Then she pushed back her rattling, bead-covered braids with one hand. "Forget magic and superheroing, Aikamieli. Go for a regular singing career. I bet it's a better life."

He shook his head fiercely, clutching the book to his chest. "Magic is in my blood! I'm the descendant of great wizards! My family has stories, but I'd have to translate them, and they're meant to be sung, so it would be awkward, but I'll try sometime if you want." He scrunched down and his voice turned hopeful making that offer. Clearly he wanted, but was afraid of rejection.

"Ask them again later. We've almost arrived," suggested Rachel. I looked out the window again. She was right. We were in a fancy part of town. Oh, and with stars on the sidewalks. The Hollywood Walk of Fame! I hardly ever went up here, but who could mistake that?

Rachel stopped in front of the theater, leaned back, and told us pleasantly, "I'll find a parking place and catch up with you. It might take a while."

We piled out. Other than a fancy sign, the El Capitan didn't look that special, being part of a rectangular grey building with other stores along the front. True, it had interesting reliefs a couple of floors up and an interestingly irregular surface, but in this neighborhood? The Chinese Theater loomed down the street, and the building next to it had Greek pillars!

I stuck my hand in my pocket. "I am so glad I've got a job and can afford tickets now. We get in line over there?"

I took two steps forward before Cassie grabbed my shoulder, sweeping her blue-tipped hair in proud amusement, and pointed across the street. "Pfft. No. We're going across the street."

Oh. In yet another display of how unimpressive the El Capitan was in context, right across from it blazed the shiniest building I had seen even in LA. It was ninety percent glass windows, held up with metal rods, and some mad architect must have designed it because every window caught the sun. It didn't blind. It was just shiny. Very, very shiny.

We scurried across in a clump when the light changed, and passed through the huge glass doors into…

…a very shiny makeup store. Okay, sure. A high-end makeup store, obviously, and not nearly as shiny as the outside, but white and silver dominated the furnishings, eye-catching around the hundreds of posters of elegantly axe-faced women in way too much expertly and exquisitely applied makeup.

It would make sense to split up, but we didn't. Cassie surged forward through the aisles, eyes devouring everything. Marcia seemed content to follow her, hands in pockets, smirking with arrogant malice at the same merchandise. Charlotte hung close to them, with the curious frown of someone who pays very little attention to makeup normally. Aikamieli, arms hugging his book with obvious abashment at being in such a girly store, tried to squeeze defensively as close to them as possible.

I trailed along, more thoughtful. The sheer variety of makeup was impressive, and I could afford it now. I wouldn't want anything bold. I had pink hair and eyebrows, I didn't need red and purple splotches on my face. My pink eyelashes were less obvious, but made mascara particularly pointless. No, maybe I could afford this, but it wasn't an efficient use of my money. Especially with price tags as much as a hundred dollars, yeesh.

Look at this stuff. I smeared a lip gloss sample on my finger, and applied it to my mouth before checking a mirror. All it really did was make my lips shine and faintly sparkle, and I looked ridiculous. Those sparkles would be so much more useful in a reflective potion. That would be interesting, and a serious challenge, but energy powers were big in the fighting type heroes and villains, right? Would there be silver powder? Of course there would be silver powder.

No, no. My strength potion was particularly difficult to make, and this place abounded in orange. Orange that would be easy to process because it was already organic. Yeeeeeessssssss....

You know, a little bit of that red nail polish over there, just that specific shade, would really simplify my healing formula. And I might not need mascara, but those mascara brushes made me wonder about concentrated, powerful chemicals that I could apply topically in tiny amounts. Wouldn't that be interesting?

Cassie's squee pulled me out of my super powered trance. She spun through an aisle with giddy delight, indicating the thousands of colors and types of makeup. She followed up with an ecstatic sigh. "I am going to knock Penny's socks off."

Charlotte closed her eyes tight, and her mouth trembled for a second. The effort of not laughing turned her voice thin and whispery. "Of course that's what this is about."

"You bet it is," Cassie answered, not ashamed, but proud. Her blue eyes glowed faintly as she explained with fierce urgency, "I told you, I have inside information. Ray's going to be leaving town, for good. There's no way I'm getting in the way of Penny's relationship while she has it, but when he's out of the picture and she's lonely, I want it firmly planted in that incredible super brain that Cassie is friendly, drop-dead gorgeous, and ready to make her life complete again."

Grinning with glee at the prospect of romantic chaos, Marcia folded her arms and leaned in on one side. "'Inside information.' You've gotten Claire on your side and she wants you to catch Penny on the rebound."

Cassie clenched a fist in heroic, or possibly villainous determination. "Priority one is that the Cog Queen, the Pigtail Princess, the Invincible Introvert, is happy. I will never endanger that. But priority two is that she be *mine*, and whatever it takes to accomplish both at once, that I shall do."

I had no idea who any of these people were. Okay, I was pretty sure they were the Inscrutable Machine, who had proven that I wasn't too young to do something big with my powers, but as people they were total strangers. It was still fun, charming, and a touch creepy to listen to Cassie's enthusiasm. I couldn't imagine what a crush that powerful and all-consuming felt like, but apparently it felt good.

Rubbing her hands together, Cassie's explanation dropped to merely enthusiastic. "First, I'll find some shades that suit me. Then I'll get my sister to show me how to apply it perfectly. I'd ask Barbara, but Penny doesn't go in for the dramatic makeup approach."

Charlotte tilted her face down so she could mime peering cynically over glasses as she smirked. "*Ruth* is going to teach you how to be subtle."

Marcia had also calmed down, and sounded honestly helpful as she raised a finger. "Lucyfar is great with makeup. It's part of that punk/goth thing she does."

Cassie waved a hand without looking up from a little cup of blue…okay, honestly, I didn't know what it was. "No good. She's in Europe. No one expects her back this year. I heard something about a lost squid."

Pouncing on a display, Cassie smeared some stuff over her lips and onto her eyelids. When she lifted her head, both had become eye-searingly light blue, with glitter like the gloss that had gotten my attention before.

"Oh, yeah. That's subtle," snarked Charlotte.

Cassie purred, "Oh, but watch this!" The blue in her pale blonde hair crept down from the tips to near the base. Electric sparks flickered inside it. A second later, the blue on her eyelids and lips turned phosphorescent, glowing softly and flickering as the occasional spark wandered across it.

I added my two bits to the conversation. "Still not subtle, but awesome."

My eyes wandered down to the tiny little metal cup in Cassie's hand, the one she'd gotten this blue stuff out of. It had gotten the same shock as the makeup on her face, and glowed the same way. Now, that was interesting. A lot of this makeup was potentially useful, but Cassie had altered this stuff, put some of her own power in it. I wasn't sure exactly what I could do with it, but it would be something amazing.

Oh, might as well. This was a sample, and samples were free, and after Cassie had altered it, it wouldn't be useful for demonstrations. As soon as she put the cup down, I snatched it up and tucked it into my potion pack.

Out of nowhere, Marcia announced, "Hey, you know what? I'm pretty sure I could bring down this whole building with a few punches."

Cassie whipped her phone out. "Look at that, it's movie time."

Charlotte took a position by one of Marcia's shoulders, and I took the other. With gentle but insistent nudges, we walked Marcia to the front of the store. Yeah, it felt good to be part of the team like this, as long as we could keep Marcia from giving in to temptation.

Cassie rushed ahead of us to the checkout counter, bought a few things, and joined us outside. Squeezed between Charlotte and I, Marcia pouted, but only a little.

As we crossed the street back to the theater, Cassie rummaged in her jean pockets. "I've got everybody's tickets here."

"I can pay for mine," I announced happily. I wasn't working for Cleric for the twenty bucks an hour, with a generously padded interpretation of how many hours I worked, but the money felt good.

"So can I, Cassie. It's fine," assured Charlotte.

Marcia's face lit up with the fiery glee of unholy inspiration. Again. "I can buy the theater from Disney. My dad would love that."

"Already got the tickets!" Cassie countered, waving a folded-up clump of papers. She twisted around to grin back at me. "And it's not that. You have to buy ahead at this place to be sure to get a seat. Not that I expect this showing to be that bad."

It wasn't. There was barely a line, and we breezed in. The place was fancy. Funny circle reliefs on the walls. Layered murals on the ceiling. Weirdly small, for all that. Not tiny and intimate, but still, way more decoration for a place the size of a regular movie theater.

We got seats all clumped together, with Marcia yanking Aikamieli into the spot next to her so she could watch him squirm.

Her plan was utterly foiled as the lights dimmed, a tenderly soft voice whispered, "Once upon a time, or maybe twice...." and on the screen some animated men's top hats turned into a rainbow.

CHAPTER NINETEEN

An hour and a half later, I staggered into Rachel's car. Finding my voice, I asked, "What did I just see?"

"The nineteen-sixties," answered Cassie with both satisfaction and wonder.

A conversation followed, but not one that made much sense to me. Marcia, Rachel, and Cassie had plenty to say about the multicolored insanity we'd just watched. It didn't filter in, just washed over me as we drove back down to my neighborhood.

One reason I couldn't pay attention was the tightness steadily gripping at my heart. The fun, easy part of the day was over. Even if Tonika's plan worked, deadly violence was barreling toward me with every minute that passed.

Rachel found my neighborhood and pulled up in front of my apartment building. As I crawled out and everyone reorganized into less cramped positions, Cassie squeezed over Rachel's lap to stick her head out the window and pout. "I'm sorry we didn't get any superheroing going. Next time."

I gave her a thumbs up. "Agreed, but I wouldn't have given up this afternoon for anything." Adding a sigh, I let my complete lack of enthusiasm creep into my face as I lied, "But, time to go in and entertain my parents."

The moment the apartment building door closed behind me, I gave up even pretending to be casual. Opening the door to my family's apartment as quietly as I could, I snuck into my bedroom, scooped up the purple book, and smushed my face into the page to teleport me to Cleric's lair.

Cleric wasn't in the front room, but my and Sean's costumes were laid out neatly waiting for us, including my gauntlet and best potion kit. I flipped the salvaged makeup dish onto my alchemy table next to the chunk of Delicious's candy shell, and scooped up my costume in my arms.

"I'm going to meet the other Pawn! I'm taking my stuff so he'll know it's me!" I yelled, since Cleric was surely in the building.

That was all true, especially the part about Sean knowing it was me. It would be mortifying to have to shake my fellow conspirator and identify myself.

I rushed down to the street corner that bordered Exposition Park and the line of shops that front the University. At every step I felt artificial eyes watching me. The cyborg had to be around here somewhere, watching me. Of course, that was the point.

My purple book sat on top of my bundle of minion clothes, but that wouldn't do me much good if—

Focus on the task at hand, Magenta, not on a crossbow bolt—

Ugh.

I reached the main street, and there at the corner waited Sean and Tonika. He looked around blankly, but she spotted me immediately, and waved. Thankfully, a second of staring at the clothes in my arms, and Sean met me with a smile that needed no introduction.

They were the blandest, least attention getting pair imaginable, her in her beige blouse and skirt, him in worn jeans and a faded grey t-shirt. His hair short and brown, hers fluffy and black. Just a pair of teenagers meeting a friend.

Switching my bundle to one arm, I pounced Tonika, hugging her to me tightly. My voice husked maybe the slightest bit as I told her, "Thank you so much for helping me. If you didn't have a plan, I don't know how I would be handling this."

She patted me on the back. This close, I couldn't see her face, but Sean beamed as if it had all been his idea.

As I extricated myself from the embrace, Tonika looked over my shoulder and around the street. "Any sign of trouble?"

"No, but the cyborg has to have seen me, and will be ready to follow." That, and checking in with my planner, had been the real point of coming here.

My nervousness took over, and I added, "If she can."

Tonika patted my shoulder and gave me a reassuring smile. "If she doesn't take the bait this time, we'll set more traps."

Tonika wasn't the one in the trap...I didn't say, because thanks to her this was merely scary and dangerous. The alternative to Tonika's plan was death.

And reanimation.

"Half robot zombie slave" didn't just sound like a nightmare, but an eternal nightmare.

Stepping past us, Sean tugged at my sleeve gently, beckoning with his head. "We'd better hurry up so the boss doesn't get suspicious."

Tonika giggled, swishing her skirt in one hand, face down but grinning, shy and impish at the same time. "He'll think the secret you're keeping is about romance. That's the way adults view teenagers."

I pictured Cleric, in his medieval armor and sword, with his ancient books and his head full of stories about knights and princesses. Yeah, his imagination would go right there. He'd imagine a love pure and noble, or perhaps guilty but irresistibly sweet. Maybe I should give Sean a handkerchief.

I barked one grim laugh. "Still, we'd better be going before trouble catches us."

Trouble. That word.

With a rush of Deja vu, I had the same inspiration I'd had with Marcia that started this crazy mess. Pulling my gauntlet to the top of my clothing pile, I checked the magnet.

It pointed southwest, straight into Exposition Park. It was Her. It had to be. My friends would be more westerly by now.

I grabbed Tonika's shoulder and shook her urgently, then

pointed at the needle. "This is a Trouble Magnet."

They didn't need any more explanation. Tonika leaned way down, studying the compass from inches away. Flat and businesslike in a way I'd never heard before, she said, "The needle is moving. She's nearby, she's headed toward the street, and she's fast. Go now."

Sean shoved his phone into Tonika's hands, blurting, "So we can keep in contact. I can't take it with me being evil anyway."

Too slow. I grabbed his sleeve and yanked. We took off running through the zigzag blocks to Cleric's little side street. We got there without incident, but I definitely felt a wave of relief as we plunged through the door into the front room.

Cleric was there waiting for us, sitting in the brain scooping chair with his sword out, point on the floor. He looked up from a floating book and gave us an expression I could not read.

Working for him, I'd discovered a vast talent for putting on a show. Out of breath, I yanked Sean forward with a grip on his arm. "I got him!"

That got the desired smile. Standing up with far more casual patience than I felt, he waved a hand toward the back of the building. "Get changed in the upstairs bathroom. I'll help your fellow Pawn. His costume is a bit more complicated, especially if he has to wear it into combat with heroes your age."

I raced up the carpeted stairway behind the kitchen, and got dressed as instructed. As I tucked my ancient Knights Templar badge into my coat, I looked at myself in the mirror. The coat and all the brown leather made me look sleek, and the gauntlet and protruding vacuum tubes and ribs of the shock absorber field added the slightest touch of menace. I flipped my dreads back, and gave the mirror a hard stare. That's right. I wasn't just some helpless bystander victim. I was a professional working to make the world a more gloriously strange place. Nor was this just a trap for my enemies. I had a job to do for that mission of strangeness.

With those thoughts calming me, I descended the stairs at an even pace, to find someone had joined Cleric and Sean in the front room.

Sean looked dressed to me, despite Cleric still fiddling with his sleeves and mask. Properly worn, the look was interesting. Not entirely human, and I could not tell at all if there was a boy or a girl under there. Maybe I would lean girl, seeing it for the first time. Perfect for Cleric's interchangeable Pawn gimmick.

The man didn't look like much. With a short moustache well into the process of turning white, a thin denim shirt and thicker jeans, the rangy old man would look entirely ordinary if not for his helmet. Even that wasn't too weird, with grey plates around the back and top, fat bumps that reminded me of very stylized animal ears, and an opaque silvery visor that was not currently flipped down over his eyes.

Cleric paused in arranging Sean's outfit, or perhaps finished. Straightening up, he waved a hand toward the new guy and introduced, "Pawn, this is Sleeper Agent."

Sleeper Agent broke into a scraggly grin. Someone had done a number on his teeth once upon a time, and there was a whole lot of gold in there. He had a wry, casual, and radiantly friendly voice. "My super power is particularly useless."

Cleric sighed, with the kind of resigned exasperation of a very serious person who was expecting this ridiculousness. Soberly, he corrected, "Sleeper Agent is not a super powered title, just his code name for this operation."

"You can use my real name. No one has cared about me since I lost my powers in the Horsemen mess," the old guy chided Cleric, giving him a cynical smirk.

Cleric returned the stare with worn patience and solemn sincerity. "I'm trying to protect the children."

Hands stuck in his pocket, Sleeper Agent leaned his back against a bookshelf and grinned at us some more. "I'm sure I'm like you kids. I don't work for Tyrant, I'm just in sympathy with his philosophy. I wouldn't throw in with an invasion, but I don't mind doing my boy Cleric here a favor now and then."

I nodded and returned the grin, because who could resist? "That's me."

Sean picked up his wooden sword where it leaned against my workbench, and held the blade up in front of his mask in salute. "I owe her, and I'm here to protect her."

If you'd asked me, I'd have said Sean was doing this for fun, but he sounded serious. I guess I didn't know him very well, yet.

Cleric took over, striding out in front of us, hands clasped behind him, feet solidly set shoulder width apart. He looked more square-faced than usual, more serious. "Transportation has been a difficult question, Pawns. There will be enough super powered witnesses to your transactions tonight that if I went myself, it would start a fight. We need freight delivery that is overtly associated with the super powered community to prevent the temporal authorities from interfering, but nothing that trumpets our allegiance. What you deserve is a phoenix and a unicorn. What you're getting is Sleeper Agent."

Not being the saluting type, I gave him a thumbs up with my gauntleted hand. "It will still be more fantastic than anything we've done before."

He nodded, still looking pained and regretful. Stepping over to Sean, he crouched down and took hold of the mask, but looked over at me. "What can you provide in potions for your guard?"

Ooh. Interesting question. I rummaged through my supplies. "Two reds and a blue, obviously. I have two itching clouds, so one for him. Glue is easy. He can have two of those. I've got half a speed potion and one strength potion, and he definitely should have those. I'll...I'll keep the sunlight potion if you two don't mind. It's hard to make. Really hard. I don't know when I'll be able to prepare another. Charging it is the easy part, and that takes a month."

I passed the potions over to Cleric, who took Sean's gloved hands and guided them to place the vials in different holstered pockets over the costume. He turned his face to Sean now. "What would you like equipped?"

Sean slipped a red vial out of its strap. "Healing." Lifting his face, he popped the lid off the vial and thumbed it into a disguised slot on the left of the mask until it disappeared. "Speed." He did the same with my blue-green potion on the right.

Next, Cleric took a box like a more angular version of my potion case off the table, and opened it up. Sure enough, it contained more potions. Fake potions. Their drab colors told me that immediately. Sean filled the empty slots, until he looked way better armed than he was. Cute.

I really didn't like my friends seeing a Pawn carrying potions just like the ones I made. On the other hand, I wasn't the only source of alchemy in LA, and Cassie and Marcia were not detectives. For Charlotte I'd just have to hope. Anyway, if Tonika was right, the question would not matter for long.

Straightening back up, Cleric clapped his hand down on Sean's shoulder. "Protect her. That is your absolute duty. Not victory or glory, her safety. Use every resource available to you. You know about her book. Escape should be your first, best instinct."

Wow. I...I was touched. Cleric knew my friends would likely attack us, and all this ceremony and preparation was because he could just barely put up with letting me face that danger.

Sean, silent now, reversed his sword and with both hands on the hilt, pressed the tip to the floor.

Satisfied, or at least troubled but accepting, Cleric flicked fingers at me, beckoning me over to the table. He laid a brightly colored booklet with lots of photos of weird objects in front of me. "Here is your shopping list, Pawn."

I lifted a hand to forestall him. "I know. Really, I know. I've memorized the list. I'm also not stupid enough to take chances on forgetting anything." So, I plucked the pamphlet off the table and tucked it into my coat by the teleport book.

That got a smile, and Cleric's approval made me smile in return.

He pointed at the door, arm extended, sending us to battle. "Go, Pawns, and return to me safely. From this moment until then, my lead Pawn does all the talking. Neither Sleeper Agent nor her bodyguard will speak."

On our way out, with his face carefully turned exactly away from Cleric, Sleeper Agent grinned and rolled his eyes.

A new vehicle had parked on the street outside. No, 'parked' did not adequately describe it. This thing was fatter than any truck I'd ever seen, and I was glad I didn't have to drive on the same street as it. Its bulgy beetle shape and dull grey surface gave the impression of thick armor. The wheels weren't visible, instead concealed by more bulgy covers, and the cab grew off the front in another bulge, with pods sticking out the top. The whole thing gave the impression of a massive animal, hunched up to spring.

Black exclamation marks painted all over it, ranging from hand to human sized, ruined that threatening aura completely. Still, nobody could mistake this for anything but a hero or villain's vehicle.

Sleeper Agent opened up the passenger side door, and Sean pushed me wordlessly in ahead of him. I had to climb up and then up some more to the high seats, but unlike Rachel's sedan this truck had plenty of room for three people in the front seat, although Sean had to fiddle awkwardly with his wooden sword the whole way. Must not have gotten any memories from The Book about that.

We drove West, a long, long way West, as sunset crept into night. The ride was completely peaceful. No one challenged our bestial tank's ownership of the road, and Sleeper Agent seemed perfectly content to be accommodating in return.

Eventually, I saw the deep, almost black shadow of the ocean ahead of us. We were somewhere between Venice Beach and Santa Monica, surrounded by brightly lit little stores and restaurants aimed at the tourist crowd, or just LA natives who wanted to treat themselves to a beach visit. This looked like the most unlikely place I could imagine for a smuggling operation. That is, until our truck turned into a ramp leading down into an underground parking garage. A guard, who looked just like a regular blue-shirted security guard except for the clover symbol on his hat, lifted the bar to let us in.

It had been a quiet trip, but now I whistled, just at the skill it had to take to get this goliath vehicle down the ramp, even if the ceiling was barely high enough for us.

A dozen or so other vehicles, ranging from regular cars to weird, malformed mad science contraptions, lurked in the shadows around the brightly lit shopping depot in the middle of the basement floor of the garage. Sleeper Agent pulled us into a random looking spot himself, and flashed us another grin and a thumbs up. "Supervillain faces on, kids."

I gave him a thumbs up back, then raised my gauntleted fist to Sean. I couldn't see his expression behind the mask, but he bumped his black gloved fist against mine firmly.

We climbed down from the bulgy tank's cab, and headed for the lights, with Sean on my right and one step behind me.

Okay, Magenta. This time it wasn't about playing ringmaster. My role was "cool and professional," so I kept my arms and legs straight, my face flat with a touch of impatient frown.

My first challenge was to not show any surprise about the displays. Standing floodlights stood between and lit up pallets loaded with...well, I'd expected robots and weapons. Most of these items, I could not identify. Crystals. Barrels of liquids. Thickly twined cables or pistons wider than my arm. Radar dishes. Ingots of metals whose faint color differences promised they could be ever so useful in my recipes.

A heap of big brass tubes was the first thing obviously on my list, but as we headed for them, I had to hesitate just a second and look over one particular display. A well-padded metal box held rows of round-bottomed glass flasks containing a goopy black substance. The label on each flask just read "Catalyst."

Oh, I wanted that. Whatever it did, I wanted it. But. Business.

We were hardly alone. Men and women, all solidly athletic and most in costumes, drifted between the displays. A good three quarters of them had mad scientist flight goggles either up on their foreheads, or hanging around their necks.

Sean and I got stares, and I drank them in. Good. We were making an impression.

"What are you children doing here?" barked an angry voice.

I stiffened, but managed not to jump. I hadn't seen anybody this close to us!

That was because no one was. A goat stood in the aisle, an ugly brown animal with black stripes and irregularly bent horns. A speaker shaped like a clover clung to an elastic collar around its neck.

Professional minion of Tyrant me did not look surprised. Nor did she care whether this beast was intelligent or just carrying the speaker. Frowning to display my faint irritation at his attitude, I told it, "You know who we are, and you were told to expect us."

The goat stared at me with its freaky amber rectangular-pupiled eyes, and chewed away at its cud.

Too hardened to be angry, either, I asked it, "Are you ready to take our order?"

"Okay," it conceded.

I strolled between the displays, pointing, and began with the pipes. "Two each of these, starting from the number eight size and going up by twos to thirty-two. That's twenty-four total. Twelve of those vibration boxes. One eighteen-inch Hazard type power core, with a turbo spike booster. Thirty-three silver core Dynar antennae. Thirty square meters of soul wrap insulation...."

The goat followed me around as I went through the order, and only seeing the objects in person, with some of the pipes as big as a man, did I realize this was a major order. Whatever. It was my job to act like I did this every day, for purposes too important for this goat to ever understand.

Only when I finished did I get out the shopping list Cleric gave me, flipping through it silently as a checklist to make sure I'd...yes, I'd gotten everything.

Sean's hand touched my forearm, getting my impression. He walked off, and I followed him to a pallet of crates I'd paid no attention to because it had nothing on our list.

Oh, ho. There were weapons here after all! Just not many. Thick, oblong looking mad science blaster things filled one box. Another held carefully stacked chainsaw swords. From a display near the end, Sean drew a sword, sleek and metal, but when he held it in both hands and touched a wooden pallet, blue light flickered and the wood charred.

Hmmm. Oh, why not? Giving Sean a gentle smile I'd shown no one and nothing else since stepping into this depot, I said, "Our employer is willing to stretch the budget for rewards to personnel. Add that to the list."

And if I was buying Sean a treat...I stalked back to the box of Catalyst flasks, and plucked one out. "And this."

The goat stared at me. Goats look naturally annoyed, which

went well with its suspicious demand, "How are you going to pay?"

Again, I made sure not to look mad. Minions of Tyrant didn't play these games. I tapped my badge. "You know how I'm going to pay. My employer has an account."

And with that, I caught a sound. Singing. Beautiful singing, outside on the street, just barely audible but unmistakable because of the liquid depth of the voice. Tonika had been right. The first thing my friends did when they left me was check again where they could find Pawns.

My heartbeat sped up, but I forced my breathing to remain steady. Sean had heard the same thing, and had his new sword low and ready, hilt held in both hands. I tried to remain, not casual, but unimpressed and businesslike as I told the goat, "Load the order onto my vehicle. My driver will deliver it. There is about to be trouble, and as my employer values courtesy, I will do my best to keep it from disrupting your business."

Speaking of trouble, I checked my magnet. It didn't point east. It pointed off north, and I could see it moving. The cyborg was here inside the garage.

Now my heart pounded in my chest, and my body felt stiff and cold. I was trapped between a hammer and an anvil.

But I wasn't trapped alone. Sean took a step forward, white mask tilting as he scanned the garage. He looked in the direction my compass was pointing, which meant he'd read the needle when I lifted my wrist to check.

From the garage entrance I heard Cassie's distant but echoing voice. "—because some people don't want to do their shopping where Spider will see everything you purchase, and know exactly what you're doing with it."

Faking calm, I strolled out to the edge of the sales depot. Sean kept perfect pace next to me, sword still low but directed toward Cassie's voice. He was slipping into the weird sinuousness of Drunken Kitty Style, but not wobbling yet.

Cassie, Charlotte, Marcia, and Aikamieli arrived, all of them in costume, and with Aikamieli leading. He had his (reputed) True Kalevala out, and was still singing, but so quietly my other friends' voices drowned him out, especially when Cassie leaped ahead of him, pointing and shouting, "There she is!"

Cassie's lightning bolt spandex glowed brilliantly in the gloom as she raised a fist at me and shouted, "We've got you, Pawns! And I see a sword this time! Prepare to be brought to Justice!"

Not far from me, a woman in a spandex bodysuit of her own, this one cut weirdly so it was all multicolor connected stars instead of solid fabric, told the man next to her, "You know, I panicked when I heard Tyrant was recruiting kids, but they really are just errand girls."

The man wore a truly tasteless costume consisting mostly of mechanical snakes wrapped around his body that showed off even more skin than the heroine. She had to be a heroine, and he was obviously a villain. With the ease of an old friend, he answered her, "I agree, but I wish it wasn't for Tyrant."

With a flutter of laughter, the heroine said, "And her friends are adorable. You have to see it happen to realize they're just kids being kids. I wish I'd gotten to do this at their age."

My heart managed to freeze even tighter at the word "friends," but no. She was merely being condescending.

The villain one-upped her condescension with amusement. "I hope they learn their lesson now. No, on second thought, I don't. I'm looking forward to the easy victories when those girls grow up."

I had way bigger concerns than pride right now, but the heroine and villain had been making no effort to keep their voices low, and Marcia didn't like it. She growled, turning toward the dismissive duo. Charlotte grabbed her by the shoulder, and turned her back toward me, voice curt and low, but audible. "We're here to bring in the villainess our age."

Still amused, the villain corrected, "Alright, I'm looking forward to the difficult victory against that one."

That's enough standing there, Magenta. Confident professional. Voice even. None of this petty bickering. I held up my gauntleted hand. "I have no interest in fighting, heroes, and I have no interest in wrecking this neutral store if I can't convince you to settle this peacefully. We'll discuss this over there." Like a lot of multilevel garages, this one had twists, and

I waved my other hand at the corner past where my Trouble Magnet was telling me the cyborg lurked.

Thank goodness for the shadows. Thank goodness for facing away from my friends as I walked, supposedly calmly, around that corner. There was no way I could keep from grimacing at the icy spike of panic as the needle of my Trouble Magnet twisted, showing me walk right past the cyborg. Where was it? I should have bumped into it! But I saw no signs, and there were not a lot of places to hide in this empty cement expanse. Even the ceilings only had a few round recessed lights.

Sean was watching the compass too, because he kept ahead of me until the needle twisted, then drifted behind me, always keeping himself between me and where it should be.

For a few seconds after we passed the corner, we were out of sight of my friends, and panic clawed at me again. I could grab the teleport book. Sean and I could disappear, and be safe.

Sure, safe for now, but giving up my best chance to be safe for good. At least I was ready for this. Supposedly.

Okay. We got completely out of line of sight of the depot and everyone in it. My friends were on a straight line with the Trouble Magnet's needle. It was time.

I swiveled, and placed my hands on my hips. Carefully, not loud, not accusing, not begging, just trying to sound like we were having a formal discussion, I said, "This will do. You are heroes. I recognize that. You came here to do a good deed and catch a supervillain."

Horribly on cue, the purple haired cyborg kicked open one of the ceiling light fixtures, leaned out of it, and fired her crossbow at me.

I reacted too slowly, but Sean didn't. As the point of the crossbow bolt leveled straight at me, he grabbed my shoulder and threw me aside. Before I hit the ground, I heard the hiss of the bolt going by, and the shockingly, painfully loud metallic clank as it embedded itself in the cement.

Then I did hit the ground, on my side, but the shock absorber in my costume made that no more painful than falling on a mattress.

Fear supplied more than enough crawling pain as the

cyborg dropped twenty feet from the ceiling and landed easily on its booted feet in the middle of my friends, already sliding a new bolt into her crossbow. Face unreadable, voice equally flat and emotionless, it said, "No. I will catch her."

I should do something. What? It was hard to think about anything but the black metal bolt within easy arm's reach that had penetrated cement by at least two inches.

The cyborg charged, her long pink-purple hair streaming behind her. As she did, she pulled the bow's string back, cocking the bolt into place. Where had she gotten it? She didn't have a quiver, or pockets. My stomach clenched at the hint her body had been altered even more than it looked.

Sean leaped to his feet, springing up as easily as a cat. Instead of shooting him, the cyborg lashed out a leg, kicking him back down and out of the way as it bent down and wrapped an arm around my middle.

Ow! It hurt to be yanked up off the floor. We were heading for the stairs. I should—

The cyborg got two steps before Sean's sword tapped it on the calf. I got a painful, twitching jolt. It stumbled and collapsed, dropping me to the floor.

Once again, the invisible field in my armor kept me from the same painful crash it suffered, and my brain had finally caught up. Looking back at my friends, I asked loudly, "So, are you heroes or not?"

A half second later, the cyborg lurched to its feet. As it did, one of its hands grabbed my ankle. The other swung the loaded crossbow toward Sean.

Charlotte's beads swarmed out of her pockets, but otherwise she stood there, with a stunned and horrified look on her face, the way any sane person would react. Cassie and Marcia were both already charging, Marcia ahead, with electricity flickering all over Cassie's body.

Sean did his kitty stagger, diving and rolling out of the way of the crossbow. It tracked back toward my friends, and Charlotte and Cassie also dove out of the way.

Marcia didn't bother, and the cyborg pointed her crossbow at that clear target, and pulled the trigger. The bolt might have teleported for all I could tell. At the same time as I heard the *thwunk* of the string, I heard the gristly *splat* and saw the base of the shaft sticking out of Marcia's chest. Just the base. She skidded to her knees, bent over, and I saw the point sticking out of her back, padded with red gunk and in the middle of a rapidly spreading crimson stain.

Sean was up, with his electrified sword out. Cassie was closing. Without time to cock her crossbow again, the cyborg had to let me go and backtrack. I crawled, then scrambled to Marcia, still on her knees, upper body bobbing as hands clumsily pawed at the arrow. Up close, it was horribly obvious how the bolt stuck through her chest just left of center. It had to be piercing her heart.

But she didn't die. She gurgled, and her face clenched in that look of insane hate. Her hands worked well enough for her to point at the arrow, and make a jerking motion. She managed to wheeze one word. "Out."

Desperate, I grabbed the point in back with both gloved hands, and yanked it through and out of her. It came out covered in red blood and slime.

Marcia started climbing to her feet, slow and wobbly, but rapidly gaining strength. I stared at the horrible black crossbow bolt, and more at the blood coating it. The sheer power of that Marcia's blood was outrageous. Except that looking at that red, which refused to completely run away or coagulate, it was clear that power didn't come from Marcia. She was full of some other power that came from outside her. Only the Trouble I'd distilled came from Marcia herself.

I tucked the evil arrow into one of the deep pockets inside my coat to stop it hypnotizing me. Sometimes a knowledge based super power did its thing at the worst times.

Able to look up now, I saw the cyborg throw its crossbow at Sean, hitting his forearm and knocking the sword out of the way. He didn't drop it, but she leaped in and grabbed two fists full of his costume, lifting him easily up off the ground and flinging him at Cassie. They both went down in a crackle of sparks.

A whirlwind of beads swept around the cyborg, swarming

up to cover her face. She didn't hesitate, grabbing handfuls, squeezing them, and dropping the shattered fragments.

It gave time for Sean to get back up. He leaped for her, sword out. He'd lost his cool, and his martial arts skill. Off balance, he was a sitting duck for the cyborg to lift her foot, catch him in the stomach with it, and toss him back behind her.

Except maybe Sean hadn't lost his cool, because as it shoved him past, the wide sweep of his sword hit it in the back. It wasn't a good hit. It didn't have to be. Blue-white flashed, a pop sounded, and the purple-haired, purple-clad former teenage girl dropped to the cement again.

"Cassie, now!" yelled Charlotte.

Not needing any more urging, Cassie lurched up and extended her arms. Bright bolts of lightning swarmed off of them to ground in the cyborg's body. It flopped until the lightning ran out. Then slowly, twitchily, that body started to rise again. Back on her feet, Cassie stood over the cyborg, pouring lightning into her.

This time, when it ran out, it only twitched, with no purpose or direction.

Marcia was fully on her feet, drenched in blood and growling, but there was no longer anything to attack. Cassie hunched over, breathing hard, sparks prickling randomly from her body.

Sean bounced back up next, although I saw the tightness of a wince in his shoulders. He took over for Cassie, standing with his electrified sword over the cyborg's chest.

That left me the least hurt, least tired, least stunned of anyone. It had worked. Tonika's plan of getting my friends to save me from my real enemy had worked. But I still had to finish things. Not bothering to fight the shaking in my voice, I nodded my head deeply. "You are heroes. You did the right thing. Now I'm going to do the right thing. This girl is as much victim as villain. Organism One did this to her. We can...no. No one can undo the damage, but we can free her from Organism One's control."

That was the last thing I desperately hoped Tonika was right about.

"I can't allow that," declared Charlotte, recovering from her own shock as I staggered over to Sean. Her beads clattered and rolled across the floor again. Behind her stood poor Aikamieli, who was even worse at this than me, and had done nothing but stare the whole time.

I at least had learned how to pretend. Giving Charlotte a sharp stare, I asked pointedly, "Do you have a way to free her?"

She pointed a thumb back at the corner of the garage. "No, but there are adult heroes right back there. We can catch all three of you and hand you over to them."

Cassie blinked blearily, and sparked, but that was it. She was out of this. Marcia had her fists clenched and started forward as gleefully as if the fight had just started. Charlotte's beads spun up into the air, obscuring everything.

They didn't hide Sean's disappearance. Beads clattered and smacked madly as he darted from his place in a blur. I could catch only his slowest, most distinct movements. He kicked Charlotte's legs out from under her, and slapped the side of her head as she fell. Then he blurred back to me, and hoisted the cyborg off the ground.

I pulled out the purple book. It fell open to Cleric's lair, where I'd put a bookmark.

"Not again!" shouted Marcia in despair, but she was much too late. I shoved the book's window against the cyborg's face. When she disappeared, I did the same to Sean's mask. He vanished, and I smacked the book up over my own face.

CHAPTER TWENTY

We stumbled and bounced apart as the book tried to teleport us into the same spot. I staggered, but didn't fall down. Instead I yelled, "CLERIC!" at the top of my lungs.

He rushed into the room in less than a second, an old-fashioned medical kit with a red cross on it in one hand, and his sword out in the other. "So, there was trouble—what is this?"

Cleric drew up short, and as he looked down at the purple clad cyborg, whose movements were more fumbling than twitching now, I blurted, "Organism One did this to her because he's angry with Tyrant for hiring kids."

Confusion did not so much as flicker on his face. He understood everything, and studied the cyborg with intent, expert eyes. His voice dropped, quiet but sharp. "You knew, and you didn't tell me."

The cyborg got an arm underneath her, and pushed clumsily up to her feet. Incredible. Organism One earned its reputation for building death machines. But I had brought this machine to a master. Books flew off of bookshelves, wrapping around her arms and legs, holding her still. With her immobilized,

Sean gave her a tap in the middle of the back with his sword. It flashed, and she jerked, then lay still in Cleric's literary grip.

Setting aside his sword, Cleric held a hand up to Sean instead. "Don't do that again. You may do permanent damage. Burning what's left of her natural brain would be difficult enough to heal, but there are only two individuals I know of who can repair implants on this level. Neither Organism One nor the First Horseman are likely to be helpful."

Cleric was upset. By now, I knew him well enough to see it in the way he slipped into teaching mode.

I clasped my hands and got to the point. "We brought her to you because you can remove her programming, right? You said The Book can wipe memories."

"Fetch a chair and The Book," Cleric answered, staring at the girl. Her head was already back up, pink plastic eyes fixed on his. He was having to focus to hold her still, even with so many books. Her modified body was strong.

Sean got the chair. I grabbed The Book, which had been sitting on its pedestal, pushed into a corner. As I carried it over, it snapped open to a pair of blank pages.

"Close it over her head, and it will erase all knowledge of Organism One," he ordered, still staring at the girl.

She did not like that. She jerked, pulling at the books on her arms and legs, twisting her head and whipping at me with her photoelectric fiber hair. That at least was an ineffectual weapon, and I slammed the book closed over her head like I was trying to squash a fly.

The effect was immediate. Her whole body jerked, going stiff. She twitched, erratically. After maybe ten seconds, she slumped into the grip of Cleric's books. Gently, he turned her around and sat her in the chair Sean had brought forward.

I looked at the page her memories were copied onto. This set look more like circuits than ever, minute and complex. So complex I would swear they were growing.

Wait, they were growing. I recognized that just in time for Cleric to reach over me, grab that page in his fist, and rip it free. I stared at him in shock. He'd just damaged his precious Book, and I could not replace a page.

Flicking on one of my Bunsen burners, he set the page on fire, then dropped it into a crucible to carefully watch it burn to ash.

All the while, he explained, "The Book does not direct what it steals itself. It takes the information the subject is thinking about. Usually that means you only have to tell someone what you want to take, and they provide it automatically without knowing they're betraying themselves. Even if they know, very few have the self-control to change the result."

With the page completely destroyed, Cleric walked more calmly over to the cyborg girl. Crouching, he laid a gentle hand on her shoulder. His mouth tightened in sympathetic pain as he studied her face. So softly I could barely hear, he asked, "Are you okay, young lady? What's your name?"

"I don't know," she answered, as bleary as someone half-asleep, although her eyes were wide open. Her voice still held that mechanical edge, but had taken on more human weak sadness. "I feel so empty."

Cleric stroked her fake hair, whispered into her ear, and stood up. His face grew tight, a grimace of moral revulsion and agonized pity. To us, now, he said, "She must have been an unwilling convert. Organism One took everything from her."

"What will happen to her?" I asked, meek and hushed.

His face slowly easing back to merely grim solemnity, Cleric answered, "I will contact the superheroes. They will understand that this is more important than their dislike of me. Someone will find a way to take care of her, and something will be done about Organism One's actions. I will not be part of either of those processes. It is not my place, nor would I be trusted. Whatever is done, I suspect it will be done quietly to prevent a panic."

Looking down at the dazed cyborg, he slid his hand over her face, closing her eyes, and whispered, "Rest. I will take you to a bed. The worst is over, and every day will be a better one from now on."

Her eyes remained closed. He bent down, slipped his arms around her, and lifted the cyborg girl up to cradle her against his chest. Cleric was a very fit man, but he did so with obvious effort. Her body full of metal was heavy.

Face still bleak, he looked down at me and Sean. His tone turned almost emotionless. "Before anything else, I want you to know that I am proud of you for saving this child. I am also angry with you for hiding this from me. You abused my trust, and I want you to think about that. I don't have time to talk to you about it right now. She needs my care."

"Go," he added, one emphatic word tacked onto an otherwise flat and blank statement.

We left. Outside, in the warm late summer night, on a sporadically lit street amidst the brighter neighborhoods on the edge of downtown Los Angeles, Sean and I stood and tried to...I didn't know. Get a grip on the world again.

Pulling off my gauntlet, I rubbed my face with a sweaty hand. My voice croaked. "I don't know how I feel. Less afraid. I hope Tonika was right, and this was enough adventure that my friends won't care about chasing me anymore."

Sean reached up and wrestled with his white, stuffed leather bird mask. After a few seconds he managed to pull it up to his forehead, and let the hood of his robe hang back. For the first time in what felt like hours, he spoke, with a groan and a lot more energy than I felt. "Keeping quiet that whole time was hard. I can't tell you how relieved I am you gave me those potions. I need so much more practice to go with my knowledge. That speed boost turned the tide, and without the healing I'm sure I'd have broken ribs. But. But! Tonika's plan worked. I can't wait to tell her." Enthusiastic now, he grinned at me and pressed, "Call my phone and ask her exactly where to meet up!"

I wished I had his energy. I could down a blue potion, but I was more emotionally than physically drained. Other people had done the actual work. Still, it was a phone call. "No problem," I assured him, because it wasn't. I brought out my phone, turned it back on because I wasn't going to be taking calls during a mission either, and in about thirty seconds pushed Sean's name on my contacts list.

"The number you have dialed has been disconnected or is no longer in service," a computerized voice announced.

Sean jerked. I held out the phone to him. He scanned the

screen, and got no relief. Clearly, it had been his number. Head tilting from side to side, he asked in increasing agitation, "Did I forget to charge my phone when I gave it to her? Even if something had happened to Tonika, a thief wouldn't bother turning off the phone, right?"

He started walking, walking fast, and I scurried to keep up. We were still in costume, and he pulled his plague doctor mask back into place. I donned my gauntlet. My coat flapped around me, less comfortable than usual because it still had the arrow and flask of Catalyst in its inner pockets. Thanks to my shock absorber field, the latter was still intact.

We hurried back down to the corner where we'd left Tonika, and saw no sign of her. Sean looked around again, even more sharply. His muffled voice sounded from behind the mask. "Maybe she went up to USC where her parents think she is?"

I had no idea what to do, so I glanced at my Trouble Magnet out of mindless reflex—and wheezed.

Its needle pointed straight into Exposition Park.

A terrible thought stole over me. Grabbing Sean's arm, I showed him the needle and said hoarsely, "The cyborg girl. She didn't kidnap herself."

Sean's back arched and he went stiff. Then he grabbed my arm back, and as the light changed dragged me across the street. His voice turned noticeably higher. "We have to save her!"

I tugged, but, well, Sean was stronger than me. "We have to go get Cleric!"

"There's no time! How long have we been gone? An hour? Two hours? How long does it take to rip out someone's mind like Organism One did to that other girl?" Sean's voice got higher and his words faster as his panicked words sprayed out.

When we reached the other side, where all the bushes formed a fence at the corner of the park, I dug in my heels. Sean wasn't going to listen to reason, and I couldn't blame him. I also couldn't leave him. If I did, I was sure I would never see him again. Or at least, I wouldn't see him human again.

So, I offered, "We'll walk around a little and watch the compass. We're only guessing it's pointing to something that has anything to do with us. There could be a huge super powered battle in Thousand Oaks deciding the fate of the world for all we know."

That sounded reasonable, and Sean slowed down, a little. I held my arm out as we took the first sidewalk turn into Exposition Park's many paths. The park wasn't dead at this hour, especially near the street, but we only got a few curious stares. After all, the only weird thing about our costumes was our height.

The needle moved. Oh, someone help us, because the needle moved visibly as we walked. The thing it was pointing at wasn't just in the park, it was nearby. As soon as that became clear Sean drew his sword, and I loaded an itching cloud vial into my gauntlet.

The needle pointed down by the aerospace museum, where the bubble fountain lay. A kid and an adult stood there, under its little brick pagoda. The needle didn't quite point at them. As we got closer, that became clearer.

My breathing sped up. I hadn't gotten a chance to completely calm down from the last crisis.

Now the needle pointed down a set of crisscrossing paths that maneuvered down a steep hill, which was almost a cliff. Bushes filled in the gaps between those tilted paths. Anything could be hiding in them. One of his hands around my wrist, the other holding his sword out, Sean followed the compass down anyway, until it twisted obviously at the bottom. We were right next to its target, with only some underbrush in the way.

Rounding a bush taller than us, we saw it: A gate, behind the underbrush, set into the hill. Thinly spaced metal bars blocked off the entrance to a tunnel almost exactly our height, closed with a normal and obvious key lock. Back inside, at full night now, I saw only darkness.

"We should really go get Cleric now," I tried again. Which made me more cowardly, that I didn't want to meet what was in there, or that I didn't want to see Cleric disappointed in me again?

Sean wasn't listening. He charged through the bushes, grabbing the bars and shaking them. His masked face turned down to the lock, and I heard him mutter, "Lockpicks. Why didn't I bring lockpicks?" before he leaned in, pressed his beak between the bars, and yelled, "Toniiiikaaaaa!"

The word disappeared into the cement-lined darkness.

He was freaking out. Anxiously, I crept in and put my hands on his shoulders, urging, "Sean, calm down. We know where she is, or at least where the danger is. It will be okay if we think our way through this."

Ignoring me, Sean slapped his hand over the bandolier built into the costume on his left side, and pulled out the orange potion. No, he was listening to me, alright, and taking it the worst possible way. He slid the strength potion into the hidden slot in his mask, and two seconds later ripped the gate off its hinges with a loud *thwung*.

Tossing the bent heap of bars out of the way, he charged into the tunnel, and I scurried after him. "Stop! Wait! Let's talk about this! We need a plan!" I shouted, while digging in my pants for my phone again. I could at least have a light.

Before I could pull it out, everything went pitch black. The park and city lights were gone, I felt the rough cement under my boots, and brushing against my dreadlocks in this short corridor. I smelled dirt and faint traces of cleaning chemicals.

I heard Tonika's voice whisper, "Got you."

And that was the last I remembered.

Chapter Twenty-One

I woke up trying not to retch.

At least I did wake up.

Yuck. I felt awful, aching and with a brain like oatmeal mixed with marshmallow, left to dry in a ditch, and then dropped in a peat bog. All of my muscles ached, including stuff like my neck and eyebrows that hardly ever hurt. My stomach twisted again, and thank goodness I hadn't eaten since lunch at school, because it would have come up.

Light was back, in a big way. I blinked goopy eyes and peered around the new room. I knew I'd been moved while I was unconscious, because whatever this hard, white stuff was that the floor was made of, it wasn't cement.

That hard white stuff made up most of the surfaces, floor, ceiling, and walls of this room. The other major accent colors were silver, and splashes of red here and there. All of it pierced my blurry eyes and it took a minute to take everything in.

First, I was lying on the floor of a cage, not of bars but transparent plastic walls with a few airholes no wider than a finger. The room wasn't all that big, and if I'd stretched out rather than crumpled up, I wouldn't have fit in the cage. On the wall opposite the cages I saw a grey metal door, some counters, a number of boxes too shallow to be called cupboards set into the wall, and stacked into the corner two freaky mechanical things made almost entirely of long, folded together metal legs.

Symbols generously decorated everything, all glaring red and unintelligible. Some were downright goofy, like a circle with little sharp arrows above it like ears, and lines sticking out from the side like whiskers. Another contender for ridiculousness would be the ovals with dots in the middle flanking a zigzag. Clumped together like they were, the markings reminded me of words, even sentences, more than mere symbols.

Sean sat in the cell next to mine, sitting against the back wall but already awake. The cell past him was empty. We had both been stripped down to our underwear, but I felt too gross to care, and I'm sure so did he.

Our costumes and equipment sat on the counter across from us, less than ten feet away. With the plastic barrier between us, they might as well be in the asteroid belt, frozen in eternal ice on Ceres.

Sean must have seen me move, and asked croakily, "Are you awake?"

I gave him the most honest answer I could. "Blaarg."

He took a few deep breaths, and rubbed both hands over his face before saying, "I think we were knockout gassed. That's incredibly dangerous, but it worked and we're still alive."

Pushing against the blandly alien white stuff that made up the floor, I forced myself to sit up. Ugh. This cell was so small. We were locked in underground. It—

Calm down, Magenta. Don't panic. You've never been claustrophobic before, and now is not the time to start.

Also, I had plenty else to panic about. Wrestling for calmness, I asked the boy who had been awake longer, "What are we going to do?"

"Escape," answered Sean immediately, then as soon as the word was out, he grimaced, wrapping his arms over his face. His spine bowed forward, and he croaked, "Except we can't. It's these memories. The ones The Book put in my head. They keep telling me what to do when locked up, but those are different cages than this. I...I even know what to do if I was locked in a Circle of Metrion."

Unwrapping his arms, Sean sat up again, holding out his hands and staring at them in horror. His fingers, curled up like claws, twitched irregularly. "Look at that. I'm not doing it. They want to draw the sigils to corrupt and subsume the circle. If I had chalk, or any kind of pigment, I couldn't stop myself from doing it. My brain is crawling with thoughts like that. I should have stored a potion useful for escape somewhere I could get to it after being stripped. I should have brought a light and checked for traps. I should—"

I cut him off, squeezing my eyes shut and clenching my teeth at my own painful confession. "I should have gone back and gotten Cleric."

Gripping his knees now, Sean gave me a frown of miserable guilt, like an all too sincere tragedy mask. His voice turned quiet again. "I wanted to save Tonika. To be her hero. A hero doesn't go back for help."

I pulled myself over to the wall between our cells, laying my hand to it, fingers spread, in the only gesture of comfort I had to give. Maybe the truth would help, bleak as it was. "I was there, Sean. You weren't trying to show off. You were scared for her, and I bet you still are."

He didn't look at me, but he did go quiet for a minute, leaning forward to clasp his hands in his lap and stare at them. When he answered, the edge of panic was gone, replaced by the softness of despair. "We've been unconscious for hours. It could have been a whole day. If Tonika is here, it's too late. I'm just praying I was wrong, that we jumped to conclusions and she's at home and I sacrificed your life and mine for nothing."

Oh, ugh. I winced, my stomach knotting again as I made myself tell him, "I heard her voice before we were gassed. We were already too late then."

Sean started shaking. Then I realized so was I, and I grabbed my shoulders to hold it down. Tonika had been altered like that poor amnesiac monster we'd freed, but hadn't been able to save. She was a cyborg slave to Organism One now. The smartest person I'd ever met, nearly the nicest, and certainly the sanest person who'd ever actually liked me had been murdered and replaced for trying to help me. She was gone.

Hands squeezed together until they turned white, his voice hoarse and droning, Sean said, "Tonika is why I did all of this. I've never met anyone like her. She was exceptional. She left all the kids who had actual powers behind. I wanted to be worthy of her. She gave me something to aspire to."

Sean went silent. I leaned my shoulder against the plastic barrier, and after what felt like a long time said, "I wanted to make an impression. To be remembered. If not for who I was, then what I'd done. All my life it's been hard to even make friends. A first impression is the only kind I get to make."

With a touch of humor—bitter humor, but it was better than misery—Sean confessed, "It took me awhile to figure out you were the only person who could be in the next cell."

That was way too normal a confession to hurt right now, so I just leaned against the clear plastic and waited. Eventually, Sean said, distant and mournful, "On our second date, before we even called it a date, I sat and watched her do her homework. That's it, that's all I did. I've never seen anyone fly through answers like that. Then some pigeons landed nearby, and she explained—"

He broke off, grabbing his head, grimacing and snarling. "I'm sorry. I'm trying not to recite some guy's idea of how a dragon's circulatory system works. I don't—I don't even know the guy's name. It's like they're my memories."

I grimaced myself, looking over at him, feeling an extra tug of guilt on top of everything else. "The Book really messed you up, didn't it?"

Sean extended one arm toward me, palm out in refusal, even as his other hand still clutched his head. He wheezed, "I love it most of the time, but..." His whole body relaxed at once. He sat up woozily, took a long, deep breath, and let it out. His eyes were puffy and red now, and tear tracks streaked his cheeks. But he was calm. "...yeah. I was looking forward to getting my learner's permit next year. Now I look at a car's controls, and they might as well be an alien spaceship's. But if I were put in an alien spaceship, I would know how to figure its controls out."

He stood up, slowly but steady. Gawky without his costume, a pale, brown-haired boy not particularly in or out of shape, he walked over to the front of his cage and ran his fingers over the air holes. Looking past them at the far wall, Sean mused, "I can even read the labels."

My head lifted and I sat up straight in sheer surprise. "What, really?"

He nodded, and his cheek twitched up in a hint of bitter smirk. "Yes. They're in Ancient Catlantian, which is a fake language made up in the nineteen twenties by a woman who used her psychic powers to invent a whole imaginary history to please rich European white supremacists. Tonika would have guesses why Organism One is using that language."

Sean grimaced again, his knees bending, weight leaning into the hand on the wall to keep him from folding up and collapsing. His body trembled for two long seconds, until it relaxed enough for him to gasp and finish, "Now she doesn't need to guess."

I climbed to my own feet. Stepping up to the front of the cell, I thumped my fist against the divider. "We'll keep trying. We'll keep trying until we get circuits implanted in our brains, and then we'll still keep trying. If anyone can rescue Tonika, it's you," I lied.

Listen to me. I sounded so vehement. I didn't believe a word of it. No wonder the compass had pointed straight here. This was Trouble I couldn't believe I would get out of.

The door opened, sliding into the wall rather than in or out. Tonika walked in. She looked almost normal, in the same bland blouse and skirt and sneakers as before. She had the same brown eyes, and black hair. The only horrible difference was a fine circuit grid of pink-purple metal around the back of her neck, running up into her hair. In places, it visibly penetrated her skin.

"Tonika!" I yelled, rushing forward to slam my fists against the barrier. Sean said nothing, frozen, staring at her.

Tonika gave me a confused, searching stare. "You are not the Pawn I captured." She followed up by looking around the room, perhaps for signs of escape.

My fists clenched harder, and my already aching heart tightened until it was hard to breathe. The real Tonika would have recognized me. Raggedly, I told the thing wearing her, "It's too late. You've erased her."

She looked back at me, still searching, and the confusion slowly faded. The thing put one of Tonika's hands on Tonika's hip. Except for that confidence, she sounded so much the same. "You continue to misunderstand my Master's motivations. Ironic, given who you serve. I am integrating slowly and with interruptions, because Organism One does not want me to be a mere host shell. It is so unusual to find anything in an unenhanced human brain superior to what he can build that I am now a higher priority than you for full integration rather than replacement."

Her gaze lingered on me for another second, unreadable. Contempt? Regret? Hope? Then she turned her attention to Sean, stepping up to his cell and placing her hands on the plastic. For him, she softened her voice, with just a touch of pleading. "You are both useful. You'll be altered exactly as much as required to make you loyal. If you accept this and join willingly, we'll be together. Not as mindless slaves, not a monkey's paw style word trick. Together the way we want to be. The more you cooperate, the better that togetherness will be."

"Stop it!" I screamed at her. "How can you do this to him? He worships you!"

Now she put both hands on her hips, incensed, and answered me, "Because Organism One wants you to join, so that's my goal." She sounded completely like her normal self, except her confidence was as alien as a sane Marcia. Her left hand lifted, and flapped at the machines folded up in the corner. She muttered some gibberish, without even looking.

With whisper-soft motor noises, it spread its pointy legs and climbed up onto the counter, scuttling over the surface to one of the sealed panels. A leg lifted toward one of the symbols next to the counter.

Tonika's neck tilted sharply to the side, glaring at the robot accusingly. At the top center of its star-shaped body a pink light went on, and it returned to its place and closed its legs together again. The light went off, and it stood immobile exactly where it had before.

I wasn't sure I could handle the hope, but it clawed its way up inside me anyway, and I heard my voice waver in what was almost a sob. "You're still in there, Tonika. You're still fighting."

She sighed, a little exasperated, but more weary than angry. "Of course. That I'm able to booby trap my own thoughts this way, with no training or genetic anomalies, is what makes me so valuable. My Master doesn't want to remove me, only render me compliant. As such, I clearly need another round of implants to establish more sophisticated control, and I might as well begin my body enhancements so it can catch up with my brain." Touching her fingertips to the plastic opposite me, she looked between me and Sean. Solemnly rather than mechanically, she finished, "When I return, you will get your first round of control implants. I suggest you use that time to think about what will be best for you after they're installed."

She left, pulling the handle to the door aside, pulling it into the wall and letting it slide back into place behind her.

Anxious about what I'd see, I looked over at Sean. He'd been silent this whole time. Now he stood in front of the wall where Tonika had spoken to him, his forehead leaning against the plastic and hand over his eyes.

"Sean…." I tried, not sure what to say.

"I'm worthless," he rasped.

"You will save her. Somehow," I insisted. There was still some Tonika left. A lot of Tonika left.

He shook his head gently, whispered, "No. She saved me," and added something in a squeaky, yowling language.

It sounded a lot like the gibberish Tonika had used moments ago, and the very same robot unfolded, returned to the counter, stabbed its foot into a painted symbol on the wall, and twisted. Silently, the cage walls descended into the floor.

Catlantian. The robots took orders in Catlantian. But they also took orders by remote control. Before the plastic wall was fully down, Sean jumped over it, lunging for our costumes. He grabbed his sword, and stabbed it into the robot. Wires crackled and snapped. Sparks flew. It fell off the counter into a heap.

A half second behind him, I pulled two of my glue vials out of the plague doctor costume's bandoliers. The pink light on the other robot went on just before I shoved the tubes into cracks in its joints. As the legs unfolded, glass shattered, and green goop splashed through those joints. Unable to balance, or move more than twitch, it also fell over on its side.

"Whatever is in control of this complex knows we're out," Sean declared. His eyes scanned over the wall, and its various signs, and his lips moved, silently shaping those words. Stepping over to the door, he flattened his hand against some of the symbols, and pulled left. They slid, as if he'd been swiping a screen, and metal bars slammed home over the door.

I said, "We need to get dressed. Fast. We need our equipment and we may need armor."

That got no argument. We struggled into our equipment as fast as possible. I didn't know how to help Sean with his costume, but if there were problems, I couldn't spot them and he didn't mention them. He did comment, "I need to activate the gas mask in my costume. If I'd thought to do that the first time—"

I cut that off, squeezing his black leather-clad shoulder. "You can't become a master swordfighter in a few days, no matter what's been put in your brain. You can't become a master dungeon delver, either."

Sean smirked, honest amusement touching his grim expression. Then he slid the mask up over his face.

We opened the door, my gauntlet and his sword ready. Nothing waited for us outside, so we peeked, then stepped watchfully out into an empty hallway.

The hall was surprisingly unimpressive. I didn't know what I expected, but a white donut ring around the diameter of a single segment bus was not it. In the half I could see it had only three doors, including the one we'd come out of, all on the outer wall. Three doors, and a doorless stairway leading up and away. From here, I could see the white unidentifiable stuff that made up the complex give way to cement in the stairway, so that had to lead to the entrance tunnel.

There still were a whole lot of red Catlantian signs everywhere, especially around the doors.

Sean voiced half my thoughts. "This base isn't very big."

I voiced the other half. "It seems stupid to leave instruction signs everywhere for robots. That's what those are, right?"

He stood still, sword pointed down one direction of the hall, while I watched the other. After a couple of seconds of silence, he said, "I know what that means. It means this place is autonomous, and is intended for visiting agents rather than one computer controller."

His masked face turned, perhaps looking at the signs, or noticing things I didn't have the Book-implanted knowledge to know were important. Thoughtfully, he added, "It's a way station, not a base."

I tapped his shoulder with my un-gauntleted hand. "Tonika."

Sean bunched up his shoulders and shook his head violently, then relaxed and let out a sigh. "Yes. False memories dragging him around."

We started moving, slowly, with Sean reading the signs we passed and me watching our back with hopefully sufficient paranoia. No shadows did suspicious things. No doors even budged. The signs stayed motionless and continued being signs.

"I don't know what I'm looking for!" growled Sean in frustration. Pointing his sword at the inner wall, he added more in desperate hope than epiphany, "Maybe...that?"

Trying not to abandon my watch, I checked. We'd circled around to exactly the opposite side of the stairs, and found the one single door on the inner wall. It was slightly bigger than the others, and had its own Catlantian signs I couldn't read.

This door didn't have a handle, a fact I didn't notice until Sean swiped a gloved thumb down a line of symbols, and it opened by itself.

The center chamber was...different. Older. The floor and ceiling were plain, worn, badly stained concrete. A machine stuck out of the ceiling, mostly a conical labyrinth of copper pipes with its blunt point halfway down to the floor. I'd have to stoop to walk under it, but it really only took up the center of the room. Inside that mass of piping, a gleaming, beautifully higher tech machine filled the empty spaces.

This had to be the maintenance room for the bubble fountain. Organism One had built a base around it.

The only other thing in the room grabbed my attention and held it. Tonika lay face-up on a surgical table made out of the white stuff, and the table grew out of a nest of bumps and blocks. Out of most of them reared thin metal arms tipped with tools or holding implants, like the arm gripping a mass of purple fiber-optic hair, two holding purple plastic eyes, and another near her left arm with a coppery rod inlaid with lots of little machines I couldn't identify, perfectly sized to replace Tonika's left arm.

We were early. She hadn't been cut open yet, despite a few knives and a whirring buzzsaw blade hovering over her body.

We weren't early enough. She had also been stripped down to her underwear, her scalp shaved clean, and her head hung over the end of the table with a dozen tiny surgical arms stuck into the plug holes left by the circuitry grown over her neck and skull.

Sean must have taken another sip of the speed potion. He bolted forward like the wind, chopping at the knives and the saw blade, hacking them apart with the edge rather than the electric shock.

The bubble machine on the ceiling spun. With an almost musically high-pitched gurgle it blew a stream of iridescent bubbles at Sean. He dodged at merely human speed, staggering away with those clumsy-looking Drunken Kitty Style steps.

The stream hit the shiny white wall, and the popping bubbles left a charred black stain. The bubble spout fired again, and again Sean dodged. This time, halfway through the stagger he lunged forward with super speed, black skirt whipping around his legs as he slid underneath the machine, twisted his sword around, and stabbed it into the gleaming high-tech stuff between the pipes. He must have picked his spot carefully, because a whole series of pops sounded through the machine, the air suddenly smelled like burnt rubber, and the bubble machine went still.

He leaned against it, panting audibly even through the muzzling mask. A deft hand popped one of my blue potions out of its slot in his costume.

Alarms went off in my head, and I shouted, "Don't! It will interact with the knockout gas withdrawal and poison you!"

The arms of the surgical bed began moving again. I grabbed the scalpel-tipped arms, yanking desperately. Two of the thinner arms snapped. Two others I wrestled with, keeping them away from Tonika's skin.

Tonika's mouth didn't move, but her voice resonated from somewhere, emphatically relieved. "Thank you both. That simplistic AI caretaker was hampering my ability to take advantage of my own brain and bring myself under control."

Under control. I'd been fighting the bladed arms, but now I looked down. The network of arms probing the back of Tonika's head fluttered, busily at work doing something horrible inside her skull. I couldn't pull them out. They'd destroy Tonika's brain in the process!

"Duck!" yelled Sean.

It took me half a second to register the command. Half a second during which he sprinted toward me. I ducked, and felt something metal scratch at the back of my neck, but my dreadlocks got in the way and I dived for the floor faster than it.

Sean arrived, grabbing an arm that had snuck up behind me, holding a purple mesh like the one embedded in Tonika's neck, and in that poor cyborg we'd rescued earlier. He hacked the arm in two with his sword, and flung the mesh to the opposite side of the room.

Picking myself back up, I joined Sean in staring at the silent Tonika, still except for the tiny arms dancing around the back of her skull.

"What do we do?" he asked, voice sharp with horror.

"I was hoping something in the memories The Book gave you would know," I answered helplessly.

Sounding as calm as her unconscious body looked, Tonika's voice said, "I was hoping you'd surrender and join me."

With a loud *clack*, the chamber's single door snapped open. A simple, scrawny humanoid skeleton stood in the entrance, looking more like a black skeleton than anything else, but without any attempt to sculpt realistic bones. It wasn't creepy, but it was plenty threatening as it stepped inside, staring at us with glowing purple eyes and extending its arms.

Behind it, two of those bug bots, each about half my height, crawled around the door jam.

The skeleton wasn't fast, or agile. Sean charged forward, stabbing with his sword, and the tip caught it in a joint between rounded chest and tubular stomach. Electricity crackled, and the robot flopped. I raised my gauntlet, pointed it at the bugs, and fired the only two vials I had loaded. Both were glue, and to my jolting surprise, both hit. The spray of green muck welded them helplessly to the wall.

If only they'd been alone. More of the bots with the poky legs, which looked like daddy-long-legs more than anything else, scurried in through the doorway. I saw two of the humanoid bots behind them, and there could be who knows how many filling the curving hall.

Sean hacked away. I had to help somehow. How? I was out of glue. Robots wouldn't care about my itching powder. I could use it on Tonika? No, she was trying to do self-surgery. The computer parts of her must be immune to pain.

My skin crawled at how sincerely concerned her voice sounded as it came out of the walls. "Sean, Magenta, it's okay. I'm not going to hurt you. I'm happy the way I am now, and you will be, too."

"Uh-huh. So happy you're sabotaging yourself," Sean barked back.

None of the robots were all that speedy, but there were a lot of them. Sean's electrified sword was keeping them bottled up in the doorway, until one of the bug-bots dropped off the door's overhang onto his sword, wrapping its legs around the blade. White and blue electricity flickered, and flickered more. The bug made a sizzling sound. But it didn't let go, and dragged the blade to the floor.

Behind it, two skeleton bots charged clumsily forward, grabbing at Sean and forcing him to roll backward, letting the mechanical servants flood into the room.

I couldn't think of anything to do. I wasn't a hero or a villain. I was an errand girl. A performer at most. But I had to do something! What? What!? I would go down wrestling alongside

Sean if I had to, but wasn't there anything smarter I could do?

No answer came to me. Instead, crisp white paper airplanes flew through the doorway. I boggled at them, until two hit the humanoid robots, scrunched up, and wriggled into the joints of its skull. Whatever they jammed, the bots stopped attacking and staggered like blind drunks. The other airplanes latched onto bug-bots, lifting them off the floor and smacking them against each other, jamming their legs and breaking off bits.

All of the sheets of paper had writing on them. More fluttered in, with the ragged edged look of pages torn out of books. They snapped around my arms and legs, pinning them in place. The paper lifted me off of the floor, and yanked me forward.

Cleric stepped into the doorway, fully armored, his face cold and angry, but with a thoughtful anger rather than uncontrolled rage. He held his sword in one hand, and wore a big backpack from which papers flew in a cloud, burying robots. The papers did that without his attention. His eyes fixed on me, and when the pages binding my arms and legs brought me before him, he laid a strong, sure, black-gloved hand on my scalp and bent my head down.

When he didn't find a purple mesh there, he sighed, closed his eyes for a single second, and whispered, "Thank you, Lord."

The pages let me go. I landed on my feet, and The Book flew out of Cleric's backpack, dropping into my arms. As I caught it, he threw his sword to Sean, grabbed the handle of the electric sword, and swung it like a golf club into a bug-bot and then a skeleton-bot coming through the door. The second hit scraped the clinging bug-bot off the blade.

He and Sean went to work. The unelectrified blade wasn't a great weapon, but the robots weren't great fighters. He knocked them away, and a few blows sliced off limbs, rendering the bots even more ineffectual. Cleric dispatched robots with swift, methodical skill, his cloud of papers holding them back so they couldn't swarm either supervillain or Pawns. One stab each disabled robots again and again and again. There were a lot of them, but he and Sean were working steadily through the horde.

Except "Steadily" wasn't good enough. Still scared, I

shouted, "Tonika is running out of time!"

"Jam something in the servos. Limit their movement," Cleric shouted back.

Just having instructions hit me like a pillow-case stuffed with a hundred pounds of relief. Dropping to my knees, I found the slots the brain probes came out of in the white surgical machine. Pulling the crossbow bolt out of my pocket, I stabbed the tip into one of those slots, angled it across to block most of the other arms, and jammed the Catalyst bottle between arrow and two other arms. It didn't completely stop their work, but it very visibly slowed the process down.

As I did, I screwed up my nose at the blood dripping from the arrow. The sheer power of Marcia's heart's blood was awe inspiring. The blood hadn't dried, caked into goo, or even run out. It still dripped from the shaft and point as if I had only pulled it out of Marcia seconds ago.

Pulling some of the purple fiberoptic hair out of the arm holding it, I threaded that through the arms in a tangled mess, restricting them further. They moved slowly now, in tiny little stabs, but hadn't stopped, and I couldn't do any better.

The one thing I'd expected even less than Cleric's arrival happened. I should have been expecting it, but I watched with stunned surprise as a hand thrust into view around the edge of the doorway, grabbing a crude skeletal head and twisting. It popped right off. Following up, Kay stepped into view, picking up a bug-bot and plucking the legs off.

I'd never seen Kay fight before. It didn't look like fighting. He meandered through the mass from behind, dismantling robots like cheap, badly made furniture. None of them had a chance to even swing at him.

"Use The Book on her!" Cleric ordered, still finishing off the rapidly dwindling robot army.

The Book. Of course! I opened it up to a set of empty pages-

"Don't trust him. He's lying to you!" shouted Kay.

I froze. He sounded absolutely positive. What?

Scowling, Cleric declared sharply, "I am not. You're saying whatever will make her stop."

Chopping the head off of the last skeleton-bot, Sean leaped

over between Kay and Cleric, sword held in both hands and pointed at my brother's chest. He stabbed twice, three times, short jabs that Kay stepped easily back from out of range.

Kay looked laughably slim and young compared to the fully grown supervillain, but he looked past Sean and addressed Cleric with fully equal and cold authority. "You're not? Then you won't mind a few questions. Why are you here?"

Electric blade held low, ready but not in combat position, Cleric stared across at Kay and answered, "To save my Pawns, and that girl."

Unimpressed, Kay asked, "Because they're people? Because they're children? Or because they're Pawns? How much are you here to recover those?" He pointed at the antique Templar badges on my and Sean's chests. "Would you have saved the girl if your followers aren't in danger?"

Cleric...didn't answer. His face stayed frozen in grim disapproval.

Kay straightened up in grim victory at that silence. Low and firm, he said, "I am going to save these children, all three of them, because they're people. Not because they're tools."

Sean lifted his sword an inch, and began swaying in that way that meant he was serious and ready for a fight. Instead, Cleric slapped a hand on the boy's shoulder, pushing him gently but firmly toward me. Still almost blankly solemn, he said, "Your job is to protect her. Not me."

Kay wasn't impressed. He didn't close the gap, just fired off more questions. "So, you won't sacrifice your Pawns. Who will you sacrifice? How much collateral damage is acceptable for your mission? Is there anyone you wouldn't sacrifice if Tyrant ordered you to?"

A few papers on the floor stirred, flowing back to Cleric rather than going after Kay. I couldn't help noticing there weren't many left. The rest had been mangled clogging robot joints. Cleric's power must not have worked on paper too damaged to be a page anymore.

Seconds went by, and Cleric still didn't answer any of Kay's questions. Instead, when he spoke, he returned Kay's probing tone exactly. "Let me ask you some questions. You'll defeat me, and save that child, and that child, and that child?" He pointed to me, Sean, and Tonika in turn. "All at once? What if those are different things? You shouted to the world what your power is, The Way. You're not the first to have it. Most of its wielders came to terrible ends, because your power doesn't care, doesn't think. On the contrary, it feeds off of that detachment. So, you say you'll save the children. From what? Transformation? It's too late. Working for me? Is that really saving them, or just what you personally want? And how will you defeat me? In a fight? I'm not fighting. What are you going to do about their friend, who right now you are denying rescue?"

It was Kay's turn to not answer, but he looked much less confident than Cleric. Then his determination hardened again. "I'll free her from Organism One."

Unimpressed, Cleric snapped back immediately, "That's it? Death frees her from Organism One. Are you going to remove the cybernetics from her brain? You can, but what if that kills her? Are you going to—?"

Kay talked over him sharply. "I see what you're doing, and I will stop you now."

The seventeen-year-old superhero in the casual street clothes advanced on the fully grown supervillain in chainmail and black tabard. Kay walked slowly, steadily, and purposefully, but not tense.

"Kay, please stop!" I yelled, my voice screechily high. "With his knowledge and your power, you can save Tonika completely!"

Kay ignored me. He reached out and took Cleric's wrists. Cleric jerked. He must have started trying to fight, but with an almost casual sweep Kay twisted him around and pinned Cleric's forearms together behind his back.

My heart, my head, my whole body hurt. We'd almost gotten through this, and now everything had turned into a disaster. "Please!" I yelled again.

Kay picked up one of the damaged bug robots in one hand, and snapped it around Cleric's arms like handcuffs. It locked as if it had been made for that purpose. Maybe it had.

Sean took a step toward them, and then a faster step. I

rammed his shoulder with mine, knocking him aside, and ran over toward the fighters, wailing, "Your power doesn't know what it's doing!"

And I slammed The Book closed over the back of Kay's head.

Kay stopped. He went still, not frozen, just not doing anything. He did say, "Okay, that's weird," in a perfectly normal tone of voice.

I held the book in place for the full ten seconds, to make absolutely sure he wouldn't start fighting again. Then I slid it off.

Kay stood there, still looking quizzical, but not upset.

I was. I boiled with it, like acid filling my arteries and spilling out of my eyes as tears. Thrusting The Book up against the bound Cleric, I begged, "Please tell me you can put his knowledge back. Please!"

Cleric turned around to face me, but before I could make sense of his expression, his eyes widened in shock. "Behind you!"

I looked. Tonika was up off the bed, and walking out the door of the chamber. Sean and I had been too consumed by the fight to notice.

The papers around Cleric's feet, which hadn't stirred against Kay, swept like snakes along the floor to latch onto Tonika's feet and ankles. As she pulled against that grip, Sean dropped his sword, and grabbed her forearms in both hands from behind. She twisted and tugged against that, and he moved weirdly, clumsily, but never lost his grip. More of the Drunken Kitty Style.

I knew what to do. Opening fresh pages, I ran up while Sean and Tonika struggled, and slapped the book over her head, crying, "You can get free from Organism One's control, Tonika, I know it!"

For a few seconds she struggled harder, but couldn't get her head loose with Sean restricting her arms. Then she went still. Then she slumped against him. I counted, and at the same time as I reached ten, she fell out of The Books' grip and into his embrace. As he held her up, I turned The Book around.

Shock jolted me. Thank goodness I had picked a spot in the

middle of the blank section of The Book. The circuitry design had spread to multiple pages, and was still advancing.

I took no risks. I ripped all of them out, and more on either side, dumping the crumpled mass on the floor. The black designs kept spreading over those papers, but only those papers. The rest of The Book remained clean, and the cement floor remained merely blotchy with old stains.

Now I looked at Sean and Tonika. He held her in his arms. She lay almost limp, only her head lifted enough to rest against his chest. He slid down to the floor, cradling her in his lap. His soft, hoarse voice emerged from the mask. "Can you remember your name?"

Tonika opened her eyes, and frowned. Hesitantly, maybe a bit embarrassed, she answered, "No, but give me a minute. I'm sure I hid it somewhere." Her hands lifted and clung to his shoulders, but she still merely looked puzzled, not afraid.

Moving down the checklist of emergencies, I turned to Kay now. He was actually smiling, with his hands in his pockets casually. Just…that's all he was doing, standing and watching me, taking no action.

The robot shackles fell from Cleric's arms, and hit the floor with a loud clunk. He headed for Sean and Tonika, and as he passed me, he gave my shoulder a quick, tight squeeze. "Take care of your brother."

It was the first time I could remember him breaking anyone's secret identity.

I hadn't been waiting for permission, but getting it gave me direction again. I ran back to Kay, took his hands in both of mine, and peered up into his face. Before I could ask anything, he shook his head, and assured me, "It's okay. Me, you don't need to freak out about. It's just that in an emergency, I expect to know exactly what to do. It's weird not knowing. But there's one thing I do know."

My brother's arms extended, wrapped around me, and pulled me against his chest for a hug. Soft, gentle, warm, he murmured, "I'm not mad at you, okay?"

It took several seconds of hard breathing to keep from crying. When I was sure I wouldn't, I twisted my head back to tell Cleric, "I thought the book didn't take away powers. I thought it would interrupt him, or make him forget he had a power."

Cleric, kneeling now beside Tonika and examining the back of her head, lifted his face to give me a solemn frown. He answered with slow, careful words. "This is a crude way of using The Book, not the way it was intended, and The Way's powers are all information."

"But can you put it back?" I begged, holding out The Book.

He must have seen enough of Tonika. Cleric stood, walked over, and opened The Book to the page I'd sucked my brother's power onto. The design was just one thick, straight line of ink on the light sepia paper, with a smudged end as if it had been drawn with a finger. Staring at that, Cleric said with unmistakable admiration, "A superhuman level of information in one stroke. Yes, Magenta, I think I can put it back, and I promise that when it is safe to do so, I shall."

With that, I lay back against Kay's chest, and didn't know what to think, or to feel.

Cleric smiled, soft and concerned and, yes, approving as he told me, "You did what you thought was right when there was no time to make a good decision. I would have been proud of you either way. I hold no ill will towards The Way. He also was doing what he believed was right."

With a deep, weary sigh, the older supervillain looked up at Kay. "But your insistence on making me the villain has cost this girl—" He flapped a hand back at Tonika, "—dearly."

Shaking his head, he crossed back and laid his palm on Sean's hood. Tilting Sean's face back, Cleric told the masked boy, "I will take her to experts. She hasn't been wiped as fully as the other child."

Tonika's hands tightened on Sean's shoulders. Her puzzled frown tightening, she whispered, "There are holes in my memory, and they scare me."

Her eyes darted around the room as she clung to him. They were still her natural eyes, at least, but when they touched on me, it was only with bafflement. She didn't know who I was. I shuddered. I heard the message in Cleric's kindness, the one he didn't want to tell Sean and Tonika directly: Her lost memories were not coming back. Her implants could not be removed. She was better off than the other victim, yes. Only some of Tonika was gone forever, and we didn't know how much.

Sean squeezed her to him, lowering his white mask to press tightly to her shaved scalp. That mask hid his expression, but not the sob in his voice. "You are the bravest person I have ever met, and I am not leaving you."

Cleric patted him again. He looked between Sean and me slowly and deliberately, telling us, "I won't ask you to leave her, but I remind you both, you are free to leave my service whenever you want. If you never want to see me again, I promise you, I understand."

We stood silent. My thoughts wouldn't come together. After a few seconds, Sean answered in a tiny, weak voice, "I don't think I can do this anymore."

Cleric stroked the hood of the plague doctor costume soothingly. "You'll have to be strong a little while longer. You need to go with me to take this girl to the people who can help her."

Yet again, the weeks of working for this strange, lonely man let me recognize something he'd hidden in the compassionate, sad expression he'd been giving me and Sean. Guilt. I swallowed, and raised my voice, looking him in his light eyes. "You're not the bad guy."

Cleric jerked an inch upwards, startled. The mask of kindness fell, replaced by a tight-mouthed, sourness. Harsh, with an anger focused solely on himself, he retorted, "I put you in unacceptable danger."

I gave him an equally furious stare, jaw stuck stubbornly forward. "I'm not leaving your service."

He wrestled his face back into calm and sorrow and gentleness, but at least let it be touched by firm command. Pointing a black-gloved finger at me, he ordered, "Right now, you must deal with the consequences of your actions, good and bad. Get the portal book. Send me first, then Tonika, then Sean to my front room. After that send The Way home. You must go home last, but hurry. This place isn't safe."

I did all of that exactly as instructed. Well, not quite exactly. When I was alone, I grabbed the arrow, Catalyst, and a lock of fake purple hair before teleporting back to my bedroom.

Chapter Twenty-Two

The sudden change of scenery could be jarring, but I'd never been more grateful to see my own bedroom in my life.

Kay had taken a couple of steps away from the landing spot, so we didn't bang into each other, but now he stood there, staring into space with a puzzled frown. It took the exact amount of time for me to register that and get worried for him to snap out of it. Laying a hand on my shoulder, my brother put his finger to my lips and said softly, "Stay here."

Stay here and do what? Until when? Kay left without explaining, opening my bedroom door and closing it behind him in near silence.

In the quiet, I noticed the faint squeak of leather when I moved. Oh, right. I was still in costume! I changed into the first shirt and skirt I could grab in my closet, and shoved my costume up onto the top shelf.

I heard my father's voice out in the apartment. Kay opened my bedroom door, looking back toward the living room and saying, "I've got her."

He held out a hand, and I took it and let him lead me into

the living room. Dad stood in the middle of the room, his clothes more wrinkled than I'd ever seen, obvious bags under his eyes. He didn't let me say anything, just grabbed me in both arms, lifting me into the air and squeezing me against him. His breathing sounded rough.

With my father's head pressed to mine, I didn't see my mother until she joined the hug, arms in lumpy pajamas around us. She sounded faint with emotion as she whispered, "Oh, thank goodness."

The hug went on and on, but eventually relaxed just a bit as Dad looked up at Kay and asked, "What happened? Where did you find her?"

Normally, this would infuriate me, but for once there were benefits in being the person no one pays attention to: I didn't have to make up a story. I did have to back it up, so I listened carefully.

"She was targeted for being my sister," Kay answered simply. Ah, yes. Superheroes were allowed to have secrets.

Dad curled a hand protectively around the back of my head, and gave Kay a shocked, worried stare. "I thought you said that's not allowed."

Kay grimaced, hands in his pockets, and with his arms drawn in looked lankier than ever. He turned his face down to the shiny wooden floorboards. "It's not. The villain who did it is not going to get another chance to break the rules."

I wasn't going to say this aloud, but I was targeted for being Cleric's assistant, which wasn't against the rules. Tonika was targeted as my civilian friend, though, and that was Getting Personal. I was pretty sure. As for it happening again, that pink haired girl, if anyone ever found out her real name, might as well be dead as far as villainy was concerned. The AI that seemed to be running the show died by Sean's electrified sword. And Organism One…would not be my problem anymore.

My body had tensed up thinking about all that, and Mom and Dad squeezed me harder. I managed to wriggle my arms up enough to press my hands to my father's shoulders and push away a few inches.

"I'm okay. I'm just shaken up a little," I lied. I didn't know it was a lie until the words came out of my mouth. I was shaken up a lot, not a little. Curling into a ball, I grabbed fistfuls of my father's shirt and buried my face in it, trying to absorb the safety of being surrounded by my parents.

They responded by holding me tighter, engulfing me.

That went on for a while. Eventually, Kay said in a quiet, carefully neutral tone, "I rescued Magenta and the villain isn't coming back, but I lost my powers in the process."

Ugh. As if my heart needed to hurt worse.

My parents didn't know what to say, either. The three of us made a silent huddle until Kay decided to continue, his tone lighter, but audibly forced. "I contacted my superhero friends. They say this happens all the time. I should get my powers back, but even if I don't, I keep the scholarship. It's my reward for the good I've already done, and losing your powers in the line of duty is something the Community respects."

I couldn't see anything with a face full of my dad's chest, but I felt his arm change position, and seconds later Kay joined the group hug. I let go of one arm, wriggling it through the knot of limbs to give Kay a fierce squeeze of my own. He wasn't just being brave about this. He was being brave about this and saving my secret identity at the same time. Even without his powers, my brother was a hero to the core.

Mom left the hug, exclaiming, "They're going to be late for school!"

"We can't possibly send the kids to school after that," Dad denied, still holding me and Kay just as tight.

Kay slid free, letting himself sound more naturally weary and sore as he said, "I'll make some phone calls. Kids get caught up in hero and villain confrontations. Schools are used to it. They just need a superhero rather than doctor's note."

Slowly, with obvious reluctance, Dad let me slide down to stand on my own two feet. His face, normally only a little less slim than Kay's, looked pouched and jowly. He sighed, blinking hard and straightening up. "I'll go to work, then."

Kay gave him a hard, scolding stare. "You didn't get any sleep."

Our father shook his head, eyes closed in cynical resignation.

"Bills don't take superhero notes."

Mom yawned, holding the back of her pink flannel covered wrist over her mouth. "I didn't get any sleep, and residency programs don't like excuses either, so I'm going back to bed." She patted Kay's cheek, and gave him a tired smile. "You've proven you can take care of Magenta."

My parents disappeared back into the bedroom. Sixty seconds later Dad emerged with his briefcase, hugged me again as he passed, and went out the front door.

Kay and I were alone. I looked up at him, not sure what to say or even what to feel.

He hugged me too, a gentle, leaning forward and arms around my head hug. With the softness of someone who doesn't have the energy for anything else, he murmured, "It's okay. It will all be okay. Call me if you need me, but I think we both need sleep."

My brother was good at pretending not to be hurt. Being a superhero must have given him practice. He covered up everything but being tired as he went back to his room.

Which meant he was really, really hurt. Guilt crawled all over me like spiders, and I might have preferred actual spiders.

But I couldn't argue with his advice. I felt coiled like a spring, but with the achy tension of someone who's been through way too much in a mere couple of hours. I returned to my bedroom, lowered the shades to block out most of the early morning light, and lay down in bed without even getting undressed.

My eyes snapped open. The white ceiling and clear plastic walls…were far away, not here. All I saw was speckly spackle above me with a ceiling fan I never dared use for fear of what the breeze would do to my experiments. Dull beige walls held shelves packed with every random object I'd ever thought might be an ingredient, not high-tech panels and red Catlantian sigils.

Everything was fine. I closed my eyes again.

My eyes snapped open. Was that white...oh, not again? I wasn't getting any sleep this morning, that was clear.

Groaning, I sat up, and went looking for my textbooks. My after-school job was taking a toll on my study time. I had homework to do, and declensions to memorize. Since I felt terrible anyway, I might as well get started on the essay questions for Chemistry. Look up stuff and copy it, that was the way. It was all I could hope to do.

That went on and on, but I had energy to use up. The surprise was that I could focus. My focus ran out around one, replaced by hunger, so I went and scrounged some of the leftover beans and hot dogs stuff my dad makes, which fills the apartment with the smell of vinegar and mustard when he makes it in a huge pot.

I ate it in my room, just in case my mother or Kay came out to check on the activity. As I spooned up the chewy, sharp-tasting stuff, I wondered for the first time: How were things going at school?

My shoulders twitched, and my appetite nosedived. I did not want to think about that question.

Why not?

I shivered again. I did not want to think about that question.

Fine. I forced myself to finish eating, and cast about for what to do next.

Well, I had one chore that definitely needed doing. Dragging my chair over, I gathered my costume from where I'd shoved it up on my closet's high shelf, with the Tyrant badge on top. I definitely didn't want anyone finding that in my room.

With an armful of that and the other holding my purple book, I teleported to Cleric's defunct knick-knack shop.

I landed in shadows, which cleared quickly. The lights were out, that's all, but the papered-over windows let in enough sunlight that my eyes caught up in mere seconds. The place looked as normal as a room packed with junk and bland, tacky antiques could. The pedestal and chair we used for memory transfers were out in the middle of the floor and knocked over, but nothing else looked damaged. The walls, carpet, and furniture lacked blood stains, black char, or violence-induced dents.

Oh, yeah, blood stains. Dumping my costume on my alchemy table, I got out the lock of fake fiberoptic "hair" and put it in a vial for storage. Then I donned a latex glove and pulled the black metal crossbow bolt out of my coat's interior pocket.

Ew. Oh, gross. It was still bleeding, still gooey and wet. The pocket was a mess, but way less of a mess than it should be with that in it for eighteen hours. The blood mostly stuck to the arrow. I found a long metal box in the shop's eclectic inventory, and tucked the bolt safely away. What an incredible power occupied Marcia's blood. Did she have any idea what she'd contaminated her body with, or summoned and been possessed by, or...?

This was Marcia. Of course she knew, and she embraced the consequences. Now here I was, stealing a tiny piece of that power without knowing what I would do with it yet.

Tired of thinking at myself, I shouted, "Cleric?"

Only silence answered me, so I raised my voice. "Are you asleep? I wish I was."

Again, nothing, so I went to look. First, I checked the front door. Locked. Then I wandered back into the kitchen. A loaf of thick homemade bread and a block of cheese sat on the table, and the chunks ripped off of them were the only signs of violence so far. I looked in the refrigerator, and wrinkled my nose at the piles of raw meat Cleric was still saving for me in case I had a spontaneous craving to create life. Next to the refrigerator sat a bunch of sealed buckets of clay with a crate full of firewood on top. Next to them were a bunch of grocery bags, five of them full of apples. Aw, that was sweet. I did badly need to refill my potion stock. Being down to two health potions was not a good thing.

I wandered up the stairs, shouting, "Cleric?" again. His bedroom door stood open. The covers were a mess, and a few books and pens and clothes were scattered around the floor, but nothing had been knocked over. The bathroom looked like the tiny little bathroom it was.

He wasn't here. Oh, well. I fetched the purple book from the front room and ferried the alchemy supplies he'd bought me home, a bag at a time. On the last trip, I brought my costume back. If he wasn't there, there was no point in...no, really, I didn't have a reason. I did it anyway.

With the last bag tucked under my crude work table at home and the costume hidden badly in my closet again, I sat down on my bed and sighed. It hurt that I hadn't gotten to ask how Tonika and Sean were doing. Hurt more than I'd expected. If I had Cleric's phone number, I'd call him, but I didn't.

I tried lying down. I felt drained now, and queasy, but still not tired. Pulling out my phone, I checked the time. Okay, school was finally out, and I might not have Cleric's phone number, but I had Sean's. With a few taps I dialed him up.

Riiiiiing.

Riiiiiing.

Riiiiiing.

Riiiiiing.

Cancel call. Did Sean not have his phone with him? Was he just ignoring me?

I wouldn't blame him for that.

My phone rang, with a jingly jangly tone I hated but kept forgetting to change. Sean was getting—no, that wasn't Sean's phone number. Where had I seen that number before?

The sad truth was, I wasn't doing anything better. I accepted the call. "Hello?"

Timidly hopeful, Aikamieli asked, "I hope this is Magenta. This is Magenta, right?"

"Yes," I answered, too dumbfounded to say anything else. I caught up fast, and tacked on the only slightly less pathetic, "Why are you calling?"

His voice cracked and fluttered constantly as he answered in a rush, "Because I want to know if you're okay. A crazy pink girl who's as tough as Marcia tried to murder you! How can you expect me not to worry? I had to call as soon as I got home from school!"

Yep, dumbfounded. Dumbfounded is what I was. At least Aikamieli couldn't see my expression of slack-jawed surprise. "How did you know?"

"Because I was there when we messed with Cleric the first time. I know you hooked up with him, and you're not the girl in the black outfit who knows how to fight," he…not quite whined, but Aikamieli sounded like that by default.

Which clearly made me underestimate him. "You're smarter than you look." Wincing at how I put that, I added hastily, "Ugh, sorry."

"But are you okay?" he repeated, emphasizing each word in turn.

I lay back against my pillow and the big "husband" style cushion that held it up. Tucking my arm behind my bed, I thought about that question. "I am, sort of. Physically. It's the other people who were hurt along the way that's torturing me."

Aikamieli sighed loudly. "I get that. It's why I called. I led the ambush to you, and I've been tearing myself apart over how it turned out. What about the pink girl? Cassie hit her with so much electricity, she should be dead!"

I shook my head, not that he could see that. "She's not dead, but that mess of a situation is not your fault. None of the really bad stuff is your fault, and might be even worse if you hadn't interfered. This is all…." I hunted for words. "It's too complicated for you to take responsibility, whether you did wrong or right."

"Then maybe that applies to you, too," Aikamieli said, his squeak suddenly soft.

I grimaced, and my heart clenched. Gripping my hand over it, I forced myself to look honestly at what I'd done. Not just honestly, but with the benefit of the doubt I would give Aikamieli. Hesitantly, I admitted, "I did my best." Pause. "I'm still scared for the people who got hurt, but maybe that's not my fault. Maybe that's only the fault of the monster that thought it was okay to turn kids into cyborgs." A few more thoughts clicked into place, and I sighed, "Or maybe I'm just trying to duck out on my responsibilities."

Still quiet, Aikamieli said, "Being a hero or a villain is too big for us. I wanted it. I still want it. But I saw your friends fight, and…."

"Come on, they're your friends too," I argued.

"No, they're not." He sounded resigned.

"Marcia likes you," I insisted.

"She likes me as a toy. Cassie only cares that I'm useful. At least Charlotte doesn't pretend she's interested." The words were harsh, but Aikamieli didn't sound angry, just sad that he had to correct me.

I waved a hand in the air, propped up my knees, and scrunched back against the pillows more comfortably. "That's not you. They're like that. It's why they can chase after being superheroes even though they're as in over their heads as we are, and it's what makes them fascinating. Like…Marcia. You have to feel it, right?"

His already soft voice turned as haunted as a sunken pirate ship carrying a cargo of mummies during a zombie apocalypse. "She scares me. She's like seeing a freight train and wanting to step in front of it."

I kicked my foot, and hmmmed. "I just think she's brave. She's not crazy. She seems crazy because she's the only person in the world who doesn't let anything intimidate her, big or small. She's not breaking the rules because she's selfish, she's breaking the rules because she's…free."

Aikamieli didn't immediately respond, so I sighed again and continued. "That's not exactly it, but I don't think I can put it any better. Now, Cassie is crazy, but it's ambition crazy, the kind of crazy that drags you in its wake to awesome things. And Charlotte is the definition of cool."

His voice stronger, Aikamieli pointed out, "You've gone further than any of them. You know that, right? I don't know how you do it."

I chuckled. "Me, neither."

Then I yawned, one of those huge, loud yawns that make your jaw hurt. It went on for a while, and when it was over, I said, quietly and sincerely, "Hey, Aikamieli? Thanks. I had a rough night, and thanks to you, I think I can get the nap I desperately need. And before I go…you should be less shy.

You're a cooler person than you think."

He didn't immediately reply, so I chose that as my moment to hang up. All of a sudden, I was tired. Gruelingly, achingly tired, and my heart hurt worse than the rest of me. Somehow, that felt like an improvement.

Chapter Twenty-Three

Tonika was not at the bus stop the next morning. I'd known she wouldn't be, but it still came as a shock, and I was painfully aware of her absence the whole time I waited.

I got a different shock when I stepped off the bus at Upper High. Superheroes flanked the front doors. Not in bad disguises holding scanning equipment. A really big, muscular guy in patchwork armor over a toga stood on one side with his arms stoically folded and his lantern jaw thrust out. On the other side, a stretched looking woman with a long tail lounged against the door frame, arms tucked behind her head. If she wore a costume, I couldn't identify it from the streaks and patches of fur, scales, metal, glowing stuff, and rubbery skin in neon colors that also made up her body. She chewed bubblegum, watching the street with insolent confidence, and blew and then popped a bubble as if smugly insulting the world.

She caught me staring. As I passed, her eyes tracked over to me. One eye tracked, the left one, which was red with a series of shifting concentric rings that looked a lot like targeting reticles. The right eye might track, but since the whole eye was ruby red, who actually knew? Her long, pointed, blue tongue snaked out, holding the wad of bubblegum and caressing it, then flicked the gum at me.

I caught the wet blob in one hand and put it into a pocket of my backpack. Waste not, want not. There had to be a multitude of mutagens in that heroine's saliva waiting to be activated.

My next shock came when I reached Chemistry. Marcia wasn't there. I took my seat, and waited for the bell to ring. She still wasn't there.

"Books away, everyone. It's test day," announced the teacher, gathering up a pile of papers to hand out.

I winced. Oh, yeah, it was Friday. Even if Marcia had been here, we wouldn't have been allowed to talk during a test, but I still felt a lot more capable with her in the next chair. Thank goodness I'd spent so much of yesterday studying. Now I just had to translate the nonsense on the test page into the arbitrary but at least coherent rules of the "ball and sticks" game Marcia taught me.

Actually, I think I did okay. When the bell rang again and I turned in my test, I headed for the door with a feeling of cautious relief. As such, I did not jump into the air or scream when a hand grabbed my shoulder just as I entered the hall.

I looked back to see Charlotte, who squeezed my shoulder with concern and leaned close to look me in the eyes. "You're back? Are you okay?"

"Is Marcia okay?" I returned.

Charlotte rolled her eyes in exasperation and disgust. "I'll tell you at lunch." That was definitely irritation and not worry. Heh. More fool me for being afraid. Marcia was always okay, even with an arrow through her heart.

Charlotte hurried away, and I looked around the passing crowd, reflexively looking for Tonika or Sean. They weren't here, of course. That took the wind out of my sails, but I headed for Latin anyway. You have to keep doing what's right even when it turns into a mess. Weird that I learned that from a supervillain.

"Everyone ready for a vocabulary quiz?" asked the teacher as soon as I arrived. Oh boy, Fridays were the best, weren't they? But I guess after all that studying, I was ready for this one, too.

It kept me busy until lunch, anyway. Marcia wasn't at the table, so I had to go through the cafeteria line rather than begging off her scraps. On the one hand, cafeteria food was less tasty than what she would have brought. On the other hand, I'd get actual variety instead of one completely random foodstuff.

With that delay, even Mirabelle was at the table before me. I took my spot, with the awkward gap now between me and Charlotte.

Everyone was quick on identification today. Cassie stared at me with lips pursed in concern as I sat down, and asked, "Are you feeling better?"

"Well enough to go back to school," I grumbled, hoping if I sounded irritated enough no one would press for details.

"Mirabelle could heal you," suggested Will, looking anxiously between me and the glass girl.

Said glass girl shook her head, and patted her sparkly transparent hand atop his regular person meat hand. I think she smiled, but she definitely sounded affectionate as well as regretful as she said, "I'm afraid this is beyond me. I can repair broken bones, but my power makes diseases worse by reassembling dead viruses."

Cassie raised a pale-yellow eyebrow at Will and snickered. "Jumped the gun there, Major League Woo Pitcher? A little too eager to flatter your feline fair?"

Will's shyness disappeared. Facing Cassie now, he propped a fist on his hip and raised an eyebrow right back. "I'm sorry, I thought you were too busy daydreaming about Penny to overhear."

Cassie jerked a thumb at her chest, scowling. "Hey, at least I chase after my perfect pigtailed goddess of mousey adorableness and unstoppable combat genius with some dignity."

The hard-muscled redheaded boy raised a hand to his ear. "What's that? Did you say you're having another blonde moment?"

That was obviously a private joke between the two. Cassie's lips flapped, so outraged she didn't have an immediate reaction. Behind Will, where he couldn't see, Mirabelle raised her hand to her mouth and shook with silent giggles.

As funny as this was, it was keeping me in the dark on a crucial question, so I asked it. "Where is Marcia, anyway?"

That blew up the play fight like a box of plunger-activated cartoon dynamite, and with just as much ridiculous drama. Will face-planted, his head dropping to the table in exasperated despair at the mere topic. Cassie put her knuckles to her forehead, then stared past me with a suddenly perplexed expression.

"Did someone mention my name?" asked Marcia, stepping over the bench to take her spot between me and Charlotte.

Cassie crossed her arms, giving Marcia a glare with only token hostility, but plenty of suspicion. "What are you doing here?"

Marcia beamed in angelic joy, slipping her arms around my and Charlotte's shoulders. "Having lunch with my friends."

Charlotte frowned at Marcia, not resisting the embrace, but with disapproval set at "official warning" level. "You are suspended."

Marcia gave me and Charlotte a squeeze, grinning as she explained, "I can't show up in class, sure, but no one watches to make sure the wrong student never enters the building."

I went to the source, and asked Marcia, "What happened?" In the process, I took a moment to look her over. She had changed. I'd been tuning out Marcia's campaign of scandalous clothing, but today her pale pink blouse and slacks were perfectly modest, and no worse than a bit rumpled.

Before answering, she picked my tray up by the corner, holding it high to throw—

No, she didn't throw it. I'd been prepared for that, but instead she just set the tray at the edge of the table out of the way, so she could lay a basket of plastic-wrapped deli sandwiches in the center of the table. Only then, as she sat down, did she happily explain, "I finally got what I wanted, for the school and superheroes to stop tiptoeing around me. I hate being treated like a fragile flower."

Mirabelle let out a sigh. Cassie gave her a lopsided grin. "Sorry, Crystal Cat, you *are* a delicate flower. Of exquisite feminine grace, even."

Will gathered up Mirabelle's hand in both of his, squeezing

it gently and giving her an apologetic smile.

Abandoning that mini-drama, I interrogated Marcia again. "What did you pull that was so awful it finally got them to kick you out?"

Scowling down at the table, Charlotte extended her arm and pointed. "That was a big part of it."

I looked. In my defense, I'd missed the teenager-sized hold in the far wall of the cafeteria because lots of kids were in the way. Someone had taped paper over most of the hole, put up a warning sign, and piled up a few boxes around it.

Quietly, Mirabelle said, "I offered to help repair the breach, but the school refused. They said I might strain myself."

Cassie smacked both hands on the tabletop loudly. "Topic over. Why is no longer important. Marcia is here, which means we can tell Magenta all about Wednesday!" She groaned, leaning back and waving her head in a circle before rearing forward again to grin at me. "The thought of having to wait all weekend was killing me!"

Ah.

Wednesday.

Right.

Sensing my awkwardness, Cassie raised a hand, her face turning sober. "First, we all want to apologize. We had a big argument—"

"Mostly with ourselves rather than each other," Charlotte inserted.

"—about whether to try to go back and get you, or let the opportunity go because we couldn't bring you along, or...what," finished Cassie.

Playing my part, I raised my eyebrows curiously. "So, I'm guessing you found either a Pawn, the cyborg, or both, and it has something to do with the new school security."

Charlotte nodded in sober respect. "Got it in one."

Leaning forward and raising my hands, I asked, "So...did you win?"

Three seconds of silence. Cassie folded her arms on the metal tabletop, and shook her head with a wry smirk. "I've been thinking about that for two days, and I'm still not sure how to answer. I got what I wanted out of it. A little bit of cool fight, a little bit of practice in real combat, and a lot of learning my own flaws. I...I ran out of lightning."

Sober now, Cassie lifted her hands, palms facing herself, and looked back and forth between them. Her voice dropped to a pensive hush. "In sparring, that's no big deal, but in a real fight...we almost lost everything. I didn't want to say it at the time, but if that cyborg had gotten back up, I would have been nothing but a target."

Charlotte rubbed her temple, setting her bead-covered braids clattering. She looked solemn and uncharacteristically abashed as well. "I'm going to have to look into being a sidekick. I froze. More than once. I didn't think I was the kind of person who does that. It was all different when Penny was involved."

"Penny would have taken all three of us down, unarmed," stated Cassie grimly.

Okay, I smirked. Cassie's hero worship of this Penny girl was adorable. But nobody else argued with her, or seemed amused.

Charlotte took a deep breath, running her spread fingers back through her braids now. Amid the rattling, she sighed, "I got what I really, really wanted. I got to do the right thing. As big a mess as it was, we saved that purple girl. The heroes have her now. That's why they're freaking out."

Taking a club sandwich in a long roll out of the basket, I set it down in front of me with a thump, and stated, "You know that I understand absolutely nothing you're saying, right? Until you give me a detailed, blow-by-blow account of everything that happened, preferably while I eat this delicious sandwich, you might as well be speaking Catlantian."

Cassie intertwined her fingers, and cracked her knuckles loudly. Grinning again, she declared, "Challenge accepted!"

Grinning too, Marcia nudged me with her elbow. "You're going to love the part where I'm murdered."

A strange sensation crept over me; the same one I'd felt shopping with my friends. I might have been on the other side, but that desperate fight had been something my friends and I did together. Did most supervillains feel like this, after the threat of death was over?

Cassie talked. Everyone else ate. Even Mirabelle ate, when Marcia flipped her a small, sparkly bead like a rhinestone. She swallowed it with a look of such ecstasy I wondered if the crystal was laced with catnip.

I went on to Social Sciences and then Algebra. The teachers gave us more quizzes, because what else were Fridays for?

When the final bell rang and I stepped out of Algebra, I unzipped my backpack and pulled out my magical purple book.

Should I go to work? I'd never had a chance to discuss my hours with Cleric after that nightmare in the robot base. He hadn't told me any of his plans after the equipment pickup. If he wanted me to work today, surely he would have contacted me?

I'd never given him my phone number. Did he know how to contact me? Yes, of course. Knowledge is what he does.

So, I put the book back and went home on the bus, like everything was normal. Sitting in a seat on a regular school bus heading South from Los Feliz, I felt awkward. Exposed. I couldn't explain why, even to myself.

Organism One was dealt with. The vigilante teenager problem was dealt with.

The danger was over, right?

CHAPTER TWENTY-FOUR

"Hello?"

Nothing. I had just gotten home from school, and everyone was out. Not really a surprise. It did leave me standing in the hall wondering...without my after-school job, what exactly should I do?

Maybe Cleric would call.

Since I was waiting, I might as well set up some healing potions to cook in my bedroom laboratory. As I lined up beakers, I popped open my potion kit. Its mouth gaped as empty as the maw of Charybdis before he picked his teeth. I had one healing potion, two energy potions, a glue potion, another glue potion still loaded in my gauntlet, and my sunlight potion. No backups. That was my entire collection. The rest were either with Sean, or stolen by Organism One's AI. I would work on that while I waited for Cleric to contact me.

He did not contact me.

At noon on Saturday, I was separating the seeds from apple cores when I slammed the core down on the table. I'd had enough. I grumbled my way through lunch with my dad and Kay, stormed back to my room and locked the door. I barely had the patience to struggle into my costume, then grabbed my purple teleport book. Opening it to the shop page, I shoved my face in against the window.

Metal bars. Bars? What was going on? I'd appeared in the shop's grey and brown front room as usual, but with a man-sized cage over the arrival spot! It was simple enough. A bunch of vertical bars, a plate for a top and bottom, and a big padlock on the door.

I'd been caught again...no. No, I had the book in my hand. I flipped it to my bedroom's page just to be safe, and the window showed the image of my room. I could get out. I just couldn't get in.

Banging my fist on the bars produced nothing but *bonk* noises. I yanked at the padlock. With that big keyhole, anybody who knew how to pick locks could probably open it in seconds. That did not include me. I didn't have super strength to rip it off, either, or any useful potions.

Thumping feet. Cleric entered from the kitchen, holding The Book tucked under one arm. He wore his sword buckled to his waist and gloves thick enough they probably included chain mail.

Face blank, the tall blonde supervillain looked down at me and said, "So, you've arrived."

I kicked the cage door, making the padlock rattle. "Yes, and can you let me out? Did you think I'd let someone steal this?" I held up the book, with both hands tightly clamped around it. Nobody was taking this precious treasure from me.

Still expressionless, Cleric pulled the chair we'd used for memory transfers out in front of the cage, and sat down. His armor clinked a lot. With The Book hugged just as securely to his chest, he said, "No. The cage is for you, to stop you from teleporting in."

I gaped at him, and squeaked, "Why? Do you think I'm not loyal!?"

The question was a lie. I knew the answer, but it hurt, and I wanted to make him say it.

He didn't rise to the emotional bait. The picture of absolute calm, he said, "I am releasing you from my service."

I tucked the teleport book under one arm and my other fist on my hip. Glaring straight into his eyes, I replied, "I do not want to be released."

Cleric stared at me, feelings hidden behind professional warrior calm.

Folding my arms over my book and my book over my chest, I did my best to replace the needling anger in my voice with sympathy. "You blame yourself for what happened to Tonika."

Cleric shook his head, calm and a little sad, but honestly so, not with blank-faced self-control. "No."

That surprised me so much I must have jerked, because Cleric took that as a signal to explain, still resigned and sad. "Fifteen years of this has been enough to learn not to blame myself for other people's evil. I did not hurt the girl and could not have predicted she would get hurt. The boy wanted a chance to taste the pain and joy of adventure, and he learned he does not like it. I feel sympathy for their pain, but not guilt."

His gloved left hand lifted and pointed a finger at me. "But *you* are my responsibility. I recruited you with the understanding you would be an assistant, and would not have to face violence and danger. I should have released you the moment I suspected you were facing harassment and danger from other children."

I should have wilted at that. I stuck out my jaw stubbornly instead. "That was my decision. I chose to face that danger, and I would choose the same way again. I...." This thought hurt, and I faltered, but I pressed on. "I didn't choose what happened to Tonika, but this isn't about Tonika. It's about me. Danger or no danger, I want to see this through."

Cleric's face went back to the stoic mask, but his tone turned soft. "Why?"

Squeezing my purple book tighter, I swept the other arm angrily through the air. "Because I'm tired of people trying to stop you from making the world a better place. And because I want that to be "us" making the world a better place."

Cleric's jaw set, his face that normally leaned toward prettiness going blocky with anger and determination. "No. It gets more dangerous here. We have entered the endgame. The instrument is built."

Whoa. In a hush of surprise, I asked, "How long?"

"I think today."

I leaned against the bars behind me, blinked, and blinked again. This was so sudden. Then I reared back up and declared, "Now I definitely want in."

He shook his head, blue eyes cold. "It is too dangerous."

My composure cracked, and so did my voice as I growled, "This is the cause that I worked for. That I risked my life and my humanity for. You can't cut me out of this now. Besides, you need my help. Right? Am I right?"

Cleric stared some more. Something went out of him. He let out a long, deep sigh, and lowered his eyes. "Yes. I always need someone I can trust absolutely, and I need someone immune to The Book's power."

I raised a naturally pink eyebrow. "Immune?"

His mouth pulled up one side into something between a smirk and a grimace. His tone took on a similar note of self-admonishment. "I was worried that it would not be safe to use The Book on someone who contributed to it. It turns out that the opposite is true. If you have any of the memories it contains, it cannot add to them."

Well. This was a strange sensation. I'd never put together that all the students whose crazy hobbies I'd harvested might be in danger, and now I felt relief knowing they were safe.

I pushed it aside, and gave Cleric another glare, demanding, "Well?"

He stood up again, clinking and creaking. There was leather in that armor somewhere. Scowling again, he asked archly, "If I take you with me, and you get in trouble, you must promise to flee, even if that means the plan fails."

"No," I answered, staring up at those stern blue eyes.

His jaw tightened. Quiet and grim, he said, "Then you can join me. Even a child should do what she thinks is right, if she's ready to face the consequences."

"I know the consequences better than you do now, and I'm still in." My voice wobbled again. Oh, yes. I knew. But I wasn't letting it stop me.

Cleric lurched into motion. He pulled a key from a pouch around his waist, and unfastened the padlock. "Then we have little time."

I pushed the cage door open. Cleric was already headed for the shop's front door, and I hurried to catch up. "Where is the machine?"

We were a team again. His explanation came crisp and authoritative, not angry. "The instrument is already at the test site. Too many of my enemies know about this location. They are watching it, and would attack the moment I showed signs of action. Come on."

We stepped out onto the eternally abandoned street, and headed down the sidewalk. Trying to look around without being obvious about it, I asked, "I thought you said they're watching."

With his long legs, Cleric stayed a step ahead of me, where I couldn't see his face. "They are. I'm using you to make them less likely to attack until it's too late. Are you okay with that?"

I grinned, even though he wasn't looking, and made no effort to hide that in my voice. "Okay? I'm proud."

Cleric was a naturally fast walker, but we didn't actually hurry. When we got off his side street, our costumes got a few curious glances from passing USC students, but no excitement. I didn't ask questions, just followed him. We were being observed, after all.

I still couldn't help but fidget with my gauntlet and my one last glue vial loaded into it.

We crossed Exposition, into Exposition Park, following its winding paths toward the bubble fountain, and…

...we were headed for the Organism One base. That had to be it.

No sooner thought than we went down the crisscrossed ramps, and Cleric stepped through the bushes at the base. The broken gate to the base's entrance tunnel still hung loosely from its hinges. He lifted it out of the way easily and stepped inside.

I did not want to go back in there.

I did it anyway. Fear was not going to stop me anymore.

The tunnel was dark and echoey, with mud squishing under our feet. It smelled of rotting garbage and sharp, antiseptic chemicals. Truly the worst of both worlds. It was also shorter than I remembered. In no time we climbed down the stairs into Organism One's abandoned base.

Definitely abandoned. Disassembled robots still lay around the hall where Kay had pulled them apart, detached spider legs and headless humanoid mannequins everywhere. No one had cleaned up anything since we'd left.

We picked our way through the robot junk, circling around to the doorway into the central room, where I found out one thing had been cleaned up. Even the ripped-up papers Cleric had used to fight still lay trampled on the concrete, but the high-tech surgical table had disappeared. Cleric didn't seem bothered, so I would trust that he took it.

Cleric reached an arm into the twisting mass of pipes hanging from the ceiling. Most of the space inside was filled with shinier computer wiring, but not all. He found something in there, something that clicked. Cement groaned, and the floor underneath the bubble machine receded. That floor had looked like one even piece of cement. It was not, and now I saw it withdraw in sections, creating a spiral staircase that led down into the Earth.

Cleric wasted no time, trotting down those steps as soon as they'd descended enough to bother. I followed, baffled by this development but trusting him. The stairs circled around, ending at a doorway arch, which we stepped through.

On the other side was darkness. Popping my potion pouch open, I lifted up the vial of sunlight, and revealed another circular stairway, with walls of massive bricks that could be concrete or stone. I wouldn't know. The place looked old. Medieval, which was ridiculous under Los Angeles, a city that had been Native American before the Spaniards arrived and never had the chance to be Medieval. Cleric brought out no light of his own, so I was torch-bearer. That would be safe enough as long as I didn't break or open the vial.

Ridiculous in concept, not in looks. In looks, it was as creepy as a spider graveyard, but still better than the base upstairs. It smelled like wet sand, with a hint of the sea.

A crude lever in a heavy base slab stuck out of the wall next to the archway. Cleric pulled it, and the stairs ground their way back up, blocking that exit.

Cleric nodded, solemnly approving and just a touch more relaxed. "There. When our pursuers become impatient enough to follow, we will have disappeared. Their first thought will be that we teleported back to my shop and this was a false trail."

He took off down the stairs, and as I skipped down them behind him, I asked, "So, where are we?"

"The Undercity," was all he had time to answer before we reached the first landing. Another arched doorway led into another dark room. The stairs flattened out for a few feet, then kept circling down.

Cleric pointed through the door. "This is deep enough. The adventures down there belong to someone else."

This new rectangular room followed the same heavy brick theme. It was old, with drifts of mud and a few spiderwebs in the corner. We crossed from it into a hall, then an octagonal room at the end. Aside from small amounts of filth, the place held no furniture. It did have side doors, but they'd all been bricked and boarded up long ago, leaving only this one path.

My small amount of trapped sunlight did not penetrate very far, but it seemed to be enough for Cleric. He led us through that one path, into a large room like a theater, descending downward in curved stages to a flat bottom. Its purpose was moot. We didn't descend, only headed to a hole broken through the heavy brick wall opposite our entrance. Past there, for two feet the cramped tunnel had a chipped, artificial look, like it had been hacked out with pickaxes to join the ancient fortress with a broader, possibly natural tunnel. Maybe natural. It smelled strongly of the sea, and glittered with crystals of salt covering the ceiling, walls, and floor. In one direction, boxes and barricades were piled up, blocking the path. We crunched along the opposite way. It curved like a worm, until it opened into a massive, pillared subway station.

It had to be a subway station. Twin tracks disappeared into smoothly artificial tunnels in the walls. Old metal benches sat against the walls. Granted, everything was old and dusted with sand and salt, and there were no stairs to the surface, but a subway station is distinctive. Cleric stepped down into the track level, and I found a rickety metal cart, like a miniature, stripped-down train engine, waiting for us. We climbed in, and he pulled some of the levers on its control panel. To my astonishment, its gauges lit up and it began chugging down the track with us in it as readily as if it were brand new.

Okay, now we had a pause to breathe, so I asked, "What is this place?"

Cleric's love of teaching kicked in. With a sudden smile, he explained, "A transit system built by the Queen of Swords. Originally pneumatic, it has been updated at least twice. When the Queen moved out, Tyrant took this system over."

"Does that mean we're headed to an actual Tyrant base?" I asked, in awe at the thought.

Cleric nodded, looking down at me with a serious frown, not angry or hiding. Acknowledging. We were partners. Okay, one very senior and one very junior partner, but still. He answered, "Yes. This is no longer a lone research project. In a few hours, the work we've done together will change Southern California. With luck, the ripple effects will make the world a more wondrous place."

My eyes went wide, then snapped shut as the wind in the tunnel flicked a speck of grit into one. Ouch. As I rubbed it out, I admitted in a hush, "I knew this was coming. I didn't think it would be so fast."

He smiled, just a little. His gloved hand patted my shoulder with the extra padding and vacuum tubes. "Your work made it so fast. You made it easy to fix The Book, to collect information, and to get parts. I was free to find out how to harness The Book's power, and do that with minimal harassment."

The cart pulled into another, smaller station. As soon as it chugged to a stop, Cleric abandoned it, again leaving me to scramble after him. This station had a door in the wall, which proved to be an elevator when he pushed a button and it *dinge*d open.

As we stood in this brightly lit, modern, fake wood paneled box with its shiny grey plate (with admittedly only three buttons, but they lit up like most elevator buttons do), I tucked my sunlight potion away. Cleric's smile widened, turned warm. Yeah, he was enjoying teaching a sidekick. "That's how it often works. Weeks, months of preparation, and then success or failure in a few whirlwind hours. I hope you're ready."

I swallowed, but looked him back in the eye. "I don't think it's possible to be ready, but I've accepted that."

He nodded, his smile now bright. "Good answer."

Chapter Twenty-Five

The door opened, and his smile disappeared. Stiff, imperious, his tabard flapping around the edges, Cleric strode through the carpeted back halls of a business. Workers gasped. Some of them saluted. A couple of them saluted me.

We got close enough to the front of the building that I saw a lobby before we turned into a side hall, and in that lobby a sign. Once again, I boggled. "King's Novelties? The company that sells rubber masks and sea monkeys? They're a Tyrant operation?"

"Of course. It's a small way of making the world a little more colorful and exciting." He was definitely holding back a laugh, but...yeah, I got it. A world with goofball novelties in it was just a little bit brighter.

We went up stairs. We circled around and went up more stairs. This place was a maze, with no stairway going up more than one floor.

Cleric caught my bemused expression as we exited the second one-floor staircase, and chuckled. "This layout is good for hiding things, makes the building less boring, and is thematic to the company."

A few more people saluted me, which was cool, but I'd had a fair walk by the time we got to the sixth floor. If this even was the sixth floor. I wouldn't put it past this building to have mismatched floors. As we'd progressed upward, the building became less clerical and more scientific, which meant it wasn't any surprise when we stepped into a big white room with a few tables with high tech equipment on them, and lots more equipment, some of it crated or covered in sheets, lining the back wall.

A college age guy in a lab coat let out a squeal when we walked in, and yanked off a pair of spectacles. He gave Cleric a shocked and agonized look. "You can't bring anyone under eighteen into the x-ray glasses research laboratory...uh, Sir!"

Ah, yes. The spectacles did have swirly lenses. Adorable.

Cleric raised his eyebrows, distracted by curiosity. "Oh, have you finally gotten them working?"

The scientist fidgeted his shoulders awkwardly, looking at Cleric's shoulder rather than meeting the supervillain's gaze. "Well...no, but we're finally making progress."

I must have looked interested, because the scientist rounded on me as less intimidating to explain to. "We've had glasses that work like an actual x-ray and let you see bones for decades. They're not good enough for medical use, unfortunately, but they work. They're part of our effort to reverse engineer the Peeping Tom Goggles of a mad scientist from the nineteen-twenties. We can now produce a version that works...uh, backwards. It makes people invisible, but you can still see their clothes."

Cleric cleared his throat. The scientist snapped to attention, which gave me a moment to sneak the spectacles out of his hands and try them on. I stifled a giggle. He was telling the truth. I saw Cleric's empty armor slap a glove down on an empty lab coat's shoulder and say, "It's time, Tom."

"Is this going to work?" asked Tom, who I belatedly noticed had a name tag with Thomas Rumpelstiltskin on it. He sounded terrified and hopeful at the same time.

Cleric's armor shifted around the neck. Probably a nod. "Yes. I've tested it. There's severe confusion at first, but you and everyone else in Los Angeles will have the knowledge of a true adventurer when this is over."

Tom's clothes didn't move visibly, but I heard him breathing hard. Having enjoyed the joke, I took off the glasses and set them on a table. Now I could see Tom's wide-eyed expression of awe.

Grave, Cleric continued, "The alignment process will be very obvious, and heroes will have time to interfere while I finalize the settings. Do you have someone who can help carry the instrument to the roof and hold off attackers?"

His voice scratchy, obviously admitting wrongdoing, Tom said, "We borrowed the Golem, Sir."

Whatever he'd done, he got away with it. Cleric left him, walking to the back of the room and pulling the sheet off the biggest of the covered objects lined up. The falling canvas revealed a massive humanoid shape, half again as tall as Cleric and so bulky it looked squat. It barely looked more carved than the kind of doll elementary school children make out of modeling clay. This one was already made out of clay, but grey, wet, and goopy. I couldn't believe it wasn't leaving globs of itself all over the floor, or just settling into a heap.

Except…it was alive. I knew before it turned its head down to look at Cleric. Something in the color, in the way it held together, made it obvious. This was life created by alchemy like mine. Crude life, but life.

I'd walked up to the thing without even realizing, and asked in a whisper, "Who made you?"

It didn't respond, and after a moment, I was glad it hadn't. The grey clay it was made of…I wanted some, but I didn't. It was nasty. Inferior. Not the way I would do this at all. Wasted effort, without enough of a mind to bother with. Anything I used a piece of this monster to make would be just as inferior.

And yet the rest of me was just going…wow.

Cleric, apparently satisfied, turned back to Tom. "One more thing. Activate the booster on the Griffith Park Observatory."

Tom jumped, literally. His sneakers squeaked when they hit the floor again. "We've been keeping that in reserve for decades! We'll only get to use it once before heroes destroy it!"

Face stony with authority, Cleric told him, "Yes. This is what we've been keeping it in reserve for."

"But with that...."

When Tom trailed off, eyes wide, Cleric finished for him. "All of Southern California."

And that was my reminder. This was serious, Magenta. As serious as it gets. We weren't playing a game this time.

That seemed to be that. Cleric whirled around with proper arrogant villain style, and walked out the laboratory door. I hurried to stay a step behind him. Golem, making only soft splatting noises when his huge feet hit the ground, trudged after us. He had to slouch to get through the door, but he slouched anyway.

Cleric clearly knew the layout of this place, because our next stop was an elevator—a big, wide elevator near the center of the building. It must be for freight, and even Golem had plenty of room as we rode it up the exactly one floor it went, and exited on the roof.

Looking around, we were near downtown, or a downtown. I didn't know LA's dense urban centers well, but this building was puny and dwarfish compared to the crowd of nearby skyscrapers. From the distance of the surrounding hills, my guess was we'd crossed underground to the exact opposite side of downtown LA.

This relatively puny building had a helicopter pad complete with big painted circle like a target in the center of its flat concrete expanse. In the center of that pad sat a pipe organ. Sort of. This contraption was obviously mad science, and I recognized many of the pipes I'd bought on Wednesday. They had been rigged together with tubes and wires, hooked to a wooden control panel that included a piano keyboard, and that was wired to the upper half of a crash test dummy, whose hands rested on the keys.

As we got closer, I saw that the dummy wasn't quite a regular crash test dummy. It was too sophisticated, the gold banding under the joints, and a pretty face, all in pale blue plastic. Its blue eyes looked eerily human, and the mouth had a slit which could open for speech. I knew that, because a number of tubes were strung from that mouth into the organ, while wires connected the dummy's skull to the stand that would hold sheet music if this were a real pipe organ.

Around the stand, between the stand and the keyboard, and all over the wooden face of the machine projected a bewildering array of controls. None of them were computer buttons or screens, either. A long row of knobs you could pull in and out, levers that could be moved forward and back between notches, levers used to swivel cones, flip switches—it was all primitive, almost medieval, and perfect for my fantasy adventure obsessed employer.

He was indeed pleased. "It's already set up! Excellent. Our people did well."

Someone must have signaled Golem, because he stepped back into the elevator, which closed behind him. Cleric set The Book, bulky and blue, several times bigger than a regular book, on the sheet music stand. He opened it up to what looked like a random page to me, and fastened clips to it from the wires that attached to the dummy's skull. Then he crouched down, and attached hoses sticking out from under the helicopter pad to valves at the base of the organ. While he did that, he talked to me, in the solemn, formal tones of a briefing. "Here is the plan: When we finish here, we will take the instrument on a freight car through the tunnels to the Ivory Tower in Hollywood. That will be close enough to the observatory to interact with the relays. Before we can do that, we have one last question to answer, which we will work out here. The process of aligning the instrument will draw huge amounts of attention, and when we reach the real activation site, we must be ready to fire immediately, before heroes can interfere. That means they will attack us here. When they arrive, you will operate the instrument while Golem and I keep them away from you."

While he talked and attached and fiddled with dials, Golem returned holding a big wooden crate that he set down behind us.

"The activating crank is inside the android shell," Cleric told me. Then his eyes widened, and as he jerked upright and whirled around, he shouted, "Pull it now!"

The crate exploded, releasing a cloud of flying books. I dove for the dummy, wrapping my arms around it, then feeling around in the open lower edge of its torso. That was full of gears, but I found a stick with a handle, and pulled. I had to pull hard, as it clicked through a number of stages to the end. When I let go, that machinery ticked and tocked. The dummy lurched upright, its hands fumbling for the keyboard.

The books from the crate formed a wall between us and the edge of the roof, and a buzz I hadn't realized I heard got louder, and louder, and louder, from "barely detectable" to the loudest noise I'd ever heard, rattling my head and stabbing at my ears. It was met by music blaring out of the pipe organ, a chaotic but weirdly pleasant ululation like a theremin in the hands of an octopus. The wall of books exploded, spraying paper everywhere.

All of that happened so fast, I wasn't sure what happened in which order. When I caught up, it was to realize the pipe organ's music had mostly drowned out the buzz, while not being anywhere near as loud and painful.

"Sun and moon forward, pull stop one!" yelled Cleric, just barely intelligible above the clamor. What did that mean? I had to figure out fast. A hero in something between a yellow and white spandex jumpsuit and actual power armor floated up into view, lifted by a round, vibrating backpack. Worse, the music from the pipe organ was running down.

Uh. Um. The pegs had numbers. I pulled "1" out until it stuck. Everything had labels. Sun and moon...those were the cones. I swung the handles until those speakers pointed at Echo. Yeah, that hero was definitely Echo. Sun and moon, stop one—yes, I was set. I reached into the dummy and hauled the lever back to full extension again.

That all took seconds, during which the haze of flying papers shot out at Echo, only to be ripped to shreds by another burst of sound. Then the pipe organ revved up again, and this time the music was not pleasant at all. It met Echo's deafening buzz, and the combined noise turned into a screech. The air itself exploded, whipping my dreads like angry snakes, shredding more papers, and sending Echo tumbling backwards.

His buzz stopped, leaving my ears ringing.

As everyone recovered their balance, a blue, fuzzy woman climbed up over the edge of the roof. Not just blue, and not just fuzzy. Deep, royal blue fur was only the dominant note in a sleek body that was a bewildering patchwork of colors and scale and skin and metal. This was the heroine I'd seen at school yesterday, and she moved with the grace of an eel.

Rather than immediately attacking, she scolded Echo sarcastically, "Finally. You know nobody can back you up when you use that thing, right?"

Cleric barked, "Sun and moon up, all stops out."

My hands danced over the knobs, yanking all twelve, and I slapped the cone handles to point them straight up. Echo did not like that. At all. He pointed both fists at the mad science pipe organ. His thick gloves vibrated, then bounced. They made a yelp noise when they fired.

They fired too late. The huge, gloppy shape of Golem got in the way. Drops of him sprayed out from the blast, but if he was hurt, I couldn't see it from this side.

"Everyone calm down!" snapped the mutated woman. I couldn't see her, but she sounded impatient, exasperated, like a teacher dealing with students who won't stop fidgeting. "Echo, get your pride out of the way. Cleric, I know you. You're a zealot, but you're not evil. Whatever that thing is, it can't be a doomsday bomb. Echo can stop it from doing its thing, and I can keep you and your monster in check for a few minutes."

Uh. I'd gotten sidetracked listening to her. I just was not good at this. I dealt with my rush of guilt by grabbing the handle inside the dummy and ratcheting it back to full extension.

The mutated woman was right. Echo did something, and the swelling music turned muted. That left the mutant woman's voice clearly audible even with Golem's slimy bulk between us. "Kid, I'm Doctor Biotic. Actual PhD, believe it or not. Don't do that again. Cleric, stop giving her orders. More heroes are on the way, and you know it. If you run now, I'll keep Echo from following. I'll also personally make sure the child escapes unharmed."

"Stops one, three, and four," barked Cleric.

As I punched all the knobs back in except those three, Doctor Biotic groaned. "Oh, come on. Look, we can all go somewhere and discuss this. I've got some capybara neural mutagen. You've never been so mellow in your life."

This time I ignored her, and pulled the lever. The android remains clumsily pressed the keys. The pipes played music. It sounded purer this time. That was the only word I could use to describe the change. Downstairs, inside the building, someone shouted.

Next to me, someone shouted. A man's voice, pained and angry, wailed, "My head—I can't—what?!" like Sean when he'd been touched by The Book.

I jumped, then fired my gauntlet at the whimpering empty spot next to the organ. Green liquid splashed over the shape of an invisible man, fastening him to the helicopter pad.

Doctor Biotic sighed loudly, the only adult in a world of children who fingerpaint on the walls with each other's snot. "So much for the easy way."

Things happened I couldn't see. Golem lumbered forward. Books flew around. Cleric yelled, "One three five nine at the street and out!"

Doctor Biotic jumped over Golem, landing on the top of the arch formed by the organ's pipes. She crouched on it with only weirdly splayed toes, one hand raised. To do what, I didn't find out. Books swarmed her, carrying her back into the air.

In a desperate hurry, I followed Cleric's instructions. Push, pull, pull, whack the handles, reach in and pull hard on the activation lever.

The mad science organ played. Strange, lovely music filled the air around us.

People screamed.

A series of loud *bangs* echoed out of the street below us.

Delighted, triumphant, confident, Cleric called back to me, "One three five eight nine and the throttle all the way up!"

I didn't move, unless breathing fast and hard counted, and my shoulders quaking. Those bangs had been car crashes. People were still screaming, some of them in pain rather than revelation. Whatever they might feel later, having so much knowledge rammed into their brain knocked people almost unconscious. If we projected this over the entire city, it might kill everyone on the freeways. Everyone working with dangerous machinery or electronics. There would be accidents everywhere. Fires.

Uh. What would it do in hospitals?

Struggling to keep my scratchy squeak coherent, I called back, "Cleric? I quit!"

"Now is a really bad time!" he answered, shock and desperation in his voice.

"You promised!" I answered. Ripping the clips off The Book, I tucked its heavy shape under one arm, and dragged my purple teleport book out of my trench coat's inner pocket. Yanking it open—

—didn't work. The covers wouldn't budge.

I ran for the elevator. It was only a few steps away. My feet crossed the threshold. I skidded to a halt and started to turn.

A strong hand closed on the back of my neck, lifting me painfully onto my tiptoes. Cleric turned around slowly, pressing the elevator buttons himself. I got a peek outside as the doors closed. No action seemed to be going on, although there were big, wet chunks of Golem splattered around.

I kicked, trying to pull myself free of the grip around my neck. That was useless. Cleric was twice my age and strong. So, I hissed up at him bitterly, "You lied to me!"

I felt him stiffen. Low, husky, and outraged, he replied, "I have never lied to you."

The door to the elevator opened. Three people sat on the floor, holding their heads and blinking at the strange new world around them. Cleric barked orders. "Get the instrument on the train *now*, and someone put stun nets over the heroes upstairs. Triple them up. Familiar physical action will help you control your new memories. Do it!"

The office workers staggered to their feet and rushed around. I saw one of them pick up a phone. Cleric stopped paying them any attention and carried me, dancing on my toes to try and keep some of the weight off my neck, through the building's maze. At least we didn't go down any stairs.

"You said I could quit! No revenge!" I gurgled, glaring up and back even though his face was out of view.

Calm, solemn, and forceful, Cleric said, "I meant it. I will not punish you for quitting, or for betraying me. I do have to lock you up until the broadcast is over, but only that long." His voice softened considerably, and he finished, "What I want to know is…why?"

"You didn't tell me people would die," I hissed. I tried clawing at his hand with both of mine, but we both knew that was no use.

He stopped, turning me enough that he could see my glare, and I could see his warm, gentle smile. That warmth replaced the pain in his voice as he said, "I am so proud of you. I applaud anyone who does what they believe is right."

Cleric started walking again, turning me because I could barely walk forward, much less sideways. His tone went back to solemn, but not upset. "I did not lie to you about that. Not even by omission. I told you my plans. I let you see what The Book does, up close. I assumed you knew that there would be collateral damage."

We entered an office. He pushed me into a chair, pulled off my gauntlet, and took the purple book out of my arms. He'd already taken The Book when he grabbed me. I'd been a little busy to pay attention to details like that. As he did, he explained, "These are yours. I will leave them outside. If you manage to escape before I return to free you, they'll be waiting."

My voice cracking, my eyes stinging, I stared up at that calm, commanding, kind face, and demanded, "How can you do this? And don't dare tell me that you can't make an omelet without breaking a few eggs."

He winced at that, face screwing up in disgust. A touch of growl entered his voice, but his anger wasn't directed at me. "I hate that phrase. It is used by people who want to brush off the damage they cause." Getting down on one knee, he looked me straight in the eyes, and said, "I am very aware of the harm I am about to do. It is much less than you think, but yes, people will be hurt and people will die. Afterwards, everyone in Southern California will be happier, kinder, and braver. Millions of people will be living much better lives. I can free them from the misery they're in now, and this is the least damaging way that I have been able to find."

I gaped at that. There was no point in arguing. He was in

preacher mode. I knew this side of him. I'd admired it. I just... had never known it would lead here.

Still softly, still a parent talking to a troubled child, he continued, "I don't require you to agree with my moral decision. I only wish I'd realized the consequences are not as obvious to a teenager just starting this life as they are to an adult who's been doing it for more than a decade. You did what you thought was right, and I'm going to do what I think is right."

He stood up, turned his back on me, and walked out. A moment after he shut the door behind him, the ceiling light went out, leaving me in absolute darkness.

Which was how my heart felt anyway.

Chapter Twenty-Six

I breathed, ragged and slow, trying to get control. Anger burned in me, threaded with the cold of fear, and sprinkled with the acid pain of losing someone I'd looked up to. But none of that compared to how afraid I was for the innocent people about to get hurt. Guilt tried to creep in as I thought about that, but if there was one thing Cleric had taught me, it was that guilt and fear and anger don't solve anything. Action solves things. And you don't have to be a fighter to do it.

He'd also taught me that I was utterly outclassed, but I was going to try anyway.

Forcing myself to stand despite the hollowness in my chest, I extended my arms and crept slowly toward where I remembered the door to be. My hands felt around, touched a desk, touched a little table, touched the wall behind it. They swept back and forth until I found the door, then up and down until I found the light switch behind it. That took way more sweeping than it should have, but eventually my fingers stumbled over the little plastic knob, and I flicked it.

Nothing happened. Of course. I felt down for the handle,

and turned it. To my great surprise, it wasn't locked and the door opened.

This pitch-black expanse was a hallway, right? I had barely been paying attention when Cleric dragged me in. Hadn't there been a bathroom? I felt along the wall, found another door and another handle, and opened it.

Yes. Bathroom. A pale green ghost-shaped LED next to the mirror gave off just barely enough light to identify the toilet and wash basin, but I still ate that illumination up like candy. Unfortunately, it didn't light up the hall and the bathroom had no other doors. I had to leave this lovely green behind and return to the darkness.

Ugh. Once again, perfect metaphor for my feelings right now. How could Cleric...be exactly the person I'd known he was, and I hadn't paid attention when people told me what that meant?

It still hurt to know that someone who seemed so good could do something so bad.

Hurt or not, tears in my eyes or not, I would keep going. My eyes weren't doing me much good right now anyway.

I kept feeling my way down the wall in the hallway. No more doors, but eventually I ran into an open space. Looking inside, I saw another light too faint to do me any good. This one was red, in the shape of four zeroes. That would be the clock on a microwave, right? So, this was an employee lounge. King's Novelties treated its employees well when it wasn't frying their brains in ways they might or might not be grateful for.

Cleric could have locked me into the office. Instead he'd locked me in with this lounge, which must contain food, and a bathroom. Great, another metaphor, this time between company policy and how he was treating me.

He was proud of me. Could I still admire him, while he did this?

You know what? That was the wrong question. I wasn't going to care. I was going to do what was right.

Between the lounge, the office, and the bathroom, and if I could find a light, Cleric had left me with enough stuff that anyone who knew how could easily break out. Except he'd done that because I didn't know and he knew I didn't know.

Keep on, Magenta. Very, very carefully so I wasn't blundering around in an open space, I faced away from the wall I'd been hugging, and walked forward until my fingers touched the hallway's opposite wall. Then I felt my way down the rough-textured wallpaper until I found another door, and that door's handle.

I twisted. This one was locked. Now I knew the shape of my cage.

Feeling around the door frame, I found another light switch, and flicked it. To my astonishment, the ceiling light turned on, showing me a crisp white hallway and shining some light into the lounge and office as well. Cleric had only broken the office light.

I banged on the door with my fist, yelling, "Hey! Is anyone out there? Can anyone hear me? I'm trapped! Let me out!"

Nothing happened, so I did it again, louder. I yelled at the top of my lungs, so loud I would have hurt my ears if they weren't still ringing a little from Echo's sonic weapon.

I kept banging for...I didn't know how long. Probably only a couple of minutes, but they felt like forever.

Nobody was coming. I stalked back into the lounge, which had its own little kitchen. Refrigerator, microwave, toaster oven, cabinets. Since I could see now, I opened up the cabinets, and found a heavy frying pan. No stove, but I wasn't going to argue. Taking it back to the hall, I used it like an axe, chopping the doorknob, and a second time, and a third.

Nothing. The knob wasn't even askew. Maybe I needed a heavier object. Or to be stronger. Or the knob was made out of some absurdly hard novelty material.

In the distance, on the other side of the door, I heard someone say, "I heard it over there."

"LET! ME! OUT!" I screamed, and kicked the door savagely, again and again.

Would that draw the voice, and whoever they were talking to?

It did. A man started singing on the other side of the door. I couldn't make out the words...no, I could, they were just gibberish.

The lock clicked. The door opened, to reveal Aikamieli, Cassie, and Marcia, all in costume. Charlotte wasn't far behind them, turned away and keeping watch on an open area with scattered desks that each had one different high-tech machine on them next to the ordinary office computer equipment.

Aikamieli looked relieved. Cassie grinned in excitement. Marcia pouted, lips pursed in not very believable disappointment.

Cassie ruffled Aikamieli's dark hair. He'd gotten rid of those ghastly three chin hairs, so it was actually cute to watch. Metaphorically glowing with delight, and literally leaving his hair standing up from static electricity, she said, "Wow, it worked. Just in time for a rescue!"

"But too late for a fight," grumbled Marcia, sticking her fists in the pockets of her hideously clashing black and white martial arts pajamas.

"How?" I asked. It was the only thought that would come.

Cassie tapped Aikamieli on the head, and turned her grin to me. "It's all him. He saw you fighting with your boss on television, got all of us together, and he has this crazy spell in his book that teleports you to the girl you're interested in's bedroom. It nearly killed him, but he still used another spell to pick this lock."

Aikamieli did look tired. His eyes bugged out with the wideness of someone forcing himself to stay awake. He was breathing hard, and wobbling. Extending an arm, he took hold of the wall and then stepped carefully forward to lean against it. If he couldn't complain about the "bedroom" comment, I knew he was really that tired.

Still scanning the entrances to the room, Charlotte commented, "It was less a teleport and more a travel spell. Absolutely bizarre. Don't expect me to describe it. Aikamieli, though—he's one hundred percent a hero."

Behind my friends, as promised, my book, gauntlet, and potion case sat on a table. I swept over to pick them up, popped out one of my blue potions, and popped the cap off, and pushed it into Aikamieli's hand.

With both hands, he blearily lifted the vial and took a sip. Blinking, the boy stood up straight and drank the rest of it down like the only water in a barren desert in the center of a boiling volcanic caldera on Mercury. When he finished, he looked so restored and energetic that he didn't need to sigh in relief.

Cassie watched this process, and the potion itself, with a puzzled frown. In the end, she gave her head a little shake, dismissing what she'd seen.

Which meant she didn't know I was me. Aikamieli hadn't told them. My friends thought they were rescuing a Pawn. Aikamieli himself might not know, since they thought there was more than one Pawn.

My aching heart softened. Somehow, that made this even more touching. It certainly was a relief. I so much did not want my friends to know that I'd had a hand in what was about to happen to LA.

Unless….

"The weapon hasn't fired yet. We would know. Can that spell take us to the Ivory Tower in Hollywood?" I demanded of Aikamieli.

Aikamieli shook his head, eyes owlishly wide. "I don't know where that is."

Jerking upright, Marcia raised her hand, putting on her crazy anticipation grin. "I know where it is! Will your spell take us to the awesome place where you and I are about to go on the craziest date of your life?"

The red-robed boy wizard kept shaking his head, leaning anxiously away from Marcia. "It would, but you can't lie to magic about that."

Marcia took a step closer to the boy, eyes regarding him hungrily, and making a sound between a growl and a purr in her throat. Voice dropped to a husk, she said, "Who's lying?"

Ignoring Marcia being weird, Charlotte shrugged. "If it works, it works."

I nodded sharply. "I'll try anything. We need to get there now. Cleric has had enough time that he could be pulling the firing lever right now."

Abandoning her watch enough to raise an eyebrow at me, Charlotte asked, "Will we be fighting your partner in the plague doctor outfit?"

"No." Poor Sean. "He was smarter than me, and quit after the cyborg horror show."

Marcia's smile turned up crookedly on one side, and her nearly black eyes searched my face, for all the good that would do her. "Sounds like you're the brave one."

Charlotte nodded. "It will be an honor fighting with you." She made it sound serious and not goofy.

"We really have no time," I snapped at all of them, pushing Aikamieli's True (theoretically) Kalevala up toward his face.

He flipped through it, but quickly, zeroing in on a page he'd used before, just minutes ago.

I threw up a hand suddenly. "Wait!"

Charlotte's curious look turned skeptical. "Weren't you the one in a hurry?"

"Printer paper. We need all the blank printer paper we can get!" I declared, in the grip of an inspiration that might just save us.

Nobody argued. My friends ran around to desks grabbing packages of printer paper, and came back with their arms loaded. Even Aikamieli held his book one-handed, with a packet of paper tucked under the other arm.

Hesitantly, Aikamieli started to read. Marcia slid her arms around his neck, watching over his shoulder with a very smug smile. The poor, innocent boy looked like he was about to hyperventilate, but his voice strengthened, launching into that superhuman singing power he had.

This song went on for a while, longer than any other spell I'd heard Aikamieli sing. When it took, it took suddenly. Charlotte was right, the experience was bizarre. We walked out of the white, science-y offices on the top floor into the brown, business-y offices downstairs, out the front doors of King's Novelties, across downtown, turned right, walked a few miles, turned left, and walked several more miles. The world moved in barely detectable slow motion around us.

That wasn't the weird part. The weird part was that we were also in slow motion. Or fast motion. Or something. The whole trip sped by in one second, maybe two, so fast I couldn't hold onto the details.

Our walk ended in another science-y hallway. This one had more of a college laboratory style, still rigorously white, but with a lot of tile and thick metal doors with windows on them lining both sides. Very institutional. We were the only people around that I could see or hear.

Aikamieli dropped to his knees, gasping for breath. That spell was rough. Marcia, arms around him, eased him to the floor gently. Leaning over him from above, she purred, "Hey, boy. About that date," and kissed him.

I didn't watch. I had more important things on my mind, and no time to waste. Power walking down to the end of the hall, I peeked out of a window. Okay, we were way high up, above the building next to us even, but that didn't tell me how far up was left to go.

Cassie and Charlotte followed me without needing orders. Seconds later, Marcia did the same. We circled around a hallway that seemed to line the outer wall of the building, until we saw an elevator. Rushing up, I stabbed the call button.

It didn't light up. The numbers above the elevator that should have told it what floor it was on were dark as well. Cleric had shut the elevators down. Besides, would it even go to the roof?

Charlotte tapped my shoulder, and pointed at the stairwell door just a little off to the side of the elevators. Storming over to it, I pushed the cross bar. Neither bar nor door budged. Great. Elevator shut down, stairs locked. I couldn't remember how we'd gotten in, with the weird time distortion effect of Aikamieli's spell.

I learned that Marcia had caught up with us as she stepped in front of me, scowled, and punched the cross bar of the door. With an awful metal *bang*, it ripped free and clattered to the floor. The door itself swung open.

We galloped up the stairs. Definitely institutional, the stairwell in this otherwise bright, clean building was bare, dingy cement. The stairs went up one floor, and stopped at a door with "Roof Access" stenciled in faded black next to it. No cross bar or window this time. This bland little metal door was just plain locked.

I stepped out of the way, and Marcia kicked the door with

a high-pitched growl like a jaguar. It didn't just burst open; it flew off the hinges and slid across the roof to bump into the doomsday pipe organ.

Cleric crouched next to the organ, hooking hoses to it that ran into a dull metal box that looked like part of the building's ventilation. Behind him, someone hung in the air, wrapped in paper like a mummy. As I watched, they stopped struggling and hung limp.

I had to remind myself that wasn't death. Cleric had choked them unconscious, not killed them, and there was a big difference between those two.

Golem, nearly mindless, stood on the far side of the mad science knowledge machine and did nothing, staring at nothing.

The exploding door had Cleric looking right at us, and he sighed in a moment of the most vulnerable frustration I'd ever seen in him. Quiet, but the only thing audible, he said, "This is exactly what I don't need."

I dropped the boxes of printer paper in my arm and pointed at the pipe organ, shouting, "Break the machine!"

"Golem. Bury them," ordered Cleric.

Cassie, Charlotte, and Marcia dropped their own paper packages. Charlotte swept her hands up, then around, and beads flew out of her pockets and spun around her. Cassie leaped forward, heading for the machine with her own arms raised.

Golem charged. It looked slow and clumsy, but sheer size made it fast. It raised its own grey, gloopy arms, each one thicker than my body.

Marcia ran to meet it. "You slime—" she started to yell, only to get a giant palmful of wet clay in the face.

She didn't let it stop her. Marcia grabbed Golem's arm, hauling it along as she charged into the mass of its body. It folded over her, engulfing her torso, but she kept running, bunched up her legs, and leaped. Marcia and Golem, stuck together, sailed up into the air, over the side of the building, and fell out of view.

Absolutely everyone, even Cleric, was left standing still and staring after them. Her voice faint, Charlotte said, "That was the most Marcia solution ever."

I had to take advantage of this moment. Lifting my arm, I fired my last glue vial at the organ. It didn't matter what I hit. I didn't have to break the machine. If I gummed up any of the dummy's joints, if I stuck one knob or key in the wrong position, Cleric couldn't fire it.

With a *ffwt* the vial flew out of the tube on my knuckles, and a colorful page from a magazine intercepted it, sweeping the vial into the air, around, and snapping it over Charlotte. The spraying green glue barely touched Charlotte herself, but her beads knocked against each other, fastening into masses that hit the rooftop and stuck.

Cassie, momentarily ignored, flared with blue-white light, pouring lightning over the pipe organ and leaving a number of black char marks. Nothing else seemed to happen.

A pair of old phone books slapped around Charlotte's wrists, hauling them behind her back and bending her in an awkward position. Cleric, walking past her, admonished, "You rely on your arms too much for control."

A cloud of papers descended, abandoning the man they'd been wrapped around and layering over Cassie. She struggled and flopped against them, spitting sparks through the few uncovered spots. Cleric tapped her on her covered nose as he passed, still unable to resist playing teacher. "Your costume telegraphs your power. The instrument is not electric and paper is not conductive."

I, like an idiot, had just been standing there as he rounded the machine toward me. I still had a second. Sprinting forward, I leaped up at the dummy, yanking on anything I could touch. I only had to break one stop, or pull off one dial!

Cleric grabbed me by the waist. I kicked and twisted as he wrapped an arm around me. Flailing to the side, I clawed at the dummy. If I could get my hand into the exposed clockwork inside and pull out a gear....

"Win or lose, I promise to return The Way's powers," Cleric murmured, quiet and close so no one else would hear.

I...I....

My thoughts hit a wall, long enough for Cleric to carry me over to Charlotte, squeezing me tight enough to feel his chainmail through my leather coat and his tabard. He set me down like a piece of furniture, jabbing the soles of my boots onto blobs of my glue, where they stuck. I would not be going anywhere soon.

Had I forgotten Kay entirely? Or had I been trying to steal The Book to save him all along, and was stunned because Cleric knew me better than I did?

I still had to stop him from killing who knew how many innocent people in his quest to help the rest, but what did I have left to do? Teleporting home wouldn't help. The potions I had left would be useless even if I hit him with them.

Next to me, Charlotte watched Cleric with similarly determined and helpless eyes. Cassie couldn't see, and was too busy fumbling at her face, clumsily pushing papers free from her nose and mouth over and over.

With a soft whirr and a green glow from his boots, a man in gleaming copper armor floated up over the rooftop. The air around him sparkled. Mech. This was the superhero Mech, and he had a forcefield, didn't he?

His voice metallic and distorted, the hero declared, "Step away from your weapon. I'd rather not melt you with it."

Cleric paused in the process of resetting the controls I'd scrambled. I hadn't done any damage, but at least he had to retune a lot of dials. He didn't straighten up and pull away from the pipe organ, but he didn't adjust anything else, either. For a few seconds, the hero and villain were at an impasse.

In that silence, Charlotte sneered. "Let's see you beat *him* with paper."

At that, Mech exclaimed, "What the—" and twisted around, then fell out of the sky out of sight.

Calmly, Cleric looked over at Charlotte and told her, "He had dollar bills in his pocket. He will also be back."

He reached back to reset the numbered organ stops. He had time to press in two before white and then yellow light and a crackling, crunching noise interrupted us all.

Lightning seethed over Cassie, not going anywhere but setting the papers holding her on fire. They had to be burning her as well, but it worked. The charred remains couldn't hold her, and she swung her arms out to pour lightning into Cleric next.

The results were a lot less impressive. He hissed and twitched, but only a few thin streaks of electricity had arched over into him, and the glow surrounding Cassie herself died out. Breathing hard, shaking, she dropped to one knee. She'd run out of juice freeing herself and had nothing left to attack with.

Beads slipped out of Charlotte's hair. They weren't very big, and they flew clumsily, but she jerked her head around to direct them as they smacked into Cleric's face, obscuring his eyes and nose and mouth and giving him a taste of his own medicine.

It wasn't working very well. More papers flew up, scooping off the beads and wrapping them up. But only two or three pages. Cassie had set fire to a great deal of paper, and the ones she burned had passed the fire to other floating pages. Cleric had much less ammunition than he had a minute ago.

Which was the desperately perfect moment for Aikamieli, wheezing, to stumble into view in the stairwell, drop to his knees, and rip open the packets of printer paper we'd brought. He flung handfuls of blank white paper wildly, sending spare sheets floating and bunched up clumps bouncing all around us.

"He can't control those! Here!" I shouted at Cassie. Pulling my last blue potion out, I threw it to her and added, "Get him!"

She'd seen what the potion had done for Aikamieli. Cassie caught it, popped the lid, and guzzled the contents.

I didn't watch that. As soon as the vial left my hand, I was crouched down untying my heavy leather supervillainy boots. Cassie was not going to beat Cleric. I didn't know what he would do, but I only needed a few seconds to wreck the pipe organ.

I found out what Cleric would do, when all those thousands of pieces of blank paper flying around stopped being blank. The word 'Tyrant' appeared on every one. Now under Cleric's control, they descended on Cassie and Charlotte like a blizzard. Lightning flared, and I'm sure a lot of paper burned, but not enough.

Except I was free, and only a few yards from the musical murder machine. In sock-covered feet, stumbling over loose paper and marbles, I ran over to it, arms reaching.

Cleric did the same, and at the last moment his arm shot in front of me, hauling me up by my waist again. I couldn't reach the dummy. I could just barely reach the wooden control panel with my fingertips.

"I'm sorry, but this is as important to me as it is to you," Cleric apologized, his face grim and sad as he pulled the last couple of stops back out and slid the throttle to maximum.

He held me off the ground, but he hadn't immobilized me, not like he had Cassie and Charlotte. I grabbed at my belt, pulled my sunlight potion out, and slapped it against the wooden front of the organ. The glass cracked, and pure sunlight spilled out in a puff of flame.

Not a big puff of flame, but it didn't have to be, because I'd splashed it on The Book.

However amazing the powers it contained, The Book itself was just paper and ink, sitting open without even its covers to protect it. The pages ignited.

Cleric sighed, sad and heavy. No longer in a hurry, he set me down on my feet and walked away. The cloud of papers scooped up Aikamieli and set him gently aside as Cleric descended the stairwell into the building.

The other papers fluttered to the floor, controlled only by gravity and the faint breeze.

Cassie, her spandex a mess of blackened holes with vivid red burns underneath, straightened up and looked around in delighted surprise. "We won? We won!" Squealing with glee, she raised a hand and high fived Charlotte, who was also grinning in delighted surprise.

Spinning around, Cassie offered me a high five. I returned it without enthusiasm. When she turned to take a step toward Aikamieli, the boy waved a hand weakly. "Pass. In fact, I think I'll nap."

True to his word, he rolled onto his side, laid his head on his arm, and closed his eyes.

I had no interest in whatever Charlotte and Cassie were saying to each other. I climbed up onto the base of the pipe organ, close enough to reach into the smoldering remains of

The Book and scoop up two handfuls of its ashes in my gloved hands.

This was all that remained of Kay's powers. I poured the ashes into a coat pocket, but that was hopeless. I would never be good enough to reconstitute that.

True to Cleric's prediction, Mech flew back up into view, with a grey-smeared Marcia sitting in his left arm. His right arm jabbed at the pipe organ, and a flickering light melted a line along the back of the pipes. That would have been enough damage to stop the instrument from firing, except that if I hadn't burned The Book, Mech would have been sixty seconds too late.

I walked away from them all, into the stairwell. As soon as I was around a wall out of sight, I pulled out my purple book and pressed my face into the panel showing my bedroom.

CHAPTER TWENTY-SEVEN

It was quiet in my bedroom. Peaceful. No one was fighting, and no one was in danger. Everything was sepia shadows. The biggest source of noise was a faint gloop from fermenting apple peels.

Peeling out of my evil minion costume, I changed into regular clothes. I folded up my costume carefully, laying the Tyrant badge on top.

Stop putting things off, Magenta. You can be brave one more time.

Opening my bedroom door, I crossed the hall to Kay's, and knocked.

Feet thumped against the floor in a rush. He yanked the door open, and threw his lanky arms around me, yanking me up into a painfully tight hug. Especially painful because Cleric had bruised my ribs. I should take a sip of my one last health potion. I should have given that potion to Cassie. I should have done a lot of things.

In an urgent whisper, Kay asked, "You're safe? You're unhurt? That was you, right?"

Surprised, I said, "You know?"

"Oh, yeah." He lowered me to the floor, rushed back to grab his phone off the bed, and brought it over for me to see the news broadcast on the screen. It's not like we could afford very good phones, but they were good enough for that.

Shaky helicopter footage replayed the foggy, zoomed in image of me struggling with Cleric over the pipe organ and the book catching fire, over and over. An anchorwoman chatted with an anchorman, "...his own Pawn, one of the girls LA's superheroes have been struggling to find, betrayed him. Betrayed him, and saved us all." She smirked. "Probably. What do you think the machine would have done?"

The anchorman's eyes scanned a paper in front of him as he answered, "We're getting reports that a mad science-based antenna unfolded from Griffith Park Observatory during the struggle. Whatever we were just saved from, it would have been huge. This will go down in the supervillainy books."

"And yet we may never know what actually happened, who that girl was, or why she saved the day," remarked the anchorwoman, wry and wistful.

"Then you know," I said quietly, as guilt crawled out like worms from my stomach.

Kay nodded. "I'm not getting my powers back."

"I'm so sorry." Tears welled up in my eyes, and I threw myself against Kay's lean chest, grabbing fistfuls of his shirt and crying into the worn denim.

He laid his arms around my shoulders, hugging me loosely for a second. Then he took gentle but firm hold of my shoulders, and pushed me away so that he could look into my clouded eyes and sniffling face. Solemn and emphatic, he told me, "Don't be sorry, Magenta. I hated my powers. I tried to explain that to you, but it wouldn't have made sense then. My powers were too dangerous to do anything with but be a superhero, and being a superhero is terrifying and depressing. For me, anyway. I would much rather take my scholarship and go to college full time. Trust me, baby sister. I am not going to miss my powers. You did the right thing."

Now he pulled me against him for another tight hug, as

I absorbed his words. My instincts insisted that he had to be lying to make me feel better. Except he could not have sounded more sincere, and after today, what he was saying made perfect sense.

Still, I clung to him and cried a little as the fact that I hadn't ruined my brother's happiness after all sank in. When I calmed down, he peeled me back again, and gave me a soft smile, asking, "How do you feel?"

"Totally unsatisfied, and I want to sleep for the next week," I answered honestly.

Kay snorted suddenly, one laugh that broke through before he could wrestle his face back to seriousness. "That is exactly how I always feel after saving the world. Go rest."

I did, plodding tiredly back into my room and collapsing onto my bed.

When I woke up again, the room was dark. It was evening. I heard my parents' voices out in the living room. Kay must have made an excuse for my long nap.

Swinging myself up and out of bed, I stood still and listened to my own emotions.

This wasn't over. I'd saved LA because I had to, but working for Cleric had never been about that.

Gathering the bundle of my costume up under one arm, I flipped open the purple book to the page for Cleric's shop, and pressed it to my face.

When I pulled the book away again, there I was in the front room of the shop as always. It hadn't changed. The cage had been knocked on its side away from the arrival spot, and a large, thick envelope sat amid my alchemy equipment, but that was all. Maybe a few books were missing from the shelves.

I didn't want to yell Cleric's name. I walked through the tiny building instead, climbing the stairs to peek into the living quarters. His bedroom was a mess, but only a few things had been taken. He'd left in a hurry.

A giggle forced its way out when I noticed that the Tyrant posters were among the few things Cleric had taken. A sigh followed it. Cleric was gone. Probably forever.

I clomped back downstairs, through the kitchen, and over

to my alchemy table. The blank envelope had been closed with a wax seal. I peeled that open, and pulled out a single sheet letter and a smaller, bulgy envelope.

In script so elegant I could barely make sense of it, the letter read:

I always admire anyone who does what they believe is right. You were brave, determined, and clever. You knew your limitations and worked around them. I sincerely hope you got what you wanted. Keep the badge. Maybe one day you'll want to wear it again, and whether as a uniform or a trophy, you earned it.

The second envelope wasn't sealed, and had written on the front:

PS: You'll need these.

I pulled out the contents. A bundle of legal typed papers looked like the deed to the shop. It was wrapped around three black, rectangular panels, unused windows for the teleport book. Also, a handful of twenty-dollar bills. My remaining pay. They weren't important, but Cleric had always been scrupulous.

My mind blank, I got out my phone, and dialed up some news sites. Tyrant Sidekick Saves LA. The Girl Who Saved Southern California. The Seed of Evil Destroys Itself. The news sites were filled with the conflict at the Ivory Tower! All of the stories mentioned me, most of them featured me heavily, and the most common photo attached was a particularly good one some lucky reporter had taken of me splashing fire onto The Book.

Before I knew it, I was grinning. I grinned so hard my face hurt. Leaning against the alchemy bench, I flipped through news site after news site, tension draining away as I watched the stories about me scroll.

This. This was what it had all been about. I doubted I would ever be crazy enough to do this again, but I had indeed gotten what I wanted: The attention of all of California, maybe the nation. Only Kay and Aikamieli knew who I was, but everyone saw me do it and I impressed them all.

Oh, yeah, definitely not crazy enough to do that again. No way. Not any time soon. But I'd succeeded.

My eyes drifted down to my alchemy kit, and I shut down

my phone and put it away. This equipment was mine, now. How much of it could I smuggle home? Bigger question: What was I going to do with this shop??? My parents couldn't find out about this, and I didn't have a part time job as an excuse to keep disappearing anymore.

Ooh, but the big positive side effect of that was that I could spend time with my friends, and not feel inferior anymore. They didn't have to know. *I* knew.

I picked up the heavy, sparkly spike of candy I'd gotten from the supervillain Delicious. Among the downsides, I was never going to collect alchemy ingredients as this job provided. The sheer power of some of this stuff! It all fit together, too, like I'd been collecting them for a purpose.

I pulled out the big glass tray I'd mixed the book restoration potion in. Cleric had taken the remaining bottle of the potion itself, I saw. I dropped the candy into the tray first—no, the blood first. Blood is life, and no blood would ever be more full of life than Marcia's. What next? The ash from The Book. It represented knowledge, even if that knowledge was now scrambled....

After a while, I had to drag the drum we'd used for ink storage downstairs, and move the congealing blob I'd created into it. As it settled into shape, I wandered into the kitchen and grabbed both bags of sugar and the bottle of honey. Dumping the sugar in, I squeezed out most of the honey, gave the bee-shaped bottle a thoughtful look, and tossed it in entirely.

Not enough. I hadn't wanted to do this, but I opened up the refrigerator and pulled out an armful of raw meat, adding that to the contents of the barrel. That would do. It was the bare minimum of mass, but it would do.

A few minutes later, I was sitting on a stool watching the drum when it gave a loud thump. Then it thumped a few more times, and flipped over. Feet, one yellow and one purple, appeared in the few inches between the open end of the corroded metal barrel and the carpet. They staggered, bumping the barrel around the furniture. Finally, the drum fell over, but as it hit the floor a gaudily covered girl slipped out with the grace of an eel.

She was short. Shorter than me, even though physically older and more developed. She had big, pointy ears, and a pointy nose. Most of her body was white, with a shiny smoothness unlike skin that still traced out the same subtle musculature a human would show. Everything that could be considered an extremity was some garish color, pink or blue or yellow or orange or purple, and the tips of her fingers were black as ink. Blue and pink freckles the exact tube shape of ice cream sprinkles dusted her cheeks. She had a lot of hair, which wasn't quite hair. Most of it came in individual strands, but they were too thick, like the purple fiberoptics the cyborg girl had for hair. Some of her hair was licorice, strung into pretty braids amid the fluffy mass.

The little homunculus kicked the drum repeatedly, making it ring. "Take that, you varlet! Uh, what's my name?"

"Snax," I supplied. It felt right.

"—wins her first victory!" crowed the creature.

Pointy nose raised proudly high, she whirled around and leaped on me, arms wrapped around mine in a fiercely affectionate hug. Up close, she smelled exactly like candy, chemically sweet with fruity touches depending on what part of her was closest at the moment. Her bare skin didn't feel quite right, a little too slick, but the warm flesh and blood and bones underneath could not be mistaken.

Affection displayed, she darted back from me, dancing on her toes around in a circle, arms extended and looking herself over as she squealed, "Eee! I'm great! I'm beautiful! Thank you! And I have powers and abilities beyond the lot of mortal woman! Watch this!" She thrust her arms forward, fingers clawed, like Cassie making lightning.

Nothing happened.

Snax jerked her arms forward again.

Still nothing happened.

Straightening up, she smoothed a hand through her heavy mane of hair and corrected, "Okay, nix on the powers and abilities, but I'm still gorgeous. And a genius. Check it, I know Sumerian!" Rushing past me, she grabbed a knife from my alchemy tools, spun it around her fingers like a magician doing tricks, then dragged the blade over the wall, leaving a bunch of scratch marks.

Slapping those marks with the handle of the knife, she translated, "It says Ea-Nasir was here and he owes me money!"

My mouth hung open. Oh, no way. Seriously? I mean, seriously?! The book could have taught me Sumerian after all!

Ignoring my tragic outrage, Snax hooked an arm around one of mine, and snuggled up against my shoulder. A happy sigh had her relaxed for exactly one second before she chirped enthusiastically, "You did it. Let's go celebrate the creation of the ultimate pinnacle of alchemy by biting the heads off of rats! Take that, philosopher's stone!" She pressed her thumb to the side of her pointy nose, and flicked contemptuously, then snickered, "Kidding. I want ice cream."

"You need clothes first," I warned, trying to catch up to events. That much was very true. Snax was definitely an adult woman, even if tiny.

"Oh, yeah, good idea!" she squealed, running like a gazelle into the kitchen, then up the stairs.

Thumps and crashes sounded above me. Lots of them. I slid off my stool, only to see Snax run back down the steps and back into the front room. She now had one of Cleric's black and white tabards draped over her body, tied with a golden rope around her waist to form a crude dress. Actually, she was so much smaller than Cleric, the result was pretty modest.

Her hyperactive face bobbed up and down, craning to look behind tables and bookshelves as she asked, "Hey, have you seen my mom?"

Oh. Uh. My homunculus wasn't immune to my power. I flapped a hand. "Actually, that's me."

The candy elf didn't give me time to explain. With good-natured cynicism, she sneered. "Uh-huh. Right. Well, when you see her, tell her I found this!" From behind her back, she pulled an oversized, ripped-out book page. It was the map to Catlantis. As I took that in, she chattered on, "And now I know my purpose. I was decanted to be the most beautiful explorer and pirate queen in history!"

"No, wait! I'm—" I tried to say, but Snax sprinted over to the door, yanked it open, and darted outside.

I hurried after her. The street looked like it always had,

deserted and entirely lacking in miniature day-glow homunculi.

I blinked, leaned back against the door frame, and started to laugh. It bubbled out of me on and on as I slid my fingers back through my dreadlocks, which were dry and fraying and I needed to moisturize badly.

The world might never know my name, but it would remember me forever.

About the Author

Richard Roberts is drawn to dark, strange fairy tales, which of course is why he got famous for his perky middle school supervillain stories instead.

That presents the two halves of his work, the fun and crazy, and the dark and weird. In both cases, he does his best to entertain, to look at old ideas to see how strange they are if you think them through, and to make a story where his characters earn their happy endings.

Bibliography

Please Don't Tell My Parents Series

Book 1: *Please Don't Tell My Parents I'm a Supervillain*
Book 2: *Please Don't Tell My Parents I Blew Up the Moon*
Book 3: *Please Don't Tell My Parents I've Got Henchmen*
Book 4: *Please Don't Tell My Parents I Have a Nemesis*
Book 5: *Please Don't Tell My Parents You Believe Her*
Book 6: *Please Don't Tell My Parents I Work for a Supervillain*

Stand Alone Novels

You Can be a Cyborg When You Grow Up
Quite Contrary
Sweet Dreams are Made of Teeth
Wild Children

Curious about other Crossroad Press books?
Stop by our site:
http://store.crossroadpress.com
We offer quality writing
in digital, audio, and print formats.

www.ingramcontent.com/pod-product-compliance
Lightning Source LLC
Chambersburg PA
CBHW030349020726
47493CB00003B/747